RED AUERBACH

BOOKS BY ARNOLD "RED" AUERBACH

Red Auerbach
Winning the Hard Way

Basketball for the Player,
the Fan, and the Coach

BOOKS BY JOE FITZGERALD

New England's Patriots
A Team History

That Championship Feeling
The Story of the Boston Celtics

El Tiante
The Luis Tiant Story

RED

AUERBACH

An Autobiography

by Arnold "Red" Auerbach and Joe Fitzgerald

Foreword by John Havlicek

G. P. Putnam's Sons, New York

SBN: 399-11893-4

Library of Congress Cataloging in Publication Data

Auerbach, Arnold, 1917-
Red Auerbach.

1.   Auerbach, Arnold, 1917-   2.   Boston Celtics
(Basketball team)   3.   Basketball coaches—United States—
Biography   I.   Fitzgerald, Joe, joint author.
GV884.A8A28   1977   796.32′3′0924 [B]   76-51377

PRINTED IN THE UNITED STATES OF AMERICA

To all Celtics, past and present,
and to the memory of Walter Brown

Preface

The idea, from the very beginning, was to present Red Auerbach just the way I found him.

At one of our first meetings to discuss this project, he and I talked about what the book would say, what areas of his life it would touch upon, and whom we would go to for recollections and insights.

"I think we should talk with the opposition," I said. "People like Bob Pettit, Jerry West, Freddie Schaus."

"Schaus?" Auerbach repeated. "What the hell do I want Schaus in my book for? He doesn't like me."

"That's why he's important," I replied.

Red took a long drag from his cigar, thought for a moment, then smiled and nodded okay.

A few days later Schaus, the former Lakers coach who is now basketball coach at Purdue University, explained to me how Red was ungracious and lucky. You'll find Freddie's observations in this book.

You'll hear from people who loved the Redhead and people who detested him. Some will tell you he was a genius and others will insist he was nothing more than arrogant and cocky. You're going to hear from the men who played for him, like Bill Russell, Bob Cousy and John Havlicek, as well as the men who played against him, like Pettit and West. You'll hear from referees, from writers, from league officials, from business associates and from Red's own family.

No critics were avoided, nor were any admirers solicited. The book, like the man, has no pretenses.

Harry Gallatin, the former Knickerbocker star and coach, once said, "Nobody has to get me up to play the Celtics. All I have to do is look over at Auerbach, that bastard!" But Indiana basketball coach Bobby Knight says, "He's one of the all-time great people. I love the guy. All somebody has to do is mention something derogatory about Red and I'm ready to go to war."

I think both Gallatin and Knight will find the Auerbach they're talking about in these pages.

Red was easy to love and easy to hate. It was always a matter of perspective. "I never knew anyone who played for Red who didn't like him," Russell said. "Of course, I never knew anyone who played against him who did like him."

There was only one thing about Auerbach that everyone could agree on, whether they loved the man or hated him: he was the most successful basketball coach of all time. No one else ever came close to his record, and the betting here is that nobody ever will.

Like baseball's Joe McCarthy and football's Vince Lombardi, the Redhead became a legend. Long after he's gone, they'll be talking about Auerbach wherever basketball is played.

This book, I hope, will help keep the record straight.

It's Red Auerbach—as he was, as he is and as he'll be remembered by the people who knew him best.

JOE FITZGERALD

Foreword

What kind of man is Red Auerbach?

Well, I've seen him laugh. I've seen him cry. I've seen him show frustration, rage and compassion. Most of the world just sees the disciplinarian, the dictator, and that's a true image, too.

You meet, and his first move is to put you on the defensive. Most of the time he succeeds. This is a definite Auerbach trait, one of his ways of immediately gaining the upper hand. Once his control is established, his tenacity of purpose takes over, and that control will be maintained until he draws his last breath.

That's the Red Auerbach I know, and I recognized him over and over in the pages of this book.

His toughness and his will to win were imbued within the men and teams he coached, almost as if by a process of osmosis. Red never asked us to give more than we could—yet he demanded every bit of what we had, and he got it.

His greatest talent was knowing how to handle men and how to react to any game situation. He would curse us, coddle us, maybe even enrage us—anything he thought would make us perform better. The results were almost unbelievable.

Red would do anything within the rules to win. And if that wasn't enough, he was perfectly willing to bend those rules, like a craftsman bending a piece of steel to the last threshold before it breaks.

He's a man of many idiosyncrasies, but he's left his mark on

9

all of us who played for him. Call it charisma or whatever you want, but Red was an extraordinary coach. We all learned little lessons from him, and I guess each of us has a special remembrance or two from the days when we played for him.

One of his favorite sayings was: "I'm not always right, but I'm never wrong!"

This positive attitude helped hang 13 flags in his domain at Boston Garden.

Oh, I know, people will speculate that he had the best talent. It's true, Red did have super players. But I don't believe any other coach could have handled that talent—and the egos which went with it—as well as he did. The challenges he faced in controlling his personnel were monumental, maybe even more so than the challenges he encountered during our ball games. I know the cynics have said, "Give another coach Auerbach's players and he will win it all, too."

Well I just don't believe that. No way.

Celtics players have come and gone down through the years, yet the organization is always able to regroup and make a new run for the title. Only one factor has been constant all along: *Red Auerbach's presence.* He is the lifeline of the team's continual success. He's our "Godfather." And as long as he's in control, the Celtics will remain in the thick of championship contention.

The array of flags hanging over our home court is a breathtaking sight, and every time I look up at them I can't help thinking Auerbach's spirit is up there, too, hovering over everything and everybody down below.

The Red Auerbach I found in this book is the Red Auerbach I've known for the past 15 years as my coach, my boss, and my friend. As you read it you'll understand why many of us loved him, why many others hated him and—most of all—why he was the greatest winner of all time.

JOHN HAVLICEK

ACKNOWLEDGMENTS

For their cooperation and assistance in the preparation of this book, the authors wish to thank: Zang Auerbach, Jerry Buckley, Frank Bellotti, Jeff Cohen, Sammy Cohen, Bob Crane, Bob Faris, Julie First, editor Hugh Howard, Irv Levin, Harold Lipton, Sadie Notes, Dick O'Connell, Bob Richards, Paul Sann, Philip Spitzer, Malcolm Sherman, Phyllis Schmertz, Len Wayne, Jason Wolf; with special thanks to John Havlicek for providing the Foreword, to the Celtics' front office staff for its many courtesies, and to all of the basketball personalities who were kind enough to give of their time.

Contents

Part Three—The Auerbach Method

Part Four—Reflections

Introduction

The room fell expectantly silent, nervously silent, as Bill
Russell made his way to the microphone and then paused to
sort out his thoughts. In keeping with tradition, the 1966
breakup banquet had no rigid format. Every member of the
team was welcome to express his sentiments, and yet it was
understood that Russell—now, more than ever, their leader—
would be speaking for all of them.

Once a celebration of their youth and their success, the
breakup banquet had become an increasingly melancholy occasion for the Boston Celtics as time slowly dismantled what
had often been called the greatest team ever assembled. Instead of saying good-bye for the summer, it seemed someone
was always saying good-bye forever. Bill Sharman left in
1961. Bob Cousy followed him in 1963. In 1964 the team was
jolted by the joint retirements of Frank Ramsey and Jim
Loscutoff. Then there was a farewell to Tommy Heinsohn in
1965.

Now, on a warm April night in 1966, only 24 hours after
they had beaten the Los Angeles Lakers to clinch their eighth
consecutive world championship, the Celtics were breaking
up again. This time the curtain was falling on Red Auerbach,
their fiery coach, who was retiring to fulltime duty in the front
office after 20 seasons on the sidelines.

He had called himself a dictator. No one in the room that night would challenge the description, though some might have felt the word *despot* would be more accurate. Others called him a genius, sometimes even while they were explaining why they hated him.

But one thing was quite generally agreed upon: Auerbach was retiring with the greatest coaching record in the history of basketball; he had produced more wins, more championships, more outstanding stars than any man before him. His accomplishments were unparalleled.

Russell, who would assume the dual role of player-coach the following season, made a few perfunctory attempts at humor and his listeners responded warmly. "My wife's name is Rose," he deadpanned. "I'm not married to any of you guys. Get it?"

The players laughed. It had been Auerbach's famous line, thrown at them again and again, whenever he wanted to get a point across. But the merriment was artificial and everyone knew it, so Russell quickly got down to the business at hand.

He talked about the Celtics, about the family feeling they shared, about the love and the pride they engendered in him. He poured his heart out in a dramatic dissertation that was both aimless and eloquent.

"It's hard to say how grown men, you know, how much they can mean to each other . . . and you guys mean so damned much to me."

By now he was crying. The audience, comprised of former players, current teammates, writers, wives and office personnel, sat spellbound. Up at the head table Auerbach kept his head bowed.

"Now you take Red Auerbach," Russell continued, his voice heavy with emotion. "Sometimes I hate him with a passion and sometimes I love him like a brother. Red has done an awful lot for me. But one of the most important things he did for me was to treat me like a man. . . . You know, in his own funny way—a lot of people don't realize this—Red is one of the greatest persons you'll ever meet. He seems like a pretty tough guy, but I'll bet he cries, too . . .

"When I took this job someone said to me, 'What did you take it for? You've got nothing to gain. You've got to follow

Red Auerbach.' Well, I don't think I'm going to be another Red Auerbach. Who wants to be another Red Auerbach? My name is still William Felton Russell. . . ."

He rambled on a while longer, then turned his back on the crowd and looked directly down at Auerbach. The Redhead returned the stare.

"I'm not going to give you any of that crap about how much we all love you and how much we're all going to miss you. Personally, I think you're the greatest basketball coach who ever lived. I think you've contributed as much to basketball as any man alive. And I know you've contributed more to this team than anybody outside of this room realizes.

"I've heard people say that the only thing that made you a great coach was Bill Russell. Yeah. It helped. But that's not what did it. This is your team, Red. You picked every one of us. And you probably had a different reason for picking each one of us.

"You did a great job. I've said this before and I'll repeat it tonight: if I had the choice, I would never play for any other coach. Just you. We've both been lucky. I've had you and you've had me. I don't think you're a genius. But you are an extraordinarily intelligent man.

"I don't want too many friends, Red. But you and I will be friends until one of us dies."

All day long Auerbach had been planning what he would say, how he would say it, but even as the hour of the banquet drew near, his mind remained blank. As he approached the microphone his face was pale, and as he started to speak his voice was hoarse and shaky.

"I don't know when I'm going to crack," he said, "but something has to give."

He waited a moment, then continued.

"Everybody says what a great coach I was, but I couldn't have done it without Russell, Cousy and all the rest of you guys. . . ."

He thanked players, writers, fans and particularly the late Walter Brown, the beloved Boston owner who entrusted the Celtics to him in 1950.

Then he sat down, buried his head in his arms and sobbed

violently. As one, retired stars like Heinsohn, Loscutoff and Cousy raced up from the audience, and active stars like John Havlicek and KC Jones rushed over from their head table seats. While Russell locked him in an embrace, the others formed a solid wall to block out the advancing horde of photographers.

Marjorie Brown, Walter's widow, leaned over from the adjacent seat and gently kissed him. "It's okay, Red," she whispered. "It's okay. We love you."

Indeed, they did. And if Russell spoke for them all, then Auerbach cried for them all.

They weren't just saying good-bye to a coach. They were saying good-bye to an era which, in all likelihood, will never be matched again.

It was a time for weeping.

PART ONE

From Brooklyn
to Boston

Chapter 1
Hymie's Kid

"My ambition was to be a teacher and a coach."

The old brown wooden three-decker tucked away at 246 Lynch Street, one of a network of side streets and alleyways running off Broadway, was no different from thousands of other urban homesteads tightly clustered throughout turn-of-the-century Brooklyn. No one would have mistaken it for a slice of the good life, but in Hymie Auerbach's eyes, it was nothing less than the proverbial castle.

Hyman Auerbach was only 13 years old when he said goodbye to his mother and father and made his way to the ship which would carry him to a better life in what everyone said was a land of opportunity on the other side of the ocean. He was at once very much alone, and yet part of a tremendous emigration which saw more than two million Jewish inhabitants flee the wave of anti-Semitism which swept across Europe, particularly in Russia where the Auerbachs made their home in Minsk. Like many of their countrymen, he and his brothers Louis and Sam eventually settled in Brooklyn, the largest of New York's five boroughs.

The new arrivals were eager to learn the ways of their

adopted homeland and they worked hard at becoming Americans. For many of them, of course, it was much too late to master the language and assimilate the life-style. The real harvest, they reminded themselves, would be reaped by the children to come.

Hymie Auerbach met a young office worker named Marie Thompson—Mary, she prefered to be called. They courted, and eventually talked of marriage. Hymie scrimped and saved until at last his nest egg was sufficient, then he ushered his bride into the third floor apartment of the home he bought on Lynch Street, up in the Williamsburg section of town. The elevated trains rumbling over Broadway provided access to the rest of New York, and right across the street P.S. 33 stood waiting for the family they planned.

The good life? As far as Hyman Auerbach was concerned, he owned it.

Victor was the firstborn, on May 7, 1914.

Arnold followed, on September 20, 1917.

Zang, the youngest son, arrived November 21, 1921.

Finally, a daughter, Florence, came on September 18, 1925.

From the beginning, Victor was the student of the family; Arnold—whom everyone called "Red"—was the athlete. Zang was a maverick, carefree spirit.

"I'd take Red with me to the playground," Victor remembers, "and as we picked sides for a basketball game, someone would say. 'Oh, let Red play—he's Victor's brother.' But it wasn't long before they started saying, 'Let Victor play—he's Red's brother!' He was a good, good athlete, and he was also very bright. Don't let anyone kid you about that. Red was a very bright kid, but he never studied as hard as he should have because he was too interested in playing ball."

He was also interested in making a buck. "Red had the strong back in the family," Zang says. "Whenever there was something laborious to do, he got the call. I think that was partly because of the fact he was also very willing to help. Red's always been a hustler, whether it was selling papers, shining cabs or helping out our old man. It was nothing for him to have two and three odd jobs going at once. And as a result he usually had some money. So whenever I wanted to bum a nickel, I'd go to him rather than bothering my father, and Red almost always had a spare one for me. He used to hide the damned things, like putting them under the carpeting on the stairs at our house. I guess the thing I think of most when I look back is the fact he was such a responsible kind of kid, even to the point of paying much more attention to our parents than any of the rest of us did."

Right before I was born my father owned a small restaurant in Manhattan, just across from Radio City. The owners once tried to get him to buy the entire building for $11,000! He wouldn't touch it. Can you imagine what that's worth today? I never let him forget it. But he was a good businessman and a hard worker. Later on he bought this little delicatessen in Brooklyn. I loved to watch him cut that bread: zoom-zoom-zoom! *He was so good with his hands. Same thing with cutting the meat. But he never had time to do things around the house—you know, build things, have fun, play games—because he always came home so tired.*

Eventually he took his money from that business and bought a cleaning and drying plant. There were about 10 guys in on the deal. And he got screwed when it went broke.

So he went to work for another plant on a commission deal. He'd pick up, say, 100 suits from customers on his route. If the plant charged him six cents to do each suit, he'd get a dime from the customer. He bought his own truck and kept that route for a number of years. I know, because I used to help him a lot.

The cleaning route went all over New York, from the 50s down to the Lower East Side. So my father and I would arrange everything in the morning. I'd get out of school and rush to get a trolley and meet him on the East Side, or maybe grab the subway and catch him uptown. We'd pick a spot and a certain time, and I made damned sure I never left him waiting too long. He was too busy for that.

It's funny how you remember things. Every piece of clothing we picked up had to be numbered. We'd use this indelible purple ink to write the numbers on the pants pockets. My father's number was 691. I'll never forget it. You couldn't make a mis-

take or you'd lose the damned suit. We'd pull up to the plant, lug our whole load upstairs where everything was dumped into these big tumblers. Later we'd go back, sort them out, put all the jackets and pants together again and then make our deliveries. We worked every day until around six o'clock, and sometimes we had to work Saturdays, too.

Eventually my father saved enough money and went back into business for himself again. He opened his own dry cleaning shop called Sunset Cleaners. I got to be pretty good at pressing pants. I can remember when I got to college and was something of a big shot there, I'd still rush home for Christmas and Easter vacations to help him in the store. I'd have two sandwiches and a big bottle of cream soda with me, and I'd show up about 10 at night and work all by myself until 8 in the morning, when the regular presser came back on the job. Here I am, a big guy at college, dating the coeds, standing up all night long pressing pants. I had to do it. Customers wanted their clothes for the holidays. If we didn't get the job done on time, they'd take their business to someone else. We got 15 cents for pressing a suit. There'd be a hundred of them piled up when I got there. By morning they'd all be done. That was $15 I made for my father. But I wasn't doing it for the money. I was doing it because he needed the help. Victor didn't know how to press clothes right, and Zang—he was an artist, which means he was in his own damned world. So I did it. It wasn't any big thing at the time. I just felt it was something I should be doing.

The only real problem I can remember is that my father thought basketball was a waste of time. He was opposed to me spending too much time playing it when I was in high school because, in his mind, I was not the son destined to go on to college. That meant I should be paying more attention to a career. I'd just tell him, "Look, I'll help you after school and during the summer, but I still want to play basketball. Basketball is important to me."

After P.S. 33, which was like an elementary school, I went to P.S. 122, and then to Eastern District High School. I think the biggest thrill I ever had in my young days was being picked for the Hall of Fame. This was something the World-Telegram

*used to do. Lester Bromberg was the basketball writer, and
each week he'd pick certain high school athletes for what they
called the Hall of Fame. You'd go down to the paper and have
your picture taken, and the next day everyone in the city would
see it. That was really something. Don't forget, I was going to
a high school that had mostly girls. We had about 2,500 students and I'll bet at least 1,800 of them were girls. We had no
football program or anything like that, so most of the athletes
in my area went to Boys High or Hamilton. Hell, we were just
a little school on a concrete lot. There were no trees outside the
door. There wasn't even a blade of grass. No one had ever been
picked for that kind of honor from Eastern District before, so
it was really kind of a special thing when it happened to me.*

*Later, when I was a senior, I was picked All-Brooklyn, Sec-
ond Team. Whenever I mention that to pro atheletes they look
at me and laugh. Naturally they've all made All-American
teams and things like that, and they think All-Brooklyn, Second Team, was some kind of joke. Big deal! Well, it so happens it was a big deal. New York City was the Mecca in basketball then. They tell me about Indiana and I say that's a lot
of crap. New York is where all of your great players were at
the time: your great LIU teams, the St. John's teams, the
CCNY clubs, the great, great NYU teams. Almost all of them
were filled with New York City kids. So I'd remind my professional friends that making All-Brooklyn, Second Team, was a
hell of a lot harder than making 80 percent of your All-State
teams in the rest of the country.*

*Whether people believe me or not, that was quite an accom-
plishment.*

*One day I was walking down the corridor at Eastern District
High and the phys ed teacher—a man by the name of Alvin
Borton—grabbed me and put me right up against the wall.*

*"Let me tell you something," he said. "I happen to know
you can be a pretty good student. Basketball's fine, but if you
think it's going to carry you through the rest of your life you're
wrong. It's nice to be a big shot, but there's no reason you can't
earn good grades, too. So if you're thinking of college, you'd
better get your mind on the books."*

I respected this guy and I knew what he was saying was ab-

solutely right, so I started to calm down a bit and pretty soon you could see my grades going up.

Then one day some kids came up to me and asked me if I'd be interested in running for president of the student body. I was an athlete—captain of the basketball team—and no athlete had ever run for school president before. We lived in our world and the real serious students—the ones who always became presidents—lived in theirs. But I liked the idea, so we started checking to see what the qualifications were. You had to have an 85 average. I was okay there because my marks were all around 87 or 88, a solid B. And you had to have a clean record. I had never gotten into any trouble, so I was all right there, too.

I got some friends to join the ticket, and we started to campaign. We already had the sports crowd with us and most of the tough guys came over to our side. But the main student body was the big question. The guy I was running against had just missed winning the year before, so everyone regarded him as a shoo-in this time.

I had to stand up in front of the whole student body and make a campaign speech and, boy, I'll tell you I was scared. I had never done anything like that before. So I started in:

"Friends—friends in the true sense of the word—in fact, I might say I'm a personal friend of the greater majority of those present here today—you may wonder, perhaps, why I seek this coveted position. . . ."

My goddamned knees were buckling, my stomach was all squirmish and I was talking in a falsetto. While I was suffering through it, I made up my mind that if I ever got to college I was going to take a speech course. Other people could get up there. Why not me?

But I was elected, the only guy in the school's history to be basketball captain and student president at once.

Then I discovered that the only damned duty I had was to get up and read the Bible at assembly time. I did it once and they never asked me to do it again.

For as long as I can remember my ambition was to become a teacher and a coach. That's the goal I set for myself when I was just a kid. By the time I graduated from Eastern District

*in 1935, we had been through the Depression and money was
very tight and, to make things worse, my father got sick right
in the middle of the Depression and missed a year of work.*

*Right around this time I got a call from Nat Holman, the
great coach at CCNY, asking me if I was interested in going to
school there. But in order to qualify for a scholarship I had to
have about a 92 average, which, of course, I didn't have. The
business of being captain and student body president wasn't
enough. I had to have the marks, too. So Nat suggested putting
me into night school for six months with a few easy courses,
then getting me transferred to the day school. But I really
wasn't interested in CCNY. That would have been like a last
resort.*

*LIU, meanwhile, contacted me about some tryouts that were
being held up there. Then I found out there were roughly 100
kids trying out for just five or six scholarships, and there I was,
only 5'9 or 5' 10. What chance was I going to have? So I didn't
go.*

*My best shot, I figured, was NYU. I liked the coach, Howard
Cann, and the NYU teams were very popular with New York
kids. Cann let me try out for a scholarship. I spent a whole day
scrimmaging and did pretty well, but then I found out that
kids who got in on athletic scholarships were automatically
enrolled in the School of Commerce. No one on athletic scholarship could enter the School of Education. I wanted no part
of the School of Commerce: I wanted to be a teacher. So I told
Cann I appreciated his interest, but I had to say no.*

*Then I heard about Seth Low Junior College, which was
part of the Columbia University system. Tuition was $250 a
year, but they'd give me a $100 scholarship. I could enter the
following February. That meant I had to come up with another
$150. I figured by entering in February I wouldn't have to take
a full course and that would give me time to find some jobs. I
worked out a deal where I could earn $12 a month working in
the gym. Then I got another job with the government's NYA
program that paid me $19 a month. The only thing I'd be tak-
ing from my parents was room and board. I'd travel to and
from school on the subway every day, attend classes, get to my
jobs and still play ball.*

Everything seemed to be fine, but after my first full semes-

ter, they announced they were going to shut down the school. The doors were closed, the whole operation was moved up to the Heights at Columbia and we were informed that Seth Low would be dissolved the following spring.

Meanwhile, I was having a good time playing basketball. There were only 175 students in the school, and I was the only one who had been any kind of a high school star at all. We had a great coach, Gordon Ridings, who later became the head coach at Columbia. Ridings put together a hell of a club and we ended up beating teams like Seton Hall, St. Peter's, Brooklyn College, St. Francis—much bigger schools, with more athletes and better facilities than we had.

The thing I remember most is finally getting my father out to see me play. It was the first basketball game he had ever seen. I was the ball handler and the other team was playing a zone, so I spent most of the night moving the ball up, in, back, out and so forth. So when it's all over I went up to him and asked, "How'd you like it?"

"It's all right," he said, "but one thing I don't understand. You're in the living room and all the action is in the kitchen! You're too far away from where the action is."

I never got over that. My father had never seen a game in his life and yet he was making a very precise observation. Of course he didn't understand anything about zones or the complexities involved. All he knew was that I was never going to score if I didn't advance the ball more.

The only thing that kept me from fully enjoying that season was one thought which kept running through my mind: Where do I go from here?

Late that season Bill Reinhart brought his George Washington University team up to New York to play LIU. Ridings had been one of Bill's great stars, so he arranged for GW to practice in our gym and to scrimmage against our team. We had a great workout and I more than held my own against his players. I guess he liked what he saw, plus I'm sure Ridings put in a very good word for me. Just before he left town he called me aside and asked me if I'd be interested in playing for him at George Washington.

"Mr. Reinhart," I said, "there's only one question. I'll be a transfer student and I know you've already got a lot of top

*ballplayers on your team. If I don't make the club, will I lose
my scholarship?"*

I've never forgotten what he told me.

"Red," he said. "I'll make you a promise. Keep your marks
up, stay eligible, and whether you ever play a game for me or
not, I'll see to it that you remain in school and leave with your
diploma. You have my word on that."

"Mr. Reinhart," I replied, "that's good enough for me."

Chapter 2
The Collegian

*"Shut up, keep working and your chance will come
again."*

Auerbach played three years of varsity ball for Reinhart,
during which time GW ran up an impressive record of 38
wins and 19 losses. As a senior, Red was the Colonials' captain and high scorer.

"He was what you'd call a heady ballplayer," according to
Bob Faris, a former teammate who now serves as athletic director of their alma mater. "As I recall, most of the kids who
came out of the New York area around that time were heady
players. They seemed to be so much smarter at the game than
the rest of us, probably because of all the playground basketball they had been involved in. I was from Nebraska and all
we did out there was run and shoot. I didn't even know what a
pick was when I came out east as a freshman. Suddenly here
comes a guy like Auerbach, setting up plays and picks and
screens for everybody and I didn't know what the hell I was
supposed to do. He was a smart, smart athlete. Reinhart was
the domineering factor, of course, but it was Red who more or
less set up our whole offense and made it go. He had quite a
head on his shoulders."

When George Washington alumni gather today to recall the good times long gone by, the ones who played and studied with Auerbach don't—as one might suspect—have a backlog of funny stories to tell about the Redhead.

Like Faris, they remember a different Auerbach.

"Years later when I saw Red on television, ranting and raving at the referees and talking tough in interviews, I had a hard time convincing myself he was the same Auerbach I knew at GW. It was like he had made a 180-degree turn. The Auerbach I knew in college would never dream of jumping up and wanting to fight a referee. You could almost say he was quiet and unassuming, certainly not a fighter."

That's the way he appeared to Dot Lewis, a beautiful coed from a prominent Washington family, who saw him as something other than a celebrated jock.

"The first time I met him was in the Student Club," she recalls. "Everyone used to hang out there between classes. I knew he was on the basketball team and all that, but the thing that impressed me most about him was his quiet, serious manner. I wouldn't say he was exactly a gentle person, but the more we talked the more I could see how very determined he was to achieve certain goals he had set for himself. There was a stick-to-it-iveness about him that I very much admired. I've always been the type who might start something and then end up saying, 'Oh, who cares?' He was just the opposite. His whole life has been goal after goal after goal. He assigns himself certain objectives, then works until he reaches them."

Dorothy Lewis didn't know it at the time, but very quickly she became one of those goals, too. On June 5, 1941—a rainy Thursday in the nation's capital—she became Dorothy Auerbach.

Zang Auerbach noticed the change in Red's demeanor whenever he met his collegiate brother.

"Sure, his attitude changed, and I think I knew why. Don't forget, we're talking about an era when money was very tight. Who the hell had any dough to send someone off to college? Certainly our old man didn't. So I'm sure the thought running through Red's mind was: *Isn't this a lucky, fortunate thing that's happening to me?* And when you're in awe of something, I think you tend to withdraw from it a bit and become overly gentlemanly or whatever you'd call it. I suspect that's why Red was so quiet and serious during those years."

Even while Auerbach was enjoying considerable success on the basketball court, he never lost sight of his overriding objective. Red still wanted to be a teacher-coach. In 1940, just as Reinhart had promised, he received a bachelor's degree in physical education. And in 1941 he added a master's degree in education.

"That was Red," Zang smiles admiringly. "He could have stopped after receiving his degree, but, no, he went on and got his master's. It was just like his basketball. Making the team was never enough; he had to practice and push himself until he was the best damned player out there. Very few projects in his entire life have ever been abandoned. When Red started something, you knew damned well he was going to complete it. He simply excels at getting a job done, and he's been that way ever since we were kids. And all the time he was studying at GW and playing ball, he was holding down outside jobs! What can you say? The man is tireless."

Bill Reinhart coached 22 seasons at George Washington, even though he missed seven years (1943–49) for an extended military hitch. Some of his teams were quite remarkable, like the 1954 and 1955 squads which had a combined record of 47–9, and many of his players went on to distinguished careers in education, government, business, science and the arts.

Still, his most famous protégé was surely the redheaded guard he befriended when Seth Low was about to close its doors.

"Reinhart was Red's first real hero," Zang confided. "He was like his priest, his rabbi, and he unquestionably made a great impression on him."

Red's adoration of his coach was not shared by all of Reinhart's charges.

"Bill demanded loyalty from his players," Faris explains, "and he was very tough on them. I think Red picked up a lot of his own techniques from him. I wouldn't say Reinhart was greatly loved by his players. Not at all. But they greatly respected him. Bill would just as soon 'break your plate,' as we

called it—which meant ordering you away from the training
table—if you were late or missed a practice or something like
that. He could be a tyrant to a kid. But he was very successful
because he was a disciplinarian and a great teacher of fundamentals. Those were his coaching secrets, and I think they
were very much reflected in Red's success later on."

In 1959 George Washington alumni arrived from all over
the country to pay special tribute to six of their brethren, men
who had risen from the undergraduate ranks and gone on to
conquer new worlds.

The six were to be enshrined in the school's Hall of Fame.

They included football great Alphonse (Tuffy) Leamans;
Vice Admiral Alfred Richmond, Commandant of the U.S.
Coast Guard; Washington Senators president Calvin Griffith:
track star Hilary Tolson; syndicated Hearst columnist Bob
Considine, who had been a great tennis star at GW; and Ar-
nold (Red) Auerbach, coach of the world champion Boston
Celtics basketball team.

*By the time I got to GW in the fall of 1937, Reinhart had al-
ready put together an excellent team. George Garber had been
All-City from Monroe High School in the Bronx; Sid Silkowitz
was a great, great star; Jack Butterworth was an All-State from
Indiana; Mike Aronson and Tommy O'Brien were sensational
high school stars from New Jersey. And all these guys had
been together since they were freshmen, so I felt like an inter-
loper. I'm sure that's how they regarded me, because I must
have gotten into four fist fights in the first couple weeks of
practice. They knew I was trying to beat them out so they
weren't about to make things easy for me. But I had come off
the streets, so they didn't bother me. I'd play real strong defense, and if it aggravated them—too bad! My problem was
making the team and keeping my end of the bargain with Bill
Reinhart. He was the only guy I was concerned about. Once I
made the team, though, everything was okay and we all became friends.*

*That first season we were 12–5. One of the losses was to
Loyola of Chicago in three overtimes, even though O'Brien
was sick and didn't even make the trip. Oklahoma State beat*

us on our own court by three. LIU beat us by four up on their little bandbox court. And Bradley beat us by three. So you see, we weren't exactly pushovers ourselves.

I'll always remember the huge disappointment I got in my senior year. College basketball was in its glory. Thousands of people used to jam Madison Square Garden to watch the colleges play. And I really wanted to play there. It was my hometown. So one day we get a wire from Ned Irish, the guy who promoted all the college doubleheaders at the Garden, and a very close friend of mine today. We had beaten Loyola of Chicago out there, and now they were coming to Washington to play us two more times. The wire says we'll be invited to play in a tournament at the Garden if we win both games. So we beat the living crap out of them twice. They had a big guy named Mike Novac, about 6'8, who was very mobile. He'd just stand in front of you and bat away every shot you took. But we ran all around him and after the game I got a very big thrill when their coach, Hank Iba, came into our dressing room and shook my hand. "You played a hell of a game," he told me. I remember thinking what a great man he was to be that gracious. Anyway, pretty soon we get another wire from Irish: COMMITTEE CHANGED MIND; HAS DECIDED TO TAKE ANOTHER NEW YORK TEAM. We were crushed when that happened.

I always felt LIU was responsible for that. They had beaten us on their court by three, and then they were supposed to play us again on our court, but a guy named Dolly King on their club wouldn't have been able to play because blacks weren't allowed to play down there in those days. That had nothing to do with our guys. We didn't give a damn what a guy's color was. We'd played with blacks all our lives. But there was nothing we could do about this situation, so Clair Bee—the LIU coach—calls off the game. And I certainly didn't blame him for that. Meanwhile he had scouted us three times. He knew what kind of team we had. He knew if we ever caught him on a neutral court up in New York—and not that little Brooklyn College of Pharmacy where he played his home games—we'd kill him and he'd lose his national ranking. That's why I was always sure he had a hand in keeping us out of the Garden that season.

I was first string right from the beginning. Then one day we went out to Ohio State and I ran into this big tough guy by the name of Hull. I thought I was pretty tough, but this guy took me into the pivot—I shouldn't have been playing him in the first place!—and leaned on me, and hooked me to death.

All of a sudden I went from being our fifth man down to being the 12th man. One game goes by and I don't get in, then another. I didn't know what Reinhart was thinking, but I knew it wasn't my place to challenge him. I didn't say a word, but I worked like hell in practice. Finally we go up to play Army and they had a guy named Brinker who was their hotshot. Out of a clear blue sky Reinhart says to me, "All right, you take Brinker." So I took him and I shut him off. After that, I was back in the lineup and no one ever said a word about what had happened.

I thought that was a good lesson: shut up, keep working, and your chance will come again.

Most of my time at GW was divided between playing ball, studying and working. I worked in playgrounds, boys' clubs, anyplace I could make a buck. Even a reform school.

I got the job at the reform school during my senior year. I had been working for the NYA—National Youth Administration, a program set up to help get kids through school, or at least keep them off the streets. Then a new thing opened up: the NYA wanted three or four young men to work about 25 hours a week at this place called the National Training School, which was really a reform school.

One of my first nights there I started playing Ping-Pong with this little redheaded kid who looked about 15. He was a nice, polite kid, I thought, and I felt kind of sorry for him. I said, "What are you here for?" and he told me he had had a little trouble with whiskey back home in Virginia. Next day I checked out his record and found out he had not only been bottling the stuff, but selling it across state lines. Plus he was involved with trafficking women. This nice little kid—I couldn't believe it.

That night we're playing Ping-Pong again and the room is getting too noisy. We had about 80 guys in this low-ceilinged basement. So I yelled out, "All right, quiet down." But some guy kept talking. So my young friend put down his paddle, turned around and smacked the guy with the hardest punch I'd ever seen. He laid him out with one shot. Then he turned back, picked up his paddle, and said, "I'm sorry, sir."

I made believe I hadn't seen it and we kept on playing.

I learned a lot on that job, especially about how to handle people. These were supposed to be kids, but a lot of them lied about their ages when they got picked up, so instead of going to penitentiaries they ended up out there. Hell, we had guys 21, 22, 23—older than we were!

There were six companies with about 60 to 80 guys each. Four were white and two were black. One of the black companies was run by a guy named Mr. Burns, and after a while I made it a point to study that man. He'd growl at them and yell, yet you could see it wasn't because he was mean or didn't like them. When the other companies went somewhere, say to a local swimming pool, everyone would be smoking and talking tough and have his shirttails out. But Mr. Burns would go somewhere with his kids and they were neat and well-mannered. He'd be all by himself with around eighty of them, while other companies had two and three helpers to keep the kids in line.

Why? Because he was fair with them. If he thought one of his kids was getting a bad deal, he'd go up to the superintendent and say, "Let's open up this kid's case again." The kids in his company actually had keys to the place. That would have been impossible in any other company, but he trusted them and, in turn, they gave him their respect. Kids from other companies were always trying to run away, but none of Mr. Burns's kids ever did anything like that. Hell, if they did the rest of their group would have killed them when they got back. That's how smooth and nice things went in his company, even though his kids were no different from any of the others when they first arrived at the school.

Mr. Burns showed me what a man can do if he's fair and honest with his people, if he treats them with respect and goes to bat for them when they deserve it.

I was almost 20 years old by the time I got to GW, which meant I had my own ideas about the game of basketball and I *could certainly think for myself. But Reinhart was smart, and I knew I was going to learn a lot from him. There are coaches in the Hall of Fame who couldn't carry his jock.*

He was a clean-living guy, and I'm not talking about the fact that he didn't smoke or I never saw him drink a cocktail. I'm talking about his philosophy. He taught me that a person is a person, and that if you treat a person with respect, you'll get respect back. Once I got to GW and started observing him, one of the things I admired was that he obviously didn't give a damn about a person's religion or color or ethnic background or anything along those lines. Six of the 12 guys on our team were Jewish, but Reinhart didn't care what you were or where you came from. I don't even know what his religion was. I do know that after he retired from GW and got tired of hanging around the house, he took a job coaching at a little Catholic elementary school and fell in love with the place. He was just an American of German descent from somewhere in Oregon, but at the end of his life he converted and he was buried as a Catholic.

One of the first things I saw him do was to admit a mistake. He had us do roadwork, running through the streets of Washington because the school didn't have a track. Personally, I've always felt that roadwork is a complete waste of time for basketball players. Coaches say it builds up stamina. I say it builds up nothing. It doesn't tone up your muscles, and doesn't increase your speed. In fact, there's a tendency to get even slower by doing roadwork. I've always suspected the real reason Bill had us do it that year was to advertise the team. Anyway, a couple of guys came up with shin splints, including me. The only time in my whole college career that I ever missed a practice was due to shin splints from running on that damned pavement. As soon as Bill saw what was happening, he made us stop it and said it was a mistake on his part.

Every drill Reinhart had was applicable to game situations. This is why I say roadwork is for the birds. The game of basketball is confined to an area 90 feet long and 50 feet wide, and you can subtract another three or four feet from every side before you get to the actual playing area. Now that's a pretty compact space. So things have got to be done in a change-of-pace manner, with the emphasis on bursts of speed, not unlike

*the halfback in football who usually gets the job done in 10-
yard to 15-yard sprints. A lot of Bill's drills were designed
with this in mind.*

*Take the long pass drill. He invented that. And I used it ev-
ery single day with every team I ever coached. Not only did it
teach certain basic parts of your game—like running at full
speed, catching the ball at full speed, throwing the ball on the
move without curving it, keeping your head up, things like
that—but it also prepared you to react instinctively, and basketball is a game of instincts.*

*Reinhart also made basketball fun at practice time by intro-
ducing little innovations every so often. Other coaches, including some great coaches I have known, make their practices
good and tough but not interesting. He got us to the point
where we looked forward to going to practice. You knew you
were going to have a good scrimmage, you were going to
knock heads, you were going to work on fundamentals and all
the rest of it—but you were going to have fun, too.*

*The best thing I could ever say about Bill Reinhart is that he
never forgot his people. A lot of his players appreciated him
much, much more after they left him than they did while they
were still in school. When you left GW, if you had kept your
nose clean and done your job, then, by God, you were prepared to coach and coach well. That was true of Gordon Ridings, Matt Zunic, Howard Hobson and a lot of other guys.*

*Reinhart taught us the way to build up a program. He saw to
it that every single ballplayer who stayed eligible ended up
with his degree. Every single one of them. I'm not sure that
any other coach can point to a record like that. You always
hear of guys who were redshirted, or left school needing a few
more hours to graduate. But Bill kept an eye on every one of
his boys, making sure they were getting the job done in the
classroom.*

*Another thing I noticed was the fact his players kept coming
back to see him again and again. GW used to play its games in
local high schools or in the old Capitol Arena. We had no
home court or fancy campus. As a result, recruiting could be a
problem. There was a time when you could sell a kid on the
idea of playing in the nation's capital, but once these guys began getting a peek at Maryland, Duke, North Carolina and*

places like that, forget it. The big campuses were a strong attraction.

So most of Bill's players came to him through former players, just as Ridings had introduced him to me. The message was always the same. Kids were assured that Reinhart would treat them fairly. Not only would he give them an excellent knowledge of the game, but he'd also be their friend and advisor.

That's a promise you could give a kid, because Bill Reinhart was that kind of a guy.

Chapter 3
Teacher, Coach and Sailor

"This thing I hold in my hand is a basketball."

Auerbach was the only member of his 1940 graduating class at GW to step right into a head coaching position. With Reinhart's ringing endorsement, officials of the fashionable St. Alban's Prep School in Washington, D.C., hired Red to run their basketball program for the 1940–41 season, during which time he'd also be engaged in his master's program at George Washington. No teaching duties were involved.

In the spring of 1941, just after his marriage to Dot Lewis and the awarding of his master's degree in education, Red at last realized a longtime ambition when he joined the faculty of Roosevelt High School in Washington in the dual role of head basketball coach and physical education instructor.

He continued to work on the city's playgrounds for added revenue and also joined the National Board of Officials. In between his teaching, coaching and playground activities, Red refereed games in the D.C. area, an avocation quite incongruous with the reputation he'd later attain as the bane of NBA officials.

None of his activities excited him as much as teaching did, and perhaps his proudest moment in the two years he spent at

Roosevelt came when the *Journal of Health and Physical Education,* a prominent publication put out by the National Education Association, printed an article in its March 1943 edition under the by-line "A.J. Auerbach," which featured an extensive plan for designing obstacle courses, complete with illustrations Red had secured from the mechanical drawing class at Roosevelt.

A faded, tattered copy of that magazine still rests on a bookshelf in his Boston office, a mute reminder of the brief but rewarding career of A.J. Auerbach, teacher.

In the early summer of 1943, with World War II raging, Auerbach enlisted in the navy as an apprentice seaman and was promptly shipped to Great Lakes for boot training. From there he was dispatched to the Physical Instructors School in Bainbridge, Maryland, and eventually to the Norfolk, Virginia, Naval Station, where he soon became a Chief Petty Officer in charge of recreation.

In September 1946, almost a year to the day after the Japanese surrender which ended hostilities, Lieutenant (junior grade) Arnold J. Auerbach received his discharge and was once again free to pursue his career in the classroom and the gymnasium.

There was, however, something new on the horizon, something he hadn't counted on, and it thoroughly intrigued and excited him.

It was called the Basketball Association of America.

The very first day I met my team at St. Alban's I could see I had a problem. I let them run around for a couple of days, going through drills and getting the feel of things, but it was so obvious that I was way, way above them. So about the fourth day or so, I blew my whistle and called them over to me.

"Gentlemen," I said, "everything I've taught you in the last three or four days I now want you to drive right out of your minds. Okay? We're going to start again."

Then I reached for a ball and held it up in the air.

"This thing I hold in my hand is a basketball," I began. "The object of this game is to take this ball and stick it into that hole over there. And after it goes through that hole, you've

got to all work together as a team to stop the other side from putting it through the hole at the other end. Any questions so far?"

They looked at me like I was a gooddamned nut, but I went right into the most basic of fundamentals and I continued to teach, teach, teach for the rest of that season.

We had a tough schedule and the team was young, so we didn't win too many games, but as the season progressed you could see them improving. The things they were doing wrong in the beginning—dribbling too high, not concentrating, not balancing themselves on defense—were getting better and better.

Many high school and college coaches apparently feel fundamentals are beneath them. Damn it, that's what this game is all about, and the time for a player to learn those things is when he's young—not in college or the pros. It's amazing how many guys get all the way up to the pro level and still make stupid errors, all because they've never been taught the correct way to do things.

The last game of that season we played Episcopal High School, a real power. Let me tell you, we were prepared! We were going to win that damned game and finish our season in glory. I decided we would play a very deliberate style because we simply weren't sophisticated enough to run with any degree of proficiency.

We led 17–16 with five seconds to go—and we had the ball: beautiful. And in those days the clock started as soon as the man out-of-bounds threw the ball in, so it wasn't necessary for a player on the floor to touch the ball before the clock started. Theoretically all we had to do was toss the damned ball up in the air and by the time it came down the game would be over.

That's not what happened. The player who was throwing the ball inbounds for my club decided to be cute. For some ungodly reason—he never did this before and I'm quite sure he's never done it since—he threw the ball behind his back, right into the hands of an opposing player. The kid from Episcopal put it in and they beat us by one point.

To put it mildly, I was very, very unhappy.

The following year, the situation at Roosevelt High School

*was altogether different. First of all, I was a permanent teach-
er and that made me very happy. College was behind me, Dot
and I had settled down, and I was about to start the job I had
waited all my life for.*

*By this time, I had some pretty definite ideas about teach-
ing. And one of them had to do with what I felt was the proper
respect and image a teacher should have.*

*Back when I was at Eastern District High School, we had
had a new, young teacher join the staff. He was the epitome of
what I felt a physical education instructor should be: nice
build, well-dressed, an authoritative voice. He was just what I
wanted to be someday. But a few years later I happened to go
back to the school and here's this same guy yelling at kids:
"Hey, you bums, get outta there!" Instead of him converting
the kids, they had converted him. That was disillusioning to
me, but it also taught me a very valuable lesson. It was still on
my mind the first day I showed up on the job at Roosevelt.*

*In addition to teaching and coaching, I also worked for the
city at Barnard Playground and Hamilton Playground, so I
spent a lot of time talking and shooting baskets with the kids.
Now all of a sudden the same kids walk into my first classroom and as soon as they see me they yell out, "Hi, Red!" I
know it's wrong and I've got to deal with it right away.*

I waited until the whole class sat down.

*"Can I have your attention, please?" I began. "I'd like to get
one point fairly clear. When we're on the playground you can
call me 'Coach' or 'Red' or anything you like, but here at
school the name is 'Mr. Auerbach.' That's not because I'm any
different now, or because I have a big ego or anything like that.
It's just that, in my opinion, the position of teacher requires
it."*

*One of the first things I insisted on was that everyone in our
gym classes should wear the same color shorts and jerseys.
They had to buy these things anyway, I figured, so why not
work out a deal where they could get them a little cheaper by
buying them from one guy? I believed if they looked good in
class, they were going to feel good about class.*

*Something else bugged me, too. About 30 kids were excused
from my gym classes. They all had doctor's notes, but I knew*

damned well the real reason most of them got excused was they just didn't like the class. Well, I liked my job and I worked hard at it, and I was sure these kids would like the program if they gave it a chance. So I went to the football and track coach, Artie Boyd, with an idea and got his permission to go ahead with it.

"Do you take a bath at home?" I'd ask each kid. He'd say yes, of course. "Good," I'd answer. "That means you have no problem taking a bath or a shower. Right?" He'd agree with that. "From now on then, every one of you who's excused from Phys Ed can sit here and study or whatever else it is you do while the group is in gym class. But twelve minutes before the class ends, I want you to report to the rest of the group, get undressed and take a shower with them."

You know what? Within a week only one kid was still being excused from class. The rest of them were out there shooting baskets or running or whatever. They figured, "Jeez, if I've got to change my clothes and shower anyway, I might as well go out and play."

The year before I got there, Roosevelt had one hell of a basketball team. They had won the big high school invitational tournament at Duke, beating Bones McKinney's team. The only problem was that most of the players had been seniors. With the exception of one sophomore who was their sixth man, all the regulars were gone when I got there.

I guess I felt a little desperate, because I started checking out the hallways and intramural games for any kid who looked big enough and coordinated enough to have a shot at making my club. One particular guy caught my eye immediately. He was about 6'5 and looked real sturdy, so I grabbed him one day in the corridor.

"Hey, boy," I said, "you look pretty strong. Tomorrow afternoon you're coming out for basketball."

He nodded and kept moving. The next day he showed up right on time and began to work out. Two days later I cut him.

His name was Bowie Kuhn.

Once I got a look at the talent I began to develop a system to fit it. I toyed with the idea of playing a very deliberate style, not quite like Hank Iba's teams, but with an emphasis on strong rebounding. I taught them how to break. But the thing *we stressed most of all was that the other team should get just one shot off before we got the ball back.*

Well, we went undefeated (7–0) in our conference and were one of four teams entered in the big Star Tournament after the regular season. Then, in the first game, we're ahead by one point with five seconds to go, and some guy takes a jump shot from 25 feet out and eliminates us.

That made two years in a row that my teams lost the final big clutch game at the last instant.

My second year at Roosevelt we had a 6–1 record in our conference, but we still finished in first place. We went back to the Star Tournament again.

What happens? We're beaten again.

Some people think winning comes easy. That's especially so if you happen to be lucky enough to win a lot. But to really appreciate winning, you've got to know what it's like to lose. Losing—especially losing three final games in a row—makes you appreciate winning.

After the war started, I decided to leave Roosevelt and go into the navy. Going into the service wasn't something I particularly wanted to do, because I was just getting started in my career, but I knew I had to. My father never had time to be real buddy-buddy with his boys because he was working so hard all the time. But he taught me an awful lot, sometimes just by the things I observed in him. And one thing we all learned from him was the importance of good citizenship, of patriotism, of carrying out your responsibilities as a man.

By the time I joined up, Bill Reinhart was a full commander down at Norfolk Naval Station and, as I've said before, Bill never forgot his people. When I got out of Physical Instructors School, he asked for me to join him down there.

The navy was having public relations problems over big league stars like Bob Feller, Phil Rizzuto and Joe DiMaggio not being shipped out. It wanted to set up a big physical education program on the base to show that every sailor was involved with sports, and not just a select few. Reinhart convinced them I was qualified for that assignment.

Within a month I had 28 tournaments going all over the

base, in everything from chess to softball to six-man football to checkers. It turned out to be a very rewarding experience for me.

As you go along through life you pick up bits and pieces of what eventually becomes your own philosophy. You learn from people and experiences. I've already mentioned how my phys ed teacher at Eastern District—Alvin Borton—got me thinking seriously about my studies; how Mr. Burns at the reform school demonstrated the power of leadership if you just treated people with respect; and, of course, how Bill Reinhart showed me what being a man of honor and principle meant.

One other man made a tremendous impression on me in those years, and I never even met him.

That was Joe McCarthy, the manager of the Yankees.

During the time I was stationed at Norfolk I got to be pretty good friends with Rizzuto. We'd spend hours talking about sports and usually that would lead into discussions about the Yankees and McCarthy.

Phil told me that McCarthy was vitally concerned with the image of the Yankees. He said Joe believed the way a team conducted itself off the field had a great deal to do with the way it performed on the field. Then he told me about the little ways McCarthy would introduce kids to his way of doing things. They'd come in from the farms and ghettos and Joe would teach them how to tip in restaurants, how to dress properly in public, how to act correctly in places like hotel lobbies. The idea made a great deal of sense to me. A guy like Joe DiMaggio actually looked and acted like a champion. If you could get a whole team to look and act the way DiMaggio did, you'd have one hell of a ball club on your hands.

I made up my mind that I wanted my ball clubs to look and act like champions, too.

My job at Roosevelt was going to be waiting for me when I got out of the navy in the fall of 1946 and the salary would be $2,900, which wasn't bad when I considered what I could make on the side. Our daughter Nancy had come along in April, so I was really looking forward to getting home, settling down and resuming my teaching career.

Then, in May, I found out that a new professional basketball league was going to start up—with a franchise in Washington. Even though pro basketball had been something of a joke before, I was always convinced the right kind of league could succeed. Tremendous crowds would come out to watch the colleges play and then all of a sudden the best players just disappeared into the woodwork. It made no sense to me.

So I sat down with Dot and we talked about it. With a new baby, maybe this wasn't the right time to be trying another career, especially one which would keep me away from home for long periods of time. The security part didn't really bother me. I had a good record as a teacher, so I could always go back if I wanted, although maybe not to Roosevelt. And there was always refereeing. I was a hustler. We'd have gotten by somehow.

But this might be a once-in-a-liftime chance. She kept insisting she didn't mind, that she wanted me to be happy. I talked about it with Dot's uncle, Selig Brez, a very successful Washington lawyer. He said, "Red, if you're ever going to take a chance, do it now, while you're young. Otherwise you're going to stay in one position for the rest of your life."

That was all I needed. I decided I would look into professional basketball, to see if maybe there was a place in it for me.

Chapter 4
The Birth of the BAA

"Mr. Uline, I can do the job."

Pro basketball was not new. The sport had its beginning in the now legendary Springfield, Massachusetts, YMCA gymnasium in 1891 and had begun to sweep across the collegiate scene by the turn of the century.

In the Roaring '20s, generally revered as the Golden Age of Sports, the pro game enjoyed its first boom. The American Basketball League was founded in the '20s, died in the Depression year of 1931 and then enjoyed a rebirth in 1933. The league featured several strong eastern franchises, including the Philadelphia Spahs (named after their sponsor: the South Philadelphia Hebrew Association), but it was the independent teams which drew the most attention, especially the New York Celtics. Though they were entered in the ABL, the Celts were principally known for their fabulous barnstorming trips around the country. In the winter of 1922–23 they had a record of 193–11! An all-black team from New York called the Rens (named after the Renaissance Ballroom, which was their home court) started in 1922 but didn't peak until the mid '30s when they put together a four-year (1932–36) record of

473–49. Included in that spree was an 88-game winning streak, snapped by the Celtics.

The most successful and, surely, the most enduring of all the teams to come out of that era was the Harlem Globetrotters, organized in Chicago in 1927 by Abe Saperstein.

The game, as the Rens' name amply demonstrated, was dance-hall basketball. Scheduling was difficult and finances were, at best, precarious.

The National Basketball League seemed better organized when it arrived on the scene in the fall of 1937. Firestone and Goodyear of Akron, Ohio, and General Electric of Fort Wayne, Indiana, provided corporate sponsorship, and 10 independent teams joined the Akron and Fort Wayne ball clubs. The NBL suffered through the war years. In the fall of 1945, a record crowd of 23,912 turned out in Chicago to watch the two-time champion Fort Wayne Pistons play a team of recently graduated college all-stars. Later that season, a new star emerged, a 6'10 giant from DePaul University named George Mikan.

The future seemed limitless, but franchise shifts and failures, the lack of facilities and publicity, and—worst of all—a general lack of interest continued to dog the sport at the professional level.

All of this activity, however, didn't go unnoticed by the men who ran professional hockey. They could see the viability of basketball as a spectator sport simply by watching sellout crowds descend upon Madison Square Garden for college doubleheaders. If the attraction of the game was legitimate, then it seemed reasonable to assume that the only thing missing on the professional level was sound administration. They were confident they could provide that, for professional hockey was flourishing under their control. And with their network of large, fully equipped arenas, they could open up shop with a minimum of complications. Basketball, they felt, would be the perfect solution to their biggest problem: dark nights, those blank dates on their schedules when no money was coming in.

Walter Brown, head of the Boston Bruins, got the ball rolling, in talks with fellow members of the Arena Managers Association; and on June 6, 1946, they convened in New York's Hotel Commodore to give birth to the Basketball Association of America.

The teams and divisions were:

Eastern Division

Boston Celtics
New York Knickerbockers
Philadelphia Warriors
Providence Steamrollers
Toronto Huskies
Washington Caps

Western Division

Chicago Stags
Cleveland Rebels
Detroit Falcons
Pittsburgh Ironmen
St. Louis Bombers

All of the buildings involved, with the exception of Washington's, already housed entries in either the National Hockey League or the affiliated American Hockey League.

Maurice Podoloff, a 5'2 realtor, banker and lawyer from New Haven, and president of the AHL, was chosen by his peers to serve as commissioner of the BAA.

Now all they had to do was find coaches and players.

Auerbach had kept his hand in coaching throughout his navy hitch. While at Norfolk he assembled a team—including Bob Feerick of Santa Clara, Red Holzman of CCNY, Matt Zunic of GW, John Norlander of Hamline, Jim Floyd of Oklahoma A&M, Ralph Bishop of Washington, Bob Carpenter of East Texas U, and Belus Smawley of Appalachian State—and brought the group into Washington's Turner Arena for an exhibition series against the all-black Washington Bears, who had just won a national tournament out in Chicago. Red's squad won two out of three.

In the winter of 1944 he was sent from Norfolk to Bethesda
Naval Hospital to do rehabilitation work with wounded veterans. In his spare time he rounded up members of the idle
Washington Redskins football team and booked exhibition
games against a squad of Philadelphia Eagles in Uline Arena,
also in Washington.

By the time he was discharged, Red had gained considerable savvy in organizing and handling teams.

So the idea of coaching on the professional level didn't intimidate him at all.

*Mike Uline was an old Dutchman who had something like
58 patents for various kinds of ice-making machines. He was
really a pioneer in that field. He used to get a big kick out of
taking me around his arena showing me inventions he had
come up with. He was really a hell of a guy and I always got
along well with him.*

*But he didn't know the difference between a basketball and a
hockey puck. He knew nothing about sports. He simply owned
Uline Arena and hired people to run his programs.*

*Uline had no idea who the Keaneys and Lapchicks were. To
him, Lapchick could have been a pancake. So there was only
one thing he could have done, and that would have been to go
to guys like Ned Irish in New York or Eddie Gottlieb in Philadelphia and ask them who he should hire to run his basketball
team.*

*For one thing, he had too much pride to do that. And he was
a shrewd businessman. If a man is your competitor, it doesn't
make sense to expect him to help you too much. There was no
way guys like Irish and Gottlieb were going to give him that
kind of help. They'd help him just enough so that they could
still beat him, and Mike was smart enough from a business
point of view to be aware of this.*

*When I got into his office he already had a lot of pretty good
applications for the job sitting right there on his desk.*

"Mr. Uline," I said, "I think I can do the job for you."

He looked at me and asked, "What makes you say that?"

*I could see that he was interested, and so I made it very sim-
ple and to the point.*

"You need ballplayers, good ballplayers, if you're going to

have any kind of success here. I can get you those ballplayers. I made contact with a lot of them in the last couple of years, and I'm sure I can convince them to come here to play. Give me the opportunity, and I'll give you a team that's competitive with anybody in this league."

He bought it, and I had myself a job.

I had some very definite ideas of how to assemble a team, and I credit Bill Reinhart with this particular bit of philosophy. Professional basketball up until that time had been a regional sort of thing. You could go from one part of the country to another and see entirely different styles and emphases. Everyone seemed to play the game differently.

Most of the teams starting out in 1946 got their players from certain areas. For instance, the Knicks got most of their guys from New York, as did Toronto; Pittsburgh got its players from the Pittsburgh area; Chicago grabbed most of its players from the Midwest, though they were smart enough to go after Max Zaslofsky of New York and make him their ball handler.

I knew that the sources of talent were quite spread out, and I was convinced you had to have a heterogenous group. I wanted my smart backcourt players from around New York and New Jersey; I wanted my runners and power guys from the Midwest; I knew the best rebounders were coming from out west. The players from each area, in addition to having different strong points, had different attitudes and philosophies and concepts. If you could get them all thinking and working together, you'd be way ahead of everybody else.

The whole process of tracking down the players I wanted cost Uline about $500 in phone calls.

I got in touch with Bob Feerick out in California. He was 6'3, but he could play guard or forward and I knew from seeing him at Norfolk that he was great at running a club, plus he could shoot. And while I had him on the phone he told me about Freddy Scolari, a real good AAU guard who came from San Francisco. Feerick got Scolari to come to Washington with him. But I wanted some New York guys in my backcourt, so I got Irv Torgoff—one of the great LIU stars in the '30s—to come over from the NBL, and I picked up Buddy O'Grady from Staten Island. The guy I really wanted was Sonny Hertz-

berg, an outstanding backcourt star from CCNY, but the Knicks got to him before I did.

John Mahnken was a good 6'8 center over in the NBL, but I knew him from the days he played at Georgetown. I got him to come with us.

I still needed help up front, so I chased down John Norlander at his home in Minnesota and convinced him to join us. He was only 6'3, but he was strong, and with Mahnken under the boards with him, he was exactly what I wanted.

There was only one more guy I had my heart set on getting: Bones McKinney from North Carolina. Bones was 6'6 and smart. He'd played in the army and been around, but I found out Chicago had already made a big pitch and he was on his way there when I tracked him down. The train had a three-hour stopover in Washington, so I hustled down to the station.

"Hey, Bones," I said, "you've got three hours to kill. Let's go over to the hotel. We'll have a couple of beers. Come on."

So we go to the Blackstone Hotel and Feerick is sitting there when we arrive. We started talking casually and then I went to work on my man.

"Bones, have you signed anything with Chicago yet?"

"No, but I told them I'd come out to see them."

"Look, Bones, you hate to fly, and you're going to go absolutely nuts taking trains all over the damned place from Chicago. At least if you're here on the East Coast you're near most of the arenas. And you're much closer to North Carolina, too."

He was listening to me, and I could see I was hitting home.

"Look," I finally said, "what did those guys offer you?"

"They said they'd give me sixty-seven hundred and fifty."

"Fine. We'll match that and you can stay right here."

He thought about it for a minute, then said, "Okay, I'll stay."

But I wasn't taking any chances of losing him again, so I brought him into the hotel's men's room and we signed a contract right there!

Now I had my team and it was time to start coaching.

Chapter 5
The Washington Caps

"Basketball, to me, is like a war."

Anyone inclined to snicker at Uline for entrusting a professional franchise to a high school coach stopped laughing almost immediately, for the Washington Caps became the scourge of the infant BAA. Relying upon a well-organized running game, and yet disciplined enough to hold the ball when necessary, the Caps ran off an early 17-game winning streak en route to a final record of 49–11, an .817 winning percentage which would not be matched until a team called the Philadelphia 76ers went 67–13 some 20 years later. Included in that rampage was a phenomenal home court record of 29–1 at Uline Arena.

Feerick averaged 16.8 points a game, second only to Philadelphia's Jumpin' Joe Fulks, who pioneered the jump shot. He shared all-league honors with McKinney, who averaged 12. Scolari (12.6) and Mahnken were named to the honorable mention squad. Though Norlander was overlooked in the honors department he averaged more than 10 points a game.

No other team had such offensive balance. The Caps also played a switching-off, helping-out *team* defense, leading the BAA with fewest points allowed. Their average winning margin was 9.9. Next best was western champion Chicago with a margin of but 3.7 points.

The BAA's unorthodox playoff format that season matched the two first-place teams against each other in the first round. Washington lost to Chicago, 4–2.

"Even at that young age [twenty-nine], Red showed he knew how to spot talent, and then get the very most out of it," marvels Eddie Gottlieb, the NBA's senior statesman who coached Philadelphia's Warriors until 1955.

It had been a shaky start for the new league. Attendance never reached expected levels, publicity was far less than what was accorded to the immensely popular collegians, and four franchises, Cleveland, Detroit, Pittsburgh and Toronto, folded.

There was a new look when the 1947–48 season rolled around. The Baltimore Bullets came aboard after quitting the dying American Basketball League. That gave the BAA eight teams. Washington moved to the western division. A draft was instituted and several top college stars arrived: Carl Braun (Colgate) and Sid Tannenbaum (NYU) with the Knicks; Red Rocha (Oregon State) with St. Louis; Andy Phillip and Gene Vance, both from Big 10 champ Illinois, with Chicago. But the biggest name to join the league was Joe Lapchick, the star of the old Celtics, who was in his heyday as coach of St. John's University. Joe replaced Neil Cohalan as coach of the Knickerbockers.

In an effort to curtail expenses, the league cut back from a 60-game schedule to 48.

Philadelphia (27–21) beat the Knicks out of first place by one game in the east, yet would have finished out of the running in the exciting west where St. Louis (29–19) was just one step ahead of Washington, Chicago and Baltimore—all of which posted 28–20 records!

The Caps, with essentially the same cast (though Auerbach finally succeeded in getting Sonny Hertzberg from New York), were eliminated in a special pre-playoff round robin series.

In 1948–49 the BAA staged a major coup by getting four top franchises to jump en masse from the rival NBL. Though it was generally conceded that the NBL had an edge in player personnel, the BAA had better locations and facilities. Indianapolis and Fort Wayne were the first to break ranks, followed shortly by the NBL kingpins—the champion Minneapolis Lakers, who featured George Mikan and Jim Pollard, and the runners-up, the Rochester Royals, led by Bob Davies, Al Cervi and Arnie Risen.

Meanwhile, Auerbach was doing some revamping himself. He sent Mahnken and reserve guard Irv Torgoff to Baltimore in exchange for two former NBL stars: 6'9 center Kleggie Hermsen and 6'2 forward Dick Schultz. He rescued guard Matt Zunic, a fellow GW grad, from the floundering NBL, drafted North Carolina State backcourt star Leo Katkavech, and picked up Jack Nichols, a sharp-shooting 6'7 forward from Washington midway through the season.

It was rapidly becoming a league of superstars—Mikan, Fulks, Zaslofsky, Davies, and others—yet Washington won the six-team eastern race without a scorer in the Top 10. Indeed, the Caps' leading scorer, Feerick (13.0), finished 14th in the race—but he was one of five Washington players to average double figures! They won 21 out of 24 in one remarkable stretch, including 15 wins in a row.

The Caps got by Philadelphia and New York in the playoffs, then went up against the Mikan-led powerhouse from Minneapolis in the championship round. With Feerick sidelined by torn cartilage, Scolari hampered by a splinted finger and McKinney shaken by a death in his family, the best-of-seven series was really no contest. The Lakers grabbed a 3–0 lead. Washington won the next two in Uline Arena. Then the Lakers applied the coup de grâce, 77–56, back in St. Paul.

In the spring of 1949 the remaining members of the NBL agreed to join forces with the BAA. The combined league would henceforth be known as the National Basketball Association.

Auerbach emerged as the premier coaching personality in the three years the BAA existed. His regular season records totaled 115–53, or a .685 winning percentage. The only other coach to win as many as 60 percent of his games during that time was Harold "Ole" Olsen, who left a Big Ten champion at Ohio State to take the helm of the Chicago Stags in the fall of

1946. Olsen's club had a record of 105–64, or a .621 winning percentage. None of the other top clubs—St. Louis, New York or Philadelphia—could come close to matching the consistency of Auerbach's Washington Caps.

"There was one very strong impression Red gave us all back when we first started out," Freddy Scolari remembers. "Maybe we knew as much as, or even more than, he did, but he was the boss and he never hesitated to let us know that. He came across as a very strong character. I think he was the shrewdest guy I ever met. He was cocky, arrogant and sometimes extremely difficult to like. In fact, I never really got to like him until years later. But I always respected him, and that was the key to Red's whole approach to coaching. He didn't care if his guys liked him or not. All he demanded was their respect and obedience. And he got it.

"Yet it wasn't hard to play for Red because he made sure we all understood what he was doing. We didn't have a hell of a lot to say about it, of course. They freed the ballplayers a long time after they freed the slaves! But we all knew and understood our jobs, and that made playing a whole lot easier.

"If anyone asks me about it today, I tell them Auerbach revolutionized this game. I still see college and professional coaches using plays—such as the out-of-bounds pass—which Red invented back in Washington.

"And he wasn't afraid to try new things. I was the only guy in our starting five who didn't go near the pivot. There was no way I could because of my size. But the other guys—Mahnken, McKinney, Norlander and Feerick—would always bring their men into the pivot whenever they got into trouble, and help would be waiting. No one else did things like that in those days.

"He created a monster in those 1946 Caps."

He also created havoc on the sidelines.

Commissioner Podoloff, in an effort to generate interest in the upstart BAA, hired a young Notre Dame graduate named Walter Kennedy to handle the league's publicity. Kennedy would go on to become mayor of Stamford, Connecticut, and later succeed Podoloff as NBA commissioner in 1963.

"I go back a long way with Arnold," he smiles. "Only Eddie Gottlieb has been associated with him longer than I have.

Everyone knew Gottlieb and Neil Cohalan and Ole Olsen and Joe Lapchick and the others who coached in those early years, but no one knew who the hell Arnold Auerbach was. But they found out very quickly. He earned the respect of his fellow coaches right away. While everyone else seemed to emphasize individual play, Arnold showed what team play could accomplish.

"But his tactics never endeared him to fans in other cities. He had the qualities of brashness, cockiness and confidence way back then, and because of that—and also because of the great success his team enjoyed—there seemed to be a great resentment towards the Caps. People called him arrogant. I never believed that, but he certainly knew how to get the officials and the fans riled up.

"He could raise an awful commotion. And, like any pro, he improved with age."

Right from the start, I was determined that if I was going to be fired or be unsuccessful, it was going to be because I lacked the knowledge or I lacked the ability. It was not going to be because of some temperamental goddamned athlete who wouldn't do what he was told, or who wanted to take over my ball club. There was just no damned way I was going to let that happen.

So my first concern was very basic: How do I get these guys to listen to me? I know what's going through their minds. They're telling themselves that they're better ballplayers than I was, and as a result they probably know more about the game than I do.

I had to impress upon them that I knew what I was doing.

"Look," I said, "my job is to coach you guys, and I've made a study out of it. That's my job—to know what's going on out there. And I've had some experience at it. You can't see everything while you're out there, but I can. If you have suggestions, give them to me. If you spot little ways to take advantage of people out there, tell me and I'll make sure we get the ball to you. Let's use all of the knowledge we've got on this team. But remember one thing: I make the moves. All you can make is suggestions.

"I know you guys are better players than I am. If I was bet-

ter than you, I'd be out there playing, too. But I'm not. So my job is coaching, and I work damned hard at it. I spend twenty hours a day at it.

"All I want you to worry about is staying in shape and playing the game. You've got enough to think about between trying to beat the man who's guarding you and trying to remember the plays.

"Let me worry about everything else, because I can see the overall picture.

"If I tell you something, I've got a reason for it. But if it bothers you, ask me about it—when the game is over! I'll listen. I'll also prove to you that I'm right. If I can't prove it, then I'll back off. I'm not a goddamned thickhead. But I am the boss. And I don't want you to forget that for a minute, because I hired you and I can fire you."

Thank God, there weren't too many problems. Once in a while a guy would step out of line, but usually I could prove to him that I was right. And if I couldn't do that, I'd just remind him that I was the boss. Either way, I won.

Take the time Matt Zunic came to us. We used to call him Mad Matt back at GW because he was very demonstrative. Matt was a sophomore when I was a senior, and I just barely beat him out for top scoring honors on the team. After the war he kicked around for a while in the other leagues. Then I said to him, "Okay, Matt, I'll give you a shot with us."

His first game with the Caps was in Washington, where he had played his college ball. After he had been playing for a while I sent in a substitute. He stormed back to the bench, threw his jacket onto the floor and yelled, "What the hell did you take me out for?"

Now I'm only three years older than him, and we've been friends for quite a while, and I know the rest of the team has heard him and is watching to see what I'll do. I didn't say anything right then. I let him sit there for about three minutes, then I spoke.

"Hey Matt, come over here," I said. Everyone's head turned.

"I'm going to tell you this just one time. What you just did— throwing your jacket and yelling at me—doesn't go here.

That's the last time you're ever going to do it and remain with this team. I brought you here, and I can kick your ass out of here just as fast. Don't you ever throw your jacket down again. And don't you ever speak to me when I take you out of a ball game. I want no more demonstrations. Understand?

"I don't have to give you a reason for any move I make. There could be a million reasons. Maybe I think there's a guy on the bench who can do a better job at that particular time. Maybe I just want to rest you. It doesn't matter. When you come out, I want you to sit down and shut up. That goes for everybody on this team."

I never had another problem with him. We've remained good friends. But that was a challenge I had to deal with as soon as it happened. I had to get the message through to him, but at the same time it gave me an opportunity to remind everyone else of what I expected from them. But you have to know when to blow your top and when to simply make your point. All I wanted to do with Zunic was make my point.

And that point was this: when I give an order, the one thing I never want to hear is "Why?"

A lot of coaches go along with the idea in that Grantland Rice poem: "It matters not that you won or lost—but how you played the game." It's a good poem, but the philosophy is a lot of crap. So is that baloney about losing coaches building character!

As far as I'm concerned, it is important whether you win or lose. And who says you can't build character when you win? As long as you're going to keep score, you've got to go out there with the idea of winning. I've always believed that. And I've always wanted my ballplayers to believe that, too. Winning is important!

I'm not suggesting you should be vicious or dirty. I've never played an injured man, and I've never wanted to see anyone get hurt.

But I'd break or bend every damned rule in the book if I thought it would help me win a ball game!

If you go into a war, you go to win, don't you? You don't know what's going to happen to you if you lose it. And you

*don't want to know. Would I die for my country? Yes I would,
if I had to. But you can be damned sure I'd try to make the
enemy die for his country first!*

*Basketball, to me, is like a war. When I first took the Caps
job I used to think about that all the time. I'd look around me
and ask myself, "What the hell am I qualified for?" I could
teach, but I had no business experience. I wasn't a musician or
an artist or a doctor or an inventor or a mechanic. So right
from the beginning, I felt there was a great deal of pressure on
me to be successful, to be the best I could be. That meant winning. So I worked hard at it.*

*I used to go home and stay awake nights, wondering, "What
will it take for us to win?" I'd list my ball club on a piece of
paper, name by name, and then I'd take the three best teams in
the league and list them the same way, name by name. I'd
study the names and consider the match-ups, and I'd ask myself, "Can my club—if I coach to the best of my ability—be in
the same class with these three?"*

*If the answer was yes, then I'd work their asses off until they
proved it. And if the answer was no, I'd analyze the lists and
try to figure out just what I needed in a trade or the draft to
make my team a champion.*

*I didn't want to improve my team to make it better. I wanted
to make it the best! I used to read these ridiculous statements
from baseball managers, saying, "Jeez, if we have a hell of a
year, and so-and-so bats .350, and someone else bats .320 and
so on and so forth, we hope to finish in the first division!" I
can't understand it. I thought the idea was to try and be the
best. First division? Who wants to shoot for the first division? I
certainly didn't. I was aiming to be the best.*

*Next to each name I'd write down what I figured we could
count on from each guy: Feerick—16 points; Scolari—12;
Mahnken—10; Norlander—11. I'd figure on so many points
from the reserves, and I'd end up with my expected total.*

Say it's 80 points.

*Okay, the other side's coming at me with all of its offensive
weapons, just like in a war. So how am I going to stop the goddamned war?*

Defense!

Forget, for a moment, things like motivation and hustle and tenacity of purpose and dedication. Those come under the heading of plain, simple preparation.

What I've got to do, under normal situations, is stop the other side from scoring 80 points, too.

So when I got to the practice floor, we'd talk about offense and defense and then I'd try to break it down for my players, just the way I had broken it down for myself while I was thinking about it at home.

Suppose, during the course of a game, Joe Blow throws the ball away five times. This was before the 24-second clock, remember. You could hold the ball if you wanted to. I'd bring this to his attention.

"You're throwing away a potential of ten points. Plus they might commit a foul, or get mad and get a technical. So really, you're throwing away a potential of as much as fifteen points. Now they get the ball and they've got the same potential to score fifteen points. Now you're talking a total difference of thirty points! How many games are decided by thirty points?"

I can see their eyes lighting up. So I carry it further.

"Let's just take it in the clutch, in the last four minutes. Suppose we throw it away twice? We're giving up four, maybe six points. And maybe the other team will score. Let's say, for practical purposes, the bulge is five points. How many games do you win by five points?"

This sounds terribly simple, I know. But there's a lot of truth to it. So they'd start thinking about it and pretty soon they'd get the message: the ball is valuable!

Another big part of our game was conditioning. I am a very strong believer in good conditioning. It's essential in order to play a fast-break offense and full-court pressing defense, which is how I've always had my teams play.

I remember we went into New York one night and the Knicks beat us. The next day the Washington papers had headlines: BETTER CONDITION BEATS CAPS! That's what Lapchick told the writers.

The next time we played New York I made it a point to bring Lapchick's comment up in my pregame talk.

"Let's get them," I told my guys. "If there's one thing we're not, it's a poorly-conditioned ball club. We're a great-condi-

*tioned ball club. Screw Lapchick and anybody else who says
we're not! But the only way we're going to shut him up is to go
out there and run them off the court. Now get out there and
show them!"*

*We did just that. We flattened them by 30 points. Later that
night I ran into Lapchick, and some of my players must have
talked to the writers or something, because the first thing Joe
says to me is, "How come you were talking about me in your
locker room?"*

I was hoping he'd ask.

*"Because of what you told the writers after the last game! It
was uncalled for. If you beat me, you beat me. That's all.
When I beat you, I don't go around telling the writers it's because your club stinks, or I'm so great or anything else. I don't
say anything at all. So what are you doing, talking about our
conditioning?"*

*I'll give him credit. He said I was right, and that he was sor-
ry, and that he hadn't meant anything personal by it.*

Joe and I ended up becoming very close friends.

*I never got along too well with the referees, which I'll get
into later on. A lot of my troubles with them stemmed right
back to those early years in Washington.*

*Here I was, going up against guys like Ole Olsen and Honey
Russell and Joe Lapchick—all great, great college coaches
with big reputations—and I was a complete nobody. I knew,
consciously or subconsciously, the referees were going to listen when a guy like Lapchick objected to a call. When he had a
beef, they were going to listen. But if I objected to something,
they'd be thinking, Who's this punk kid? I was very much
aware of this, and I knew I had to figure out a way to coun-
teract it.*

*So I became a fighting type of coach. On and off the court, I
was going to back my ball club right down to the wire! They
were the guys I was going to have to win with, and I was
damned well not going to let them get the short end of the
stick—not for any reason, but especially not because the referees thought they could ignore me. In their minds I'm sure
they were convinced I couldn't possibly be as smart or know as
much as Lapchick and those other guys.*

Goddamn it, when Joe protested a call—especially in Madison Square Garden—it was as if his word was Gospel!

He'd get mad and kick a bucket of water and the officials would give him a reprimand. I'd start to say something and they'd hit me with a technical. This shit went on all the time. One night he got mad and reached into his pocket, took out some change and threw it all over the court! If I did that, it would cost me $100. All he got was a warning.

See, I was smart enough to appreciate that New York was the core of the league. It still is. And knowing a little bit about the human psychology, I knew that the referees had to be affected—even awed—by the New York media. New York was the Mecca. All the magazine stories and all of the wire stories came out of New York. When we traveled, we didn't even bring a trainer. When the Knickerbockers went on the road, they had a whole entourage of newspapermen with them. So there was no way New York was going to get a bad shake from the referees.

If anything bad happened to the Knicks, or if Joe Lapchick happened to be upset by something, hang onto your hats! God forbid anybody offend New York. If a little sportswriter from the Post *or the* Star *in Washington criticized the referees, who cared? More to the point, who knew? It got buried. It meant nothing. But if a New York writer criticized the officials, the whole damed country heard about it!*

So these officials were smart enough to recognize this, and careful not to antagonize the powerful New York machinery.

That's why one of my greatest thrills was taking the Washington team into Madison Square Garden and knocking Lapchick's guys onto their asses. But in order to do that, I had to be sure we got at least a fair break in the officiating. At home I'd hope to get an advantage, maybe by getting the crowd worked up, but on the road all I was looking for was a fair break.

That's when I started to get a reputation for fighting with the officials.

The refs would make a couple of bad calls, or they'd miss a couple of obvious ones, so I'd pop off and let them have it. I knew it would cost me a technical, but in my mind it was a strategic technical. And after I got it, I'd try to control myself again. I knew my ranting and raving wasn't going to make them change their minds on a particular call. The idea was to get the next call in our favor!

It was just my way of letting them know I was aware of what was happening out there, too, even if my name wasn't Lapchick or Olsen. I wanted them to know Auerbach was no dummy either.

Chapter 6
A Tale Of Tri-Cities

"A little knowledge is a dangerous thing."

A few days before Christmas 1948, the Caps played the lowly Providence Steamrollers, the worst team in the league, and beat them by a 102–77 score. The win gave Washington a 20–2 record.

"The Caps are so all-fired superior they're becoming a bore," Washington columnist Shirley Povich noted a few weeks later. "When they win game after game this way, the fans' reaction is 'So what?' "

The Caps had 59 points by halftime, and a great shot at the BAA record of 117, set earlier in December by Mikan's Lakers against the same hapless Steamrollers. But Auerbach elected to rest his top guns, including Feerick, who had scored 24 points in the first 28 minutes and was taking dead aim on Carl Braun's BAA mark of 47.

That strategy fascinated Boston columnist Harold Kaese, who proceeded to interrogate the Redhead after the game.

"Why did you pull Feerick out of the game?"

"Why not? Why should I ask everyone else to feed Feerick the rest of the game? I'm not interested in records. I just want to win and keep the players happy."

"But won't that make Feerick unhappy?"

"Look, he's played for me long enough to know that the team comes first."

Towards the end of that 1948–49 season rumors began sweeping Washington, suggesting a mutiny was brewing on Auerbach's ship. One paper ran a banner headline reading: CAPS STEWING OVER RETENTION OF COACH. The story reported that several players were openly hostile towards their boss.

"The whole thing stems around one or two players," Red insisted to sportswriter Bill Fuchs. "They didn't have as good a year as they had last year, and they became disgruntled when I started using other men in their places. Well, the other men came through, and that's all I'm interested in."

At the center of the maelstrom was Red's old navy buddy, Feerick, now nearing 32 and bothered by a persistent leg injury. Word had it that the perennial all-star had an eye on Auerbach's job.

"It's a long story," Freddy Scolari recalls, "but I think Red made a mistake with Feerick. He made Feerick bigger than Red Auerbach in some ways. Bob was Red's own creation. Somehow, some people got the feeling they could get along without Red as long as Bob was there. They were very wrong, of course."

At the conclusion of the season Auerbach quit the Caps and Feerick was immediately named player-coach. The issue, publicly, was a contract dispute between Red and Mike Uline. Privately, however, no one doubted an insurrection had succeeded.

Uline, who had cast his lot with Auerbach because he admittedly didn't understand the game, now felt independent enough to bid farewell to the man who had brought him the finest three-year record in the BAA.

He would later regret the decision.

Within days of his departure from the Caps, Red was contacted by Billy Werber, a former major league infielder, who was now a member of the athletic board at Duke University.

Duke had a delicate problem. Gerry Gerard had been its basketball coach for the past seven years, during which time the Blue Devils compiled an excellent 116–63 record. But Werber had learned that the popular Gerard was suffering from a terminal illness. While Duke had no intention of replacing him—at least not until Gerard made the suggestion—a replacement had to be found and kept waiting in the wings.

Auerbach agreed to go to the Durham, N.C., campus as an advisory coach and an assistant professor of physical education.

In September he moved Dot and Nancy to their new home in Academe.

Back in the NBA, Ben Kerner had high hopes for his franchise. Kerner had been a hustling advertising executive in Buffalo when he formed his Buffalo Bisons basketball team in the early '40s. In December of 1946 he decided to jump into the sport on a full-time basis and moved his whole operation to Moline, Illinois, where he entered his team in the NBL under the unlikely name of the Tri-Cities Blackhawks. Sharing a rooting interest with Moline were the towns of Rock Island, Illinois, and Davenport, Iowa.

In 1946–47, under coach Nat Hickey, Tri-Cities was 19–25. When Hickey got off to an 8–12 start in 1947–48, Kerner fired him and hired Bobby McDermott, and the Hawks went 22–18 for an overall season's record of 30–30. Late in the 1948–49 season the Hawks were 25–20. Not content with moderate success, Kerner promptly canned McDermott and brought in a local high school coach named Roger Potter to finish out the schedule. Under Potter the team was 11–8.

Now, in 1949–50, Tri-Cities joined the other five survivors of the NBL—Indianapolis, Anderson, Sheboygan, Waterloo and Denver—in the new NBA. It was a very exciting period for pro basketball and Kerner had no intention of sitting back and watching the parade go by. He wanted a winner, and when Potter's team lost five of its first six games, Ben reached for his handy hatchet and another coach's head rolled.

Auerbach was unhappy and restless at Duke when he got the phone call from Kerner, offering him a two-year contract for $17,000.

He quickly accepted, shipped Dot and the baby back home to Washington, and made his way to Moline.

"Auerbach is the answer to our problems," Kerner assured the press conference he convened on November 9 to introduce his fourth coach in less than three years. "He's going to look over this club, decide who to keep and who to let go. Because of his reputation in pro ball he will be given full authority to trade and build as he sees fit. This is the man to tell us what we need here."

One newsman had a significant scoop the next day, however, for he overheard Red telling Kerner: "I'll give these customers a real show if you'll pay the fines!"

The *Davenport* (Iowa) *Democrat* identified Auerbach as "the Easterner."

"People used to yell out, 'You New York sonofabitch!'" laughs Sid Borgia, one of the best known NBA referees. "Fans today have no idea what it was like back then. You know what would happen years ago? We'd go out to Sheboygan or Waterloo and the local team would be playing the Celtics or Knickerbockers. First of all, those people hated anyone who came from the East. Right away that's against you. And if you happened to be Jewish on top of that, you really caught hell. Me, with my name Sid, I was an immediate target. They figured I had to be Jewish with a name like Sid.

"So one night I'm in Waterloo, and they had had a riot or something in the previous game, brought on by a referee's decision. Now the whole damned town is antireferee! Anyway, the players come onto the floor and the announcer starts in. He introduces both sides. Then he waits until everyone is quiet, and he says, very distincly, 'Now ladies and gentlemen, the referees assigned to tonight's game by the NBA are . . . '

"He introduces the other guy first, some local ref.

"Then he pauses again, and says, '. . . *and from New York City . . .*'

"Christ, they start right in, booing my ass off!

"He waits, then says, '*Sid–neee . . .*'

"Not Sid! Oh, no. '*Sid–neee!*'

"Do you know it took fifteen minutes to clear the shit off the floor before I could toss up the first ball?

"Those were the days, my friend."

The local fans took quickly to "Auerbach from New York" when the Blackhawks defeated Waterloo 99–89 in Red's first night on the job. The 99 points represented a new team scoring record.

Two weeks later a record 6,156 fans jammed the Wharton

Field House in Moline—hundreds were left beating on the doors outside—and the Blackhawks responded with a 104–88 romp over the division-leading Indianapolis Olympians.

Auerbach was wheeling and dealing all the while. Within six weeks he had completed deals involving a total of 28 players! Only three of the players he inherited would remain by the following March. Among his key acquisitions were two old Washington Caps: John Mahnken, whom he got from Fort Wayne, and Jack Nichols, whom he plucked from Mike Uline in midwinter.

"Kerner and Auerbach have seemingly fitted together like hand and glove," AP writer Joe Ives observed. "Auerbach has spotted the talent and Kerner has gone out and gotten it." Tri-Cities made more player transactions that season than the other 16 NBA teams combined.

If there was any doubt over who was running the show, an incident in a game against the Anderson Packers quickly cleared the air. The first period had just begun when Red decided to substitute Don Ray for starting forward Warren Perkins. In a scene reminiscent of the Matt Zunic affair, Perkins objected vehemently upon his return to the bench. Auerbach immediately ordered him out of the arena and into the locker room.

"I've got six thousand coaches in the stands," he told writers later. "I can't afford another one on the team. So I suspended him from tonight's game for rank insubordination."

Perkins was back in the lineup the next game and Red never had any more difficulty with the ex-Tulane star.

The highlight of Auerbach's winter came late in January when he led his revamped Blackhawks into Uline Arena for the first time. The crowd lustily booed the Redhead—who wore a new suit for the occasion—as he ranted and raved and berated the officials from start to finish. Just before the final buzzer signaled Tri-Cities' 85–81 triumph, Auerbach looked over at the press row and shouted: "Boy, am I going to sleep good tonight!"

A day or so later a Washington paper ran an angry letter from a Caps fan, part of which read: ". . . I have spent many

a $5 bill for two front row seats to watch the Washington
Caps. I have always enjoyed it until this year when Bob Feerick took over and tried to remake the best team in pro basketball . . . There were a lot of things that Red Auerbach did
that I couldn't agree with, and at times I was very much dis-
gusted with him, but now that I have seen what Feerick has
done to the Caps, I realize what a great coach Red was and
still is. His record with Tri-Cities proves that."

The Caps, with Feerick, McKinney, Scolari, Norlander and
Don Otten, the seven-foot Bowling Green star whom Auerbach traded for Nichols, wound up 32–36, their first losing
record ever.

Halfway through the following season the club was disbanded.

Observers familiar with both Kerner and Auerbach kept
waiting for an explosion. Ben was an inveterate meddler in his
team's affairs while Auerbach demanded nothing less than total autonomy as coach. From Day One they were on a collision course.

The inevitable confrontation reads like a very predictable
script. Kerner had a notion that Boston's Gene Englund, a 6'5
forward who starred at Wisconsin, was a more valuable prop-
erty than Mahnken, one of Red's personal favorites. He kept
urging Auerbach to make the trade, but Red was adamantly
against it. Then one day while he was on the road with his
club, Auerbach received the following telegram: HAVE TRAD-
ED MAHNKEN FOR ENGLUND —WILL ASSUME RESPONSIBILI-
TY—BEN.

Red finished the season, including the playoffs—in which
Tri-Cities lost two out of three to the eventual runner-up,
Anderson—then walked into Kerner's office and quit.

"He was a great coach, and he worked at it day and night,"
Kerner remembers. "That Englund trade was the only problem we had."

Then Kerner laughed. "We had an understanding when he
was in town. But when he was out of town there was no understanding. Seriously, though, things were different back
then. Owners were much more involved because basketball
was their only business. This was my whole livelihood. I had

nothing else. So some of my own thinking had to go into the franchise."

Thus Auerbach, who started the season as the ex-Caps coach, ended the season as the ex-Blackhawks coach.

But he didn't remain unemployed very long.

Walter Brown, the man who pioneered the BAA in 1946, was on the brink of disaster with his Boston Celtics. He had already lost too many games and too much money. Then, he lost his coach, too, when Alvin "Doggie" Julian accepted the head coaching job at Dartmouth.

Brown intended to try one more season—1950–51, and Auerbach was the man he wanted to coach his ball club. But Kerner still had a second year left on his contract with Red.

Maurice Podoloff, the diminutive commissioner, stepped in. "Podoloff called me and told me about Walter's problems," Ben explains. "He said I'd be doing a great thing for the NBA and for the Celtics in particular if I allowed Red to go to Boston. Red wasn't going to stay with me anyway, and I had an awful lot of respect for Walter Brown, so I called Podoloff back the next morning and told him it would be all right with me if Walter contacted Red. But I told him I wanted to talk to Auerbach first.

"Despite our differences, I liked Red. I told him what had happened and then I said, 'Good-bye—and don't louse it up!' "

I don't really know when the trouble started in Washington. We were winning—winning big, as a matter of fact—and we were doing it as a team. Everywhere you looked that season, someone had a superscorer, whether it was Mikan in Minneapolis, Braun in New York, Fulks in Philadelphia or Zaslofsky in Chicago. But my teams don't play that way. Sure, Feerick could have been right up there with the rest of them if we had geared all of our plays to him. Bob was a great, great scorer, and at 6'5 he was bigger than most of the guards who played back then. No one could have stopped him from scoring 25 or 30 points a night if that's what we had wanted him to do.

But that wasn't what I wanted. I've always believed in a bal-

anced attack, for two reasons: one, you don't suffer as much when your big man has an off night; and two, it tends to keep everybody happy. Hell, Scolari was a great shooter, too. So was Nicholas. And McKinney didn't mind scoring once in a while. Neither did Hermsen or Hertzberg.

What am I supposed to do? Tell nine guys to work their asses off on defense, but then forget about the offense because we want to make a superstar out of the 10th guy?

Feerick never complained to me, but I was told he became very upset that night I sat him down when he had a chance to break Braun's scoring record. Later on I heard from some of the guys that he sometimes talked about wanting to be traded. I didn't lose any sleep over that. Ballplayers talk that way all the time, especially when they think they've been abused. Feerick was getting one of the best salaries in the league. There was no reason to believe he really meant the things I kept hearing.

That was just the beginning. Later I found out he had met privately with Uline, and soon there was speculation about him replacing me as coach.

As soon as the playoffs ended I went in to see Uline. I had planned on asking for a three-year contract long before any of these troubles began. I gave him a good, competitive team, just as I had promised, and I felt my performance merited that kind of contract. With the possibility of a disciplinary problem to deal with, I was even more determined to have the front office back me up. A third consideration was that the nucleus of my club—Feerick, Scolari, McKinney, Norlander—was getting older. It was time to begin thinking more about the future.

"Mr. Uline," I said, "I'll come right to the point. I think I've done a good job for you and I think I deserve a three-year contract this time."

"You're right, you have done a good job," he told me, "but you know my policy, and you know the reasons for it. As much as I'd like to make an exception in this case, I'm not going to. All I can offer you is another one-year agreement."

A few years earlier he had given a hockey coach a long-term contract and the guy had never produced, or something like that, and Uline got stuck paying him anyway. So he said he'd never again give anyone more than a one-year package.

But I was sure that wasn't his reason for saying no to me. I was quite certain he had already made up his mind to give the job to Feerick, but he couldn't very well fire a coach who had just brought him to the final round of the playoffs. If he wanted me badly enough, I figured, he'd have been happy to give me the contract I asked for. But by sticking to his guns the way he did, he was putting the burden on me. He knew I wouldn't settle for one year again. I'd quit first. That would solve his problem without putting him into the role of a bad guy. I could stay or I could go. The choice was mine. But we both knew damned well that there wasn't any choice at all.

There were a lot of things I could have said at that moment, a lot of advice I could have given him. There was no way in the world that the players were going to react properly to Feerick's leadership. I knew that. Bones knew it. Scolari knew it. Some of the players even came up to me before the playoffs ended, when all of the papers were talking about "unrest," and said, "Gee, Red, don't let it happen!" See, Bob was a wonderful player, and despite his injuries I still felt he could be effective for another couple of years. But there was no way he could play and keep track of everything that was happening and make substitutions and keep the guys motivated all at once.

But if I started telling these things to Uline, it would have looked as if I was just trying to save my own skin. I'm not even sure he would have believed me. It was something he'd just have to learn for himself.

"Okay," I said, "you've got a guy here who thinks he can do my job, and meanwhile you're thinking that you can save yourself an extra salary by making him a player-coach. I'll agree that it's one way to cut expenses, but I'll also guarantee you it's the biggest mistake you're ever going to make with this team."

Then I shook his hand and headed for the door.

"Good-bye, Mr. Uline. And good luck."

I was still looking around for something when I got the call from Duke. Right away I liked the idea of going there—until Billy Werber explained the Gerry Gerard situation. All of a sudden I wan't so sure. But Billy assured me there would be no awkwardness. "Gerry will remain head coach," he ex-

plained. "You'll have plenty of duties to keep you busy, like teaching a phys ed class and maybe coaching the handball team. And anytime Gerry needs help, of course, you'll be around to pitch in."

Dot was all for the idea. For the first time since we'd been married we would have a normal home life with friends and neighbors and a routine schedule. The move would be good for little Nancy, too, because we found out she had an asthma condition. The North Carolina climate would be better for her, we were told. And, of course, I would be doing the kind of work I wanted to do.

So I told Werber I'd take the job.

It was no good. Gerry had cancer, and he was taking regular cobalt treatments for it. He suffered, but he hung in there in a magnificent display of courage and determination. The whole situation was tearing me apart inside. I couldn't sleep at night. This guy was my friend, and here I was sitting around waiting for him to die. I know that wasn't exactly the way it was, but that's the way I felt. I couldn't stand it.

I guess I began feeling that way when I'd show up in the gym and kids would come over to me, wanting to discuss some aspect of the game. These were Gerry's players, not mine, and I had no damned business giving them advice or tips. I couldn't blame the kids. They figured I was a pro coach and that I had all the answers. But I'd always tell them, "Gerry's your coach, and he's a damned good one. Go ask him and see what he thinks."

Finally I stopped going to the gym altogether.

That's when I heard from Ben Kerner. Talk about an answer to a prayer! I had made up my mind to leave Duke, anyway, and now here was an opportunity to get back into pro ball. The timing was perfect.

Once I got Dot and Nancy headed back to Washington, I went out to Illinois to meet my new ball club.

Maybe the weight of the Gerry Gerard situation, on top of the unpleasant way things ended up with the Caps, had worn me down. I don't know. I had always been very confident of my abilities and very strong in my convictions, but shortly after I arrived in Tri-Cities I went through a period of depression.

I found myself worrying too much. We'd lose a game and it would bother me all night long. Was it the players' fault we lost? Common sense says it can't be their fault all the time. So maybe it was my fault. Did I make a bad move, or forget to make a key substitution, or fail to motivate them properly?

One night, after a loss, I was sitting by myself in the arena. It was dark and quiet, and I was trying to analyze the whole situation, when Ben came over to me. I don't quite remember if I was having doubts about my own abilities, or just wondering how in hell I had allowed myself to come back into pro ball with such a lousy team. Ben sensed I was troubled, so he sat down with me and we began to talk about the ball club.

We started discussing possible trades and moves we could make, and suddenly I could feel myself getting excited again.

I snapped out of my mood that night, and never thought about those things again.

We rebuilt the Blackhawks. We got Gene Vance to come out of retirement and we went after guys like Nicholas and Mahnken. When I traded away Don Otten there was all kinds of criticism in the press, but Kerner stood behind me 100 percent. Ben was a great salesman and I think the trading activity really excited him. I'd tell him who I wanted and then he'd go out and get him.

Little by little we could see a new team taking shape. A big win here, a sellout crowd there—things were happening fast. There's no question that the biggest thrill of all for me—and I think maybe for Ben, too—was the night I took the team into Washington and we kicked the shit out of the Caps! Don't misunderstand. I liked a lot of the guys there. But there's something very special about returning home as a winner. It's the same feeling I had the first time my Caps beat the Knicks in Madison Square Garden. Those are triumphs you never forget.

I had a lot of admiration for Ben Kerner. I've often said if he was still active in the NBA today the Players Association wouldn't get away with its one-sided attitude and selfish demands. He was a businessman, and no businessman would stand for the ridiculous situations we've seen in recent years.

Ben was from the old school of NBA owners—guys like

Walter Brown, Eddie Gottlieb and Danny Biasone. The Black-
hawks weren't just an investment to him; they were his livelihood. *He put his whole life into that team, and as a result he*
always had this fear: How can I put everything I own in this
world in the hands of another person?
  The answer, of course, is that he couldn't. I used to try kid-
ding him. I'd say, "You know, Ben, a little knowledge is a dan-
gerous thing." But it made no impression. He wanted to have
his hands into everything involving his ball club. As long as he
and I were in agreement, it didn't matter. I'd suggest going af-
ter a certain player. He'd concur, then he'd be on the phone the
next minute trying to work out the arrangements. And he was
damned good at that end of the business.
  I don't know where he ever got the idea that Englund was a
better player than Mahnken, or that we even needed a guy like
Englund on our ball club. The first time he brought it up I put
my foot down. "Absolutely not!" I said. "We need Mahnken."
  He kept pestering me about it, and I'd try to explain that
Englund was only 6'5 while Mahnken was a solid 6'8. John
was a good center, plus he knew our plays and our system.
What would happen if we got into a playoff game and Jack
Nichols, my starting center, fouled out? What good would En-
glund be to us?
  The trade made no sense at all, but I could see that Ben was
determined, so just before I left on a road trip I made him
promise that he wouldn't make any moves without consulting
me.
  I couldn't believe it when I got that telegram.
  I didn't want to make a big scene then because the team was
just starting to jell and the playoffs were only around the cor-
ner. I knew what I'd have to do, and my decision was greatly
reinforced when Nichols did foul out of a playoff game. Even
if he hadn't, my mind was made up.
  The day after we were eliminated I paid Ben a visit.
  "Ben, I'm not going to stay," I said as I sat down.
  "If you don't, you can't coach in the NBA next year, because
we've got a two-year contract,"
  "I don't care. I'll go back to college if I have to."
  "But why?"

"We've got a problem here. You apparently don't appreciate my knowledge. If you're going to make all of the decisions here, then you don't need me."

With that, I got up and left.

I was back where I had started a year before, out of a job. Once again I considered returning to teaching. Pro ball, it seemed, was not the answer.

Then Walter Brown stepped into the picture. The Boston Celtics, he explained, wanted Red Auerbach to be their coach.

PART TWO

The Story
of The Celtics

Chapter 7
Walter Brown's Woes

*"They loved him because he was Walter Brown. And
so did I."*

By the spring of 1950 Walter Brown had very few allies left
in his noble crusade to keep the Celtics alive. Indeed, the man
who personally breathed life into the BAA in 1946 still remained what in the Scriptures is referred to as "a prophet
without honor in his own country."

Everyone had tried to warn him that basketball just
wouldn't catch on in Boston. It was a baseball town in the
summer and a hockey town in the winter. There was so little
interest in basketball that the city's high schools didn't even
include the sport in their varsity programs.

"Kids from Boston would go out to Great Lakes or somewhere like that for their military training in 1941, 1942 and
1943 and they wouldn't know what to do when someone
brought out a basketball for recreation," smiles Joe Looney, a
longtime sportswriter for the old *Boston Herald.* "While kids
from Madison, Wisconsin, were throwing in hook shots, our
guys would stand around scratching their heads."

Outside of Boston it was a different story. Most suburban
towns had popular schoolboy teams and when they went into

Boston Garden for postseason tournaments the attendance figures were astounding. Crowds also flocked to the building whenever topflight college teams, like Bowling Green, made appearances.

Brown had been a hockey man all of his life. He was president of the immensely popular Bruins. He also founded a unique organization called the Boston Olympics, an amateur hockey team created to provide the U.S. Olympic Team with a steady source of talent. In their heyday, the Olympics drew capacity crowds into the Garden on Sunday nights.

So his friends were aghast when he brought up the idea of adding basketball to the building's busy agenda.

"We used to scoff at the game," recalls Howie McHugh, now in his thirtieth year as publicity director of the Celtics. At that time McHugh, who had been an All-American goalie at Dartmouth, was serving as coach of the Olympics and publicist for the Garden. "Nobody knew what basketball was all about. We thought it was a sissy's game, and I wanted no part of it."

But Brown was determined, so one day he called McHugh into his office and informed him he was about to become the PR man for the new team in town.

"But you don't know anything about basketball," Howie pleaded. "How are you going to run a team?"

"That's why I'm bringing you into it," Walter answered.

"Great," McHugh sighed. "I know half as much as you do."

They tossed around a few names for the franchise. Brown wondered how "Unicorns" or "Whirlwinds" might do, while his chagrined PR man held out for "Olympics," figuring it would at least get the hockey crowd's attention.

"Wait a minute," Brown said. "I've got it. The *Celtics.* We'll call them the Boston Celtics! The name's got a great tradition, and, besides, Boston's full of Irishmen. We'll put them in green uniforms and call them the Celtics."

The Celtics got off to a very late start in rounding up talent. While people like Auerbach in Washington were assembling their rosters, Brown spent most of the summer of 1946 waiting for Frank Keaney to accept the coaching job. Keaney, whose "firehouse" brand of fast-break offense had electrified New

England, decided—upon his physician's advice—to turn
down the job at the 11th hour and remain at the University of
Rhode Island. By the time Brown wooed John "Honey" Russell away from Seton Hall, most of the good talent was already
spoken for and Russell had to settle for a second-rate roster.

The Celtics finished last in 1946–47 and next-to-last the
year after. Brown lost $200,000 in those two seasons.

Meanwhile, Holy Cross, a small Jesuit college in nearby
Worcester, blossomed into a national collegiate power, winning the 1947 NCAA championship and compiling a 26–4 record in 1948. Even the hockey nuts of Boston stood up and
took notice. In an obvious attempt to cash in on the Holy
Cross pandemonium Brown replaced Russell with Alvin
"Doggie" Julian, the Crusaders' popular coach.

Doggie's approach didn't settle too well with the older,
more sophisticated pros. They simply didn't respond to his
leadership, and he was just as disenchanted with them. Only
the pathetic Providence Steamrollers kept the Cs out of the
cellar in 1949, and in 1950, after Providence had disbanded,
Boston fell to the bottom of the six-team eastern division.

In despair, Julian quit without notice and returned to collegiate ball as head coach at Dartmouth. Almost simultane-
ously, the directors of the Boston Garden voted to withdraw
all support of the Celtics, leaving the shambles entirely to
Brown, who by this time had lost nearly $500,000!

"Friends were begging Walter to give it up," says Marjorie
Brown, his widow. "And, truthfully, I was, too. We had just
finished paying off our house mortgage when the Celtics came
along. Walter owned stock in the Ice Capades and we used
those dividends to buy the home. By 1950 he had sold most of
the stock and remortgaged the house. Almost everything we
owned was locked up in the Celtics. One day I said to him,
'Walter, what's going to happen to us if it's all lost?' I was
worried. All of our friends were worried, too.

"But Walter loved that team. I've heard people say he hung
on because he was stubborn, or because he was too proud to
admit failure. That wasn't it at all. The Celtics were his idea
from the beginning, and he just never stopped believing in
them."

During the second week of April 1950, Brown made a series

of phone calls to radio and newspaper sports departments around the city, summoning his friends in the media to a mid-morning meeting in his Garden office. When all of the invited guests had been seated, he laid his cards on the table.

"Lord knows I don't know anything about this game," he began, "but you fellows do. You're my friends and you've been closer to this team tham anyone else. So who do you think I should hire as coach?"

Roger Barry, now semiretired after a long career of writing for the suburban *Quincy Patriot-Ledger*, recalls that session well.

"If you knew Walter," he smiles, "you'd know that what he did wasn't as unusual as it sounds. The man was completely informal, without any pretensions whatsoever."

Several names were bandied about, but three seemed to draw the most support: Buddy Jeannette, the Baltimore coach; Art Spector, the well-liked Celtic forward who would soon turn 30; and Auerbach.

"The more we talked, the more stories kept popping up about Red," Barry remembers. "Like the night his Caps came into the Garden and fell behind by twenty points in the third period. Feerick reported to the scorer's table and Tony Nota, the timekeeper, kidded him about forgetting this one. 'You think so, huh?' Feerick snapped at him. 'We're going to win this thing.' And they did win it. In those days if you fell behind by twenty on the road, it was all over. But Auerbach's teams never gave up, and that was a point everyone seemed to agree on."

By the time the meeting concluded, the consensus pointed towards the Redhead.

One other factor weighed heavily on Brown's mind. When the Garden washed its hands of the Celtics, he decided to look for a partner, someone who might share his faith in the franchise.

"He was desperate," Sammy Cohen, a close friend and sports editor of the *Boston Record*, recalls. "I introduced him to a broker in Boston who was willing to put up twenty-five thousand dollars. That was big money back then. But the guy wanted to know all about the business end of things, like how much popcorn was being sold, and this discouraged Walter.

He wanted someone who'd be enthused about the team itself. In his mind that was what was needed most. So he turned down the broker's offer."

He went to see Lou Pieri, a longtime business associate who owned and operated the Rhode Island Auditorium and its principal attraction, the AHL's Rhode Island Reds. Everything had been neat and orderly in Pieri's world until Brown persuaded him to jump aboard the BAA bandwagon in 1946. Pieri's Steamrollers lost almost $300,000 before Lou gave up on them in the spring of 1949.

Now, one year later, here was Brown beseeching him to give basketball one more go with a team that was only one step above the abominable 'Rollers.

Lou liked Walter. More important, he trusted him. So he agreed to invest $50,000, on one condition.

"Hire Auerbach," he said, "and we've got a deal."

When I walked out of Ben Kerner's office I was crushed. I really was. Damn it, I had done a good job, but once again I had the rug pulled out from under me by circumstances I couldn't control. By the time I got back home to Dot and Nancy I was really blue.

You can imagine what it meant to me the day I got the call about the Celtics' situation. I didn't know Walter Brown at the time, but I had heard a lot of good things about the man. And the idea of working in Boston was particularly attractive because it meant I wouldn't be that far away from home.

So I said yes.

Walter didn't pull any punches. He told me exactly how bad things were up in Boston. It's funny: the more he described his problems, the more I began to admire him. Most guys in his spot would try to sell you a bill of goods. They'd make everything sound rosy, as if you were the luckiest guy in the world to be getting the opportunity to coach their goddamned teams. Then as soon as you started to lose, they'd fire you and blame their troubles on the coaching.

Walter didn't operate that way, and I appreciated his honesty.

"I'm not going to try to kid you," he said. "We've got troubles, Red. I know you're interested in security. I wish I could

*offer you some. Believe me, I would if I could. But I don't
even have any security for myself. That's how bad things are.
All I can promise you is that you'll be treated fairly and I'll
back you all the way. If we're still in business next year, we
can talk about raises then. That's the picture. What do you
say?"*

How the hell can you say no to a man like that?

I didn't know where Walter had picked up all of his information about me, but I wasn't too surprised when I heard that
Lou Pieri was in my corner.

Right after I left the Caps, around the time I was looking for
a college job, Lou called me up and asked me if I'd be interested in coaching for him at Providence.

The year before, his team lost 42 out of 48. You can check it.
That's how awful they were. Then they lost 48 out of 60. (The
league had lengthened its schedule.) I never beat them as
badly as some of the other clubs did because I just didn't believe in rolling up the score that way. I wanted to beat them,
not humiliate them.

"Mr. Pieri," I said, "I'll level with you. You've got the worst
team I've ever seen in my life."

"You don't have to tell me that. I'm well aware of it," he
said.

"I know, but let me finish. You need a lot more than a coach.
You have to start all over again, right from the bottom, and I
know you've already lost a bundle. I don't know how much it
would cost to build a contender out of what you've got up
there. Maybe $300,000. Maybe more. You've got to decide if
you're willing to invest that much money on top of the losses
you've already absorbed. Frankly, I'm not sure it's worth it.
That's my honest opinion."

He didn't say anything for a moment or so. I don't think he
expected that kind of an answer from me.

"Red," he finally said, "I appreciate what you've told me.
It's excellent advice, and I'm going to think about it."

A couple of days later he announced the Steamrollers were
going out of business.

Walter and I had our occasional differences, but in my eyes
he was a magnificent human being who personified everything
good in sports. I learned a lot from him. Believe it or not, I

learned humility. I saw things in Walter that made lasting impressions on me, things I've tried to copy in my own life. He taught me that a man is a man. He once told me, "Take a man for what he is and what he does, and never mind anything else you've ever heard about him."

He never cared a damn about a man's color or religion or nationality or anything else. He just cared about the man. And what I observed in him only cemented my own feelings along those lines.

Through the years his players truly loved him. They didn't love him for his money. Shit, he was broke most of the time and everyone knew it. They loved him because he was Walter Brown. And so did I.

There was only one thing I demanded in the beginning. I wanted to run the show. If I didn't have complete authority over the players, I told him, then I wouldn't have their respect and obedience.

He agreed. He was too busy to be a real general manager anyway, and he knew it. He was involved with the Bruins, the Garden, the U.S. Olympic Committee, the Boston Athletic Association (which runs the Boston Marathon), and the professional ice shows, not to mention all kinds of charities and civic activities.

Plus he was a hero-worshiper, and that bothered me. To me, players are players, and that's what they get paid to be. They are not people to be adored and admired by their bosses!

Although he was a hockey man in the beginning, he became obsessed with the Celtics. The more he understood the game, the more he began to appreciate it. The more the team struggled, the more determined he was to see it survive. All of this was very good. But when he started to fall in love with the players, someone had to crack the whip or we'd have ended up with a bunch of happy guys in last place!

So I told him, "Walter, give me the authority I need."

"Okay," he said. "You've got it. Now go to work with it."

Chapter 8
Boston Meets the Redhead

"I don't give a damn for sentiment or names."

"I'll never forget the first time I met Red," Sammy Cohen says. "He had just arrived in town with his wife, so Herb Ralby, a sportswriter who worked on the side for the Garden, brought them to old Braves Field. I was standing there when the three of them walked up to me. I don't remember just what Red's words were, but I remember thinking this was the freshest bum who had ever come into town! He was like a sailor who had been out to sea for three years and had just gotten back on land. There was a cockiness about him, and he made it very plain that anyone whose heart and soul weren't into basketball was no good, in his book. I couldn't believe what I was hearing. I remember wondering how the hell a nice girl like Dot wound up with a stiff like this.

"That's exactly what I told Walter the next day, but he just laughed and told me I'd get used to Red.

"Of course, I did. We became very close friends over the years. But you could have bet me anything that night and I'd have said he wasn't going to make it in this town. Too fresh."

Brown hosted basketball luncheons every Monday in the Hotel Lenox, and his first guest of honor that season was the new coach of the Celtics. Red sat patiently at the head table as each of the local college coaches addressed the gathering. He took special note of Boston College coach Al McClellan's lament over the new NCAA rule which said substitutions could be made only during official time-outs.

"Time is automatically called when a player is injured, isn't it?" he asked McClellan moments later.

The coach nodded in agreement.

"Then why not have your players fake an injury so you can get a substitute in there?"

A chill fell over the room. "College coaches can't teach anything like that," McClellan replied. "It wouldn't be ethical."

Auerbach glared at him. "Don't give me any of that crap about college ethics! I know plenty of college coaches who'll bend the rules just as far as they'll go."

With that, the Redhead was off and running, scoffing at the colleges' soft 30-game schedules and criticizing his fellow coaches for their lack of imagination.

Brown, except for an occasional incredulous look in the speaker's direction, just nursed his tumbler of lukewarm water and rode out the storm.

At another luncheon Colby College coach Lee Williams, now the executive director of the Basketball Hall of Fame, rambled for 10 minutes about the excellent quality of officiating he had observed, and further noted he had found no reason to complain about a call all season long.

Then Auerbach got up and looked directly at Williams while addressing his remarks to the audience in general. "Any coach who doesn't complain to the referees once all season just isn't doing his job!"

Little wonder that Brown admitted that Red might be "the world's worst public relations man."

In fairness, Red was a marked man the day he pulled into town. Although he wasn't officially introduced to the press until an April 27 luncheon, he had assumed control several days earlier, just prior to the 1950 college draft.

There was a bumper crop of talent that spring, but no one in New England was even concerned with names like Paul Arizin, the national scoring champion from Villanova, or Dick Schnittker, the 6'5 star of Ohio State's Big 10 champs.

Red's new home was Holy Cross country. The Crusaders had just completed a brilliant 27–4 season. They were the top independent team in the country and they had just made their third trip to the NCAA tournament in four years. Of all the stars to emanate from the little Worcester campus in recent years—George Kaftan, Joe Mullaney, Dermie O'Connell—none could hold a candle to Bob Cousy, the electrifying playmaker whose floor work brought crowds to their feet and won him first-string All-American acclaim in every major poll, and who now was about to graduate. An adoring Boston press was already predicting he'd turn the pro scene upside down with his ball-handling magic. Surely Cousy was the answer to all of the Celtics' ills.

There was just one problem. Auerbach didn't share that enthusiasm. Brown had promised him complete control, and now Walter had to fulfill that pledge by going along with Red's choice of Charlie Share, the 6'11 giant from Bowling Green, in the first round of the draft.

When the media learned of the impending sacrilege a roar of outrage, a cry of betrayal, swept across the city. Brown was excoriated by every writer in town, including those who laughed when basketball came to Boston four years earlier. No one was laughing now. Not take the Cooz? Had Walter lost his mind? True to his word, Brown stuck by his guns and insisted that Auerbach knew what he was doing. Privately, it can be assumed, he simply *prayed* Red was right.

Auerbach must have privately gloated when seven other teams—Philadelphia, Baltimore, Washington, Chicago, Minneapolis, Indianapolis and Syracuse—followed his example and bypassed Cousy in the draft. That was sort of a public vindication. Ben Kerner, drafting ninth, finally took Cooz.

A few days after the draft was completed, when the Cousy snub was a *fait accompli,* the new coach pulled into town and was promptly ushered to the Hotel Lenox by a very relieved Walter Brown, who, along with the rest of the western world, anxiously awaited Red's logical explanation. The press was hurriedly convened for what was the largest gathering of writers and broadcasters in the team's four-year history. There wasn't a smiling face in the mob.

Brown formally introduced Red, who began his remarks by

genially noting, "I've always had a hankering to come here."

A score of arms shot up, and one was selected at random to deliver the volley.

"How come you didn't want Cousy?"

The room fell quiet as Auerbach smiled faintly, obviously anticipating that first question. Then he leaned into the microphone.

"I don't give a damn for sentiment or names," he replied evenly, returning the hard stares as he spoke. "That goes for Cousy and everybody else. The only thing that counts with me is ability, and Cousy still hasn't proven to me that he's got that ability. I'm not interested in drafting someone just because he happens to be a local yokel. That won't bring more than a dozen extra fans into the building. What will bring fans into the building is a winning team, and that's what I aim to have."

So that was it. The greatest collegiate star in New England history had just been summarily dismissed as a "local yokel!"

In the howls which followed, Red turned to Brown and was overheard demanding: "Walter, am I supposed to win or am I supposed to please these guys?"

Brown let out an anguished sigh. "Just win, Red. Just win."

The Cousy stir was basically a provincial *cause célèbre.* Outside of New England there was general agreement that Auerbach's decision had been a correct and proper one. "Cousy's a great ballplayer," noted referee Eddie Boyle pointed out to *Boston Record* columnist Dave Egan, "but six-foot-one guys are a dime a dozen in this league and six-foot-eleven players are not."

Of much greater concern to the rest of the NBA was Walter Brown's selection on the second round of drafting.

Only four years earlier Branch Rickey broke baseball's color line by bringing young Jackie Robinson up to the Dodgers, but the NBA was still an all-white circuit in the spring of 1950. That certainly wasn't because of a shortage of black talent, because teams like the Globetrotters, the Rens and the Washington Bears had played before packed houses all over the country in their heyday, and the collegiate scene was producing more and more superb black talent. Publicly, of course, NBA officials denied any "gentleman's agreement" existed, but privately they wondered what effects racial integration might have on team morale and fan attendance.

None of them, therefore, was prepared for what happened when the Celtics' turn came to draft on round two.

"Boston takes Charles Cooper of Duquesne," Brown announced.

There was an awkward silence in the room. Then a fellow owner looked at Walter and asked, "Do you realize Mr. Cooper is a Negro?"

"I don't care if he's plaid!" Brown snapped back. "All I know is this kid can play basketball and we want him on the Boston Celtics."

Cooper, 6'5 and an excellent shooter, had led the Dukes to the semifinals of the NIT. He'd go on to play four sound seasons with the Celtics and two more with Milwaukee and Fort Wayne before retiring in 1956.

The day after that 1950 draft Brown received a telegram. THANK YOU FOR HAVING THE COURAGE TO OFFER ME A CHANCE IN PRO BASKETBALL. I HOPE I'LL NEVER GIVE YOU CAUSE TO REGRET IT.

The draft and the advent of Auerbach were not the only big happenings that spring.

Five teams announced they were folding: Sheboygan, Waterloo, Anderson, Denver and St. Louis. There was a rush to secure the services of the unemployed stars, such as Red Rocha and Noble Jorgensen, a pair of 6'9 veterans. But the biggest plum was unquestionably Easy Ed Macauley, the 6'8 all-star from St. Louis whom many experts regarded as the second best center in the league, next to Mikan.

Ned Irish knew his Knickerbockers were knocking on the door of a possible dynasty with stars like Carl Braun, Dick McGuire and Harry Gallatin, but Connie Simmons, a veteran of Honey Russell's two teams in Boston, just wasn't the answer at center. New York was one good pivotman away from serious title contention, so Irish pulled out all the stops in an effort to get Macauley, even offering to buy the entire Bombers franchise, but his fellow owners awarded Macauley to Boston on the basis of the Celtics' obvious need for talent.

The move sounded quite magnanimous, to be sure, but there were two very practical reasons for the decision: one, many owners resented the powerful New York establishment; two, no one was at all interested in recreating anything like the Mikan scourge which had just rolled to a second successive playoff championship.

For Brown and Auerbach, it was an early Christmas present.

By early October, with the season's opener just three weeks away, things were quiet around the Garden as Brown attended to his administrative chores and Auerbach continued mapping plans for his first campaign in Boston.

Then a bombshell fell upon the league when a sixth team—the Chicago Stags—decided to call it quits. This was completely unexpected. In addition to representing one of the major cities in sports, the Stags had been an excellent team. In four years under Ole Olsen and Phil Brownstein their record was 145–92, a .619 winning percentage, and they had qualified for the playoffs every season.

Once again there was a scramble for players. Several opted for lesser known leagues and a few dropped out of the game altogether. Three remained: Max Zaslofsky, the perennial super-scorer; Andy Phillip, one of the best playmakers in the game; and a rookie named Cousy. Immediately after the announcement that Cousy had been drafted by the Tri-Cities Blackhawks, owner Ben Kerner traded Cooz to the Stags. Suddenly, just days before the opening of the season, Cousy found himself waiting to find out who his *third* employer would be, and he hadn't even played his first professional game.

The Celtics, Warriors and Knickerbockers were all clamoring for rights to Zaslofsky, each insisting Max would best serve the league's interests in their particular city. When the squabbling showed no signs of subsiding, an exasperated Commissioner Podoloff settled the feuding in the most democratic manner possible. Each name was printed on a slip of paper, then all three slips were placed inside Syracuse owner Danny Biasone's hat.

Irish, reaching into the hat first, at Brown's invitation, drew

Zaslofsky's name. He let out an involuntary scream. The prospects of returning home with a four-time all-star, a former St. John's standout, a native New York Jewish kid were dazzling.

Gottlieb reached in next and won Phillip. He was happy, too, though nowhere near as ecstatic as Ned.

Brown didn't bother to reach in. He was left with Cousy.

The City of Boston was very hostile towards me when I arrived, mostly because of the fact that I didn't share everyone's opinion about Cousy.

What the hell did these people know about basketball, anyway?

Believe me, those writers and fans were actually convinced that Holy Cross or some other good college team could beat my ball club! They didn't have the slightest appreciation of what professional basketball was all about. All they knew was Cousy, Cousy, Cousy, and if you didn't agree with them, they had no use for your opinions.

Well, it so happened that I knew the game and I knew talent when I saw it, and their wonderful Mr. Cousy wasn't what I was looking for.

And they never forgave me for saying so.

Sure, he could pass and do all kinds of fancy things with the ball, but I watched him play against the Globetrotters one night and he must have thrown the ball away 20 times. Now what good is all that fanciness if the other team ends up with the ball?

Maybe Cousy would adapt to the pros and maybe he wouldn't. At that point I couldn't have cared less. I wanted Charlie Share.

I talked it over with Walter and he wasn't very happy at first. After all, Cousy's Holy Cross teams had filled Boston Garden. That had to make an impression on him. Then all the writers kept filling him up with their ridiculous opinions. These guys laughed at Walter when he organized the Celtics. Now all of a sudden they're telling him how to run the team.

Before Cousy, the Celtics kept putting local names on their roster, hoping to attract some interest. Look it up. They had guys like Ed Leede from Dartmouth, Tony Lavelli from Yale,

Saul Mariaschin and Wyndol Gray from Harvard. They even took three of Holy Cross's biggest names before Cousy— George Kaftan, Dermie O'Connell and Joe Mullaney—and they still couldn't win games or draw fans.

So it was perfectly obvious that hometown heroes weren't the answer in the pros. That's the point I kept stressing to Walter when we discussed the 1950 draft.

Going along with me wasn't easy for him. He knew he would catch hell from everybody in Boston, but he had promised me I could call the shots and he meant it. His word was good, even if it was killing him to let Cousy get away.

Then, right after the draft, all those teams started to fold and we ended up with Macauley. If I'd had Macauley before the draft I might have let Share go and taken a chance on Cousy.

Anyway, the whole thing had died down and people were finally getting off my back when Chicago announced it was quitting the league. I had a second chance, with Cousy available again, and I could have my cake and eat it, too. Everybody had a reason why we should rush out and grab Cousy's contract.

But Zaslofsky and Phillip were proven pros. They were all-stars. Cousy still hadn't proven a goddamned thing to me, except that he had a lot of friends who were getting on my nerves. There was no way in the world he was as valuable as either one of those other two guys. You didn't see New York and Philadelphia screaming to get him, did you?

Well, we ended up with him anyway. Fine. Now I've got to decide what to do with him. I knew the guy had all kinds of talent. But having talent and being able to fit that talent to your team's needs are two different things. If this kid was going to be throwing the ball all over the goddamned joint, I didn't want him. It might excite a few fans who don't know what the hell's going on out there anyway, but it certainly wasn't going to win any ball games for us.

The writers kept asking me what I was going to do with Cousy and I kept telling them that was completely up to Cousy. If he could control himself, play good defense, and do what he was told, then maybe he would become a good professional player. I said I hoped he would. But if he didn't do those things, I said, I was going to run his ass right off the team.

My views weren't very well received, but I didn't have time to worry about that. I was too busy trying to put my team together. I'd worry about Cousy when we got to the practice floor.

Chapter 9
A Winner Takes Shape

"I knew I had a superstar on my hands."

"There he is, Auerbach!" a piercing voice boomed. "Now he's going to show you what everyone's been talking about. He's going to turn this game around, Auerbach. Just watch him."

The heckler was Clif Keane of the *Boston Globe*, the strongest Cousy booster in town and Auerbach's principal bête noire among Boston sportswriters down through the years.

The scene was Cousy's first practice with the Celtics and it drew a lively, curious crowd of onlookers who wanted to see (a) Cooz cast his magic among the pros, and (b) the interaction between the celebrated rookie and his overbearing coach.

"He's still got to show me," Auerbach grumbled.

"He'll show you," Keane persisted. "Don't worry about that."

"Red was controversial right from the start," Roger Barry remembers, "and nothing irritated him more than writers. To be truthful about it, we didn't know that much about basketball around here. We were so far removed from other parts of the country in basketball sophistication it wasn't funny. He kept complaining that we were thinking Holy Cross while writing Celtics. Guys like Clif, of course, were always second-guessing him, and when that happened Red would really take the sizzle. Fortunately, Walter usually had a calming, restraining influence on him."

"Arnold is not your stereotyped coach," Cousy smiles. "He's not the kindly figure people associate with someone like Knute Rockne. Arnold has an image all his own. We chatted very briefly when I first joined the team. I don't remember all of the things we talked about. That first conversation was rather perfunctory and to the point. There were no difficulties or anything like that, but I know I left the room with the very strong impression that there was no sentimentality involved in Arnold's communications with his players."

"There very definitely was a problem between Cooz and Red in those early days," Ed Macauley insists. "Here you had this great, great ballplayer coming out of a local college with tremendous love, admiration and loyalty showered all over him by the fans, and especially by the news media. Auerbach saw this as a threat to himself, as a potential threat to his authority, and I think he very quickly realized that he was going to have to be the dominant factor in the picture.

"In later years there was a great example of what happens when a coach doesn't take charge. I'm talking, of course, about the people who *tried* to coach Wilt Chamberlain.

"Red saw possible conflicts arising out of the Cousy situation, so he didn't wait for Cooz to prove him right or wrong. He immediately went out and challenged everyone involved—the fans, the writers, Cousy himself—and there is no doubt in my mind that he did it in order to establish his domination of Cousy right away. I'm sure Red felt that if he didn't dominate Cooz, Cooz might dominate *him!* Now that might have been a mistake. It's hard to say, looking back. Auerbach might have created an awkward situation that could have been avoided.

"But ninety-nine percent of the time there was no problem at all. They could have had real trouble. But Cousy respected Red. We all did. And, in the end, that was all that mattered."

An interesting insight into the Auerbach-Cousy brouhaha comes from Freddy Scolari.

"I can't climb inside anyone's head," Freddy says. "But I

wouldn't be surprised if somewhere in the back of Auerbach's mind there was the memory of the Bob Feerick situation in Washington. Feerick became so big that Uline made the mistake of thinking he didn't need Red. And Cousy was a lot bigger in Boston, even as a rookie, than Feerick was with the Caps. I don't think Red intended to be burned twice."

Andy Duncan, a 6'6 forward from William and Mary, was acquired from Rochester in the summer of 1950. He got a first-hand lesson in Cousy's popularity when the Celtics played a preseason exhibition game up in Worcester, the nerve center of Holy Cross euphoria. Duncan took a terrible spill in the game and had to be carried off the court on a stretcher, semi-conscious. As the attendants made their way through an exit the sheet covering Duncan flopped a bit, covering part of his face.

Just then a young boy bolted from the corridor, ran up to the stretcher, pulled back the sheet and peered into Duncan's eyes.

"It's okay," he shouted to his friends. "It ain't Cooz!"

Despite the aggravation of second-guessers and hecklers, Auerbach maintained an open-door policy at all of his practice sessions. He wanted the writers to see what he and the players were doing, and reach, Red hoped, a better understanding of the game.

"This is what makes a basketball player, see?" he said one day to Jack McCarthy of the *Boston Herald,* wiggling his hands in front of the newsman's face. "Hands. You've got to have the *touch!* Max Zaslofsky has it. And so does Macauley. That's what makes Ed so good. Most of these big clowns today don't have the balance of an anteater, but Macauley is an athlete!

"And he's got guts. Early last year when I still had Don Otten we played a game against the Bombers, and I told him just how I wanted him to handle Macauley. 'Look,' I told him, 'you weigh two hundred fifty pounds. So just lean on him a little bit. And use your right elbow on him when you're getting ready to shoot.'

"So Otten does just what I told him to do. He knocked Macauley right off the court.

"But here's the point. Macauley came flying back, got the

rebound and charged Otten all over the joint for the rest of the night.

"That's what I mean by having guts. Watch him."

Writers covering the team were regularly treated to such impromptu dissertations.

"That was Red's way of educating us, without being too obvious about it," Roger Barry explains. "I can't recall ever spending time with that man when I didn't learn something. What a brain he had. He'd point out the smallest details and then tell us why they were so important. I thought he was the smartest basketball guy in the world."

Cousy wasn't the only "new look" to the Celtics when they gathered in the fall of 1950. Red had spent a good portion of his summer wheeling and dealing, just the way he had a year earlier when he and Kerner rebuilt the Tri-Cities squad. In both instances, the result was almost a complete metamorphosis.

Tony Lavelli, the 6'3 Yale alumnus from the basketball-crazed city of Somerville, which is just over the line from Boston, had been something of a local hit during Doggie Julian's final season. In addition to scoring almost nine points per game, Tony occasionally entertained the customers with half-time performances on his accordian.

"He's gone," Auerbach replied when writers asked where Tony fitted into his plans. "He's not tough enough to play pro ball, and I've got no time for sentiment."

Lavelli hooked on with the Knickerbockers that fall.

Gone, too, were Kaftan and Mullaney, the Holy Cross stars, along with guards Howie Shannon, Jim Seminoff and Johnny Ezersky. Forwards Bob Doll and Art Spector were also trimmed from the roster.

Only Sonny Hertzberg, Red's old favorite from the 1948–49 Caps, and Ed Leede, a 6'3 swingman, survived the Redhead's axe.

Bob Donham, a 6'2 guard from Ohio State, joined Cousy and Cooper in the ranks of rookies. Macauley, of course, came from the ruins in St. Louis. Red talked the Rochester Royals into releasing Andy Duncan, then swung a deal with Kerner to get 6'9 Kleggie Hermsen.

Charlie Share, meanwhile, decided he had a very limited future in Boston, so he opted for a career with Waterloo, the ex-NBA entry, which now played in a loosely organized circuit called the National Professional Basketball League. That was fine with Auerbach. He was very content to go with Macauley and Hermsen.

Share's selection in the draft soon paid grand dividends, though, when he had a change of heart midway through 1950–51 and made plans to rejoin the NBA with the Fort Wayne Pistons the following season. Red had no objection—as long as Fort Wayne owner Fred Zollner was willing to pay what Auerbach felt was a reasonable price for Charlie's rights.

The price Red asked was Bob Harris, a 6'7 forward—immediately. The former Oklahoma State star was promptly dispatched to Boston where he played in the Celtics' final 56 games. "He gave the Celtics four good seasons and two sharp elbows," *Boston Herald* writer Joe Looney mused with a grin.

Fort Wayne also had the rights to a baseball player named Bill Sharman, who had played with the Caps before their demise. Red asked Zollner to add Sharman's name to the deal, just to sweeten the pot. Zollner quickly agreed. He needed a big guy like Share. Sharman was only a 6'2 guard who divided his time between pro basketball and playing the outfield for the Brooklyn Dodger's top farm teams. It was common knowledge that Sharman was very close to winning a tryout with the "Boys of Summer" Dodgers and if it came down to a choice between the two sports, he would surely lean towards the greater fame and fortune in baseball. What did Zollner have to lose?

Then Auerbach came up with one final thought. Brown, he explained, had taken a financial bath over the past four seasons, and times were understandably tough for the Celtics. An extra $10,000 would certainly come in handy for meeting operating expenses. Zollner did what any right-thinking millionaire would do if a gun was aimed at his head. He paid the ransom.

Auerbach then used the $10,000 to purchase brawny 6'5 Bob Brannum in the summer of 1951, after it had become apparent that a *policeman* was needed to keep a protective eye on Cousy, Macauley and Company.

The trade was a nifty piece of work. In exchange for Share—whom he didn't want, anyway—he got Harris and Brannum, two good cornerman who'd make substantial contributions in years to come, and Sharman, now generally regarded as one of the finest backcourt shooters of all time.

"Hockey people, which is what most of the owners were in those days, could never have finagled transactions like that," Joe Looney marvels. "Neither could coaches coming right up out of college. Red had put in so much time on DC-3s, Pullmans and day coaches, he knew where all the talent was, and he always knew exactly what he wanted."

The Celtics lost their first three games in 1950–51, then reeled off seven wins in a row—an unheard-of feat in Boston. On January 7 they had a record of 19–15. Two days later the Washington Caps, with a disastrous record of 10–25, went out of business. Red grabbed Bones McKinney, who had replaced Feerick as coach, and talked him into coming out of retirement. Bones agreed.

The Celts won six of their next seven, for a 25–16 record. They finished in second place, just *one game* behind eastern division champion Philadelphia. They had the fourth-best record (39–30) in the 10-team NBA.

The season represented a total turnabout by a franchise which was on the brink of extinction only 12 months earlier. The fact they lost a stormy playoff confrontation with New York did nothing to diminish the enormity of Auerbach's achievement.

Colonel Dave Egan, the legendary *Boston Record* columnist, was fascinated by the Redhead. And Egan was not known for tossing bouquets around. Indeed, he once drew national fire for suggesting the MVP Award should go to the Boston cabdriver whose hack almost ran down Casey Stengel in the days when Old Case was managing the downtrodden Boston Braves. His feuds with Ted Williams were legendary. Egan, who graduated at the top of his class from Harvard Law School, was at once both brilliant and vituperative. Little wonder he was feared in Boston. And little wonder he stood tall as Auerbach's chief defender and admirer in the Boston press during those early raucous months when Red's program was just getting off the ground.

We knew, long before the unforgettable Georgetown classic and long before the Sugar Bowl was even a speculative glitter in the eye of Boston College's John Curley, that Frank Leahy was bound for the mountain peaks. We know now, as Syracuse, Fort Wayne and Minneapolis and the giants of the game come striding toward Boston, that a winner has been forced upon us in the person of Red Auerbach of the Celtics, and that he will do for professional basketball in this town of ours what Frank Leahy did for intercollegiate football. . . . We know this not by anything he ever has said, but by the performance of his team. . . . This is not a team of ballerinas and prima donnas and temperamental, selfish stars. They are young and hungry and full of heart, and they play the rambunctious, enthusiastic, blood-and-thunder basketball which only the young and the hungry and only the hearty can play. . . . —Dave Egan, *Boston Record*, 1950

That would have been an entirely appropriate summary of the 1950–51 season, except that it overlooked the continuing drama which clouded Auerbach's opening day of practice and then nipped at his heels the rest of his way through the schedule.

Joe McKenney, writing in the old *Boston Post*, added the proper postscript in his account of the team's breakup dinner: ". . . the former Holy Cross star's name, however, was mentioned more than any other as attending members of the Cousy A.C. took issue with Auerbach for his seeming lack of appreciation for Cousy's talents in the past season. The coach defended his handling of Cousy. . . . No blows were struck, but the verbal bout ended in a draw with some writers insisting that Cousy is one of the greatest of all basketball players . . . and Auerbach insisting that he still has a lot to learn."

Give me credit for this much: I'm not dumb! Okay? I could see Cousy had great talent, but I had to control him. If I hadn't been able to harness this great, great talent, we'd have wound up with a wild-ass, sulking athlete who never would have realized his full potential.

Guys were writing in the papers that I didn't know anything about the fast break, and that Cousy was going to show me how it was done. It was absolutely ridiculous. I played fast-break ball for Bill Reinhart. That's the same system I used when I had Feerick, Scolari and the rest of those guys in Washington. I've been a fast-break man all my life. But the fast break isn't wild, uncontrolled, run-and-gun basketball. At least it's not supposed to be. It requires discipline and concentration and coordination with your teammates.

Cousy went out there on the first day of practice and threw the ball all over the place. What the hell good is that?

I had to get a message through to him. He was getting 90 percent of the publicity as it was, and unless I stepped in right away and put my foot down, he'd keep getting fancier and fancier without any appreciable results.

So one day I took him aside and had a talk with him.

"Bob," I said, "will you agree with me that guys like Macauley and Cooper are pretty good athletes with good, quick hands?"

"Sure."

"Well then, will you please tell me why they can't catch your passes? How come they're hitting those guys in the head, or bouncing off their chests, or just missing their fingertips?"

He could very easily have told me to go to hell, or complained to the writers, or blamed all of his problems on the other guys. We both knew that everyone in Boston, including the press, would have taken his side. He could have made my job unbearable and disrupted the ball club at the same time.

But he didn't.

He looked at me and asked, "What am I doing wrong?"

Right then I knew I had a superstar on my hands. I wasn't about to tell him that, of course. His head was big enough, thanks to the writers. But he still had a champion's attitude, a champion's heart.

"Look," I explained, "I have some very definite ideas on the proper way to hold a basketball, the proper way to shoot a basketball, the proper way to pass a basketball and so on. I'd never recommend your style to a kid. In fact, I'd kick his ass if I

saw him trying that behind-the-back crap. But the important thing is, it works for you. Some people do crazy things in this game and get away with it. Okay, if it works, I'll buy it. I'm broad-minded enough to know that there are exceptions to every rule.

"But, damn, there is no exception to this: when you pass that ball, make sure someone catches it! The prettiest pass in the world is no good if someone doesn't catch it. And nine times out of ten, if a pass is not completed, it's the fault of the passer.

"It's wonderful to fool the defensive man out there. But you're fooling your own teammates, too!

"The answer is communication. They'll catch your passes— even blind passes—if they know they're coming. It's something that doesn't come overnight. It takes time. But until Hertzberg and Macauley and the rest of these guys get to know your habits, and you get to know where they're liable to be in every situation, you've got to hold back on the fancy stuff.

"Now if you're going to play for me, and do the things for this team that I think you can do, you've got to start making sure those guys can hold onto those passes of yours. Remember, I don't care if you pass with your head! Just make sure they catch it. Otherwise you're going to end up sitting on the bench, and that's not going to help you, me or the ball club."

I've never believed in yanking guys out of games because of mistakes, but in Cousy's case I sometimes had to sit him down, just to get him thinking about what he was doing out there. Every time it happened, the fans and the press climbed all over my back. A few times they wrote things like, Cousy supposedly left the locker room in tears. What the hell kind of writing is that? Suppose he did? Big deal. There was a lot of pressure on Cooz and I'm sure there were times when he became completely frustrated. Maybe it got to him once or twice; I don't know. I never saw it happen. And if I had, it wouldn't have changed things. As I said before, he was no good to us unless we could harness all of that talent.

Down deep inside, though, I was just as excited as the writers were. Cooz would go out there and pick the whole team up by its bootstraps. You couldn't always see what he was doing to make it happen, but by God you could feel it.

No, he wasn't the greatest damned thing I'd ever seen in my life when he came out of college, and some people never forgave me for saying that. The truth is, Cousy didn't really become great until his third season with the Celtics.

After that, he was the best I ever saw for our type of game.

I remember telling Walter at the start of that season that our biggest problem was educating the public. People weren't going to come to our games until they developed an appreciation and a respect for what we were doing.

So we decided to conduct clinics throughout our preseason exhibition schedule. All over New England, wherever we went, I'd stage clinics in the mornings and scrimmages at night. It wasn't easy. I was knocking myself out, but I figured it had to be done.

I wasn't unaware of the fact that certain friends of mine in the media were watching these clinics, too. If they picked up a few points, all the better. You know people believe what they see in the papers, so getting sportswriters to write intelligently about the game could only help promote the team and bring people into our building.

But I still kept reading crap from guys like Clif Keane, things like, "Holy Cross could whip the Celtics right now."

He really believed that. He used to tell me, "Auerbach, those kids up there would whip your ass!" He wasn't the only one who felt that way. A lot of people honestly believed we couldn't beat a good college team. That was too much! How was I supposed to sell my ball club when people actually felt there was a better attraction out there in Worcester? I thought it was fantastic that a little school like Holy Cross could go down to New York and beat all those giants—Navy, CCNY, Oklahoma—for a national championship, but let's get one matter straight.

When you're talking about college teams and professional teams, you're talking about two entirely different worlds. There's no comparison. Even the worst professional team is loaded with guys who were great in college.

The only way I was going to prove my point, however, was to prove it on the floor, where everybody could see for himself. Right after Cooz joined us, I arranged a scrimmage with Holy Cross, and I made sure all of the writers were there to watch it. Then we kicked their butts.

That stopped most of the nonsense about which team was better, but we faced the same kind of problem up in Maine, New Hampshire and Vermont when we traveled there to play our exhibitions.

People would challenge me to let their local teams play the Celtics! They'd have one or two kids who had played some college ball, and a couple of others who were high school hotshots, and they'd actually think they could beat us.

So, okay, I'd have my guys go out and cream them by 50 or 60 points. They got the message. Afterwards, these same people would come up to me and say, "We didn't know you were that good."

These were just plain, decent country folks—good people— who had no idea what big-time basketball was all about. I didn't want to rub it in. I just wanted them to realize what the Celtics had to offer.

Now you might think that winning by 50 or 60 points was rubbing it in. Not at all. We could have beaten them by 100 points. I just wanted to beat them badly enough to show that the NBA has the greatest basketball players in the world.

Some people would say that's bad business. They'd prefer to play a customer's game, like customer golf, where you win by just four or five points. That way the opponents aren't convinced you're beyond them, so they invite you back again the following year.

That's what the pros used to do in the old days. Teams like the Renaissance and the Original Celtics would barnstorm all over the country, winning by two points, four points, five points. The home crowds would go nuts thinking they almost beat these famous visitors. They couldn't have beaten those teams once in a million years!

I wasn't interested in exciting the crowds that way. Beating the Berlin, New Hampshire, team by four points would destroy everything I was trying to accomplish by visiting these towns in the first place.

I wanted to sell these people—and the Clif Keanes of this world—on the idea that you'll never see a better basketball team than the Boston Celtics.

That wasn't just a sales pitch, because I happened to believe it was so. Maybe we weren't the best right then, but that's what we were aiming for.

Chapter 10
Always a Bridesmaid

"It was frustrating as hell."

Auerbach made good on his promise to deliver an exciting product. For the next five seasons, 1952–56, Boston scored more points than any other team in the league.

Sharman and Brannum joined the cast in 1951–52, along with big John Mahnken, whom Red found in Indianapolis, where John wound up shortly after the infamous Englund trade.

Red agonized over Sharman's fate throughout the summer of 1951. Bill had broken all of Hank Luisetti's Pacific Coast scoring records during his remarkable career at USC, but he had also been a good enough baseball player to pocket a $10,000 bonus from the Dodgers organization. Now he was faced with a dilemma. Should he head south for a much-needed season of winter ball, or should he remain in the States and give the NBA another go? He had been the Caps' leading scorer (12.2) at the time of their demise, and the idea of playing in Boston alongside guys like Cousy and Macauley intrigued him.

Auerbach dispatched McKinney to seek out Sharman and convince him the Celtics were for real. Bones had played against Bill in college. Sharman agreed to visit Boston and talk it over, and while he was at the Garden he walked onto the court in street clothes and casually took a few shots. Swish! Swish! Swish!

Red convinced Brown to sign this handsome stranger for the then astronomical figure of $14,000, a veritable fortune for a team whose coffers were almost empty.

Sharman, Auerbach insisted, would be worth every cent. Indeed he was.

At first Sharman shared playing time with Donham, but then, at the start of his second season, 1952–53, he teamed with Cousy on a full-time basis and they went on to become the greatest backcourt combination in basketball history.

"Willie was perpetual motion out there," Cooz explains. "He never stopped moving without the ball. For a passer like me, this was the ideal situation because I could always pick him out. And once he got the ball, of course, he was the greatest shooter who's ever come along."

The two formed a mutual admiration society.

"It worked out so well for me," Sharman says. "Cooz was a magician. I knew if I kept moving he'd put that ball into my hands somehow."

Looking back, Sharman laughs: "We roomed together for eight years and I can recall just one disagreement in all that time. And it was a misunderstanding at that. We were all in a huddle and someone said something about passing. I don't even know who it was. But I do know I yelled out, 'Pass the ball!' I didn't mean it to sound like Cousy wasn't passing enough. It simply involved some play we were trying to work on. Anyway, Bob misinterpreted it, and I could tell he was mad. The next four or five times down the court he whipped the ball at me kind of hard—too hard—but right on the money every time! He wasn't so mad that his passing was affected, because this was a guy who paid attention to details. I'm the same way. That's why our abilities complemented one another's to a T."

And Ed Macauley made three. He finished in the Top 10 scorers list every year he played in Boston. One year (1954) he led the league in field goal accuracy, and another year (1953) he missed the title by an .001 margin.

The Cousy-Sharman-Macauley show became sports' best-known triumvirate since Tinker-to-Evers-to-Chance.

But every year they came up short, just reaffirming and reinforcing Auerbach's primary rule of thumb: individual honors don't mean a thing if the team doesn't win.

Oh, the Celtics did their share of winning in the early '50s, but there were no championships. In 1951–52, they had a 39–27 record, and finished second in the East; in 1952–53, a 46–25 record, finishing third; in 1953–54, a 42–30 record, and second place; then in 1954–55, a 36–36 record, and another third; finally in 1955–56, a 39–33 record, good for second place.

"We'd bust our asses," Cousy recalls bitterly, "and end up with nothing when it was all over."

Nothing, of course, refers to the playoffs. Three times in a row the Knickerbockers knocked them out (1951–53), then Syracuse did the honors the next three times (1954–56).

"We always respected Boston," New York's Carl Braun points out. "You knew you were in for a high-scoring game whenever you played the Celtics because the Lord just doesn't often give the shooting brilliance of a Sharman and a Macauley, or the all-around brilliance of a Cousy. Yet in our hearts we always knew we could beat them when we had to."

The explanation was obvious.

"If you had come to me back in 1952 and said I was not a good rebounder, I'd have said, 'Like hell I'm not!'" Easy Ed explains. "I was working my tail off out there. But let's face it, I just wasn't big enough to take the pounding. We'd do all right early in the season because we'd just run those big guys into the ground. But by playoff time all that running would take its toll and fatigue would set it. And I just couldn't handle some of those monsters we faced."

Auerbach tried countless tricks to offset Boston's lack of muscle, and he employed a host of backup talents.

Brannum had a specific assignment. The only way more cumbrous foes could cope with Boston's speed was to lean and hold and shove. If they got away with it, the Celtics' speed—their best weapon—was effectively neutralized. Brannum's job was to stop the manhandling. "He's the only guy I ever knew who would get mad before a season started and never smile again until it was over," Auerbach joked. "No one ever wanted to mess around with him. No one!"

That still left Macauley on his own against the Sweetwater Cliftons of the East and the George Mikans of the West.

In 1952–53 Red brought in Gene Conley, a rugged 6'8 prospect, but a year later Conley quit the NBA to pitch for the National League Braves. In 1953–54 old friend Jack Nichols came aboard. He had starred for Auerbach at both Washington and Tri-Cities, but at 6'7 he wasn't going to be the answer. Red even took a brief nine-game gamble on Ed Mikan, George's 6'8, 230-pound kid brother, but that didn't pan out. In 1955–56 he heard that Arnie Risen, Rochester's 6'9 veteran, was about to retire, so he got in touch with him and convinced him to come to Boston for a final season or two, just to give Macauley an occasional breather. Arnie agreed.

But nothing changed, despite Red's frantic search for an answer. The Celtics remained the fastest, highest-scoring bridesmaids in the league.

"The criterion for judging any coach—from Little League to major league—is whether or not he gets the most out of his talent," according to Cousy. "There's absolutely no question in my mind that Arnold did that with us during those seasons. We just didn't have the horses to go all the way. It's like the old saying about not being able to make chicken salad out of chicken shit. It just doesn't happen on the professional level. Auerbach brought us as far as we could possibly go."

No one felt the frustration any more than Auerbach. By 1955 he had assembled all of the components of a great, great team—save one. And everybody in the NBA knew which part was missing.

Cousy, Sharman and Macauley were bona fide all-stars. Nichols and Risen were excellent coming off the bench for short stretches. Brannum had retired, but Red found a more than worthy successor in Jungle Jim Loscutoff. And in one of his grandest coups he drafted all three of Kentucky's top stars—Frank Ramsey (6'4), Cliff Hagan (6'4) and Lou Tsioropoulos (6'5)—in the spring of 1953, even though they each had a year of eligibility remaining due to Adolph Rupp's decision to redshirt while the Wildcats sat out a one-year NCAA tournament ban for recruiting violations. Their original graduating class was 1953, Auerbach noted, which made them eligible. The league immediately passed a rule prohibiting any such shenanigans in the future, but Red didn't care at that point. He had his three players.

There was only one thing he didn't have.

"Damn it," he muttered to *Boston Globe* columnist Jerry Nason moments after Syracuse eliminated Boston from the 1956 playoffs. "With the talent we've got on this ball club, if we can just come up with one big man to get us the ball, we'll win everything in sight."

He knew the man he wanted. For three years he had been keeping very close, very quiet tabs on the kid's performances, thanks to a cluster of West Coast confidants. Could he get him for the Celtics? That was doubtful. He wisely played his cards close to his vest and said nothing, lest he alert the competition to what he believed was the best-kept secret in basketball.

His only slip occurred late in the winter of 1956 at one of Brown's weekly writers' luncheons.

"I was sitting there next to Red," Sammy Cohen smiles. "By this time he and I had become very close friends and I knew he was after someone out in California because he used to make telephone calls from my home at three and four A.M. He never told me who he was talking to, or what he was talking about, but I had a pretty good idea.

"So now Floyd Wilson, the Harvard coach, gets up to speak about some tournament his team played in out west, and someone in the audience asks him what he thinks of this kid Russell who played for San Francisco. Suddenly Red got very tense. Wilson began to describe Russell, and then he said Russell would never make it in the pros.

"Red leaned over to whisper something to me, but he was so mad the whole room heard him. 'He's full of shit!' he said. Everyone looked over at him, and Wilson got all red in the face, but Auerbach never said another word. He had already said too much."

* * *

All those years we had Cousy, Sharman and Macauley together, I kept thinking there had to be a way we could do it, a way we could beat those bigger teams with our speed and finesse and execution, but the same fact kept coming back at me: you can't score without the ball. We simply weren't able to control the ball, especially before the 24-second clock came along in 1955.

I couldn't ask my guys to give me any more than they did. We were hustling and winning games and putting on a good show. How could I complain about Cousy? He was fabulous in those years. No, that doesn't mean I was wrong in 1950. It means he developed. Everybody talked about his passing and his scoring, of course, and rightly so—like the night he just dribbled away the last 23 seconds and we beat the Knicks by one, or that afternoon in the playoffs against Syracuse (1953) when he gave us 50 points and we won in four overtimes. Cousy did things with the ball that nobody else has ever done. But what people don't realize is that Bob also began playing defense and switching off and setting picks. He became a complete ballplayer, even though one area of his game got all of the attention.

He really came on strong when he got Sharman next to him. Bill was the ideal guy for him to play with. I've always said he was the best pure shooter I've ever seen from anywhere around that foul line. Plus he was just super on defense, the best I ever had in the backcourt until KC Jones came along.

Macauley fit in perfectly with them on offense. He was fast, had great hands and was a good, good shooter. But then he'd get murdered at the other end of the floor.

Year after year I'd sit there and the same thing would happen. We'd break camp in great condition, get the jump on everybody else and have a good season. But around February we'd start running out of gas.

It was frustrating as hell.

Now Walter was getting a bit panicky because the dough was running out and we still weren't taking in that much at the gate. He wasn't like a lot of these other owners who had vast sums of money at their disposal, or wealthy buildings like Madison Square Garden to back them up. He was on his own. There was one whole year he owed me $6,000 and I never *asked him for it because I knew he didn't have it. A few times Cousy and those guys had to wait for their paychecks, and one time he had to hold off giving them their playoff money— which wasn't too much, anyway—in order to meet some operating expenses.*

I never complained about it and neither did the players. We knew this guy was staking his entire life on the success of the Celtics, and every time we lost it tore him apart. He was our biggest fan and our best friend.

He was also our worst critic whenever he let that famous temper of his get loose. But that was just the way he was, and you had to love him in spite of it. See, we understood him, and we knew he didn't mean the things he said. After a while it got to the point where the writers even stopped quoting his outbursts because they knew by the time the papers hit the streets Walter would have apologized and forgotten all about it.

That doesn't mean we didn't have our run-ins, though.

Take the Ernie Barrett situation, for instance.

Ernie was 6'3 and just out of Kansas State when he joined my team in the fall of 1953. I already had Harris, Brannum, Nichols, Cooper and a big guy named Don Barksdale, who I picked up from Baltimore, all fighting for playing time up front. All of these guys were veterans. Not only was Barrett a rookie, but he was also very small to play in a corner. I had Cooz and Sharman as my guards, with Bobby Donham— another veteran—backing them up. So that pretty well took care of the backcourt.

We got off to a slow start that season and were only about .500 when December rolled around. So naturally I'm going with my regulars, trying to get everything together. We went on the road for four games and lost a couple of them, and Barrett didn't play at all.

The next morning I stop by Walter's office and he hits me with, "What am I paying ten men for if you're going to lose with eight? I might as well save myself two salaries."

Now that really burned my fanny.

"Walter," I said, "is that you talking, or is somebody putting words in your mouth?"

"Nobody tells me what to say!" he says. "I think for myself."

Now he's really mad, and so am I.

"What you're talking about, in essence, is my handling of the team, and I don't like it. You're criticizing my substitutions. Have Keane and those other guys been talking to you?"

Anyway, we both started yelling and then I walked out and headed down the hall to my own office.

A little while later—and if you knew Walter, you could picture this very easily—he sticks his head in my door and says, "Hey, Red, come on, let's go to lunch. I'm buying."

"I'm not hungry."

"Ah, come on. You know better than to listen to me."

We didn't talk again for three days. Right after that happened, I worked out a deal for a side job with a cellophane company called Cellu-Craft. Allie Sherman, the coach of the Giants, and Sid Luckman and a group of other sports people were already involved in it. I had an arrangement which let me devote as much or as little time as I wanted, and I got paid a commission on whatever I sold. In fact I've still got a couple of accounts today.

Why did I do that? First of all, I could use the extra dough in those days. But it was more than a money thing with me.

Walter Brown—and I've said this a million times—was one of the greatest men who ever lived. But he was also a very emotional guy, and since I'm built the same way there was always the chance that someday I might fly off the handle and walk out. If that had ever happened, I had to have someplace to go, something to fall back on.

You have to understand the situation back then. Walter's office door was always open. Anybody could just walk in, sit down and have his attention, including my friends in the press, who never got over that Cousy thing. So they'd walk in and say something like, "Well, I see you've lost four in a row. Shades of the old Celtics!"

Shades of the old Celtics, my foot. In my first year here I built this team from 30 games out of first place to two and one-half games out. I was supposed to listen to this crap from the writers? But, see, Walter did listen. So I made up my mind that I was not going to be solely dependent upon a man who could be influenced by these other people when I was on the road.

That was one time I was really angry with him.

I can remember another time when we lost a few tough games and Walter came storming into my office bright and early the next day. "How the hell can we lose like this with the kind of money I'm paying these guys? I'm sick and tired of it."

I've got a temper and all that, but I can also be kind of sensitive, and things like this would really hurt me sometimes. Here I was doing a fantastic job for him, and working harder than most people ever realized, and I certainly wasn't any happier about the losses than he was.

"Walter, that kind of talk isn't warranted. I don't deserve it."

"Ah, hell, I know it, Red. When I get excited I talk that way. I even talk that way to my wife."

I had to laugh. But I got the last word in.

"Walter," I said, very seriously, "please remember that I am not your wife."

He broke out in the biggest grin you'd ever see in your life.

We did have a serious problem with the team. We weren't going to go anywhere until we solved the little matter of controlling the basketball.

That's where Mr. Russell came in.

People first noticed him during his junior year at San Francisco when his team won the NCAA Tournament. They lost a game to UCLA early that season, then won their last 26 in a row. The next year they went 29–0 and won the NCAA championship again. No team had ever won 55 games without a loss, and everybody was talking about Russell.

I first heard about him when he was a sophomore, long before the win streak and the championships. And the man who told me about him was Bill Reinhart.

"Red," he told me, "I just saw a kid who's going to be great."

Reinhart had such an eye for talent, that if he said that, it had to be true. So I began to follow Russell's career very closely. Occasionally I'd talk with his coach, Phil Woolpert, and I had friends who'd go to his games and talk with other coaches. All of the reports were good. I was told he was a great rebounder, and a great, great defensive ballplayer.

Then one day Freddy Scolari called. "Red, he can't shoot to save his life, but he's the greatest thing I've ever seen in my life on a basketball court."

Barksdale retired in 1955 and went back home to the West Coast, so I asked him to check out Russell's toughness for me. Being a smooth hero in college is one thing, but it is something else to have to mix it up under the boards with the giants in the NBA, all of whom are quite skilled with their elbows and knees.

"No problem there," Don told me later. "I've watched this kid take some pretty good shots. He can take it, and he can dish it out, too. You won't have to worry about anybody pushing him around. He just won't allow it."

Pete Newell, who was coaching at California, assured me Russell was even better than all of the things I had read about him.

These people—Reinhart, Woolpert, Newell—were great judges of talent. I respected their opinions. And Scolari and Barksdale were two of my own guys. They knew the kind of players I liked.

Long before the 1956 draft, I knew exactly who I wanted. I needed someone who could get that ball off the boards and into Cousy's hands, and once I found him we were going to own this league. I was sure of it. And I was sure Russell was that someone, the guy I had been looking for all these years.

The question was, how were we going to get him?

Chapter 11
Russell to the Rescue

"This kid is really something."

Ben Kerner—though he adamantly rejects the suggestion—made a serious mistake the day he let Auerbach get away, for the third-place team Red patched together in that remarkable buying-and-trading spree of 1949–50 quickly fell upon hard times once he left the scene.

In the next five seasons Kerner went through six coaches, but the Hawks wound up in the western division cellar every single year. In the fall of 1951 he abandoned Tri-Cities, hoping to find more receptive audiences in Milwaukee. But his product remained unattractive and fan interest was minimal, a bad situation which grew intolerable two years later when baseball's Boston Braves packed up and followed Ben to the brewery capital, sweeping the city off its feet and driving the Hawks even further into the background.

So he moved again, this time to St. Louis for the 1955–56 season. Under coach Red Holzman the Hawks finally climbed out of the cellar, but only by a scant margin of two games over the lowly Rochester Royals. The people of St. Louis proved to be just as discriminating, however, which meant they weren't about to support a bad club either.

So the draft of 1956 was vital to Kerner. He would get second pick and he'd have to use it wisely, knowing full well that the future of his franchise hung in the balance.

Auerbach huddled with Brown. There was a possibility, he explained, that something could be worked out with Kerner which would result in Boston getting the St. Louis pick, but first Red had to know what Rochester planned to do with its first choice. If the Royals intended to take Russell, there was no point in worrying about Kerner's pick.

Brown got in touch with his good friend Les Harrison, the Rochester owner, and asked him to confide his plans. The Royals, Harrison said, didn't feel they could meet Russell's estimated $25,000 salary demand (which the Globetrotters were more than prepared to offer), plus they felt their rebounding strength was adequate with Rookie-of-Year Maurice Stokes around. They were going to draft Sihugo Green, the excellent Duquesne guard.

Walter relayed the news to Red. Auerbach called Kerner, offering him Easy Ed Macauley in exchange for Ben's draft choice.

The trade made sense, Red carefully pointed out. Ed was a St. Louis boy who had gone on to a spectacular career at St. Louis University. His appeal as a gate attraction was enormous. He was also a genuine NBA all-star. The fact he was weak under the boards would be easily offset by the presence of Bob Pettit, Chuck Share and Alex Hannum in the same front court. Plus Russell had made it known he intended to play in the Melbourne Olympics, meaning he would not be available to any NBA team until December. Could Kerner afford to wait that long?

Ben mulled it over and was almost ready to agree when he remembered Auerbach's bit of finagling in the 1953 draft. The Kentucky stars Red took that year went on to play another season of college ball and then went into military service. They were due to be released soon. Ramsey had already played a little bit with the Celts (1954–55), but Hagan was a full-fledged rookie.

"I want Hagan, too," Kerner said. "Then you've got a deal."

"He's yours," Auerbach replied.

They hung up in agreement.

One hitch remained, unbeknownst to Red.

"Just before we went into the 1956 playoffs," Macauley explains, "my one-year-old son, Patrick, contracted spinal meningitis. He had gone into convulsions and we'd rushed him to Children's Hospital in Boston. When the doctors diagnosed him and told my wife Jackie and me what the story was, we were really shook up. So as soon as the playoffs ended we had him transferred to specialists near our home in St. Louis. I wasn't even sure if I'd ever play again at that point. He was going to need constant care.

"So all of these things were going through my mind one day when the telephone rang. It was Walter. And he sounded awful. 'Ed,' he said, 'I've got some bad news. Red has a chance to trade you to St. Louis for the rights to Russell, but I don't want to make the deal because I just can't imagine your not being a Celtic.'

"I don't have to tell you, I was touched by that.

"But at the same time the move seemed like the best thing for me. I could continue playing ball and still be near Patrick. And I'd be playing in my hometown where I had lived all my life. So I told Walter to go ahead and make the deal. 'Are you sure?' he said. I told him I was.

"And then he did a very beautiful thing, so typical of him. 'You haven't signed your contract yet, have you?' he asked. I said no. 'Good, I'll give you a nice raise then and they'll have to honor it.'

"But I told him not to do it. Do you know why? Because Walter would sit down, think about it, realize he wasn't being fair to Ben, and then reach into his own pocket and pay the difference. That's the kind of guy he was. Just a super individual. So I told him I'd work out my own contract arrangements with Kerner and we let it go at that.

"But I've always believed in the back of my mind that if I had ever said, 'Walter, how could I not be a Celtic?' he wouldn't have allowed Red to make that deal."

The territorial draft rule was still in effect in 1956, allowing teams automatic rights to players who starred in nearby colleges on the assumption their natural gate appeal would be beneficial to the league. One of that spring's many talented graduates was Tommy Heinsohn, a strong 6'7 scoring star who had led Holy Cross to an NIT championship as a sophomore and then won All-American honors in both his junior and senior seasons.

Tommy weighed 235 as a senior.

"If he doesn't take off some of that weight, he might as well stay home," Auerbach informed the Boston press as draft day neared. "He's got no business weighing two thirty-five, but when you're a big star in college you get to thinking you're indispensable and can do any damned thing you please."

Writers—many of whom recalled Auerbach's disenchantment with an earlier Holy Cross star in 1950—rushed to Heinsohn for a response.

"It was the coach's idea I should be big and strong," Tommy replied. Then, assuming his services were not wanted in Boston, he got on a plane and met with representatives of the Peoria, Illinois, Caterpillars, one of the better AAU teams of the day.

Realizing he might have overplayed his hand, Red quickly summoned Cousy and told him to get in touch with Heinsohn, explain how the press had botched up the story and then bring the young man into his office the following morning so he could personally make amends.

Cousy obeyed. "Don't pay any attention to that stuff in the papers," he advised his friend on their ride into Boston. "That wasn't what Red meant at all. He wants you on the team. We all do. Wait till you meet him. You'll like him."

They had a pleasant meeting, and when they got up to leave Heinsohn was satisfied that Red's bark was surely worse than his bite.

Just as he started to close the door behind him he heard an abrupt shout: "I want you to report at two seventeen—and not one pound more!"

Everything went smoothly the day of the draft. Rochester took Green and then Red announced Boston's selection was Russell of San Francisco. Russell, of course, wasn't around. The Olympics owned him. Heinsohn was on hand to meet the writers. "It was the damnedest press conference in the world as far as helping a kid's ego goes," he remembers. "Almost ev-

ery question they asked me was about Russell. Had I seen him
play much? Was he as good as everyone said? Did I think he'd
make it in the pros? And I told them the truth. 'I've never seen
anybody who could play basketball the way this guy does,' I
said."

Red wasn't finished dealing yet. He picked up Andy Phillip, a great playmaker, just turned 34, whom Fort Wayne decided it no longer needed. Auerbach had plenty of young
bloods lined up for the coming season—Russell, Heinsohn,
Ramsey, Loscutoff—and the league's premier backcourt in
Cousy and Sharman. He wanted the steadying influence of
veterans and Phillip fit that bill perfectly, along with Nichols
and Risen.

"What Red did that summer was fantastic," Cousy says.
"He got exactly what he wanted, exactly what we needed. After six years of not winning a damned thing in the end, I went
into that season believing we really had a shot at all the mar-
bles. I felt that way *before* Russell joined us. I couldn't wait to
get started."

Not everyone shared Auerbach's conviction that Russell
would succeed among the pros.

The owners didn't. "There's no question Red was the first to
realize what Russell could mean," Eddie Gottlieb says. "Russell was not a scorer in college, and that made him a question
mark when he came into our league. A lot of people said, 'He
can't shoot, he can't score, so what good is he?' But Red recognized a way he could take advantage of Russell's defense and
rebounding and get big results which he couldn't get from
him in any other way. He saw things in Russell that a lot of
people didn't see. And he knew just how he planned to use
him. So you've got to give the man credit. He was the first to
spot Russell's real greatness. He saw things nobody else saw
back then."

The players were skeptical, too. "Guys kept asking me
about Russell," says Willie Naulls, who graduated from
UCLA in 1956 and was playing with the Knicks by the time
Russell arrived. "They thought he was a stiff. I'd tell them
they were in for a surprise, but they just laughed. To people in

the East, including the media, people like Russell, KC Jones and me were just farm boys from the West. They really believed Neil Johnston and Harry Gallatin and Johnny Kerr were going to eat him up. I'd just laugh and tell them those other guys had better go out looking for work because Russell was going to take their jobs away. The people in California knew that. And Red knew it, too. Everybody else was going to find out later."

Russell returned from a Gold Medal performance in Melbourne midway through December.

"Walter Brown came out to the airport to meet me that day," he remembers. "He didn't have to do that. Those are things you never forget."

Nor did he forget his first contract talk with his new coach.

"Those were formative years," Bill explains, "and Red did a lot of things which were extraordinarily important to me. Like the day I signed that first contract. He said, 'You're probably worried about scoring because everyone says you can't shoot well enough to play with the pros. Does that bother you?' And I said, 'Yeah, I'm a little concerned about it.' Then he looked right at me and said, 'I'll make a deal with you today. I promise as long as you play here, whenever we discuss contracts we will never, ever talk about statistics.'

"And we never did."

On Tuesday, December 18, Russell sat with Auerbach in Madison Square Garden and watched St. Louis beat Fort Wayne in the opener of a doubleheader.

AUERBACH: "I want you to watch Mel Hutchins. He's one of the best big men in the league. See him block that guy out? Now watch him tap the ball. See?"

RUSSELL: "Why didn't Houbregs take the hook? Doesn't he do that anymore, or do they break your arm if you hook in this league?"

AUERBACH: "No, you can. But you've got to pick your spots."

RUSSELL: "Will they try ducking underneath you on the rebounds?"

AUERBACH: "They'll try anything. But mostly the big guys will just try to block you out. Watch Rocha go up for his shot.

See Macauley block him out? The thing for you to remember is that you don't have to worry about getting every rebound like you did in college. You've got Risen and Heinsohn and Loscutoff out there to help you."

The first period ended. St. Louis had 31 points. "This sure isn't possession ball, is it?" Russell laughed. Auerbach shook his head no. The game continued.

AUERBACH: "Keep your eye on Pettit. He'll give you a lot of faking. Usually he'll end up taking a jump shot, but first he'll try to fake you and then run past you. Let him fake. Most of the time you'll be better off making him go over you."

RUSSELL: "What about Foust?"

AUERBACH: "He'll go right or left, but then step back for the jump. And he won't hook. And he's got no left hand at all. Now watch the pushing. See? They'll all try to go for a spot if you let them. So just force them out and they'll probably pull away. Then pick up the man coming through."

RUSSELL: "Share?"

AUERBACH: "Power, that's all. He'll dribble a little bit, but only to better his position."

There was a rough exchange under the boards.

AUERBACH: "The first thing they'll try to do is to push you around. Just rap 'em. That's all."

RUSSELL: "Is there any danger in jumping real high for a rebound?"

AUERBACH: "These guys are pros. They'll belt you around, but nobody's malicious. Nobody is going to *try* to hurt you. But on offensive rebounds be cute—fake, then go up."

They continued to watch until it was time for the Celtics to get ready for the nightcap against the Knicks. Auerbach buttonholed Commissioner Podoloff. "Can Russell sit on the bench with us?" Podoloff smiled. "Okay. But every once in a while point out something on the floor, then wave your finger at him. It will look good." Auerbach beckoned to his star pupil. "Good. C'mon, let's get out of here."

As they left Podoloff shouted an afterthought: "You won't mind, of course, if I fine you $25 for the privilege."

Auerbach looked over his shoulder and grinned. "He'll be worth it."

*   *   *

Four days later, the Saturday before Christmas, a crowd of 11,052 turned out at Boston Garden to welcome Russell in his pro debut. The Celts had a 16–8 record at the time.

Red kept him on the bench for the first five minutes of the game, then sent him in with a thunderous ovation ringing in his ears. Boston trailed by 16 points halfway through the final period before staging a thrilling comeback which was climaxed by Sharman's winning jump shot at the buzzer. Russell played just 21 minutes, during which time he scored six points and grabbed 16 rebounds.

But the topic of conversation that had everyone buzzing after the game was an entirely different skill: the blocked shot. In that furious fourth-quarter rally, Russell had blocked three of Pettit's patented jumpers, a very appropriate introduction to what would soon be recognized as a new era in the NBA.

The Russell Era had begun.

On New Year's weekend the Celts played two games against the defending champion Warriors who were led by Neil Johnston, the NBA's leading scorer for the past three seasons. In the first game Russell had 34 rebounds. In the next he held Johnston scoreless for 42 minutes. The word spread throughout the league.

"I'm a shooter," Macauley explains. "Carl Braun is a shooter. So are George Yardley, Neil Johnston and the others. To be a great shooter you must be able to concentrate. There can be only one thing on your mind when you go up for a shot: the hoop. And this is where Russell changed things. Now you had two things to concentrate on: the hoop, and 'Where is he?' We used to kid about it. As soon as he left a game you'd walk around telling everybody Russell's gone. That meant you could relax again. Now everything was normal. You could drive down the center, fake and shoot. But when he was out there you'd have to stop for just a split second to see where he was, and in that split second one of his teammates would catch up to you. That's what Russell's biggest asset was: the element of distraction."

Like a snowball tumbling downhill, the Celtics just kept running faster and faster and faster.

"The more we won, the better we got," Sharman explains.

If the Cousy-Sharman matchup was a stroke of genius on Auerbach's part, the Cousy-Russell combination was nothing less than a work of art. The most exciting offensive personality in the NBA had now been joined by the greatest defensive player the game had ever seen.

"Russ allowed my playmaking instincts to express themselves fully," Cooz points out. "All of a sudden I didn't have to be quite as careful. It wasn't like every damned pass was life or death out there. Now we could afford to gamble, whether it was in passing, shooting or playing defense, and when you can play that way, when you're doing your thing and everything's flowing, you're going to do everything better. That's what Russell gave us. He gave us that extra leverage which made us the great team we became."

On January 4, just a fortnight after Russell's arrival, Ramsey returned from the service. The rich got even richer. Later that month they'd win 13 out of 15. By season's end they'd be 44–28, the best record in the league.

The playoffs? They couldn't come fast enough. Especially not for a certain Redhead who had long since grown weary of watching other teams and other coaches walk away with all the honors.

Now, he was quite certain, it was his turn.

I made it my business to find out what kind of a guy Russell was. Never mind the rebounding and the defense and all of the other things my friends kept telling me about him. I wanted to know about Russell as a man. What was he like? Was he coachable? Those kinds of things, because I think those qualities are just as important as basketball skills when you're bringing a new member onto a team. He's got to be able to work with the people you've already got or else what the hell good will he be?

So I asked plenty of questions and I liked the answers I kept hearing. He was very proud, very intelligent, very determined. And it was just these characteristics that helped us get him.

Lester Harrison was a good man, and maybe he didn't even realize what he was, in effect, doing, but he made a very big mistake by going out to visit Russell and taking Dolly King *along with him. Dolly was a great player for Clair Bee back at LIU. I played against him. He also happened to be black. Russell interpreted King's presence as Lester's way of showing him that blacks were welcomed in Rochester. So he told Harrison he wouldn't settle for less than $25,000. He knew he was pricing himself out of the Royals' picture, and that's exactly why he did it. The Globetrotters, meanwhile, made the same type of mistake. Abe Saperstein, their owner, went out to San Francisco for a talk, and all the time he was there he directed his comments to Woolpert, Russell's coach, while Russell sat there like a dummy. In both instances Russell felt he was being talked down to, that neither Harrison nor Saperstein gave him credit for being smart enough to talk their language and arrive at his own conclusions.*

I thought that was beautiful—beautiful because it told me so much about the character of this kid, and beautiful because it also eliminated the Royals and the Globetrotters from the picture and gave me a chance to shoot for him.

I have always operated on the theory that no player is bigger than the team, but when you see a player you really want, you should spare no effort in the world to get him. There were theories in pro ball then that said a guy like Russell maybe couldn't cut it. He could rebound and play defense, but when most people compared that to a guy like Walter Dukes—who could rebound, run like hell, shoot well, and was quick, too—all of a sudden Russell became a question in their minds. But I knew this kid was fifty times better than Dukes or any of those other big guys—at least on my team he would be.

We drafted Russell, but I couldn't talk with him about a contract or anything like that until after the Olympics. If I talked any kind of business with Bill I'd be jeopardizing his chances to go to Melbourne. That is ridiculous and someone should put a stop to it, because it's still going on.

You can't sign a contract before you play in the Olympics. Why not? Who are they trying to protect? Not the kid. That's for sure. Suppose a kid plays in the Olympics and gets hurt. Then what? But if he signs a contract first, and then plays with the blessings of his team—and the teams would go along with it; it's great publicity for them—he's protected in the event something happens to him. If they're really interested in the kid's welfare, isn't that better than the situation they've got now? So he signs a contract. As long as he hasn't played professionally, what's the problem? No one can tell me these rules are set up with the kids' best interests at heart.

As long as I'd drafted Russell I figured I might as well take a peek at him, so Walter and I flew down to a benefit game the Olympic squad was playing at the University of Maryland. It was the first time I had ever seen the kid play and he stunk out the joint! No offense, no defense, nothing. They had some high school kids on the other team and they looked better than my guy. I looked at Walter and he looked at me and neither one of us said a word.

Then a great thing happened. I had invited Russell and a couple of his friends to have dinner with Walter and me at my house after the game. We got there first and waited. Pretty soon they arrived and the first thing Russell did was stick out his hand towards me and say, "I'm sorry."

"For what?" I asked.

"For the way I played tonight. I don't usually play that way. It's the worst I've ever played in my life and I'm sorry you had to see it."

"Look," I said, "I've had people watching you for a long time, and you know who they are. So don't worry about it. I know what you can do."

Then he started apologizing to Walter and I jumped in again.

"Bill, let's drop it. But just for the record, the fact you feel this badly about it tells me you're my kind of guy. I don't like to look lousy either. So just do your job over there in Melbourne and then get your ass back to Boston. We're all looking forward to seeing you there."

Later on, when they were gone, I turned to Walter and said, "We can stop worrying now. This kid is really something."

And he just smiled and nodded because he knew it, too.

Right from the beginning I think Russell felt at ease in my presence and with our ball club. Nobody catered to him. I simply told him what I expected him to do. That was the note we started out on. Arnie Risen played a big role in those early weeks. He had been around since the league started and he *knew a lot of the little shortcuts, the tricks you pick up after a while. He knew the habits of the big men Russell had to face. It was a beautiful thing to watch the two of them working together like that.*

Some things just can't be taught. Little by little as the days went by I began to detect this fierce pride Russell had, this incredible urge to win. I never once saw him looking at the sheets to see how many rebounds or assists he got. All he cared about was winning the games and, baby, that's what the name of this game is. You tell a man that, and you hope he understands and appreciates what you're saying. But no one had to tell Russell what it was all about. He came to win.

What made this guy so special? A hundred things.

Take his rebounding. He's the greatest rebounder who ever lived, and please don't give me any shit about Chamberlain's totals. Those are just numbers. On the court, in the situations where it really counted, there's never been a man who could hold Russell's jock when it comes to controlling a rebound.

You see, every time the ball went up in the air, Russell rebounded or boxed out or did something. He was never a spectator. If he found himself out of a play, the very least he would do was box out. But usually he'd release his man and move in to dominate the boards.

He brought something to my attention that very first season. We were talking about rebounds and he said, "You know, Red, everything in rebounding is timing and position, because 80 percent of all rebounds are taken below the rim." Goddamn it, I thought, that's a very, very significant observation and it showed me the way this man thinks about the game. He's reduced basketball to a science. Russell's rebounds were not accidents. He knew exactly what he was doing.

Rebounding was only part of his genius. When he began to block shots it was a brand new ball game. He didn't block shots the way all of the other big guys used to do it—and still do it. He would block the shot by reaching underneath the ball, or on its side if he had to.

Most shot-blockers are what I call shot-swatters, like Chamberlain was. They hit the ball any way they can, and it sails out

of bounds or it bounces onto the floor where anybody who
reaches it first can pick it up.

Russell made shot-blocking an art. He would pop the ball
straight up and grab it like a rebound, or else redirect it right
into the hands of one of his teammates and we'd be off and running on the fast break. You never saw Russell bat a ball into
the third balcony the way those other guys did. Sure, it looks
powerful and the crowds go nuts, but all it's doing is interrupt-
ing play. When Russell blocked a shot he not only took the potential basket away from the other team, but almost always
kept the ball for his own team.

Yet there was more to it than that. There's a way to cope with
the average shot-blocker. If my team is facing some big giant
who likes to smash the ball, I just say, "Throw it over his head
so he can't reach it." Then my center, who's standing behind
him, can catch it and have an easy dunk shot. That's the normal way to get around a big man's advantage. But other teams
couldn't do that against us because Russell wouldn't leave his
man alone while he went out to block a shot. He'd stand right
next to him and wait until the ball left the shooter's hand and it
was too late for the shooter to change his mind. Then in that
split second he'd go up and make the block.

He began instilling fear in the hearts of other players. I
mean that. He didn't react normally, and as a result no one
could predict what he was going to do, which bothered the hell
out of everyone. When other big men anticipated blocking a
shot, the shooters could sense it, so they'd come off a screen,
and pump or double-pump, to upset the blocker's timing. But
Russell never fell for that pump shit. He wouldn't even make a
move. He'd just stand there and let the shooter make the move.
Talk about intimidation! The shooters didn't know what the
hell to do. He bothered them without even moving. There were
times, so help me, when Russell wasn't even in the game, but a
shooter would drive to the basket, see Satch Sanders's arms
out of the corner of his eye, and he'd blow the shot!

I'll bet that 80 to 90 percent of the shots Russell blocked
ended up in our hands, whereas Chamberlain and those other
guys were lucky to save maybe 30 percent.

*   *   *

Now we were ready for anything anybody wanted to throw at us. We had had the best damned scoring team in the league even before getting Heinsohn and Ramsey. The only thing that had killed us in the past was not being able to control that basketball. Russell would take care of that little problem for us.

We had everything we needed. Now it was just a matter of going out and getting the job done.

Chapter 12
Diary of a Dynasty

"This is the greatest team ever assembled."

"People are forever looking for dynasties," Bill Russell observed, "and yet most of the time when a dynasty comes along, no one's expecting it because there are always challengers around and the picture's continually changing. In our case, first there was St. Louis, then Philadelphia, then Cincinnati, then the Lakers, then Philadelphia again, then the Lakers again. There was always *someone*. And what happens is, before you know it you're two-thirds of the way through your dynasty and suddenly people begin to respect it. But you see the people involved with it never think of it in terms of a dynasty because they realize that there are no miracles in sports. You work for what you get."

The Celtics won 11 world championships in 13 years, a record of excellence unmatched in the history of professional sports. And they did it in the NBA's most competitive era, before expansion and rival leagues and longer schedules drained the game of much of its vitality.

In the seven years following the conclusion of the dynasty, no team has been able to win even two consecutive champion-

133

ships. Indeed, the only team in the entire history of the NBA—other than the Celtics—to win consecutive titles was the Minneapolis Lakers, champions in 1949, 1950, 1952, 1953 and 1954. But George Mikan, its 6'10 superstar, had no peer—as Russell did in the person of Wilt Chamberlain—to contend with, nor was there a 24-second clock to keep him moving.

The Celtics dynasty was born on the eve of the NBA's emergence as a major league of national stature, and it flourished with the arrival of Chamberlain, Elgin Baylor, Oscar Robertson, Jerry West and a host of spectacular talents. The league Boston so thoroughly dominated was well stocked, well balanced and well equipped to knock the pins from under any superpower, but that never happened. At one time or another in that 13-year span the St. Louis Hawks (51–28 in 1961), the Los Angeles Lakers (54–26 in 1962), the Cincinnati Royals (55–25 in 1964), the Philadelphia 76ers (62–20 in 1968) all came up with outstanding teams, teams good enough to win championships, yet none of them was able to dislodge Boston.

The Celtics, in a word, were awesome, and it's quite likely their record will never be equaled.

1957

By playoff time the Celtics were in full stride. Heinsohn, the NBA's Rookie of the Year, was starting up front with Loscutoff. Tommy, in addition to being a completely uninhibited shooter, proved to be an especially effective offensive rebounder, while Loscy, also a good rebounder, spent much of his time setting immovable picks and screens. Ramsey, who could play at guard or forward, became Red's "sixth man," a then unique role which would eventually catch on with other teams. He was the first player off the bench, usually five minutes into the contest, and his specific function was to maintain or accelerate the game's pace.

Because of the way the league was imbalanced—all four western teams finished under .500—the C's most formidable playoff competition appeared to be their first round opponent, eastern division runner-up Syracuse, the team which had eliminated them the past three years.

Their opening game, played before an ecstatic crowd in

Boston Garden, was nothing less than a seminar in Auerbach's first belief: the team concept. Ramsey scored 20, Heinsohn 19, Cousy 18 and Sharman 17. Russell contributed 16 points, 31 rebounds, 12 blocked shots and three assists.

Boston won, 108–90, and went on to sweep the series in three games.

Call it justice or call it irony, but out of the western division chaos emerged Ben Kerner's St. Louis Hawks, who featured— in addition to Bob Pettit—Easy Ed Macauley, averaging almost 17 points a game while playing mostly at a forward position.

After a split in Boston the teams reconvened the series in St. Louis. Prior to the third game, Auerbach summoned referees Sid Borgia and Arnie Heft and demanded that they check the height of Boston's basket. They found it to be exactly 10 feet from the floor. Kerner, convinced Auerbach was merely trying to arouse the crowd and stimulate the Celtics, yelled, "You're really bush!" Whereupon the Redhead charged his ex-boss and landed a solid haymaker.

"Look at that," the shaken Kerner said, pointing to a rapidly swelling lip. "Nothing happened." Then he shouted at the retreating Boston coach: "What's more, you can't punch either!" By now the lip was bleeding.

Commissioner Podoloff, surrounded by writers and outraged Hawk fans, said, "I must ascertain the facts." He did, and later fined Auerbach $300.

The series went to seven games and the finale was pure Hollywood as Boston won in double-overtime, 125–123.

"We've been trying to get to the top for seven years and now we're finally here," Cousy said. "People are calling us great. But now we've got to do it again, just to show that we're the greatest."

1958

A new face was added to the cast this season, thanks to a tip Red got from old friend Bones McKinney, who was now coaching at Lake Forest. "This kid can shoot," Bones exclaimed. "Get him if you can."

No one knew who Red was talking about when he drafted

Sam Jones of North Carolina College, but the 6'4 rookie, perhaps the fastest man in the league, would become one of the all-time great NBA scorers.

The Celts won their first 14 games that season and never looked back, finishing with a 49–23 record. Five of their members—Sharman, Cousy, Heinsohn, Russell and Ramsey—had scoring averages ranging from 22 to 16 points a game. Russell led the league in rebounds while Cousy led it in assists.

When Boston methodically rolled over Philadelphia in the eastern finals, four games to one, the stage was set for a rematch with the Hawks. Hagan, the throw-in in the Russell deal two years earlier, was now a bona fide star, averaging almost 20 points a game.

The series went six games, but was actually decided in game three when Russell—soaring high to block a Pettit shot (which earned him a goaltending call)—crashed to the floor and severely injured his left ankle.

Though the Celts fought gallantly, they couldn't shut off the St. Louis attack and the Hawks wrapped it up with a 110–109 victory in game six, led by Pettit's 50-point performance.

At the breakup dinner tht spring, three old troopers—Risen, Nichols and Phillip—announced their retirements.

1959

Amidst all the ballyhoo surrounding the joint drafting of Russell and Heinsohn in 1956, people generally overlooked the third choice Auerbach made, especially when the little-known rookie never showed up.

KC Jones, a 6'1 guard, had been Russell's teammate at San Francisco. While the big man was anchoring the famed Dons' defense up front, KC was raising similar hell with his ball-hawking tactics in the backcourt.

After a tryout with the Los Angeles Rams and a military hitch behind him, he was reporting to the Redhead for duty.

So was Gene Conley, the same 6'8 Gene Conley who left the team in 1953 to pursue a pitching career. After appearing in the 1958 World Series he decided to combine the two sports and rejoined the Cs that fall. With Risen gone, Gene was the perfect backup for Russell.

Again Boston got off to a brilliant start and by New Year's Day the record was 23–9. Late in February Auerbach agreed to conduct a clinic for one of the local papers. Hundreds of kids showed up to hear his lecture on defense, then sat back and watched his Celtics score 173 points—still an NBA record—against the Lakers and their standout rookie, Elgin Baylor.

At season's end Boston owned a 52–20 record.

Syracuse, strengthened by the addition of George Yardley (the NBA's first 2,000-point man the year before), won every game on its home court to force a seventh and deciding contest in Boston Garden for the eastern division playoff championship.

"Red gave the greatest pep talk I've ever heard before that game," former Cs trainer Buddy Leroux remembers. "My eyes were wet when I left the room, and I had heard a thousand pep talks in my lifetime. But nothing like that one."

In the second period the Celtics found themselves trailing by 16 points. "There was nothing we could do," Cousy later recalled. "The shots just weren't falling in." On the contrary, they reached for their bread and butter—defense—and kept chipping away. Russell fouled out midway through the last quarter and Conley, in his finest hour as a Celtic, took over in the pivot and turned in a flawless effort. The final score was Boston 130, Syracuse 125.

Baylor's Lakers had pulled off a stunning upset in the west, knocking the Hawks out of the picture and setting up a Boston-Minneapolis title showdown.

The Celts became the first team in league history to sweep a championship series in four games. "I'll tell you something right now," Laker coach Johnny Kundla said in the wake of his team's rout. "It's going to be a long, long time before anybody beats that crew over there."

1960

If Russell's debut in 1956 caused a stir around the league, the reception awaiting Wilt Chamberlain could only be compared to a tremor. At 7'1 (and many insisted he was taller), 275 pounds, the Philadelphia rookie was the most awesome figure to arrive on the scene since George Mikan's day.

Wilt lived up to his incredible advance notices by scoring more than 37 points a game and carrying the Warriors to a 49–26 record, third-best in NBA history.

Boston, meanwhile, won 11 of its first 12 and, beginning late in November, ran off a 17-game winning streak, tying the record set by Auerbach's Caps back in 1946. The Celts wound up with a 59–16 mark, the best the league had ever seen.

The battle lines were drawn for what would become the epic rivalry in basketball: Chamberlain vs. Russell. It would bring into sharp focus the two prevailing schools of thought: you build your system to fit your stars or you fit your stars into your system. For years Auerbach was the lone proponent of the second approach.

The Warriors got past Syracuse in the quarterfinals, then fell to Boston in six games. The final game, in Philly, went to Boston, 119–117, when Heinsohn tipped in an offensive rebound at the buzzer.

St. Louis, now coached by the retired Macauley, pushed the Celtics to a seventh game in the championship series, but then was overwhelmed by Boston's great versatility, 122–103. Ramsey scored 24, Heinsohn 22 and Sam Jones 18. And Russell chipped in with 22 points and 35 rebounds.

"I'm not much for talking about other players," Pettit said, "but I'll take my hat off to Bill Russell as a basketball player and a man anytime I'm asked to. Today he played it like a gentleman. He made us respect him every minute he was out there."

1961

More than ever the NBA was becoming a league of superstars now as Oscar Robertson and Jerry West, fresh from their spectacular Olympic showing in Rome, joined the ranks of Chamberlain, Baylor, Pettit and Schayes. West and Baylor would be Laker teammates in Los Angeles, where owner Bob Short had just relocated the historic Minneapolis franchise.

The Celtics had a newcomer, too, although he hardly got noticed outside of Boston. His name was Tom Sanders— "Satch" to his friends—and he was a painfully shy 6'6 string bean from NYU who was so terrified of Madison Square Garden crowds in his college days that he wanted no part of the NBA. Indeed, his mind was made up to accept a management training offer from the Tuck Tape Company and to play on its AAU team.

Then he received a visit from the Redhead.

"He talked to me like a father," Satch smiles. "He said a job was something I could always get, but that the chance to play pro ball comes just once in a lifetime. That made sense to me. Then he said Loscy's back was hurting and Conley was getting tired of two sports, and he kept stressing there was room on the team for me. By the time he got done I envisioned myself rushing to the rescue of the world champions. Then I got to training camp and found 50 forwards fighting for my job!"

Satch's particular forte? Defense.

Boston posted a 57–22 record in winning the eastern division race by an 11-game margin over Wilt's Warriors, though Chamberlain increased his scoring average to 38.4.

Syracuse, 38–41 in the regular season, shocked everyone by eliminating Philadelphia in the quarterfinals, but was no match for the Celts who won their series in five games. Sharman, playing his final season in Boston, had 27 points in that fifth contest and an even 100 for the series. But the big story, as always, was Russell, who put on another Herculean show in the finale with 25 points, 33 rebounds and six blocked shots. "He's in another world," Nats coach Alex Hannum marveled. "There's nobody else like him."

The championship series opened with Boston beating St. Louis by 34 points (129–95) and was mercifully over in five games.

The Celts had their third consecutive world championship and their fourth in five years.

"This is the greatest team ever assembled," Auerbach declared in the winners' crowded locker room. "And there are two reasons for it. One is the way we all get along together. On some teams the players can get into each other's hair over a long schedule. That doesn't happen here. And the other reason we're so damned good is the quality of our guys. We've always got somebody ready to explode. Any one of my guys can tear you apart. One night it's Tommy. The next night it's Sam. Or maybe it's Sharman or Ramsey or Cooz. And then there's

Russell. With most teams you can win if you stop one man. Stop Chamberlain and you win. Stop Baylor and you win. But nobody can stop the Celtics that way! That's why we're the best."

1962

Carl Braun, after 12 grand seasons with the Knickerbockers, closed out his career with a final year in Boston, just the way Risen, Phillip and Nichols did earlier. It was another Auerbach trademark which would surface again and again.

The other big change in the Boston picture found Sam Jones stepping into Sharman's vacated spot in the starting lineup. Did the transition affect the team? Hardly. Jones averaged more than 18 points a game, one of six Celts to average in double figures that season.

But everyone was talking about Chamberlain, and with good reason. On an early March night down in Hershey, Pennsylvania, Wilt scored 100 points against New York. His *average* was a mind-boggling 50.4 points a game!

The net result? Boston, with a 60–20 record, finished 11 games ahead of Philadelphia again, and in head-to-head meetings the Celts beat the Warriors eight times in 12 games. They also won six out of nine from the Lakers, who relied almost exclusively on the guns of Baylor (38.3) and West (30.8).

Auerbach's lads were proving it was still a team game.

Of all the playoffs in all the years of Boston's dynasty, however, none would have more tension than the 1962 episodes, for the Celts would almost lose their crown twice.

Philadelphia disposed of Syracuse in opening round action with Wilt scoring 56 points in the final game. Then the Warriors landed in Boston for what promised to be a dramatic confrontation. Though Chamberlain got the lion's share of attention, his supporting cast was quite impressive, featuring a backcourt of Tom Gola, Guy Rodgers and Al Attles and a front court of Paul Arizin and Tom Meschery.

The clubs split the first two games. Then Russell got into foul trouble in game three and Auerbach sent the brawny, but undersized (6'5) Loscutoff out to contend with Chamberlain. Less than two minutes later Jungle Jim and Wilt got into a shoving match which was quickly broken up. "It's okay for Wilt to lean on people, but no one's supposed to lean on him," Loscy later fumed. "Bullshit on that." Boston won by 15, then Philly squared the series at 2–2 in game four.

Tempers flared again in game five when Sam drove on Wilt late in the final period. He got hit on the chest as he went by, so he snapped at the big guy. Wilt, obviously tired and no doubt irritated by the Celtics' lead, shouted back and began moving towards him. Sam reached for a photographer's stool and waved it menacingly over his head. "If I'm going to fight him," he explained afterwards, "I'm not going to fight fair." The Celts won that one, 119–104, but the Warriors evened the series at 3–3 two nights later.

The seventh game in Boston came down to the final minute, when Wilt scored a three-point play to tie it up. With two seconds left, Sam threw in a jump shot from fifteen feet away and Boston won, 109–107.

The series with the Lakers followed the same script through four games. But Los Angeles won game five, and now the action moved to California with Boston just one defeat away from elimination. But the Cs, down 10 at the half, won by 14 to force a seventh game.

It was a thriller.

A great Laker rally tied the score at 100–100 with only five seconds remaining. Ramsey tried to win it for Boston, but his shot missed and Los Angeles got the rebound. Time out. Then the ball went to Frank Selvy, who had the hot hand, and he fired a shot from the baseline. The Garden was absolutely still as the ball struck the near rim, hopped over the mouth, bounced off the far rim and was gathered in by Russell, sending the game into overtime.

Boston was in full control from that point on, and won, 110–107, for its fourth world championship in a row.

1963

This was the year that John Havlicek came and Bob Cousy left.

Before the season even started Cooz let it be known that he would call it quits after this, his 13th campaign, and then take over as head coach at Boston College. The early announcement was intended to stimulate BC's recruiting efforts.

Havlicek's Ohio State teams went to the championship game of the NCAA Tournament in each of his three varsity seasons. In 1960 they beat California for the title, but in 1961 and 1962 they finished second to Cincinnati. Everyone knew their names: Jerry Lucas, Larry Siegfried, Mel Nowell, Bobby Knight.

But Havlicek? "When I got to Ohio State I realized everyone there had been a thirty-point scorer in high school, so if I was going to do much playing I'd have to find something else to contribute."

When draft time rolled around all of the big names were quickly scooped up: Billy (The Hill) McGill, Wayne Hightower, Dave DeBusschere, Len Chappell, Terry Dischinger, et al.

Then Auerbach went for the kid nobody seemed excited about. "We know John can run and play defense," he explained. "We'll teach him anything else he has to know."

The Warriors, meanwhile, left Philadelphia when Eddie Gottlieb sold them and took up residence in San Francisco, meaning they were no longer in the eastern division. With a 58–22 record the Celts coasted home, 10 games in front of second-place Syracuse.

All that remained was the playoffs once they got off to a 13–3 start—with one notable exception. On March 17, St. Patrick's Day, Boston officially said good-bye to the Cooz in what's been properly called the most emotional sporting event in the city's history. In a 43-minute pregame ceremony, dragged out by sobs and embraces, Cousy cried and thanked the fans. Walter Brown, trying to inject some levity into the proceedings, spread his arms and said to the crowd: "Think how I must feel. I'm the guy who didn't want Cousy. What a genius!"

Brown was a little bit careless with history. It was the guy who followed him to the microphone who once shunned this "local yokel." As Auerbach approached the mike he and Cousy exchanged gulps and glances. "What can I say?" Red hoarsely whispered. "There's Mister Basketball!" Then he wrapped his arms around the star and they both wept.

* * *

The up-and-coming Cincinnati Royals pushed the Celts to seven games before succumbing to Sam's 47-point performance in the finale.

Meanwhile, the California press had been steadily beating its drums, proclaiming Los Angeles as the "basketball capital of the world" because of UCLA's fabulous record and its belief that the Lakers were at last ready to dethrone Boston. Los Angeles coach Freddie Schaus confided certain likely strategies to the writers, several of whom wore a path to Red's door for his reaction. "Look," he said, waving his cigar, "they can talk all they want to and try anything they want to, but we're still the champs and they've still got to beat us."

They didn't.

Boston won three of the first four games and then wrapped up its fifth consecutive championship with a 112–109 victory in game six at Los Angeles. It was the same old story. West and Baylor combined for 60 points, but Boston's scoring looked like this: Heinsohn 22, Sanders 18, Cousy 18, Havlicek 18.

When the Los Angeles writers came into his locker room, Auerbach was waiting for them. "All year long all I've been hearing about is the Lakers this and the Lakers that. But we're still the champs, aren't we? We weren't beaten this year, and I don't expect anybody's going to beat us next year either."

1964

With Cousy gone, KC Jones moved into a starting lineup that already included Russell and Sanders. More than ever, *defense* was the byword in Boston.

Willie Naulls, a seven-year veteran (and five-time all-star with the Knicks), was brought aboard.

Havlicek (19.9) led the team in scoring, yet never started a game! He had taken over Ramsey's "sixth man" duties and the team never missed a step in the transition, as it 59–21 record indicates.

The playoffs that year were merely perfunctory as the Celts took four out of five from Cincinnati in the eastern finals, and then four out of five from Wilt's Warriors in the championship round.

The New York Yankees won the World Series five times in a row from 1949 through 1953. And the Montreal Canadiens won the Stanley Cup five times in a row from 1956 through 1960.

But now the Celtics had won the NBA championship six times in a row. They were the longest dynasty of all, and they still showed no signs of slowing down, not even with the announced retirements of two old stalwarts: Ramsey and Loscutoff.

1965

On September 7, 1964, five weeks before the season opened, Walter Brown died after suffering a massive coronary at his summer home on Cape Cod. He was 59.

When the Celtics appeared for their first game each man had a strip of black cloth sewn onto the left strap of his jersey. In case the significance was missed, Russell made an announcement. "We're going to win this championship for Walter Brown," he promised.

Then they went out and rolled up their finest record ever, 62–18. They averaged 112 points a game. Their opponents averaged 104. They beat Cincinnati, which finished second in the East, eight out of 10. And they beat the Lakers, winners in the West, seven out of 10. Six of them had scoring averages in double figures. All in all, it was easy to overlook the fact five key members of the club were now in their 30s.

The Celtics were growing old, but they were still the champions.

The Syracuse Nats, Boston's perennial nemesis in years gone by, had moved to Philadelphia a season ago, replacing the departed Warriors. They now went under the name Philadelphia 76ers. In the winter of 1964–65 Chamberlain was traded from the Warriors to the 76ers, bringing him back to his hometown. He had his best supporting cast ever, with Chet Walker and Luke Jackson in the corners and Hal Greer and Larry Costello in the backcourt.

Although the 76ers finished a distant third in the regular

season, they were the only team in the league to give Boston any trouble. The series between them ended up tied at 5–5. So their playoff meeting promised to be a classic. Tied at 1–1, 2–2, and 3–3, the series came to a seventh-game, winner-take-all battle in Boston Garden.

Early in the last period the Celts moved ahead by eight, 90–82, but Philly fought back and cut the margin to one, 110–109, when Wilt scored with four seconds to go. Boston got possession. Russell, standing beside the 76ers basket, attempted to throw the ball into play, but his pass hit a support cable. Officials ruled it was Philadelphia's ball. No time had elapsed, so the 76ers immediately called for a time-out to set up a last-ditch play. All the Celtics could do was wait.

"I'll never forget this," Buddy Leroux, the trainer, says. "Russ walked into our huddle and said, 'Somebody bail me out. I blew it.' And I remember thinking that was so typical of our team. No one made excuses or alibied. We didn't operate that way."

Greer, Philadelphia's excellent playmaker, was to throw the ball in to Walker. Then 6'9 Johnny Kerr would set a pick and Walker would pass it back to Greer. Hal carried a 20-point scoring average. It was a good play. And if the shot failed, Wilt was there for the rebound.

It didn't work out that way, for Greer's in-bounds pass to Walker was intercepted by Havlicek on a perfectly timed leap. John batted it to Sam, who dribbled out the clock, and Boston won the series.

In the ensuing pandemonium Russell raced over to Havlicek's side and planted a kiss on his forehead.

The Lakers series was anticlimatic. Boston won it in five games. The string of world championships now stretched to seven in a row.

That summer Heinsohn announced his retirement.

1966

Two years earlier sportswriter Bill McSweeney, writing in the *Boston Record,* first raised the question of Auerbach's ability to continue wearing so many hats. In addition to being general manager, Red handled radio and TV negotiations,

Garden lease negotiations, league responsibilities and scouting chores. Brown's death left him in charge of the whole operation. The load was enormous; added to the strain of coaching and constant traveling it was almost impossible, both mentally and physically.

"It is questionable how much longer Auerbach can go on," McSweeney noted in 1964. "Over the past few years he has grown grayer and balder. His eyes are deep-set, his face covered with worry wrinkles. He doesn't eat. He doesn't sleep. And he takes the losses much harder than his players. . . ."

On the eve of the 1965–66 season, Red announced this would be his final year on the bench. "I'm announcing it now," he explained, "so no one can ever say I quit while I was ahead. I'm telling everyone right now—Los Angeles, Philadelphia, everyone—that this will be my last season, so you've got one more shot at Auerbach!"

Hoping to offset the loss of Heinsohn, Red hired Don Nelson, a 6'6 forward who had kicked around for three fruitless seasons in Chicago and Los Angeles. Every other team in the NBA turned thumbs down when his name appeared on the waiver wire. Then Auerbach stepped in, and Nelson went on to give the Celtics 11 outstanding seasons.

Boston held onto first place through the holiday season and on into the dead of winter, but the 76ers—with Wilt on hand for a full campaign—remained just a step or two behind. In early March the rivals met head-on and the 76ers swept a home-and-home set, finally vaulting ahead of Boston. Neither team lost again, and the final records were Philadelphia 55–25, Boston 54–26.

For the first time in 10 years, the Celts were not eastern division champions.

That meant playing a preliminary series against Cincinnati, a best-of-five affair. The Royals won games one and three, but twice the Celts fought back to even the count, and then Sam came through with 34 points in game five as Boston wrapped it up, 112–103.

The much-heralded showdown with Philadelphia was a clinker. Boston routed the 76ers in five, winning the first two games by margins of 19 and 21.

"This might sound like a crock," Russell advised reporters,

but this is a team game. It's not me against Wilt. It's a team
thing."

Once again it was Boston against Los Angeles in the final
round.
The Lakers won the opener in Boston in overtime and coach
Freddie Schaus correctly observed, "This is the best team
we've had in Los Angeles in my six years there."
After the game Auerbach ordered all of his players to report
to a news conference the following morning downtown, and
speculation was rampant. The new coach would be announced. That was widely surmised. But who would he be?
His name, it turned out, was Bill Russell.
"We're like a family," Red explained. "It wouldn't be easy
bringing in someone from outside and making him a part of
the family. Russ can do the job. He'll make a great coach."
The next night Boston clobbered the Lakers by 20 points to
square the series, and an irate Schaus refused to talk with
writers. "We should have gotten more credit for our win Sunday," he fumed.
The papers, of course, had ignored LA's win and focused on
the Celtics announcement. Psychologically, it was another
win for the Redhead.
Boston went on to win the series in seven games.

1966, Postscript

After a very quick round of handshakes in his locker room,
Auerbach left the Garden, closing the door on 20 years of
coaching. He returned to his apartment, accompanied by his
friend, New York columnist Milton Gross. As soon as he arrived he picked up his phone.
"I want some wonton soup, egg rolls, spareribs, roast pork,
chicken wings with oyster sauce and steak kue. . . . Auerbach! Who the hell do you think it is? And hurry. I'm starv-
ing."
Then he disappeared into the kitchenette and began skin-
ning a potato.
"What are you doing?" Gross asked.
"Making French fries. What's it look like? I make 'em the

way my father used to and I do it well. I like to make my own.
It helps me to relax. Then after I eat I'm going to go to bed. I
just hope I can sleep."

Gross studied him for a moment, then broke the silence.

"What if you had lost this one?"

Auerbach kept on peeling.

"Would you have cried?" Gross persisted.

Red turned to face him. "Cry? I don't know. I might cry later anyway. I've fulfilled my life in basketball. Now why don't
you get out of here and leave me alone?"

1967

Two grand veterans joined the club this year: Bailey Howell and Wayne Embry, both 30 and both five-time all-stars.
The 6'7 Howell was a power forward in the Heinsohn mould,
providing scoring and rebounding strength. Embry, a massive
6'8, was an ideal backup for Russell, the best since Conley left
in 1961.

Regardless, the 76ers were untouchable this time around,
even though Russell's aging Celts compiled a 60–21 record.
Philly posted a 68–13 mark, the league's highest winning percentage (.840) to date.

Boston beat New York handily in quarterfinal action, but
fell to the 76ers in five games.

The string of titles had been snapped at eight.

1968

The 76ers, defending their crown, ran up a 62–20 record,
tops in the NBA, but only managed a 4–4 split in meetings
with the Celtics, who finished second at 54–28.

After a hard-fought preliminary with Detroit, Boston took
on Wilt and Company in the eastern division finals. When the
76ers swept games two, three and four for a commanding 3–1
lead, everyone assumed school was out. The Celts would have
to win the next three, two of which were scheduled for the
76ers' home court. It was not likely to happen.

But it did.

The Cs went on to beat the Lakers in six, bringing the world
championship back to Boston for the 10th time in 12 years!

1969

The NBA was suddenly rich in super teams, all of whom viewed themselves as logical successors to Boston's throne. Los Angeles owner Jack Kent Cooke, determined to bring it all home this time, sent three players to the 76ers in exchange for Wilt, giving the Lakers a seemingly invincible punch of Chamberlain, West and Baylor! In the east the young, exciting Knickerbockers of Frazier, Reed, DeBusschere and Bradley were coming on strong. So were the Bullets of Unseld, Monroe and Johnson. And even without Wilt, the 76ers were formidable.

Boston finished fourth at 48–35, the final qualifying spot for the playoffs.

But the old champs went out and shocked the 76ers, eliminating them in five games.

And then took on New York, a team which had beaten them six times in seven tries that season. Boston prevailed, 4–2.

So for the seventh time the NBA championship round would feature Boston and the Lakers. But this year all of the smart money said the Lakers had too much, and when the Celts lost games one and two it seemed the experts were, indeed, correct.

But they weren't. Boston recovered to tie the series at 2–2 and then carried it to a seventh game, which it won by two points.

The count was now 11 world championships in 13 seasons. But it was the Last Hurrah. The dynasty was over.

Early that summer Russell walked into Auerbach's office and said, "Red, I've had enough. I'm going to hang 'em up." Auerbach let the impact of that statement slide by. "Do me a favor," he said. "Think it over for a while and then we'll talk about it."

Russell had thought it over. Physically, he was still the most imposing player in the game, but mentally, he was exhausted. He had no more to give. The August issue of *Sports Illustrated* explained his feelings dramatically, in a by-lined cover story entitled, "I'm Not Involved Anymore." In it, Russell formally announced his retirement.

Auerbach still wasn't convinced. For one thing, he knew Russell's financial situation was shaky at best, and he couldn't imagine Bill turning his back on the $300,000 he'd earn by remaining another season. In a typical move the Redhead suggested, "Why don't you pick up another ten thousand by selling them a story on 'Why I Changed My Mind'?"

Russell smiled, but nothing could change his mind.

His departure, of course, was the death knell of the dynasty. Even with the retirement of Sam Jones that same summer, there might have been hopes for another miracle in 1970 with Russell on the job. Without him, the club was competitively dead.

Even so, Auerbach didn't beg him or plead with him or confront him with emotional pressures.

"I held no ill feelings toward him," Red recalls. "That man produced for every nickel he was paid here. How could I have told him he owed me or owed the Celtics anything? He owed nothing. That's the way I honestly felt. I think I knew Russell as well as any man alive. He played with tenacity of purpose and conducted his private life the same way. He'd make up his mind to do something, and as long as it made sense to him he would have the balls to do it, whether it made sense to anybody else or not.

"I just couldn't say to him, 'Russ, you caught me short. Please stay. We need you.' A man should do what he feels he has to do, and Russell felt this was something he had to do. He always wanted to quit on top. That's what he was doing and I understood.

"This might sound like cornball schlock, but I wanted to maintain my dignity as a man in his eyes. The two of us have had a great, great relationship. I wasn't going to ruin it by lowering myself in that hour.

"So I accepted his decision, even though it killed me to see him walk away, knowing he was still the best damned player in the game.

"As soon as he left, I called Tommy Heinsohn, gave him the coaching job, and started planning for the future. As far as I was concerned, the glorious past was all over. It had just walked out the door."

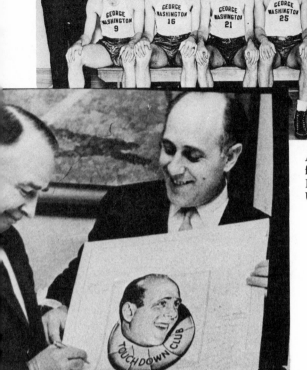

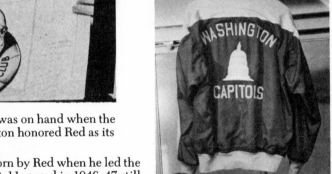

Auerbach (second from right in the front row) when he played for Bill Reinhart on the George Washington University team in 1938.

Bill Reinhart, by then retired, was on hand when the Touchdown Club of Washington honored Red as its man of the year.

The warmup jacket worn by Red when he led the Washington Caps to a 49–11 record in 1946–47 still hangs in his office as a memento of past triumphs.

Red poses with his Washington Caps team.

Ben Kerner, owner of the Tri-Cities Blackhawks, who hired Auerbach in the 1949–50 season, only to lose him when the Redhead quit in protest of front-office interference.

Walter Brown was all smiles when he announced the hiring of Auerback to coach the fledgling Celtics in 1950.

Auerbach pauses for a chat with Commissioner Podoloff (center) and Jocko Collins, the NBA's referee-in-chief, during a pregame warm-up in 1955.

Easy Ed Macauley (left) and Bob Cousy join Red in one of many public clinics staged during the early fifties in Boston—all designed to sell the game of basketball to a then-indifferent city.

Bob Cousy interrupts his coach's postgame analysis for an impromptu shampoo following another world championship.

A 1956 photograph of Auerbach's dream team. Left to right are Tommy Hein-sohn, Bill Russell, Bob Cousy, Bill Sharman, and Frank Ramsey.

By 1962, when this victory party occurred, the Celtics had won their fifth world title in six years. The celebrants (left to right) are Carl Braun, Bob Cousy, Bill Russell, Tom Sanders, KC Jones (sitting), Auerbach, Frank Ram-sey, Tommy Heinsohn, Gene Guarilia (kneeling) and Sam Jones.

The famous victory cigar came to be known by Boston fans (and uneasy opponents) as a sure sign of another Celtic victory.

Commissioner Walter Kennedy, an old friend, enjoys a laugh with the Redhead. Kennedy's first official act as Maurice Podoloff's successor, in the fall of 1963, was to fine Auerbach a league record of $500.

As a rookie, John Havlicek never buttoned his jacket. When Auerbach called his name, John had no time to waste, so he made sure the jacket fell off as he left the bench.

Auerbach perfected the art of arguing with NBA referees, though he never excelled in avoiding fines. During his career, he paid more than $17,000 for his temper. Here he exchanges pleasantries with Earl Strom (top), Sid Borgia (center) and Mendy Rudolph.

Walter Brown meets Auerbach at the airport to personally welcome the team home following a successful road trip in the winter of 1964. Brown died the following Labor Day.

In the midst of the celebration following the 1965 championship, Auerbach pulled a silver medallion from his shower-soaked pocket and held it up before a national television audience. He expained it had been Walter Brown's religious medal. Brown's widow gave it to Red at the start of the season and Auerbach carried it with him to every game and practice. No one knew that story until the Redhead's emotional explanation that afternoon.

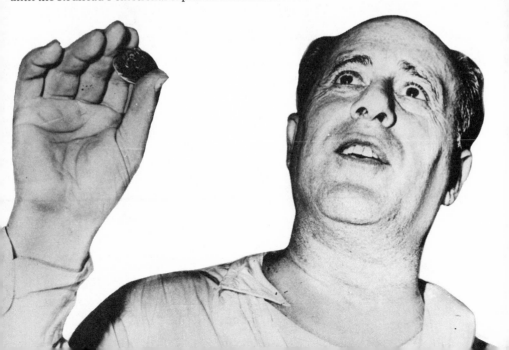

The familiar signs—the cigar, the rolled-up program, the clenched fists—were all present as Auerbach led his aging champions through the 1965–66 campaign, but as the season wore on it became increasingly obvious the dictator was nearly worn out.

Jubilant Boston fans raced onto the court following the dramatic 1965 victory over Philadelphia in game seven of the Eastern Conference playoff final. John Havlicek, foreground, stole an in-bounds pass with four seconds to go, thereby preserving a 110–109 Celtics win.

Auerback lectures on one of the finer points of basketball while John Havlicek stands by to demonstrate during a State Department visit to Burma.

Opposite: Auerbach is despondent when he learns that the Celtics have lost the Eastern Division title by a one-game margin to Philadelphia in 1967.

Above: Bill Russell's famed Number 6 is about to be hoisted to the Boston Garden rafters, alongside Sam Jones' 24. The seats are empty because Russell insisted the ceremony be conducted before the public was allowed in. (Left to right) John Havlicek, Russell, Auerbach, Tommy Heinsohn, and Don Chaney.

The Redhead in his office
during a quiet moment.

Before training camp convenes, the Celtics team i
put together, in Red's office, on draft day. Sittin
next to Red is Bob Schmertz, the popular owner wh
died in 1975.

Visiting players and fans see Boston Garden as a shrine with its rows and rows
of championship banners and its own special Hall of Fame, where the following numbers are majestically retired: 22 (Macauley), 14 (Cousy), 23 (Ramsey),
15 (Heinsohn), 21 (Sharman), 25 (KC Jones), 24 (S. Jones), 6 (Russell), 16
(Sanders), and 1 (Walter Brown).

Auerbach
confers
with owner
Marvin
Kratter
prior to a
1966 game
in Boston.

Film producer Irv Levin is the corporate head of the Celtics today, along with partner Harold Lipton, but like all Boston owners since the day Walter Brown brought Red to town in 1950, Levin and Lipton allow the Redhead a free rein in running the franchise.

A meeting of
three
basketball
legends:
Auerbach
with college
coaches John
Wooden of
UCLA
(center) and
Adolph Rupp
of Kentucky.

In thirteen of the twenty seasons between 1957 and 1976, the NBA championship trophy has occupied a corner of Red Auerbach's office. The smiling Redhead poses proudly next to the symbol of his remarkable achievement.

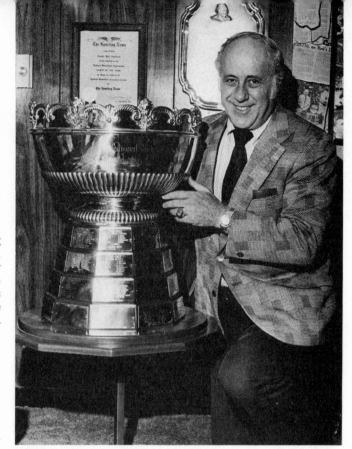

NBA Commissioner Larry O'Brien presents the 1976 championship trophy to the Boston Celtics, represented by Auerbach, coach Tommy Heinsohn, and captain John Havlicek.

Red has allowed himself to get much closer to his players and their families since his retirement. Here he poses with Chris Havlicek, eighteen months old.

Flanked by two of his greatest protégés, Bob Cousy and Tommy Heinsohn, Auerbach recalls the days of his remarkable dynasty during a visit to the sports flashback series, "The Way It Was."

Bill Russell and Red's ladies—Dot, Nancy, and Randy—are on hand for Red Auerbach Day at Boston Garden, commemorating Red's one thousandth coaching victory. The day was January 12, 1966, when Boston beat the Lakers.

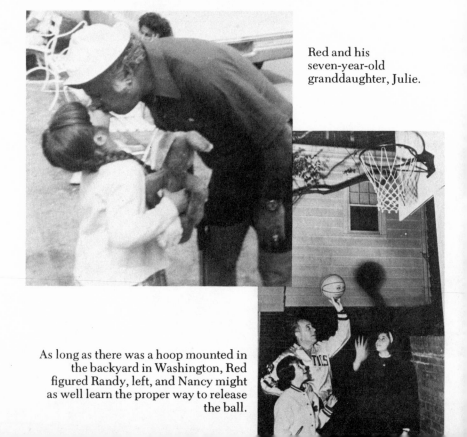

Red and his seven-year-old granddaughter, Julie.

As long as there was a hoop mounted in the backyard in Washington, Red figured Randy, left, and Nancy might as well learn the proper way to release the ball.

PART THREE

The Auerbach Method

Chapter 13
Proper Selections

"He has to be my type of kid."

The names changed as the years rolled by, for sports are particularly susceptible to the ravages of Time. Most pro athletes are born at 21. Most are gone 10 years later.

So it is with the Celtics. The standard gets passed from Bob Cousy to Sam Jones to Jo Jo White; from Ed Macauley to Bill Russell to Dave Cowens. It's a continual process of regeneration. A Brannum is replaced with a Loscutoff; a Sharman with a Jones; a Ramsey with a Havlicek; a Heinsohn with a Howell.

Yet, somehow, the beat goes on in Boston. For 27 years the Celtics have been the longest-running success story in sports, sustained by the most famous roster in basketball history.

Only one factor has remained constant in all that time.

Red Auerbach.

Since the spring of 1950, when he arrived to find the franchise teetering on the brink of extinction, Auerbach has been its sole authority. The Boston Celtics have been his creation. Institutions, we're told, are reflections of the people who serve them, and the Celtics are no different. Indeed, they're the spittin' image of the man who rounded them up, whipped them

153

into shape and sent them out to conquer a hostile world that stretched from Madison Square Garden to the Forum in Los Angeles.

We've followed him along the road from Brooklyn to Boston, and we've seen what his talents have wrought.

Now it's time to explore the ways he did it.

He began, of course, with the players.

"Red always told me he'd deny this if I ever wrote it," Roger Barry smiles, "but back in the beginning, in 1950, 1951, 1952, I know for a fact that he used to call chiefs of police and coaches and headmasters in small towns no one ever heard of, just checking up on guys he might be interested in. What kind of kids were they? Did they ever get into trouble? Did they hang around with rough crowds? Things like that. He wanted to find out all he could about them, just in case he decided to draft them. Now I knew he was doing this, and he knew I knew it, so one day we talked about it and I asked him what the reason was. I never forgot his answer. 'The selection of material is more important than the handling of it,' he said. 'If you get the right guys in the beginning, you won't have any problems later on.'

"That was so typical of him. Red never overlooked the smallest detail."

Scouting was a problem in the early days. Red hardly had time to hop a plane for a first-person inspection of the leading college seniors. But he did have a network of trusted friends around the country and he relied heavily upon their advice. Ex-players formed the nucleus of his talent search. Scolari and Barksdale helped scout Russell; Bobby Donham recruited Loscutoff; Bones McKinney found Sam Jones.

"Red felt free to call on us," Scolari explains, "because he knew we would look for the same things he would look for in a kid. After all, we played for him, so we knew better than most people what he demanded. And then once we found a kid, he'd sometimes ask us to pay him a visit and talk about the good things the kid could expect if he joined the Celtics.

"Believe me, Red wasn't lucky to get the type of players he had down through the years. He knew what he was doing every minute. Sure, we helped him, but I'll bet there was an awful lot of advice he got from other sources that he never accepted. You've got to know whose advice to take. And you've got to be willing to take it. Red was smart that way. Not lucky. Smart."

"Lucky?" Ed Macauley repeats incredulously. "Look at the man's record! When you're talking about a great, great team like the Celtics, I can assure you there are no easy answers. Don't even bother looking for them. There was nothing simplistic about Auerbach's success. He knew how to handle talent, but he also knew how to spot it."

Havlicek, though one of the least celebrated seniors of 1962, had an attractive calling card. "Red knew Ohio State was a championship ball club," John explains. "That told him I was used to winning. One year alone there were six of us who had been NCAA champions."

Don Nelson was a different story. "I thought my career was over," he remembers. "I couldn't believe it when Red called and said he wanted me. Let's face it, when you clear waivers you're all done. Why did Auerbach pick me? He could have had Jackie Mooreland instead of me. Jackie was bigger (6'7), had much better stats and had been around the league longer than I had. Yet Red picked me.

"I believe he sees things in certain players that no one else sees, or maybe no one else bothers to look for. It's something inside a player, something other than talent alone. Look at the people he's picked up late in their careers: Bailey Howell, Wayne Embry, guys like that. Look at a player like Paul Silas. What do you see when you look at men like that? You see dedication. You see someone who wants to win very badly. I'd like to think that's what Red saw in me, too.

"You just don't find many bad apples on the Celtics. He's made a few mistakes, sure, but very, very few. When you look at the Celtics, you're looking at a bunch of winners."

Few people had a better view of the Celtics—the dynasty Celtics—than Jerry West, the spectacular Lakers guard who never knew what it was to beat those Boston teams in a playoff series.

His testimony on the subject is eloquent. "Why did they beat us every time? I've looked back and thought about it often. I've reflected on so many situations, times when everyone knew we had the superior ball club—we had proven that during the season—and yet, again they'd beat us. I've tried to understand it, and now I think I do. After watching so many games over so many years, I'm convinced the *quality* of the player is the most important thing of all.

"When two teams are equal, or nearly equal, and they come right down to the deciding moments of a seventh game—when winning and losing is on the line—that's when the quality of the players might mean more than their talent alone.

"The Celtics, I think, were just a cut above everybody else in their desire to win. I really believe that. They had that hunger, that pride, that *want* to achieve, and it made them better than everybody else in a clutch situation.

"And that's where I give Auerbach a tremendous amount of credit. What he accomplished in the selection of his players was just remarkable. That's one reason why I'm one of his biggest fans. He knows how to go into the draft and come out with exactly what he needs, but more important than that—someone who will fit into his system and play the same way everybody else does.

"I won't get into names. But just think of some of the great players who've lost to the Celtics over the years. And ask yourself why it happened. To me, it gets right down to the quality factor again. Everyone wants to win. But some athletes will try, lose and then say, 'Well, we gave our best.' And then they'll forget about it! Well, if you can forget about it that easily, maybe the quality of the person you're talking about is not what's needed to achieve Boston's kind of success.

"You see, the Celtics were always totally dedicated, totally involved, totally prepared to sacrifice whatever was necessary in order to win. They never went about things in a half-assed way.

"And that's their real secret, I think."

I've been lucky enough to have friends—good friends—in this business, especially when it comes to finding new players for my team. Here again I've got to pay tribute to Bill Reinhart, because so much of what I learned from that man has helped me later in my career.

I made it a point to develop a system of my own, like Bill's,
one in which my old players would be instrumental in helping
me, too. Who knows you and your techniques better than one
of your players?

I also kept in touch with many of the college coaches. I'd
call them and I'd lecture at coaching clinics all over the country, getting to know these men and getting a better understanding of who was doing what in college ball.

This was very important to me. You have only so many
chances to find good new players each year, so you had better
find out all you can about each kid on your list.

Even today, I go to places like Kentucky, Maryland, Indiana, and I can see why those teams are successful. Watch their
benches during a game. Everybody is involved. That's the way
it's got to be, because this is a team game. I've been to some
schools where the athletes acted as if they were doing the
school a favor by participating. This is one of the things I tell
coaches all the time: you're better off forgetting a guy like that
and getting someone else who's only 50 percent as good, but
will bust his ass for you.

When I'm scouting young players, the first thing I do, of
course, is ask myself: What do I need? I analyze my team and
try to figure out exactly what I need.

Let's say I'm looking for a certain type of forward and I've
got two in mind, but I just can't decide which one to take. On
the surface they appear to be pretty equal.

So I consider where they've played, and for whom they've
played. Most coaches, you see, are under great pressure to
win, and I'm talking about all the way back to the high school
level. But at what expense do they do this? Are they concerned
about developing their players, or is their first goal to win every game in the book? Quite often it's the second approach. So
what happens? The players end up holding the ball all of the
time, playing possession, staying in zones. The kids get into
ruts and it's very hard to scout them. Nobody knows what they
can do. As a result very few kids who play in those systems
ever make it to the pros because they never get out of those
ruts. Jo Jo White happens to be one of the exceptions.

That's why I was so high on Ramsey, Hagan and Tsioropoulos that year I took all three of them. Just knowing they

played for Adolph Rupp told me they were motivated and fundamentally sound.

I also liked the idea of getting kids who had played on championship teams, or at least teams which went to tournaments. There's a better chance this kid won't choke in the clutch. He's played before big crowds in big games and he's had to make the big play. That's important. It means he has a feel for winning.

By far the most important thing of all is that he has to be my type of kid: he can absorb coaching; he will listen to what you're telling him, and then go out and do it. And he's a good kid on and off the court. You find that out by talking to people who've had a chance to observe him. You don't want someone who'll be bitching all the time. Unfortunately, a lot of kids who are great in college become real pains in the ass later on. I want a kid who was great, but who never stopped being nice.

Most of all, I want a kid who's willing to pay the price, who's willing to work at winning, who wants to win so badly that he'll give me everything he's got.

I want a kid like Frank Ramsey, like KC Jones, like John Havlicek.

They are my type of people.

Chapter 14
Contract Time

"The Celtics just cared about winning."

The argument was getting nowhere fast. Jack Nichols, beginning his third season with the Celts (1955–56), had a fixed figure on his mind when he sat down to discuss his contract with Auerbach. Red had a figure in mind, too.

The figures, however, weren't even close.

"Look, Jack," the exasperated coach finally said, "if that's the amount you have to have, then you might as well forget playing here. It's out of the question. Absolutely impossible."

Nichols was just beginning his rebuttal when Auerbach was summoned out of the office momentarily. In his absence, Walter Brown happened by, noticed Nichols sitting alone and stopped for a chat.

"How's everything, Jack?" he asked.

"Well, not so good right now. We're having real problems with my salary."

Brown asked for the specifics, so Nichols told him what he wanted and what Red was willing to pay.

"Oh, hell," Walter said, as if he was dealing with a triviality. "I don't think your figure is unreasonable. Why don't we shake on it right now and get it over with?"

By the time Auerbach returned Brown and Nichols were deep into an unrelated conversation.

"Okay, Jack," he said impatiently. "Let's get back to what we were talking about. As I told you, there's no way . . ."

"Red, Red," Walter interrupted. "We've already solved that. We can pay Jack what he wants."

Nichols excused himself, smiling as he left.

Auerbach turned to his boss. "For Christ's sake, Walter. How the hell am I supposed to run a ball club with this stuff going on?"

In the fall of 1958 Gene Conley took his check for $4,500— the losing share each Milwaukee Brave received in that year's World Series—and used it as a down payment on a $40,000 home. Then he called his old coach in Boston.

"Hey, Red, can you use another good basketball player?"

"Can you still play?"

"I think so."

"What have you been doing the last couple of years?"

"Oh, playing some down at the Y!"

Auerbach laughed. The first time he saw Conley was in October 1952, when Gene—at Sharman's urging—went to the Harvard Indoor Athletic Building and tried to win a job with the Celtics. It was the first time he had played basketball in two years, yet his quickness, his good hands, his mobility for a big man (6'8, 225) immediately impressed the Redhead. He was stunned when Gene quit basketball a year later to concentrate on his pitching career.

When Conley called, Arnie Risen had just retired. The Celtics needed a backup man for Russell, and Conley fit the bill.

"How much do you weigh?" Red asked.

"The same as I did five years ago."

"Okay. If you want to come here for a tryout, you can. But we're not going to pay your way."

Conley came, and the minute he stepped onto the court it was obvious he could still do the job.

All that remained was agreeing on a contract. Before Auerbach had a chance to bring that matter up, Gene stopped by the Garden for a visit with Walter. Their conversation, naturally, got around to money.

"What do you want for a salary?" Brown asked.

"Gee, I don't know what you're paying these days. I know what you were paying in 1953, though, and I want more than that."

"So name a figure."

"Well, how about twenty thousand?"

"You've got it."

When Auerbach heard of the deal he hit the roof, but he couldn't very well stop it. So he bided his time. Angrily. Angry at Brown for playing Santa Claus again, and angry at Conley for sitting on Santa's lap.

On November 18 the Celts were playing Detroit in St. Louis, and that morning Conley got a phone call in his hotel room.

"Gene," Auerbach began, "you're not helping the club that much, and we've got this guy Swain [first draft choice Ben Swain, 6'8] , and Walter paid you more than we can afford. What I'm trying to say is, I'm going to have to let you go. But listen: stay in shape, because maybe I can use you later on."

Conley packed his bags and flew home to Milwaukee.

On November 22 his telephone rang. It was Auerbach again. Boston had won two and lost two in Conley's absence.

"Ben's not playing that well," Red began. "Are you ready to come back?"

"Are you kidding? You bet I am."

"Good. There's only one problem. We've got to cut your pay."

"How much?"

"In half."

Conley returned, played a major role in that spring's playoffs, and was given a bonus at season's end.

"I knew what Red was doing all along," Gene remembers. "He was letting me go, just so he could cut my pay in half a few days later. But I wasn't really mad at him. Hey, deep inside I knew I wasn't worth twenty thousand. Not in those days. Even the stars weren't making that much. But lovable old Walter wanted to make me happy. So Red waited and made his move. And what could I do? There were no agents and lawyers back then. It was a case of take it or leave it. So I took it."

* * *

As agents began arriving on the scene in the early '60s, when the ill-fated American Basketball League first surfaced, they were generally viewed as a sign of the more affluent times. Owners and general managers were resigned to their presence in negotiating sessions.

The only man who balked was Auerbach and he was characteristically adamant on the subject. As late as June of 1967, long after the issue had died on every other front, he continued to fight off the interlopers—which is exactly the way he pictured them.

"I have always dealt with my players directly and I have always treated them fairly," he explained in a June 5, 1967, *Boston Record* article, under the banner headline: AUERBACH DEFIES AGENTS. "I see no reason to change my way of operating now. I will not deal through agents, and I want no agents sitting in when I'm negotiating with my players. If these players want agents, that's their business. But I draft them, and they're the ones I'm going to talk with."

In the end, of course, the agents made their way into Red's office, but there was no Welcome Wagon awaiting them.

"I was on guard," admits Larry Fleischer, the most prominent of all basketball agents. "His initial hysterical position—allowing nobody to represent his players—suggested to me that he had a desire to take advantage of the people he was dealing with. Prohibiting a player from using an attorney is wrong, and very few industries in the world—if any—would allow that kind of nonsense to go on. So it had to put me on my guard."

For a year after Walter Brown's death in 1964 the team was operated by his widow, Marjorie, and Lou Pieri, but in the summer of 1965 they sold the club. It was the first of eight ownership changes in the next 10 years. At times money was so tight that the Celtics couldn't even pay their telephone bill.

"Red's reputation is that of a hard negotiator," says Jason Wolf, his longtime personal accountant. "But he also has a fine reputation for going to bat for his players against management. I know there have been instances—after Walter's death, of course—where he has gone to his boss and insisted certain players had to get more money than management wanted to pay.

"One thing really bothered Red a lot. Someone like Walt Frazier might get talking to a Celtic and ask him what he was making. And when he found out he'd say, 'Boy, are you underpaid!' And that would tend to undermine the player's faith in Red. I know that hurt him badly."

The Auerbach guidelines for assessing players' worth never varied. It's been the same since 1950 in Boston, 1949 in Moline, 1946 in Washington.

"What Red asks, in effect, is this," says Norman Blass, a New York attorney who has represented several Boston players. "Is the player a winner? That's what he wants to know. And statistics don't always tell you that. Most contracts nowadays are negotiated by people who are not basketball people. They're business people. But Red has grown up in basketball, so his philosophies and ideas are much different than those you'll find in most front offices. He has a different way of determining values. Tell him so-and-so scored twenty-five points a game and it won't make a damned bit of difference. Red knows what a player has done, or has not done. And generally I've found him to be fair. He's tough, but fair. And his word is good. If you double-cross him, watch out. But if you're open and honest and reasonable with him, he'll treat you the same way."

Beginning with my very first job in Washington, I had enough ego and enough balls to insist that I be given full authority over my players' contracts. I was very strong on this point. I believed it was necessary if I was going to have complete control of my ball club.

It's very easy to put out in home games. The crowd is friendly, and the player is comfortable because he's slept in his own bed and eaten in his own home. Don't underestimate what those things mean in a long season. It's natural for players to perform better at home. The owners see them play at home, of course. Very few owners watch their teams play on the road. So the picture they get is often distorted. But a coach sees his players all the time, at home and away, against good teams and bad teams, and he knows exactly what a player is contributing. Road games count just as much in the standings as home games do. So the way my guys performed away from home counted very heavily with me. And I was the only one in a position to make that judgment.

When I sat down to discuss contracts with my ballplayers, the subject of road games came up almost immediately.

We had a rule on our team. I didn't want anyone to bring his statistics in with him when we sat down to negotiate. I didn't want to see them or even hear about them. For one thing, I never believed them. A lot of statisticians cheat on things like rebounds and assists, trying to build up their own guys. So what the hell do the numbers mean if you've got that crap going on? What is a steal? What is an assist? If a guy gets a rebound and hands it to another guy who then dribbles down the floor and makes a basket, do they give the first guy an assist? For what? But some teams do. As far as I'm concerned, the only true statistic is foul shooting.

Another bad thing about statistics is that you get so caught up in them, so worried about records and things like that, that you end up forgetting about the goddamned game. This happens all the time in sports and it's wrong. It's terrible.

I'll give you an example. One day Gene Conley and I were driving along up in Maine someplace and we had the World Series going on the radio. Early Wynn was pitching for the White Sox and in the very first inning he got something like a 9–0 lead. If you can't win with a 9–0 lead you don't belong in the World Series.

So I turned to Gene. "Get him out of there," I said. "Bring in somebody else and then come back with Wynn again tomorrow. That way you get to use your ace twice in a row."

Conley says they can't do that because he won't get credit for the win.

"Piss on the win!" I said. "Let's win the goddamned Series. What the hell do I care who gets credit for the win?"

But Gene insists that's the way it's got to be. So now we get to the fifth inning, and by this time Chicago is leading 11–0.

"Hey," I said. "Now he gets credit for the win, right? Get him the hell out of there. He's an old man and it's cold in Chicago this time of year."

Conley says no again. He says they can't take him out because he's got a shutout going.

I just looked at him. "You're shitting me!"

Well—so help me—the old guy won the game, but he hurt his arm and didn't do a damned thing the rest of the Series. That just strengthened my belief that the win comes first. Every other statistic means nothing.

When I sat down to talk to my players they understood. "Your salary," I'd say, "depends on what I've seen with my own two eyes. Until the day your statistics can tell me how many points were scored in the clutch and how many came in garbage time, I don't want to see them."

No one on the Celtics ever got paid according to how many points or rebounds or assists or anything else he might have compiled. Each man got paid according to how well he did what we asked him to do. What was his contribution toward making us a better team? That's all I cared about. In our system, the guy who set the good pick was just as important as the guy who made the jump shot. Or take guys like KC and Satch. If they could stop people like West and Baylor from getting their normal amount of points, wasn't that worth as much as if they both scored 20 and let Jerry and Elgin toss in 100? Every man on our team had a job, and every man's job was recognized and appreciated when it came time to discuss contracts.

Walter and I had most of our confrontations over contract negotiations. He was in love with his players and he dealt in emotions rather than hard business facts. He wanted to make decisions, and yet he realized he didn't know enough about the game. So he'd talk with me about the club and we'd go over the contracts together. Then he'd get talking to one of the guys and his heart would take over. He'd figure, "Red wants to pay this man ten thousand, so if I pay him fifteen thousand and make a mistake, I'm really blowing just five grand."

The ballplayers were no dummies. They'd wait until I left town, then get good old Walter out on a golf course. It happened all the time. Then I'd get back to my office, expecting to resume salary discussions with somebody, and Walter would come in and say, "Gee, Red, I just did something and I know it was wrong." He never had to tell me what it was that he did.

Finally I brought it to a showdown. "Walter," I said, "this is ridiculous. Every time a ballplayer has a little bit of trouble getting something from me, you step in and give him whatever he wants. Now, besides ruining everything I'm trying to accomplish with this club, you're also making me look stupid. So let's have an understanding. Either I sign all of them, or I sign none of them!"

He said, "You're right, Red. I'll keep my big nose out of it from now on."

We never completely solved that problem, because right up until the day he died Walter loved the Celtics, much more than he could afford to love them.

Through the years a lot of stories went around about what a tough, shrewd negotiator I was, and down deep inside they always hurt me a little bit. I wasn't being shrewd at all. I was trying to watch the money because we just didn't have that much dough to work with.

I'm always amused to read about the Knickerbockers trading a Mike Riordan for an Earl Monroe. Damn it, that's no trade. That's a $40,000 salary being swapped for a $200,000 salary. In my book it's a $160,000 purchase.

We couldn't make purchases like that.

People kept comparing us to the Yankees, but there was one big difference. After every season the Yankees would go out and buy someone like Johnny Mize. The Celtics couldn't do that. We had to depend upon what we got out of the draft and on any old players we could convince to postpone retirements. The most I ever spent for an older player was the $6,000 I paid to get Wayne Embry. We simply didn't have any cash reserves to go to if we came up short. Believe me when I say we were winning world championships some years when we didn't have a goddamned dime in the bank.

New York won two lousy championships (1970, 1973) and look at the guys who were bought for those teams: Dave De-Busschere, Dick Barnett, Earl Monroe, Jerry Lucas, John Gianelli. Believe me, there are a lot of owners in this league who'd gladly spend a million dollars of their own money just to walk around with a championship ring on their finger. That's the kind of ego thing a championship is. But Walter and I had to deal in the financial facts of life. That's why it always hurt when people said I was tight.

* * *

As far as the agents go, I finally had to give in on that, even though my personal view of them never changed. Sometimes you've got to bend with the times. I can remember some of the great old coaches, guys like Nat Holman, saying, "Anybody who shoots one-handed will never play for me!" But then a different breed of cat comes along and you have to back off just a bit.

One of the first agents I ever had to deal with came into my office one day with his client. This kid wasn't even a high draft choice. So his man starts in telling me all about the kid and how he's going to help the Boston Celtics win another world championship. I didn't say anything. I just puffed on my cigar and let him do the talking. Then he got down to the meat of his pitch. His kid wanted so many extra dollars if he scored X number of points, and so many extra dollars if we won X number of games.

That was enough for me.

"Just a minute, Buster!" I said. "If making my ball club isn't enough incentive for this kid, I don't want him. Now get the hell out of here."

They got up and left and the next day the kid signed with another team.

It was okay with me. If that was his attitude, he wasn't my type of kid. But I'll always wonder how things might have turned out if that damned agent hadn't come along, or if he had just shut up and allowed the kid to talk with me alone.

Chapter 15
Respect & Discipline

"I never expected my players to love me."

The Celtics, as Red was always quick to point out, lived under a dictatorship.

It was that way in the early 1950s when the Auerbach regime took over.

"Red intimidated most of the people who were around him," Ed Macauley says. "You always had this feeling in the back of your mind that if you challenged him, he was just as apt to say, 'Okay, let's close the door right now and settle this.' And there was no doubt about who would come out second! You were always just a little bit afraid of Red, and that's the way he wanted it. He was the boss and everyone knew it."

The situation hadn't changed when Willie Naulls arrived in 1963.

"We were playing a game down in Providence," Willie remembers, "and we had a three-point lead with ten seconds to go. In the huddle it was decided that we'd go into a semizone and make the other team shoot over our heads. There was no way we were going to lose. Well, my man got the ball and I jumped up in the air with my hands down by my side and I shouted to distract the guy. The referee blew his whistle and said I committed a foul. The guy's shot went in, then he made the free throw to tie it up, and we lost in overtime. Auerbach was all over me after the game, but I never answered back, even though I was convinced the ref blew the call. See, Auerbach was the boss. Period. And when he talked, you just shut up and listened. That's how it was on the Celtics. You did what Red told you to do."

That's not to suggest the Boston players were reduced to automatons.

"We could talk to Red," Ramsey says. "He listened to our suggestions. Many times I'd go over to him on the sidelines and say, 'Hey, Red, I think it might work better if we did such-and-such.' He wanted his players to contribute their ideas. He encouraged that.

"But once he started to talk, that was it. He was the boss and he had absolute power to do whatever he wanted to do with us. And the only response he expected was obedience.

"If you want to know one of the real secrets to the success of that team, it was this: we had respect for authority, and everyone on the ball club recognized Red as that authority. He was master and I never dreamed of questioning him.

"And if you think that sounds funny, let me assure you that you have to have that kind of discipline if you want to go on winning the way we did. Today it seems so many players think they are smarter than their coaches. No one on our club ever thought that for a minute. If Red said to do it, we did it, because we knew he knew what he was talking about. It was as simple as that."

The Redhead ruled with an iron fist.

"That's the way it's got to be in athletics," Macauley feels. "And that's why the whole sports scene seems to be coming apart today. You don't see many disciplinarians like Auerbach, McCarthy and Lombardi, do you? But look at their records, and look at the records of their players later on, and then tell me their approach was wrong.

"It's quite simple to understand. It's like a war. The enemy is over the hill or across the trenches and the sergeant yells, 'Okay, let's go!' Now what happens if one half of your group wants to talk it over, and the other half decides to go a different way?

"It's no different in sports. Whether you agree with your coach or not, somebody has to be the one who says, 'This is the way we're going to do it!' If you ask five players how they want to do it, you're going to get five different answers and it just won't work.

"A good team needs a strong leader. That's what Auerbach was."

But the discipline was fathered by a respect the players shared for Red; the respect made obedience a natural reaction.

"Red can be very annoying at times," Russell smiles. "He's annoyed me more than once. When it happened I'd just look at him, and I've been told I have a *look* that people understand.

"What Red and I shared is, I think, the most essential ingredient in any relationship. We shared a mutual respect. He knew I was a man and I knew he was a man, and that's the way we treated each other.

"Was I submissive? I'm not sure that's the word I'd use. You see, in order to lead you have to know how to follow. Why should I challenge Auerbach? Why should I question him? What was there for me to gain? There was never any reason for it. He was the coach and I was the player. That's the way this game is set up. There are coaches and there are players. I understood his function and he understood mine, and we worked very well together.

"In my mind, he was the best coach in the history of professional sports. Period. So why would I want to tell him what to do?"

Auerbach's command was manifested in very subtle ways. It could be seen even in an act as simple as taking off a warm-up jacket.

"This is something I try to point out to younger players today and sometimes I'm sure they think I'm crazy," Havlicek says. "But it's not crazy at all. When Red wants you, he wants you *now!* This is what Ramsey explained to me when I became the sixth man. That meant I had to be ready to go the minute he called my name. I've seen guys waste almost a whole time-out just getting ready to report. You weren't supposed to have your jacket buttoned up and your arms through the sleeves. That meant you'd have to waste time later on. I'm not kidding. This was a big thing. So I'd take my pants off, and I'd just drape the jacket over my shoulders. The minute he yelled, 'Havlicek!', I'd jump and the jacket would fall off as I ran to get the scorer's attention, letting him know I was going into the game. That way I didn't miss out on anything.

"And this is how Auerbach's players were trained to respond."

It's one of Red's proudest boasts that he handed out just four fines in the 16 years he coached the Celtics.

Three were levied concurrently when he caught a trio of players breaking curfew.

The fourth fine was handed out to Sam Jones, though to this day Sam insists it was a miscarriage of justice.

"Red hit me for five dollars and I still say he was wrong," Jones explains. "Every time we get together I remind him about it, but he just laughs.

"We had a rule on the team that said you couldn't eat pancakes on the day of a game.

"Well, we played Syracuse on a Saturday night in Boston, and as soon as the game ended we caught a plane back to Syracuse for a return game Sunday. As soon as we landed, Russ, KC and I went looking for a place to eat and ended up in some greasy spoon. The three of us ordered pancakes, but I got my order in while they were talking. Naturally mine arrived first. I just started to take a bite when I heard this voice yell, 'That will be five dollars!'

"I look around and who the hell's standing there but Auerbach. So I said okay, I might as well pay the five dollars and enjoy my meal. He looks at me and says, 'Take another bite and it'll cost you another five dollars.'

"Meanwhile, Russell and KC are yelling in to the kitchen: 'Cancel those orders!'

"I was the only one who had to pay."

But if the rules stated no pancakes on the day of a game, what was so unfair?

"It was two o'clock in the morning!" Sam replied.

From the day a player first joined the Celtics, he understood that discipline was a very big thing with us. There were no loudmouths, no complainers, no dissenters and no goddamned clubhouse lawyers like they have on the other teams.

When I told someone to do something, I wanted it done, and I wanted it done immediately. We live in a democracy and I believe in democracy, but in sports you can't have a democracy because there just isn't time for one. So my word was law. If you had to call a meeting everytime you wanted to make a decision, you'd never get anything done.

What is discipline? Discipline is just a proper response to authority.

I'd had these little sayings I'd use, like "I may not always be right, but I'm never wrong!"

I told the guys right away that I wasn't worred about keeping them happy. There were 12 of them and only one of me, so it was a lot easier for them to study me and find ways to keep me happy than for me to satisfy all of them.

Different sports have different disciplinary needs. Football, for instance, is a very regimented type of game and very unexciting to prepare for. A guy spends an hour rolling on the ground, running into a dummy, doing 100 sit-ups. That's not interesting. Or you get 10 guys together and have them push a truck up a field! Wonderful.

But basketball is a game of fun, whether you're playing 1-on-1, 2-on-2, or doing shooting or dexterity drills. Even working out all by yourself can be fun. So most basketball players love to play the game.

Yet to be successful, a certain amount of discipline has to be involved. One thing I insisted on was this: whenever I told someone to do something, I never wanted to hear the word Why. And that went for everybody, including Russell. As great a player as he was, he never pushed his weight around. Sure, he had his own kind of personality, which is characteristic of all great athletes, but there were no double standards on the Celtics, contrary to what a lot of people might think.

You can have big discipline without 100 rules. The way to get it is through respect, respect for the team, respect for one another and respect for the coach.

I never expected my players to love me. I just wanted them to respect me and to obey me. If you can win their respect, then everything else comes rather easily. But you don't get respect by demanding it. You can get obedience that way, but not respect. When I was thinking of a new play I'd discuss it with them at practice. And when a guy had a suggestion to make, I'd always listen and consider it. I never kidded myself into believing I had all the answers. I respected their knowledge of the game.

When the time came to make a decision, the responsibility belonged to me and nobody else.

This is a point I make quite clear at my basketball camp. Kids hear me suggesting a certain way to do something, then go back to their schools where maybe their coach has a different idea. I don't want them saying, "Auerbach says to do it this way." That would be wrong. So I repeat myself over and over: "If your coach says to do something a certain way, then—right, wrong or indifferent—that's the way to do it because he is your coach."

If you can show your players you know what you're talking about, and explain things to them as you go along, discipline will just follow naturally.

People will usually follow someone they respect.

But if that failed I could always fall back on my standard line: "I hired you, and I can fire you!"

Years ago, right after Arnie Risen joined us, we took a train to someplace or other and shortly after we got going Arnie ordered a cocktail. Everyone else just looked at me, because I didn't allow that when we traveled as a team. So I called the trainer over. "Tell Arnie to drink the cocktail," I said, "and then never to order another one as long as he's a member of the Boston Celtics. If he orders anything other than a beer or Coke from now on, it's an automatic fine."

I didn't want to embarrass the poor guy. He just didn't know the rule. You've got to know when to be tough and when to be reasonable.

The time I fined Sam for eating the pancakes was more of a joke than a fine, even though Sam didn't think so. I wasn't upset that he ate the damned thing, or planned to eat it. But once he knew I was in the same room, it would have been wrong for him to eat them. It would have been like flaunting the rules in front of me, and I wasn't about to let that go.

So I hit him for $5 and everybody had a good laugh over it. Except Sam.

The only other time I made a fine stick was the night I caught three of my guys breaking curfew. We had just finished a long road trip on a Saturday night. I planned to get up at dawn, fly home to Washington and meet the club at practice on Monday. They were going to fly home later Sunday morning.

I was walking across the hotel lobby just before daybreak and I happened to spot my friends sitting in the coffee shop with three broads. I decided to walk in, and the minute they saw me they almost died. Finally one of them got up the nerve to speak.

"Red," he said, "I'd like you to meet so-and-so's cousin and her friends. We're on our way to church."

"That's nice," I smiled. "Well, I've got to be going. Nice to meet you ladies, and I'll see you guys Monday."

The look I gave them told them Monday couldn't come fast enough for me.

At practice, I blew my whistle and called the three church-goers over. I was quite sure everyone knew what the story was and was waiting to see my reaction.

"Look," I said. "I want to make one thing very clear, okay? I am not going to fine you birds for breaking curfew. It was the last night on the road and you're entitled to relax sometime.

"But I am going to fine all three of you for insulting my intelligence! Now get to work."

Everyone was smiling. What would I have accomplished by screaming about curfews and fining them heavily? I'd have upset the whole team.

This way I got my point across and still let them know I wasn't an unreasonable man.

It was a dictatorship with feeling, I guess.

Chapter 16
The Team Concept

"Little things can destroy a team."

Wayne Embry noticed right away how different things were in Boston upon his arrival in the fall of 1966. His ego had been crushed in Cincinnati. He had been a captain and five-time all-star for the Royals, but their perennial inability to dislodge Boston as eastern division kingpin somehow convinced management that Embry was dispensable. At 6'8, they concluded, he was too small to get the job done in the pivot, so they cast their lot with rookie Walt Wesley and veteran Connie Dierking, both 6'11.

"My confidence," he remembers, "was destroyed."

Then Auerbach found him and brought him to Boston for a new lease on life at the age of 30.

"The first thing I noticed was the manner in which you were treated in Boston," he says. "You were now a Celtic, one of Red's guys, and you knew he'd bust his ass to do anything in the world for you. Even if you were horseshit, Red made you think you were the best player in the league. And in his own mind I think he really believed that anyone wearing the Green and White was someone special. If I played only two minutes and grabbed just one rebound, he'd be sure to point out that I was making a hell of a contribution."

In the Celtics' scheme of things, that *was* an important contribution.

"There was no way I was going to be a big scorer," Gene Conley says, "but I took great pride in the things Red asked me to do, because I knew it all added up to victory in the end. One night we were playing the Royals and Red told me to stay with Embry and let Russell guard a corner man. 'Don't let Embry near the boards,' he said. And I didn't. Russell ended up with almost fifty rebounds. He hung around the basket like a cat. When the night was over my back was bruised, but I had done my job. And everyone knew it."

The team concept received more than lip service on Auerbach's clubs. It was considered gospel truth.

Satch Sanders expressed it neatly.

"Around my third or fourth season I started thinking about all-star teams and all that jazz, so I started shooting more and pretty soon I had my average up to nearly sixteen points a game. Red didn't say anything to me. Then one night I scored something like twenty-two, twenty-four points and we lost. On the ride home that night I thought about it and I began to realize what we had going for us. Each man was a specialist, and it only took one man crossing over to another man's specialty to spoil the balance of that beautiful machine. That's when I realized the broader picture was so much brighter than my own little picture. It taught me a lesson: do what you do best. All the extras, like headlines and ovations, just don't count as much as winning. It was a much bigger claim to say I was part of the world champion Celtics than to say I averaged thirty-five points a game.

"I never again bemoaned the fact I wasn't an all-star. I just told myself, 'Satch, you contributed.' "

The team concept was never more clearly demonstrated than in the area of player helping player.

When Sam Jones arrived in the fall of 1957, both Cousy and Sharman had reason to regard him as a threat to their own security. "But this is what made those teams so great," Sam says. "If Cooz or Sharman got hurt, they wanted me to go out and play as well as they had, so they helped me learn the system and they gave me little tips."

A few years later Havlicek arrived as the obvious successor to Ramsey's sixth man assignment. "I was a little bit insecure the first day I walked into training camp," John recalls. "Most rookies feel that way. But it didn't last too long, because so many people were so willing to help me.

"Especially Ramsey. Frank told me all the things I had to do, what to watch out for, how to take advantage of situations in a game. And yet the papers kept saying I was going to take his job!

"I was really inexperienced at the guard position, so whenever I'd bring the ball down I'd keep my body between the defensive man and the basketball. Consequently, my back was turned and I couldn't see all of the players on the floor. As soon as Cousy noticed that he came right over and began working with me. That was one of the things he was so great at—watching every man on the court to see who was open—and it was one of the things I had to learn. He was a very big help to me.

"But this was an attitude Red created and encouraged on all of his teams. The emphasis was never on the fact someone might take your job away. Instead, veterans were made to realize that rookies could prolong their careers by taking some of the burden away from them.

"It became a unified team effort. And the only thing that mattered was winning."

"When Willie Naulls came to Boston he discovered there were four other men on the floor," KC Jones laughs. "He saw what it meant to play as a team and one day he told me he never enjoyed the game on the pro level until he became a Celtic."

Johnny Most, the club's legendary play-by-play man, has

been high above courtside for every game over the past 24 years. No one knows the team any better.

"People often ask me to explain how these guys keep winning. It's quite simple. The Celtics have always been able to instill in their players the idea that the ultimate victory belongs to the group, not the individual. And so they have pride in themselves as a unit. Corny? Sure it is. But what the hell's wrong with being corny? There's nothing sophisticated about what these guys have done. It's the oldest formula for success in the world: they function with pride."

If someone else said it, you'd want to laugh.

"That's right," Sanders said. "But it's true. The things other people laughed at were the things the Celtics believed in."

Not only the reserves felt that way.

"Why were we so good?" Russell asks. "Because we were a team. That's it. We were a team. We all recognized that and understood it, and when you do, you find that all the other things just aren't that important. But you've got to be men to play that way. You can't be needing false praise and pats on the back all the time. You can't be needing someone to tell you you're okay. I *know* I'm okay.

"My concern was the Celtics. Period. That's it. We were the Celtics. I wasn't playing for Boston or playing for the NBA. I was playing for the Celtics. And the only thing that counted with me was the Celtics. We were a family. Maybe I could have made another million dollars playing someplace else, but I couldn't imagine wanting to play anywhere else. I was a Celtic."

I was very concerned with the way my players got along, both on and off the court. If they had a card game going, for instance, I'd make sure that nobody was losing too much dough. I didn't want anybody being hurt by a teammate. That's very bad for a ball club.

I had a system of rotating roommates for a long time. I wanted these guys to get to know each other. One of the nicest things that ever happened along those lines occurred way back in 1951 when Bones McKinney joined us from Washington. That was Chuck Cooper's first season and, though I wasn't re-

ally worried, I was a bit apprehensive about the way he'd be received. There weren't any problems at all. The guys loved him.

But my boy Bones was a dyed-in-the-wool Southerner from North Carolina. The first day he arrived that January he called me aside.

"Red," he said, "Ah hear ya drafted Cooper."

"That's right," I told him.

"Well, Ah don't know who ya got the kid roomin' with, but Ah'd like to room with him for a while."

I started to tell Bones that it wasn't necessary because of our policy of shifting roommates, a policy I had back in Washington.

"Ah know 'bout the policy," he said. "But Ah still think it'd be nice if he stayed with me. Do ya know what Ah mean?"

I knew what he meant, all right. Cooper and McKinney roomed together and became great friends.

The thing I was most determined to avoid was cliques. There were going to be no goddamned cliques on the Celtics! That stuff can kill a ball club quicker than anything else I can think of.

For example, years ago when we'd play the Knicks, Dickie McGuire (who I thought was the next-best passer to Cooz) would throw the ball to Gallatin the major portion of the time. Why? Because every time Braun got the ball, he would throw it to Vandeweghe. Poor Sweets Clifton used to get it by mistake. There were two cliques going on in that ball club and that's why we used to beat their asses. We knew what they were going to do with the ball, so we just played to their weaknesses.

You can also have black cliques, white cliques, even wife cliques. One wife will say to another wife, "Your husband is terrible. He never passes the ball to my husband." That stuff goes on all the time.

Having the players like each other wasn't as important as making sure they respected each other. Take Cousy and Russell. At one time they were very buddy-buddy. Russ used to go to Cooz's basketball camp. Then a rift developed, brought on, I think, by the press. Russell wasn't getting his just due. It wasn't Cousy's fault, but nevertheless he and Russ weren't the pat-on-the-ass buddies they had been and I picked it up right away. The problem wasn't that they were mad at one another or that they stopped talking. Their social existence just cooled off.

I watched very closely, but there was no big problem, for the simple reason they had a tremendous respect for one another. Bill had a great respect for Cousy as a passer, a playmaker, a fast-break guy, and Cooz had an equal amount of respect for the things Russell could do.

Cousy kept getting a tremendous amount of publicity. Russell wasn't ignored, but the papers never played him up the way they fell all over Bob. Maybe if Russell had been a white Holy Cross hero it would have been different. I don't know. I do know it took some of those damned writers 20 years to fully recognize Russell's greatness.

I went out of my way to point out things Russell was doing, and Cousy never resented it because he was getting so much coverage anyway.

This is what I mean by the little things that can destroy a team.

So I kept a very close eye on who was friendly with whom, which guys tended to drift from the group, which situations were potentially harmful. Was it any of my business? You bet your ass it was.

The other area that was very important to the team way of thinking was convincing guys that their contributions were appreciated—no matter what the fans and writers were saying.

Take the bench, for instance. On a lot of teams they make a big deal out of the "starting five." If you don't start, it implies you're not as good or as valuable as the next guy.

That's not the way we looked at the men on our bench in Boston. Our "starting" lineup in the minds of every one of our ballplayers was the lineup that finished the game, not necessarily the one which began it. And when you think about it, it makes sense.

This is where my idea of the "sixth man" came into the picture. Psychologically, as soon as you pull one of your five starters out of the game, the other team is going to let down

*just a bit. That's when I wanted a guy like Ramsey or Havlicek
to get out there and run them into the ground.*

*All around the league, everybody starts his best. Suppose I
don't start my best. Suppose I start 80 percent of my best.
Now, after five, six, seven minutes go by, it's time to substitute. Their 100 percent is getting tired, and so is my 80 percent. In goes their sub and in goes my sixth man. What happens? They've decreased their proficiency while I've increased
mine.*

*It doesn't always work, of course. It depends on your per-
sonnel. But it's a good concept.*

*You do not have to weaken your team when you make a sub-
stitution. You can be strengthening it. It all depends on how
you use your people.*

*Having the right kind of people is important, and I don't
mean only people with talent. A team has got to think like a
team or else all these goddamned theories go sailing out the
window.*

*Look at Loscutoff. He was a much, much better player than
people ever gave him credit for. He could shoot and he was
pretty fast for a guy his size, but there's only one ball in the
game, and I already had guys who could put it into the hole
for me. I needed Jim to set picks and box out. He was great at
that, but who the hell ever writes stories about setting picks?
It's not a glory job, but it's necessary.*

*Or how about Conley? I wanted him to go out there and get
the ball whenever Russell needed a breather. That's all. He
had to appreciate his role and his limitations while at the same
time appreciating Russell's greatness. Don't forget, Gene was
a marvelous athlete himself—the only guy I know of who has
championship rings from two sports! It took a certain type of
personality to do what we asked him to do.*

*Guys like KC and Satch hardly ever got recognition, yet the
jobs they were doing out there were fantastic. I convinced each
one of them that his best contribution to winning came through
his excellence in certain phases of the game. Sure, that was
egotistical on my part, but I was right, and I knew if I could
convince them of my theories, we were going to be one fabulous ball club.*

If they didn't go for it, of course, I had an ace up my sleeve. I controlled the salaries. Every one of them knew that his salary was totally dependent on what I believed was his contribution towards winning. This is the way to win, I told them.

We became a team because it made good sense. We lived as a team, we traveled as a team, we played as a team, we thought as a team, and, most important, we won and lost as a team.

But mostly won, I might point out.

Chapter 17
Training Camp Blues

"If you faint, it's your fault."

Willie Naulls had his Celtics' baptism on the campus of Babson College in the fall of 1963 and he's never forgotten the experience.

"I thought Auerbach was absolutely crazy," he smiles. "We ran. And then we ran some more. And then we ran and ran and ran after that. And that was on the first damned day of camp! There was no way in the world I could have had any doubts about the kind of basketball team that man was building. Hell, I never did that kind of running before in my career. I couldn't believe what I was seeing."

"Willie didn't know that Red tried to kill you right away," Ramsey explains. "I lived right near Babson at that time, so Willie would come over to my house between the morning and the afternoon sessions and we'd get a bite to eat and maybe watch TV for a while.

"Well, that first day Willie had himself a big lunch. I tried to warn him, but like I say, he didn't know Auerbach. We went back that afternoon and Red had us running and jumping all over the place. Then, with no rest at all, he made us get down and start doing pushups.

"That was too much for Willie. He just threw up and then passed out, landing right in his own mess. A couple of players stopped what they were doing, dragged him off the court, then went back to their pushups. Poor Willie was laying over there with puke all over him.

"We laughed all day about that."

The Celtics, as Ramsey suggests, knew what to expect.

"Training camp," Sanders notes dryly, "was never my favorite activity. In fact it was a weight on my mind all summer long. Oh, it was great that first day we arrived. Picture day. All the photographers were running around and the writers were asking questions about the glory of the Celtics and all of that. But we knew that all the pictures and articles and no-cut contracts in the world were not going to spare our bodies from the aggravation ahead.

"We spent the first day of camp just running around to see who fainted first. On the second day the body was really aching and the legs were tightened up. By the third day we were in the worst condition of all. The muscles were so tight it was hard to walk. It was even hard to sleep. On the fourth day you were still in pain, even when you were sleeping, but you could begin to feel it ebbing. By the fifth day it was almost gone. And on the sixth day we were ready to go again.

"It was the same thing, year after year. No matter how much work you did during the summer to keep in shape, you still had to face the tension, pressure and pain of Auerbach's camp. That's why no veteran was ever foolish enough to let himself get too much out of shape in the off-season. Training camp was a bitch and there was no sense in making it any harder than necessary. In the best of times, it was awful."

In the 1940s the word first spread. Freddy Scolari was more commonly known as "Fat Freddy" during his playing days. Washington columnist Bob Addie once suggested Scolari resembled "a well-fed bartender."

"I had a funny build," Freddy shrugs. "My body was thick and my legs were thin. But fat? I don't think I was ever fat. There was no way you could play for Auerbach and still be fat. He worked our tails off. Just ask anybody who played for the Caps, or played against them, and he'll tell you those Washington teams were never out of shape.

"As soon as training began, Red was a nut on conditioning."

As the '50s rolled along, the reputation grew. Auerbach's team was a running, fast-breaking, pressing team, and everybody knew it. But the pace was set long before the season opened.

"When I rejoined the team in 1958 I knew what to expect," Conley says. "But I had no idea of what was coming when I first reported to Red in 1952. Wow. I never took such a beating in my life. Red would toss the ball to me and tell me to move with it, but Brannum and Mahnken would be clobbering me from both sides. And on top of that I had to run and run and run. When I got back to my room that first night I had blisters as big as silver dollars on my feet. I had to *roll* out of bed the next morning. When I got to the gym I was certain they'd put me on a sick list or something, but Harvey Cohn, our trainer, just popped a needle into them, let the water pour out, taped some hot packs onto my feet and told Red I was ready to go again!"

By the time the dynasty got under way, Auerbach's methods of running a training camp were as established as Captain Bligh's methods of running the *Bounty*—and the analogy is not at all inappropriate.

"He was tough," Sharman says. "Very, very tough. The minute he saw someone slowing down he'd step in and raise hell. I can clearly remember the way he'd do it, too. He'd say, 'Is this the year you're going to let down? Is this the year you're going to coast?' Then he'd push us even harder.

"Red was convinced you could steal a lot of games early in the season if you left camp in great condition. And believe me, the Celtics always left camp in great condition."

Did it work? One year they started off by winning 14 in a row. Another year they won their first 11. And check a few of the records they compiled by New Year's Day: 34–4 (1960), 29–5 (1962), 25–5 (1964), 31–7 (1965).

Like most of the Redhead's schemes, it worked quite well.

I had a standard opening speech I used at training camp each year. It went like this:

"Gentlemen, you are the world champions. You've heard all of the accolades all summer long. You've had the prestige. You've had a good time. But now everybody's out to knock your jocks off. It's unfortunate, but true. They're all out to get you. Now if you want to let them get you, just try living off last year's reputations. This is going to be an even harder year because everybody's after our asses and after them good. They got all the hotshots in the draft. We got last pick. So now they think they're as good as we are. Fine. Let's see them take these rings away from us. We know what it is to be world champions. They don't. So what we have to do is go out there, meet them head-on and say, 'You're damned right we're the world champions, and if you want this title you're going to have to take it from us.'"

That was my opening salute, so to speak. Then I'd go out and bust their balls. A lot of times I'd use little forms of psychology. Like they'd be scrimmaging real hard and real long and I could see that they couldn't go much more.

"Okay," I'd say. "Is everybody tired? Beautiful. Now we're really going to get in shape. Let's see twelve more baskets!"

Everybody would groan.

"Goddamnit," I'd yell. "That's the only way you're going to get in condition."

Sometimes I'd ask them if they were tired and they'd say No.

"Really?" I'd tell them. "Great. Let's do forty more!"

In other words, whether they were tired or not, I was going to push them harder.

And every time it looked like one of them was going to protest, I'd just remind them: "It's your club, not mine. It's you they're after."

A lot of them puked and fainted, but that was their problem, not mine. Every year, before they left town, I'd warn them what to expect. "If you puke, it's your fault. If you faint, it's

*your fault. If you come in heavy, it's your fault. We're only go-
ing to have a month to get ready, so you'd better be in shape
the next time I see you. If you're not, your ass will be grass and
I'll be the lawn mower! I'm giving you ample warning. I'm
treating you like men. The rest is up to you."*

Sure, I was tough, but I have never consciously played an
injured man—not in training camp, not in practice, not in a
game. And I never will. All I want is the okay from the doctor.
After that, if a man plays himself into exhaustion, he plays
himself into exhauston. Big deal. Nothing's going to happen to
him. He'll pass out. That's all. You cannot baby these guys. I'll
warn them to report in shape and not to drink too much water
during a rest period. I'll warn them not to eat heavily before a
game or a workout. If they aren't smart enough to heed my
warnings, whatever happens to them is their own damned fault
and they'll get no sympathy from me.

I remember one time I was coaching in the annual Maurice
Stokes Game up at Kutsher's Country Club and Ray Felix was
on my team. About five minutes after the game started he
grabbed hold of one of the support posts and puked his brains
out. I looked over at him and ignored it. "Get back in the
play!" I yelled.

That night my wife started to give me hell. "How can you be
so callous?" she says. "You didn't even go over to see if Ray
was okay."

"Dot," I told her, "that man ate seven pieces of pie at dinner! He's a professional athlete, and if he's that stupid, then let
him vomit. Let him get as sick as he wants to. There's no way
I'm going to hold his hand."

To play the kind of ball I wanted, my teams had to be in
condition.

Back in the days when the old Philadelphia Warriors had
Joe Fulks, everybody double- and triple-teamed him and he
still led the league in scoring. So I'd figure, the hell with him.
Let him have his points. Instead, I'd press his teammates all
over the joint. We pressed Arizin. We pressed Neil Johnston.
This was unheard of back in those days. No one pressed a
whole team over the whole court for a whole game. But my
teams did. I was the first man in these United States ever to do
that, with my Washington Caps in 1946.

People really began to notice it around 1959, 1960, when I had Sam and KC on the bench, backing up Cooz and Sharman. That was beautiful. Cousy and Sharman would start out with all their finesse and be doing a great job. Then I'd send Sam and KC out in a full-court press. The other guys would be all worn out trying to cope with those two. Then, bang! Cousy and Sharman would return to pepper the nets and knock them dead.

In order to play that kind of basketball you've got to be in better shape than the next guy. If he gets tired, his game is hurt. Take shooting. It's a matter of touch. The man goes up, releases the ball and follows through in one fluid motion. If he's tired his hand gets a little shaky, his control is off, his timing is gone. There is a lot of difference between shooting when you're fresh and shooting when you're exhausted. My teams were trained to run, to press, to beat the other guys' brains out with their hustle.

And that's why my training camps were so tough. The only way to get in that kind of shape is hard work. Lots of hard work. And that's what I gave them. Human nature being what it is, most players don't like that system. One of Cousy's cute little tricks was to hang around Walter Brown's office three or four weeks before camp opened, just hoping Walter would send him on an errand that would cause him to miss the first few days of training. Sometimes Walter would forget camp and do it, and I'd have to step in and blow my top at both him and Cooz.

Athletes would much rather play themselves into shape.

Take baseball players, for instance. I tell (Red Sox GM) Dick O'Connell and my other friends in baseball: "You know, you guys amaze me. You live in the past. They've had training camps down there in Florida for fifty years now and nothing's changed. Sure, you need the warm weather. I'll buy that. But what's this bullshit where the players take their wives and their golf clubs and spend their afternoons sitting by the pool and their evenings in the local nightclubs? Are you trying to get in shape or are you running a goddamned country club?"

In my mind, that's ridiculous. I've even heard of situations where baseball players were singing in nightclubs during spring training! You can bet your fanny no Celtic ever felt like singing after a day in our camp.

The whole idea of guys playing themselves into shape is absurd. Only one person could really get them working hard enough so that it would do some good. Me.

I have one other theory. I think it is a complete waste of time to bring 20, 25 players into camp. Usually I'd bring 13 or 14 at the most, and that was only because I wanted extra players around in case someone got hurt and I wanted to run a scrimmage.

Limiting your squad is just common sense. Say you're running a two-man drill and you've got 14 men. You've got two going out and two coming back, so you're using four men at once. It's 4—8—12—boom! Start all over, with the extra two guys starting the next series. But if you've got 20-odd guys standing around, they're only in operation once every six times, where in our system the players were running once every three times. That's much better for timing and conditioning. What good is it if a guy runs up and down the court and then has 40 seconds to rest? With us, you were lucky to have 10 seconds.

They got tired in my camp. I'd watch them. I knew a guy like Loscutoff couldn't keep up with a Havlicek if they happened to be paired off. I just wanted to make sure each guy was running up to his potential.

When I spotted someone dogging it, I broke in.

"Are you shitting me? That's false hustle! What am I supposed to do, stand here like a watchdog and tell you you're a bad boy and make you take 20 laps? That's a lot of crap. I won't do it. I don't have to do it. I am not married to any of you guys. Remember that. There's going to come a time when all of you will have to leave this team. I'd hate to think that time is now. But if you've got the idea you can take it easy and pace yourself just because your name happens to be Joe Blow, I've got news for you. You've got to make this ball club every year, and that means getting ready right now. Have I made myself clear?"

My favorite training camp story came in 1961, the year Carl Braun came to us to finish up his career.

About the third or fourth day after we got started, my friend Ramsey came up to me and said, "You must be getting soft, Red. This is the easiest camp we've ever had."

That bothered me. Was I really slowing down? Was I getting softer in my old age? Was I too preoccupied with other duties? I began asking myself some of these questions.

Then I heard about Braun and I felt better. He had almost collapsed on the court, I was told. So he moaned to one of my veterans: "This is worse than all 12 of my New York camps put together!"

I always got a kick out of that remark.

Chapter 18

A Matter of Execution

"A play does not have to succeed to be good."

Once conditioning and discipline were understood and established, Auerbach's house was in order.

Then *execution* became the order of the day. They had been given their orders. Now they were expected to carry them out. Crisply. Efficiently. And successfully.

"Everyone had the same thought in his mind," Havlicek explains. "You didn't want to be the weak link which broke down. You knew everyone else was prepared. They expected the same thing from you. On a lot of teams when the game boils down to one last shot or one last play, no one is too anxious to get the ball. But we didn't feel that way. We all had confidence in one another in those situations. If you took the shot and missed, that wasn't the important thing. Anybody can miss a shot. What was important was executing properly so that you at least got a good shot away. Failing to execute properly in a situation like that was the biggest mistake you could make on our team. That's why we worked so hard on execution. We wanted to know what we were doing at all times so there would be no panic or confusion when a big play was needed."

"Red is a mathematician," Russell points out. "He's better at that than anybody realizes. It was one of the keys to our success. He always figured out the odds, always reduced the risks to a minimum. Very little was ever left to chance."

"A key word in Red's approach to the game was *simplicity*," Naulls said. "We played very simple basketball. He never overcomplicated anything. Most people do that and it's a mistake. Basketball is really a simple game.

"I'll give you an example. The other team is shooting a free throw, okay? So Red would have me run down to our basket and wait. The free throw is taken. Russell grabs the ball and fires it to KC, directly on a plane extended from the free throw line. KC is breaking towards the middle as he takes it. If my man moves up to stop him, KC hits me and I've got a jump shot. If not, KC keeps going for a layup. In a two-on-one situation like that, everything is automatic if you know what you're doing. And Red's guys always knew what they were doing. All of the Celtics became *thinking* ballplayers. We'd go into a huddle and Russell would ask for the 'sucker play.' That's when his man was overplaying him too high. Russ would fake like he was going to jump, then push the guy a bit and take an easy lob pass for a dunk."

Simplicity.

"We had one or two options on every play, but that's all," Havlicek notes. "Red always said if you had to pass the ball around four or five times, then it was a bad play to begin with. He wanted us to get into situations where we immediately got a shot out of the play, or maybe made one or two quick passes and then took the shot. But other than that, anything else was a waste of motion."

The bread and butter of Auerbach's offense, of course, was the fast break, a weapon which the Celtics turned into an art form with their grace and precision.

Contrary to a widely held public opinion, it didn't begin

with the marriage of Russell's rebounding and Cousy's playmaking. Red was first schooled in the fast break while playing under Bill Reinhart.

"I'm not suggesting what we had was anything comparable to what the Celtics had many years later," Bob Faris points out, "but our first thought at GW was to run, run, run. Reinhart wanted that ball brought downcourt as quickly as possible. He never allowed a guard to bring it down thump-thump-thump. We ran with it, and then if we didn't get the two-on-one or three-on-two, we'd back off. That's the way Red played in college."

And it's the way he coached, right from the start.

"He had the fast break long before he got Russell," Eddie Gottlieb smiles. "Russell just made it a hell of a lot better."

Better? When he teamed up with Cousy, and the two of them were flanked by marksmen like Sharman, Jones, Heinsohn and Ramsey, the Boston fast break became the most exciting show in basketball.

"For sheer excitement," Ben Kerner says "you just couldn't beat those great teams Red had. The way they'd run and move that ball was an everlasting thing to see. It was thrilling to watch, even while they were beating you. No other team ever played that way."

And if the machine broke down, Red was quick to spot the problem.

"One year, late in my career, I was off a bit with my shot," Ramsey remembers. "So Red had me play one-on-one with Heinie until I nearly dropped. Then he called me over and said, 'Here's what you're doing. You can't jump as high as you used to, so you're releasing the ball too quickly.' And he demonstrated it for me. Sure enough, he was absolutely right. The next day he worked with me on shooting one step sooner. Everything fell into place after that. Red was great that way. If you had a problem, he could usually solve it."

As much as Boston's awesome scoring feats were celebrated, the lifeblood of the dynasty was its defense.

Once again, simplicity was the byword.

"In order to teach you how to block out properly," Havlicek says, "some coaches will describe the moves of the legs, the reverse pivots, the crossovers and things like that. But Red would say, 'Stick your forearm into his chest, get your ass against him and don't let him get the ball!' That's how simple he made things. Then you were expected to go out and do it."

The players called it a "funnel" defense, for everyone overplayed towards the middle secure in the knowledge Russell was there to atone for their mistakes.

"They had no inhibitions whatsoever," Lakers coach Fred Schaus recalls. "They could dive and slash and knock people down and gamble for interceptions—guys like Ramsey, Satch and KC, especially—because if their man happened to get past them, what did he end up with? A fifteen-foot jump shot with Russell's hand in his face! To hell with their scoring. That team became a defensive giant."

In the fall of 1962 Conley joined the New York Knicks and suddenly discovered what life was like with the have-nots. "I played with the Celtics and against them," he says, "so I had a much broader view of them than most people. Believe me, it was their defense which killed you. I never saw so many arms and legs in my life. You'd be holding the ball and all around you there was pressure: Satch's arm coming this way at you, Havlicek's hand coming from the other direction, KC running up behind you—and, of course, Russell just standing there, waiting for you to make your move. If you couldn't handle the ball against that team, forget it! You were dead. Red never allowed them to stand around or drop their arms. So it was like playing against eight men whenever you tried to score against Boston."

Some would say Conley was guilty of understatement.

"Either I'm seeing double or there's ten of them out there!" Hot Rod Hundley gasped to Schaus one night as he returned to the LA bench.

After the fundamentals were imparted—offense, defense, execution—there was one more thing Red emphasized.

"He taught us not to accept losing," Cousy remembers. "Society tends to frown on sore losers, but Arnold taught us that was a lot of garbage. Being a sore loser, he kept telling us over and over, was not a bad thing. His idea was that only losers accept losing."

* * *

I've never been much for Xs and Os and all kinds of fancy diagrams. Throughout my whole career I believed that the fundamentals of this sophisticated game of ours are still what separates the men from the boys.

I never believed in gadgets or gimmicks. I've had people tell me stupid things like, "Why not practice with heavy sneakers so you'll feel better when you put on the light ones for the games?" What bullshit! That's like the old thing about hitting yourself on the head because it feels so good when you stop. I feel the same way about these rebounding collars they put on the rim. To me, that's not a true rebound. You've got to determine through instinct, through continual association with situations, that the percentages say a shot taken from the right side will bounce to such-and-such a spot, and then you react accordingly. See, Russell had things like that down to a science. But there aren't any shortcuts. You've got to watch and study and learn.

There were certain things I expected my ballplayers to know. During the last five minutes of play they must know the score, they must know how many time-outs are left, they must know how many fouls have been called against the other team and against their own team, too. They must be aware of what's happening at all times out there.

Execution ties in very closely with communication. If you have too many plays, too many picks, too many intricacies in each play, the execution will suffer. It takes too damned long to teach all of that, and the players will forget half of what you tell them anyway.

Keep it simple. *That was my rule.* You have one move, away from the ball, a little pick, pop a little shot, very simple. But timing was everything. And coordination with your teammates, too, of course.

Years ago when I first started in this league, 99 percent of your plays culminated with a guy going in for a lay-up, working a give-and-go or something like that. I believe I was the first one to devise plays which culminated in fifteen-foot jump shots. Why? Because I felt that, percentage-wise, my guys should hit 45 to 60 percent of those shots, especially if the shots were not expected.

In all my years of coaching the Celtics we had just six plays, six basic setups, and every one of them involved the center. The "1" and "3" had the center in a high post; the "2" had the center on a pick; the "4" made the center into a passer; the "5" involved him more indirectly; and the "6" play went directly to him. The big man was always involved, whether as a shooter, a passer, setting a pick, screening out, whatever.

You have to study the psychology of people. Here's a big guy—Russell or anyone else—who breaks his ass getting you the rebound and throwing it downcourt. Now if the play is over every time he joins you at the offensive end, he's going to be pissed. How many times is he going to run down there and find out you don't need him? After a while, he'll just stop getting you the ball. Setting up my six plays the way I did was just my unobtrusive way of keeping the big man involved, keeping him happy.

Here is an excellent example of the importance of proper execution. I go on these State Department tours every year, conducting clinics, and I always bring a few NBA players along in addition to a group of my own guys. One year Oscar Robertson was part of the team. I was late joining them because of the draft or something back home, so they're playing without me over in Poland. Oscar said, "Let's use the Celtics' plays because we all know them." And they did. They ran the "2", the "3" and all the rest of them. This wasn't too surprising. When you've faced a team as many times as Robertson, Pettit and guys like that faced the Celtics, you get to know something about them.

Early the next season we had a game scheduled against Cincinnati and my guys are all upset about the plays. "Oscar knows them," someone says. "What are we going to do?"

I told them not to worry.

"Call a '1' play," I said.

So they ran the "1" and it didn't work. Oscar switched in.

The next time-out I told them, "Okay, this time call a '1' but run the '1R' instead."

That meant a reverse off the "1."

So Cooz comes running down the floor and yells, "Let's get a '1.'" They ran the "1R" and left everybody standing there while we got an easy lay-up.

We had options off of each setup, so altogether there were 26 plays we could run. But the basic six setups never changed. For instance, on the "2" play you hit the corner man, get the ball back, the center makes a screen and then it goes either way. Now a "2-0" play—two-oh—meant a "2" to the outside, and a "2-1"—two-eye—meant a "2" to the inside. It was really quite simple.

One day my bright squad got it in its head to change the numbers. Sharman and Ramsey were the two guys really pushing for this. "We can fool them," Sharman says.

In my own inimitable way, I said no. "It won't work. It'll be too confusing. These plays have been ingrained in your minds for too long now."

They kept insisting, so I gave in, but only to prove to them that I was right and they were wrong. Before the game we agreed to move all of the numbers up one. So a "2" was a "3" and so on.

The game starts and they call a "2." Three of the guys ran the old "2" and the other ones ran the new "2." I let this go on for three plays, then I called a time-out.

"Everybody bend over and close your eyes," I said.

Then, slap-slap-slap-slap-slap! I ran the back of my hand right across their mouths—not trying to hurt them, just to stress a point in a kidding way. "Throw it all out of your minds," I said. "As of right now we're back to the old system. A '1' is a '1,' a '2' is a '2,' a '3' is a '3,' a '4' is a '4,' a '5' is a '5' and a '6' is a '6.' Okay now. Have you got it?"

I ran through every play in that minute, including the options, and no one ever suggested changing them again.

Like Russell used to say when he was coaching, if something's been successful for years, why change it? I couldn't agree more.

One other thing I told them was that a play does not have to succeed to be good. We never forced plays. If one didn't work, we tried something else. The play is merely a beginning. If it works, great. If not, go to the options. A play might be good just because it opens up something else.

If your play doesn't work, do you hold the ball and panic? No. The idea is to have continuity. Keep moving. Try something else. If worse comes to worse, throw it to the guy in the *corner and yell,   "Hey, take a one-on-one; time's running out!"*

A good team should never, ever panic out there.

But plays were for special situations: if the fast break didn't work, or if we were playing for the last shot of the period.

The fast break has to become a way of life. It's automatic. It's ingrained. Anytime our team gets the ball, whether it's on a rebound, interception or whatever, we immediately know exactly where to head on the floor.

The ideal fast break occurs after the rebound. You make the outlet pass, you fill the lanes, your trailer follows you down. Everybody understands that. We've taught it to millions of people. But that's not enough. You want to be ready to fast-break all the time, not just when the situation's perfect. We practiced for hours and hours. Lift your head when you release the ball, so you won't throw it away. Make sure you don't curve the pass. Other teams don't work on fundamentals like that and they end up wasting a fast break because the passer curves the throw and it sails out of bounds.

When you fast-break, the advantage should be all yours. If a team knows you're going to fast-break, they probably won't crash the offensive boards because they're afraid they'll look ridiculous if you beat them back downcourt. So when they take a shot, they're stepping backwards instead of forward. There's an immediate advantage.

When you get the ball, the first thing to do is look before you pass. This is very important. It doesn't slow you up that much. You're only taking about a fraction of a second. If you just throw by instinct, there's a good chance the other team will pick off your pass. Ideally, you start the break down the side where the rebound came. But if you look first and maybe spot a teammate breaking into the open, that's got to be the best two points in the world. If you don't look, you don't see him. The break is no good if he has to yell, "Hey-hey-hey!"

The second thing is to throw the ball properly.

The fast break is just basic fundamentals, based on hustle, conditioning and working together as a team.

Cousy just happened to be the best guard who ever lived when it came to execution of the fast break.

But a Cousy isn't indispensable. I ran the fast break in Washington with Feerick and Scolari, who was certainly no speed demon. You don't have to have a Russell. Wes Unseld was great at getting a quick pass away.

What you do need is discipline, an understanding of the fundamentals and, again, conditioning.

Defense is something else again. It's much harder to teach offense than defense. Defense means work. You play defense until you get the ball. It's like pursuit in football. When a guy knocks you on your ass at the line of scrimmage, you're supposed to get up and continue in pursuit until the ballcarrier is taken down or the play is whistled dead. That's very basic. Your defensive responsibilities are not complete until you get the ball.

Suppose we're in a full-court press, working hard, and the other team pulls off a series of perfect moves and scores. What then? You work harder, because you know eventually you're going to make the other side tired. You're going to wear them down. Then they start throwing bad passes and missing easy shots. You've got to outlast them. That all comes back to proper conditioning.

If you check, you'll find out most great sports teams were also great defensive teams. Even the great old Yankees played defense. Everyone ooohed and aaahed over the home runs DiMaggio, Henrich and those guys kept knocking out of the ball park, but that was a lot of crap. I'm sure you'll find that New York won more one-run games than any team in the league.

No matter how powerful you are and no matter how good your players are, there is no substitute for that getting-down-to-the-ground-and-sacrificing type of defense. If you can get great players to do that, then you'll have super players.

We'd watch the other teams closely, and every time we saw someone loafing on defense, we'd run the ball right up at him. A lot of big scorers would give you false hustle on defense, trying to save their energy for all the spectacular offensive moves they liked to make. Show me a player who thinks he can rest on defense and my team will kill him. You can't rest on defense.

But in all of these areas—setting up plays, running a fast

break, playing defense—*the biggest danger is in overcoaching. Don't give your players too much. Don't confuse them. This is a mistake so many young coaches make today. They want to be great strategic leaders. That's a lot of bullshit. The coach's biggest job is to get his players in shape and then keep them hustling. Forget the fanciness.*

If I've said it once, I've said it a million times. Goddamn it, you've got a hole over there. You've got to put this ball into that hole, and then stop the other team from putting it into the other hole. And the easier you do that, the better off you are.

Chapter 19
Referees vs. The Redhead

"I was no more guilty than they were."

Red Sox general manager Dick O'Connell, one of Auerbach's close friends, happened to be in New York one winter's night when the Celts were playing the Knickerbockers, so Red invited him to the game as his guest. It was a typical Boston-New York encounter in the mid-'60s with the Celtics holding a 22-point lead in the closing minutes. Then, with no apparent provocation, the Redhead stormed off the bench, got into a raucous shouting match with the officials and was promptly ejected.

Later that evening over a quiet meal, O'Connell asked him why in the world he created such a fuss with the contest almost over.

"We've got the same referees tomorrow in Boston," Red replied between bites. "I want them on their toes."

❋ ❋ ❋

"Was he unreasonable?" Mendy Rudolph repeated, amazed there could be any doubt. "Look. Red was a fighter. That's the only way he knew how to coach. That was his style, his personality. There were some games when he'd sit on his hands and never move, but I can remember an awful lot of nights when he was absolutely wild. I couldn't even tell you how many times I had to chase him out of ball games. He was tough on officials, no question about it. First of all, he always thought his judgment was better than ours, and most calls are judgment calls. He knew we weren't going to change our minds, but that didn't stop him from going nose to nose every time a call went against Boston.

"But he was cute. He never expected to get a call reversed. But he did think his tirades would help swing the next call his way.

"He was something. I'd work one of his games on a Tuesday and he'd be perfectly sane. I'd see him again on Thursday and he would go nuts the first time I blew my whistle.

"The only time it ever bothered me was when he came out to challenge me on a rule interpretation. Red knew that damned rule book as well as anyone—better than most people, in fact—and when he started yelling about a rule, you knew you had to be on your toes.

"But judgment calls? No way. That's when I'd say, 'Good night, Red. Go take a shower!' "

Auerbach was fined more than $17,000 for his battles with referees over the years.

He got into a violent shouting match with Arnie Heft in 1954 at Rochester when a call against Macauley at the buzzer allowed the Royals to win at the free-throw line. A writer flagged him down later and asked what had transpired out there. "I will admit my remarks were strong," Red said, "but they were not abusive." The writer persisted. What had he said? "I told the sonofabitch he was stupid and incompetent!" A wire soon informed him he was fined $100 by Podoloff.

When the Celtics lost their 1958 opener to New York, 127–125 in overtime, Auerbach was thrown out of the contest in the fourth period for protesting Heinsohn's sixth foul by charging onto the court and calling Richie Powers "a choker." The standard fine at the time was $35. Podoloff nailed Auerbach for $150, citing extenuating circumstances. "How come every other coach in the league gets normal fines or maybe just warnings, but Podoloff always finds a new twist for me?" he raged.

When Boston absorbed a rare defeat in New York in 1962, Red gathered the writers around him and proceeded to point out that Rudolph and Norm Drucker were "biased" and "chokers." This time Podoloff solicited $350.

In addition to the $300 fine he paid for punching Ben Kerner during the 1957 playoffs, Red also made the headlines midway through the series by charging at referee Jim Duffy in an impromptu airport meeting.

The NBA instituted a new rule in 1961–62, prohibiting a coach from getting to his feet during a game. In a November contest against Detroit the Redhead jumped up to protest the abuse he said Cousy was receiving. Joe Gushue called a technical. When Red screamed over that, Gushue gave him a second T and ejected him. Podoloff immediately fined him $200 and issued a stern warning that his next expulsion would result in a three-game suspension. Auerbach was furious. "Why doesn't he say *anyone* getting two evictions will be suspended?" he demanded. "Why just me?" Two nights later, as the Celts were losing for the first time that season, Drucker called an early technical on Red, then hit him with another one when he threw his program onto the floor in disgust. Podoloff carried out his threat and suspended the Boston coach for three games.

But for sheer drama, emotion and theatrics, nothing could hold a candle to the Auerbach vs. Sid Borgia Show.

They were both 5'9, balding, loud and animated, and when they stood jaw-to-jaw it brought the house down.

"I was a very emotional referee," Sid explains. "And I was a very proud referee. If anything happened during the course of a game which I felt was belittling to me or my profession, I became very belligerent. And if it happened in Boston, of course, the crowd was all over me, and that, in my mind, was a form of intimidation, so I became stronger and stronger. Goddamn it, nobody was going to intimidate Sid Borgia on the job! Nobody.

"So now we come to the Redhead. Red would try every damned trick in the book to upset the officials, to harass them, to intimidate them. Now frankly, I wouldn't give you a nickel for any coach who wouldn't bitch when he thought he had a bitch coming. But every time I blew my whistle Red thought he had one coming. And he'd elaborate on it immediately.

"Whenever I tried to explain my point of view to him, it always ended up with him telling me, 'You're full of shit!' It never failed. And because he was so damned loud, everybody in the joint heard it, so that's when I'd call the technical. It was embarrassing to me. Not only that, but if he got away with it, everybody in the league would be telling me I'm full of shit!

"So one night I happened to meet him in an airport coffee shop. There was only one seat open, right next to him, so I grabbed it. We started talking and he said to me, '*Jesus Christ, you're always picking on me.*' I said, 'Red, do yourself a favor and do me a favor, too. The next time we start yelling at each other, instead of telling me I'm full of shit, just say, "You're full of bananas!" Okay? I'll understand what you mean, but I won't have to chase you because it won't be embarrassing to me.' He said okay, he would do it.

"Don't you know, the very next night I'm working one of his games and we get into a good one. And what happens? He goes right back to the old word again!"

Boston fans found out early what Auerbach was going to be like. In November, 1950, his first month on the job, Red was fined $75 for "conduct unbecoming a coach."

Was his behavior really unbecoming? Not the way his players saw it.

"One of the great things about Auerbach is that he's always fighting for his players," Sharman told a writer in 1960. "The players appreciate that. If I got a bum call and my coach didn't back me up, I wouldn't feel very good about it."

"In the third game I played for the Celtics I found out what kind of a man Red is," Russell says. "The referee called goal-

tending against me and Auerbach came storming out onto the
floor, arguing like mad. It cost him a technical foul. He didn't
have to do that. That's when I realized here was a guy who
was 100 percent for me and the rest of his team, and you can't
help liking a coach like that."

In early 1952 Red was fined $100 for "delaying tactics," ac-
cording to Podoloff, after his team held the ball and prevented
Rochester from breaking a club scoring record. After the game
Macauley spoke with reporters. "This is no Boy Scout move-
ment," he said. "Whatever Red does, he does for us, and we
think he's the best damned coach in the league. So if we get
the credit when we win, then we think we should share in his
setbacks, too. We've all decided to chip in and pay the fine for
him."

Red confessed he was "flattered," but Podoloff warned the
Boston players they'd be fined for insubordination if they
paid a cent of Auerbach's penalty.

"Red's got to be stopped when he behaves that way," the
commissioner concluded.

On October 1, 1963, Boston had an exhibition game against
the Knicks in an Oceanside, New York, high school gymnasium. Mendy Rudolph worked the game with a rookie ref
named Manny Sokolofsky.

"There was a new rule in effect that year," Rudolph remembers, "and Manny called it against the Celtics—and he was
right. So Red called time-out and rushed onto the court to protest vehemently. I told him Manny had been correct, so let's
get on with the game. But he was adamant. He wouldn't leave
the floor. I said, 'Look, Red, it's only an exhibition game. We
can talk about this later.' He wanted to talk about it right then
and there. So I threatened him with a technical and he dared
me to call it. Bang. He had his T. 'Now will you please start
acting sanely and get the hell out of here so we can finish this
game?' I said. He wouldn't move. He just kept on bitching. I
told him he had one more chance before I tossed his ass out of
the game. 'If I go, I'm taking my team with me!' he said.

"What could I do? I said, 'So long!'

"And I'll be goddamned if he didn't turn to his club and

say, 'C'mon, we're getting out of here!' The whole Boston team walked out. Now it's just me, Manny and the Knicks standing around, and the poor promoter was going out of his mind. We have no Boston Celtics!

"I waited and waited, and finally I sent word in to the locker room that I was going to call it a forfeit if Boston didn't come back. One by one the Celtics started to reappear, and eventually we finished the game."

The next morning, bright and early, Walter Kennedy got a phone call. It was his first week on the job as Podoloff's successor.

"Walter," the familiar voice began, "how the hell are you? Hey, I'm in New York today. How about having lunch together? It's been a long time. How's the new job going?"

An hour later Kennedy's phone rang again. It was Mendy Rudolph.

"Walter, are you sitting down? I've got something for you, baby. This is a first in the history of the NBA and you're the commissioner."

Kennedy stiffened. "What is it, Mendy?"

"Auerbach pulled his team off the court last night."

"It took me a while to catch on," Kennedy laughs. "Whenever Arnold had been a bad boy the night before, I could expect a phone call first thing the next morning. He'd want to know how I was, and when I was coming to Boston again, and if I had found any good new Chinese restaurants. We'd have a wonderful talk. But within an hour I knew I'd be getting another call, telling me he had been thrown out of a game and raised hell and wouldn't leave and did this and did that.

"But he always got me warmed up first by beating the referee to the phone and then talking about old times. How could I get mad at him?"

Mad or not, Kennedy had little choice in the matter when it came time to hand out fines.

In his first official act as commissioner, he fined Auerbach $500—a league record—for the Oceanside incident.

"It was a situation that had to be handled immediately," Walter explains. "What Arnold did just could not be tolerated. So I sent him a wire, informing him to make out his five hundred dollar check to league headquarters.

"When he received it he called me right back, ranting and raving as you can imagine. But do you know what really irritated him? He said, 'How the hell can you fine me five hundred dollars and then add "Kindest personal regards" at the end?'"

The Auerbach-Referees war never ended. Some calls *in favor* of his Celtics even caught his fury, like Borgia's famous "forced walk" infraction.

"I still say I was right," Sid maintains. "Here's what happened. There was a question as to whether the Boston player committed a foul or the opposing player walked. The Boston man bumped the other guy, making him walk, and yet I didn't think the contact was sufficient to call a foul. But I couldn't very well penalize the player who walked. So I yelled, 'That's a forced walk. He walked, but you made him.' And I let the other team keep possession.

"Oh, boy, wouldn't that get the Redhead steamed up! 'You're making up your goddamned rules again,' he'd yell at me. And I'd say, 'Red, what would you prefer me to do? Call a horseshit foul on your man?'

"I thought it was just good common sense on my part. As usual, Red didn't see it my way."

On February 13, 1966, a "Red Auerbach Day" was celebrated in Boston Garden in honor of the retiring Redhead. Ceremonies took place at halftime. One of the speakers was Cousy.

"Red," he said, getting a laugh from the crowd, "I sweated out the whole first half, wondering what we'd do if you got kicked out early and couldn't come back to accept these gifts." Auerbach smiled.

Then in the third period he received a technical, making his Day complete.

The following year, fully retired, he was asked by the league to coach the eastern division all-stars in place of Dolph Schayes, the fired Philadelphia coach. Red eagerly agreed to return to the bench for this nationally-televised special occasion.

Just before the first half ended he got into a shouting match with referee Billy Smith. Technical foul. In the third quarter he resumed his battle with Smith, jumping up from the bench and stamping his feet. Smith gave him a second technical foul, making Red the only man in history to be kicked out of an all-star game.

Walter Kennedy went up to him later that night. "I'm going to waive the fine," he smiled. "Call it the league's going-away present to you."

You've got to realize one thing when you're talking about referees. You can be the best damned coach in the world and have the best-prepared team in the world, but if you don't get your fair share of breaks—by that I mean an equal distribution of the calls—the referees can destroy you. They can absolutely destroy you. They've got too much power in their hands. Everything being equal, one team might be six or eight points better than another team. How many lousy calls does it take to turn a game around? Is it a travel or not a travel? Is it a charge or a block? You take that ball away from me four times when you shouldn't have taken it away, and there's the game.

I'll never forget the clutch game my team had up in Minneapolis one year. Johnny Logan was a great former player with the Bombers. He also played at Tri-Cities the year after I left. He was a big tough guy, about 6'3, who had been an army tank corps officer. Then he decided he wanted to be an official, and he's working this game at Minneapolis.

We're three points up with 15 seconds to go and we've got the ball. The Lakers call a time-out and the whole joint is jumping because they hardly ever lost up there. In six seasons they lost only 18 home games. With their narrow court and big guys like Mikan, Pollard and Mikkelsen, you never had a chance. But we were going to win this one.

All of a sudden Logan blows his whistle: "Technical foul on Boston!" He said we took too much time in the huddle. Apparently he yelled over to us and we didn't hear him because of the crowd, so he makes that horseshit call. In 30 years of pro basketball I've never heard that call made any other time. It was a once-in-a-lifetime thing.

The Lakers got the ball, made the technical and—the rules were different in those days—put it back into play to Mikan, who scores and sends the game into overtime. We end up losing.

I went berserk. I caught up with Logan and challenged him physically. "I'll fight you, you sonofabitch, no matter what it costs me! How could you do this? A former ballplayer! You stupid bastard!"

I just went crazy and some of the ballplayers grabbed me and pulled me away from him.

"I've got my heart and soul into this game, and then an idiot like you takes it away from me!"

I called him every name in the book. Today we're friends, but I've never gotten over that.

I had another incredible situation back in the 1947 playoffs, my first season in pro ball. We were facing Chicago in the opening round. We had beaten them five times out of six in the regular season, so there was no question which club was better. One of the refs was Pat Kennedy. To me, he set the pattern for all referees. He was a fabulous, fabulous guy: a real showman, but he always had the game under control. And he was 100 percent ethical. I don't know who the other ref was, but he made 11 straight calls against my Caps. Chicago had a big guy named Gilmur who just grabbed McKinney and never let go of him. Bones couldn't pass, couldn't cut, couldn't move. Pat looked at me, kind of embarrassed, when the other guy started making those calls. What could Kennedy do? I blew my stack something awful, and that jerk never worked in our league again. But the damage was done. We lost the series.

I made it my business to know all I could about every referee, to study him, to analyze his personality, to anticipate the way he might call a game.

Referees became a big part of my pregame talks. Suppose, for instance, the Celtics are on the road and I find out Borgia's doing the game. I would talk about him in our locker room.

"Okay, we've got Borgia tonight. Don't challenge him. He's going to give us a shake. We already know that. He's got balls on the road. So don't aggravate him. Don't antagonize him. Play tough, but stay away from him. That doesn't mean I want you to be a bunch of Casper Milquetoasts out there. If he blows one, let him have it. But that's it. Don't keep it up. Don't try to make him look bad. He's not going to give us the next call just because you bitch and moan. Borgia doesn't operate *that way. He likes to think he's in charge. Let him be in charge. He likes action under the boards, so don't be afraid to really hit. He's not going to make any crappy calls. Okay. Any questions?"*

You had to understand these people. Mendy Rudolph had a great deal of ego. His hair was always neat and things like that. He ran around like he was Mister King out there. Borgia was just plain tough. He was always on top of the game and he had supreme confidence in himself.

Most of your referees were inferior athletes, guys who could never do much in sports themselves. So they've got frustrations. Now you give them a whistle and a little bit of authority and they think they're big shots. They control you. You must do what they say. It's like a little guy who becomes a cop. Give him a whistle and a badge and all of a sudden he's King Shit. Referees are like this. I was smart enough to know it. Now and then you get someone like a Cal Hubbard or a Hank Soar, but most officials are just frustrated jocks. I didn't want them taking their frustrations out on me or my ball club.

How much can they affect a game? I'll show you. We'd play a game on a Tuesday night and end up shooting maybe 60 free throws. That's warranted. You're a fast-breaking team, so you drive to the hoop, you get fouled and you've got to shoot. It's expected. Then we'd go out on Wednesday, play the same style of ball and end up taking seven free throws.

I'd go to league meetings and raise hell. "How can these guys have this much discrepancy in their interpretations? How can it be? It just doesn't make any sense at all."

Some refs liked to referee the score. Boy, would that get my ass. Everybody subconsciously roots for the underdog. If you've got no emotional tie with either team, you're going to pull for the one that's 12 points down. If my guys were leading by 25 points, I wanted that game officiated the same way as if the lead was one point. For one thing, I wanted my subs playing under proper game conditions, too. But get a good lead and pretty soon some refs are letting everything go out there, hoping to make the game close again. I'm not suggesting they were dishonest. It was just a psychological thing.

I used to tell myself that if I ever got 12 points down I was

going to throw in all my reserves. That way people would feel
sorry for me, thinking I've given up. Next thing, I would get a
break here, a foul there, and I'd be only six down. Then I'd
rush my horses back in and we'd win the game!

Who says referees are right all the time? Sometimes I'd go
out there yelling and screaming, then they'd explain their interpretation to me and I'd say, "Goddamn it, you might be
right." And I'd walk away. I've done that.

But they've never done it. Never! If I rushed out there to
give someone hell and he just looked at me and said, "I blew
it, Red," what could I do? I'd have no more argument. But
they'd never admit they blew a call. They'd say, "That's the
way it is!" I remember thinking I'd like to be as infallible as
they are. Those guys were only human, so why didn't they act
that way?

I'll never forget the day I was coaching in Washington and
the ref runs by our bench and yells, "Technical on the Washington bench."

I asked him who the foul was on.

He said, "The little paisano."

I said, "Do you mean Scolari?"

He said yes, Scolari was the one.

"That's great," I said. "For your information, Scolari's not
even here today. He's in bed with a cold."

The guy looks at me like he's going to cry or something. But
did he say he was wrong? No way. He said, "Well, someone on
the bench said something so the foul still goes."

What happened was he heard someone in the stands saying
something, but rather than admit his mistake he just got stubborn.

Whenever people asked me if I didn't feel sympathy for
those guys, if I didn't feel a little bit guilty giving them hell,
I'd just tell them stories like that.

I was no more guilty than they were.

My best run-ins came with Borgia. Personally, I thought he
was a good official. I'd put him and Pat Kennedy up at the top.
But I used to fight like hell with him.

Take that "forced walk" crap. It made sense. He was 100
percent right in his thinking, but 100 percent wrong in his call.

Sid was a damned good commonsense referee, but he was not hired to be a commonsense referee. He was hired to enforce the rules as they were written. I fought him all the way down the line about this.

"If the rule is no good, change it. But when you're out there on the floor, you've got to referee the rules we have. You are hired to enforce the rules, not to write them!" I'd tell him this over and over, but we'd still have forced walks and forced backcourts every time Sid worked.

The fact that rule about walking was changed is proof that Borgia was right. But he was wrong at the time he made the call. He admits contact took place. Then he says it was not enough contact. What's that supposed to mean? The rule didn't say anything about how hard you had to hit someone. What's hard enough? What's too soft? How hard do you have to push to make someone walk? I'd say, "If there's contact, call it. And brushing someone is a form of contact."

Sid wanted to judge each case by itself, and that's the problem with officiating. There's too much judgment on the part of referees. Borgia and I fought over that more than anything else.

The other guy I was always fighting with was Podoloff. He was a brilliant man, and I really believe he always had the welfare of the league at heart, but he was another one of these little guys with power. Every time I'd get kicked out of a game he'd send me a wire which would go like this: "Due to extenuating circumstances, you are hereby fined two-hundred and fifty dollars."

Joe Lapchick would kick a pail of water all over the floor and get a technical. A regular technical. But Auerbach? I paid extra dough because of "extenuating circumstances."

I pulled Podoloff aside one day.

"Is it normal to get thrown out of games?" I asked.

He said no.

"Well, then, obviously there's got to be extenuating circumstances! Why don't you ever ask me what they are before you fine me?"

No one can ever convince me I wasn't a scapegoat. I had a reputation as a fighter, so the word went out: If you want to referee in this league and make a name for yourself, control Auerbach.

I can guarantee you I didn't do enough to get thrown out of a lot of those games. But I had a name, an image, and a lot of those guys felt they had to prove something when they worked my games. So they spent half the night watching me instead of watching the goddamned game.

I think the funniest thing that ever happened involving officials was one night in Boston when Borgia made a couple of bad calls. In those days once you called a time-out you could walk onto the floor to talk with the refs.

So I went out to midcourt, looked at Sid and said, "Godamn it, how can you be so bad? You're the worst incompetent I've ever seen."

He looked at me and said, "Same to you!"

I turned back and went at him again. I really let him have it. I must have thrown half a dozen insults at him.

He looked at me again and said, "Same to you—in spades!"

Now I'm laughing to myself, but as I get back to the bench I start thinking, "Wait a minute. That sonofabitch had the last word." So just before play resumed, I called another time-out and headed back to midcourt. Now the crowd is on its feet and roaring, thinking some big strategic move is taking place. Another time-out. Auerbach must really have something on Borgia now.

"Sid," I said, talking very quietly now, "you've got to be a stupid man."

He looked shocked. "What's with you?" he says. Before I was yelling and jumping around, but now I'm talking very soothingly to him.

"You and I have been fighting and feuding for all these years," I said. "While we're out on this court I have no use for you and you've got no use for me. We're enemies. But you just saved me three hundred and fifty dollars. If you hadn't said, 'Same to you—in spades!' I would have cussed some more and you could have hit me with a technical. Then I would have gotten madder and you could have thrown me out. But you didn't do that. Now, Sid, how does it feel knowing that you have just saved me—your enemy—all that dough?"

Then I stamped my foot real hard, turned around and walked away. The crowd went out of its mind and Borgia didn't know what the hell to do.

It was the damndest thing I ever saw.

I was the first one to come up with the strategic technical foul and later, the strategic ejection from the contest.

Sometimes the game would start and I'd just sit on the bench, not making a move, like the pilot who flies by the seat of his pants. I had to get a feel for the game. That wasn't always automatic. So I'd make a substitution and nothing would happen. My team falls behind. I'd make another move. Nothing. I start juggling the lineup and nothing seems to work. We're flat, and there's no way in the world we're going to win.

So I'd find something to gripe about. You can always find something. I'd yell and scream and jump and the crowd would get going and everybody would get excited. Sometimes that would snap us out of it.

If not, then I'd figure it's a good time to get out. That's when I'd go for the ejection.

The ref would run past our bench and I'd yell, "No wonder you're working such a horseshit game. You're not hustling!"

You tell a referee he's not hustling and it's like waving a red flag. He'd just glare at me.

"And that's another thing," I'd say. "What the hell are you looking at me for? The game's out there."

I can see he's getting very close to letting me have it. So the next time he runs by, I yell, "Did you get my message? It still goes."

That's it. "Technical foul!"

I just sit there staring at him. Next time down the floor I get on him again.

"I see they didn't teach you guys anything about rabbit ears! You don't know a goddamned thing about what's happening out there because you're too busy listening to me instead of watching the game."

Naturally, I'd get the second technical, which means I'm gone.

But for the same price I figure I might as well really go after him, so I'd run out onto the floor, yelling and waving my arms

and getting red in the face. Cousy would rush over and grab
me, and sometimes Russell would put his arms around me and
pick me up off the floor. "Put me down, goddamn it!" I'd
scream. By now I've raised holy hell. The crowd is screaming
at the referees, the other team is all upset and my own guys are
suddenly motivated as they see me getting kicked out.

But the important thing is I bet we won 80 or 90 percent of
those games I was kicked out of. I never had the ego to believe
they went out and won them for dear old Red, their buddy. On
the contrary, they probably wanted to win in spite of me, just
to show me they could do it.

I didn't care about that. All that mattered to me was that we
won the ball game.

Chapter 20
Practice Makes Perfect

"It's what they hear and absorb that really matters."

Early in the fall of 1969, long after Auerbach had retired to the front office, rookie forward Steve Kuberski—no shrinking violet at 6'8, 220—was taking a merciless pounding from veteran Bailey Howell during practice sessions. One day, after just such an encounter, he went out to lunch with trainer Joe DeLauri.

"Jesus, that guy is murdering me," the newcomer moaned.

DeLauri, who began working with the Celtics during Auerbach's last season on the bench (1966), had to smile. "Why don't you hit him back?"

"Me hit Bailey Howell?" Kuberski said. "Red would have my neck when he heard about it."

"That's what you think," DeLauri counseled. "Auerbach would take a bite out of his cigar and be the happiest guy in the world."

Kuberski pondered the advice, and the following day he

leveled Howell with a Pier Six forearm, bringing practice to a temporary halt while Bailey picked himself up off the floor.

"I was right," DeLauri remembers. "As soon as I saw Red and told him what had happened, he broke out in the biggest damned smile you ever saw. He loved it. He said it was just like old times."

Indeed, practice sessions in the heyday of Auerbach's dynasty often resembled a gathering of the Hatfields and the McCoys. Some of the fiercest rivalries in the NBA were carried on behind the closed doors of a Boston workout.

"Sometimes we'd get bored, so we'd play a little three-on-three and kill each other for a dollar," Ramsey smiles. "Especially Heinie and me. We always seemed to be paired off. I was smaller than him. So he'd shove me and I'd shove back just a little bit harder. Before you knew it, he'd get mad."

"Ramsey used to love that," Sanders insists. "Tommy could take a lot of punishment, but you could always hit a hair root with him that would reach right into his nerves. And he'd get pissed. Ramsey was great at doing that. It wasn't unusual to see those two coming to blows.

"And that's what Auerbach loved. He really did. It kept everybody sharp and made practices serious. Yet Red was always careful not to promote it to a point where the players were on edge. He controlled those confrontations, just like he controlled everything else."

Life was no more tranquil in the backcourt.

"Whenever he had certain players vying for the same job, Red always matched them up in practice," Sharman recalls. "So it was me against Sam, or Cooz against KC. He knew it was only natural for us to take practice less seriously the more we won in league games, so he'd look for little ways to motivate us, to get us keyed up. Sure, it was just a practice, just a scrimmage, but you knew Red was watching, and you knew there was a possibility your playing time in games could be affected by what he saw, so you didn't want to be shown up. As a result you ended up playing almost as hard in practice as you did in a regular game."

"Everybody knew Cousy and Sharman had a lock on those starting jobs," Satch observes, "but still it was necessary for them to go out and prove it to Sam and KC every day."

One day, in the middle of a fast-paced scrimmage, a stray elbow hit KC on his left eye and sent him sprawling.

Auerbach pulled the cigar out of his mouth. "Now *that's* the way to practice!" he shouted enthusiastically.

The lone exception to the rule was Russell, whose aversion to practicing was second only to his distaste for losing.

"He was the worst practice player I ever saw in my life," Willie Naulls says. "Sam used to get hysterical when Red made the rest of us run our asses off while Russell just moped around. He'd say, 'Look at Russell! Look at Russell!' And the rest of us would just laugh."

For cynics always on the lookout for double standards, it might have appeared that Russell was something of a privileged class when it came to workouts. But his teammates—Sam's howls notwithstanding—didn't see it that way.

"We knew Russell had to play forty-five minutes a game," Ramsey explains. "So he was entitled to rest. But everybody else needed the work. So sometimes we'd ask Red to let Bill be the referee. Once in a while, just to break the routine, Red would have the little guys—Sharman, Cousy, KC, Sam and me—play against the big guys: Heinsohn, Loscutoff, Russell, Conley and Sanders. We'd play for half a dollar a man, or maybe ten laps around the gym, and then you'd see Russell go to work!"

"He'd play Ping-Pong off the backboards," Naulls said.

But practice was often as much a seminar as a scrimmage. It was a time for learning, for planning, for developing.

"Games are won in practice as much as they're won on the floor," Russell notes. "That's when everybody gets a chance to have an input. In fact it's quite important that *everybody* have a say. And Red, despite his image, happened to be a great listener."

Like every other part of his domain, Auerbach's practices were characterized by discipline and by organization.

"When he showed up on the court and blew his whistle, he had instant command," Havlicek says. "Then he would tell us exactly what he wanted us to do. A lot of coaches will waste time elaborating and going into the most minute details. They become very boring. But not Red. He'd tell us what to do and then we'd do it. There were no ten-minute or fifteen-minute explanations. You just did it, or kept on doing it until you got it right. Usually we'd warm up with a three-man drill, then work on the long-pass drill, then go into our scrimmage. After that you'd shoot a few free throws and go home. It rarely lasted more than forty-five minutes.

"But in those forty-five minutes he had the complete attention of every player. He could accomplish more in a shorter period of time than anybody I've ever known."

I had one very important rule regarding practices. When I came through the doorway and walked onto the court and blew my whistle, I didn't want to hear another sound. I didn't want to hear any balls bouncing, any shots being taken, not even any laughing and joking. I wanted immediate attention. They were to stop whatever they were doing and come over and gather in a semicircle around me. And I didn't want anybody sitting down on a basketball or stretching out in some crazy position.

I wanted them to stand there, shut up and listen to me.

That wasn't any big ego thing on my part. They knew I wouldn't keep them any longer than I had to, so the idea was to get right down to business and then get the hell out of there.

I never believed the length of time meant anything in practice. If you kept the players too long they'd get fidgety and uncomfortable.

If we were going to work on a new play or a certain pattern, I'd explain in a very soft, slow voice just what I had in mind. Then I'd ask, "Do you understand what we're going to do? If you don't, then ask questions. Don't just nod your head if you're not sure."

Communication is everything in coaching. It's not what you say that counts. It's what they hear and absorb that really matters.

It helps to know when to be sarcastic and when to be humorous, when to be mean and tough, and when to be calm and soft. You must employ a change of pace in this business, just to keep your players off guard. You don't want them to know how you're going to react.

One day I came out to start a practice at the Cambridge Y

*and nothing went right. Everyone seemed to be loafing. Espe-
cially Russell. So after about 10 minutes of this crap I blew
my whistle and said, "All right, everybody out of here! Get
downstairs and get dressed. I don't want to see another shot
taken. Now go!"*

*For three days I never said a word about it. I kept them won-
dering what I was going to do.*

*Do you know what I did? Nothing. Absolutely nothing. If it
wasn't there, it wasn't there. They just didn't feel like practicing that day. A coach has to be smart enough to see that. He
can't be thinking, "I am the great Ichibod Honcho. How dare
they do this to me? When I say jump, they must jump!" That's
a lot of bullshit. I'm motivating these guys for 82 games. It's
hard to maintain the same intensity for practice. That's why I
always kept my practices short. I figured 10 minutes of good
hard scrimmaging was worth more than two hours of their
fighting me and my fighting them. If we had had a good, brisk
workout, I felt it was a job well done.*

But that day they just didn't have it.

*Then we met for another practice, the first one since I kicked
them out of the gym three days earlier.*

*"Gentlemen," I began, "we will not discuss what happened
the other day. All I want is a good tough practice today. Now
let's get started."*

Right away Russell starts giving me false hustle again.

So I blew the whistle.

*"Goddamn it, Russell," I yelled, "you destroyed practice
the other day, but you're not going to destroy this one! I am going to get a cigar and go up there and sit in those seats, and
we're going to stay here until I see a good twenty-minute
scrimmage. I don't give a shit if it takes an hour, two hours,
three hours or all day."*

Then I went up into the stands, lit my cigar and sat down.

*They started to play and after about eight minutes I had to
laugh. I walked back down and blew my whistle again.*

*"Jesus Christ, Russell! What am I going to do with you? I
didn't mean for you to play that hard."*

*He must have blocked 9,000 shots. He wouldn't give any-
body a shot within 18 feet of the basket. Nobody. He'd block
the shot, get the rebound, throw the pass, beat Conley to the*

*other end, stuff the ball, run back on defense and start all over
again. It was like his best playoff game ever!*

I said to myself, "If I don't stop this right now, he's going to
leave his next ball game right here in the YMCA."

So I tried to make a joke out of it. "Russell, you give me a
coach's dilemma. I want you to hustle and play hard so we can
get our timing down. What happens? You screw around and
nobody can get anything done. Then you get mad at me and
tear up the goddamned practice like this, and ruin it the other
way. You're making my job tough. I don't even know how to
analyze this. Can't you just give me a happy medium?"

Russell just hated to practice, but Russell was an exception.
Certain players can get into bad habits if they don't practice
hard. Their shooting goes bad, their passes are terrible. But
Russell's skills weren't the kind that you could really practice,
so I'd shut my eyes to a certain amount of his false hustle. So
would the rest of the team. We knew he was going to give us 48
minutes of playing his guts out during the games.

Plus he had to practice against the same person all the time.
I could put KC against Sharman, then Sam, then Ramsey.
Same thing with the forwards. Tommy could play Loscutoff,
then Sanders, then Havlicek. Russ always had to play the
same guy, and in those years when Conley was his backup, he
was afraid. Gene would swing his elbows all over the place.
They were friends and all. That's just the way Conley played.
Even Loscutoff was afraid around him!

But every once in a while I'd really get on him. "You big
shvartzeh sonofabitch! All the plays revolve around you.
When the rest of these guys see you loafing, they want to loaf,
too. You're ruining it for everybody. Now start moving."

He'd stand there and give me the famous Russell look, but
in all of our years together, he never once answered back.

The whole idea of my practices was to simulate game conditions as much as possible. This was something I began in my
first year with the Caps.

I'd give them an actual game condition—"White team:
you've got the ball; two points ahead; 30 seconds to go"—and
we'd throw in the foul situation and number of time-outs left.
They'd run their play and then we'd all discuss it.

Some of the veterans who came here, guys like Risen, Phillip, Braun and Embry, couldn't get over it. They had never practiced in real-life situations.

Doesn't that make a lot more sense than standing on the sidelines and telling somebody to run 10 laps? There were very few things that ever came up in a game that caught the Celtics by surprise. We had done our homework. We were prepared.

Chapter 21
The Pregame Talk

*"No matter what happens tomorrow night, you're
still my guys."*

The locker room pep talk has a niche all of its own in American sports folklore. There was, of course, Rockne's legendary exhortation to win one for the Gipper. And each fall New Englanders are reminded of the words of The Sainted T.A.D. Jones, football coach at Yale from 1916 through 1927: "Gentlemen, you are now going out to play football against Harvard. Never again in your life will you do anything so important!"

Unfortunately, no records were ever kept of Auerbach's locker room oratory, for he believed in the sanctity of the locker room; it was a family place, and what was said and done behind those doors was no one else's business.

But once in a while, the words filtered out.

❈ ❈ ❈

The California press was gleefully predicting a 200-point performance by Freddie Schaus's western division all-stars in the 1963 classic at Los Angeles. Schaus had a starting lineup of Pettit, Bellamy, Chamberlain, West and Baylor. Auerbach's eastern squad was generally pictured as a lamb en route to slaughter.

"But Red did a soft-sell in his pregame talk," an eastern star later confided to New York columnist Milton Gross. "He played on each man's pride with the virtuosity of a Segovia plucking softly at guitar strings. He even reminded us that some of us perhaps disliked him personally, but he said for this night alone he wanted us to feel that we were *his* guys. And he said it wasn't for personal reasons. He just felt our professional pride couldn't allow us to be discounted the way Schaus and the California writers had been doing all week."

Russell, with 19 points, 24 rebounds and five assists, was named MVP as the underdog eastern stars shot down the favorites, 115–108.

With a few seconds left in the game, Auerbach leaned over to the press table and said, "I don't think they'll score two hundred. Do you?"

"Red was very wise," Sanders says. "He always stressed how strong we were, how great we were. He never frightened us with reports of how great and strong the other team might be. He believed in a totally positive approach.

"I remember one night we were sitting in the locker room just before one of those seventh-game playoff situations. No one was talking. Each man was alone with his thoughts. Then the door opened and Red walked in. Right away he could feel the tension, the nervousness, the uncertainty. He put his hands on his hips and looked at each of us like we were all crazy. I'll never forget it. Then he said, 'If you guys are nervous, how the hell do you think they feel, having to play us?'

"It was beautiful. The typical Auerbach point of view."

His moods ranged the whole length of the emotional spectrum. The 1965 playoffs were a good example.

That was the year Havlicek stole the ball from Greer, foiling what might have been a last-shot Philadelphia world championship. The game, indeed the whole series, left the Celts drained.

Then came the Lakers for the final round, sans Baylor, who injured his kneecap against Baltimore a week earlier and had to undergo surgery. With the Philadelphia menace put to rest, and the prospects of token opposition from LA, the players naturally let their guard down.

When Auerbach walked into the locker room prior to game one, he encountered a giddy, giggling group of Celtics.

"When he saw that, he got pissed," KC Jones remembers. "He really let us have it. And he was right. We were wise-cracking and fooling around. Hell, we felt relaxed. It was hard not to feel that way, knowing Elgin wasn't going to play. Red went up one side of us and down the other. He said if we didn't smarten up we were going to get knocked on our asses by the Lakers. He reminded us they were still plenty tough, and maybe they'd be even tougher trying to make up for Baylor's absence. He said they wouldn't lie down and die for us, and he was not going to stand back and watch us lose the goddamned game in the dressing room.

"It was quite a talk. When he got through, all the smiles were gone."

Then the Celtics went out and won by 32 points, 142–110.

The Redhead had been much more subdued a few days earlier. Philadelphia, getting great efforts from Walker, Greer and Jackson to go along with Chamberlain's omnipresence, tied their series at 3–3, forcing a seventh game in Boston. Once again momentum had shifted and the 76ers—powerful, explosive, deep, confident—were just 48 minutes away from dethroning the perennial champs.

The morning after that sixth-game loss the Celtics gathered for a light practice. Writers, photographers and hangers-on crowded around. Was this, at last, the death throe of the dynasty? One by one the players got dressed and taped. Few words were exchanged. Some faces were grim. Some expressionless.

Then Auerbach arrived. He ordered trainer Buddy Leroux to clear the locker room of everyone except the ballplayers, and he told him to lock the door shut.

In a barely audible voice, he gave his pep talk one day early.

"Okay, listen. I just want to let you guys know one thing. No matter what happens tomorrow night, you're still *my* guys and you always will be. You've given me eight great years, so one ball game isn't going to change the way I feel about you. I think you're the greatest guys in the world, the greatest team in the world, and I'm going to continue believing that after tomorrow night.

"That's all I'm going to say. I just wanted you to know it."

If I had to pick the biggest danger in coaching, I'd say it was overcoaching. *One of the ways to avoid it is to make sure that you don't fall in love with the sound of your own voice. I tell this to young coaches all the time. It can't be emphasized enough. Get your point across and then shut up. Otherwise you begin saying things which aren't meaningful, just to carry on the conversation. A guy becomes a successful coach and suddenly he wants to become an orator, too. He's got to have his 15 minutes before each and every game, come hell or high water.*

What happens? After so many games and so many years, the players get turned off. He starts in and they're thinking to themselves: "Here comes his bullshit again!" Now his motivation is actually working in reverse. They don't hear a thing he's saying. I've said this a million times: communication is not what you tell them, but what they hear you say.

I used to change the amount of time I talked according to the game, the situation, the standings, a whole lot of things. Sometimes I'd talk two minutes, sometimes eight, sometimes 10. I'd change the inflections as I went along. Sometimes soft, sometimes hard, sometimes a combination. Every game is a separate entity.

I sometimes wouldn't say anything at all, and that would motivate them. They'd think, "Gee, Red doesn't want to talk about this one. Let's show him we can do it anyway."

What do you say? There is no one answer. You've got to be able to determine what the team needs at a particular moment. You can get your point across with humor, with sarcasm, with ridicule, with appeals to their pride. Maybe one night you'll yell and the next night you'll talk softly. Sometimes you'll get technical. Other times you'll be very general.

And sometimes you just don't know what the hell to say. It's happened to me more than once.

One night I walked in not knowing what to say. I killed some time, looked at the clock, went to take a leak, came back out and still had no idea what I was going to say. Then I saw Russell drinking a cup of tea. He had his big goddamned hand wrapped around his little cup with his pinky stuck up in the air.

"Before we start on the intricacies of this ball game," I said, "I want you all to look at Russell. He thinks this is a goddamned tea party! Will you look at Mister Russell's pinky. Isn't he delicate? Aren't we, the hoi polloi, lucky to get this lesson in etiquette?"

I gave an eloquent speech on the proper way to drink tea.

Another time I spotted Sharman eating his pregame piece of chocolate. He was just like Russell with the tea. Every night the two of them had their piece of chocolate and cup of tea.

"Tell me," I began, "has anybody in this room ever been offered a piece of chocolate by Bill Sharman? I haven't. Have you, Ramsey? Have you, Loscy? How about you, Heinie? See what I mean? He sits there every night eating his chocolate, getting energy like Mister America, and he's never offered a piece of it to any of his teammates. He's got to be the cheapest sonofabitch who ever lived."

I went on and on about that piece of chocolate. Then someone banged on our door and said it was time to go.

"Now there you go," I yelled at Sharman. "You've made me lose the whole impact of my pregame talk with your goddamned chocolate bar. Now we've got to go out there and play and I never got to say what's on my mind. Okay. Get out there. Maybe you'll know what you're doing anyway."

Then I'd stamp my feet and leave.

Sometimes those were the best pregame talks of all.

Chapter 22
Inside the Huddle

"God help anyone I caught not listening!"

The fruits of Auerbach's labors were on display to the world for the entire 48 minutes each game consumed. But it was in the single minutes set aside for time-outs that the secret of the Celtics' success was really explained. And it was easy to miss if you weren't looking for it.

Sid Borgia didn't miss it.

"I watched every NBA team, night after night, year after year, and I got to know how each one operated. I'd see teams go into their huddle and everyone would start talking at once. Or the coach would talk and no one would listen. Or some would listen while others went looking for towels and cups of water.

"But that never ever happened on the Celtics. Not once in all the years I watched them.

"When Boston went into its huddle, only one man talked and everyone else listened. And that man was the Redhead.

When I say everyone listened, I mean the five players who were on the floor and all the rest of them who were on the bench. And during those years when Boston kept winning championship after championship, Red was surrounded by some of the greatest stars this game has ever known.

"When you hold the greats of the game in the palm of your hand, then you are truly the master of the ship. Red was the master in Boston.

"That's one reason why I always respected the man as a really great, great, great coach—even though he could be a sonofabitch to me!"

That's not to say his players took a vow of silence, however. On the contrary, their advice and opinions were frequently solicited.

"Don't take that business of keeping quiet at face value," Macauley cautions. "To visualize all of the Celtics standing around not uttering a sound would be unfair to Auerbach. See, part of his great ability to handle his players was his skill in drawing upon their thoughts and ideas. It was like the football situation where the quarterback comes out of the game and the coach asks if he has any suggestions to make. The men in the game have a better feel for the tempo than anyone else. Red was smart enough to recognize that. He never hesitated for a second when it came to asking us our opinions.

"But ninety percent of the time he knew what he wanted done out there. And one hundred percent of the time, the final decision was his. There was never any question about that."

Gene Conley vividly describes a typical time-out scene in front of the Celtics bench.

"You've got to remember that we had so many superb basketball minds on that team. Guys like Cousy, Russell, Heinsohn, Ramsey and Sharman were some of the smartest players in the world. So the whistle would blow and we'd all gather around Red.

"Cousy would start in: 'As soon as I take the ball, Tommy, you run over there and I'll flip it to you; and Loscy, you pull your guy out of the lane. . . .'

"He'd be halfway through his plan and Russell might break in: 'I think it would be better if Sharman took it out, then Cooz could . . .'

"Meanwhile Heinsohn's insisting: 'I'll be over in the corner. Get it to me. I *know* I can make the shot!'

"Then all of a sudden—and I can remember this so clearly because it happened so often—Red would hold his hand up for silence. He'd been collecting his own thoughts all the while. He'd say, 'Everybody listening? Okay. Here's what we're going to do.'

"He'd just take charge. A lot of coaches—especially in tight situations—might back off and let their stars decide what to do. That way the responsibility on them wasn't as great. But that never happened with Auerbach. When the game got down to the nitty-gritty, this man was excellent. He knew how many fouls had been called on every one of his players and every one of the opposing players, too. He knew the entire time-out situation. And all this time he's psyching out the refs and keeping his eye on the clock. Just check the records and see how many games the Celtics won in the closing minutes. He knew precisely what he was doing. He knew who should take the shot, who should put the ball into play, who should set the pick, who should stand in such-and-such a spot—and what to do if the play didn't work.

"It's a fact. The man was a brilliant strategist."

It wasn't surprising, then, that the Celtics paid attention when the Redhead began to speak.

"We all had great confidence in him," Ramsey explains. "Red would sit down and figure out the odds on every possible situation. Nothing was overlooked. So when we got into a game and a time-out was called, especially late in the fourth quarter of a real tight ball game, he would know what we should do and we accepted his leadership without question. Nine times out of ten, it turned out he was absolutely correct.

"Sometimes, after the games were over and we were all back in the locker room, or maybe at practice the following morning, we'd ask him: 'Red, how come you did that?' And he would give us the most wonderful explanation.

"After a while, you never even thought of second-guessing him."

Somewhere along the line I picked the image of a loud, tough, pushy kind of guy, but my players will tell you I very

*seldom got mad in the huddle. You can't communicate when
you're mad. You can motivate, perhaps, but you can't communicate, and the name of this game—first and foremost—is
communication. When you tell them something you want a
reaction. So you've got to make sure they understand you.*

I had certain rules for my huddles. First, my ballplayers did
not sit down! At the very end of my coaching career I changed
that rule a bit, only because many of my guys were getting older and needed the extra rest. But for years and years you never
saw a Celtic sit down during a time-out.

I wanted to show contempt for the other team. They had to
sit down. They were tired. They needed rest. But we were in
superb physical condition. The Boston Celtics were not tired.
The Boston Celtics did not need rest. We were ready to run
right back out there and chase their asses up and down the
court. It was like Muhammad Ali standing in his corner between rounds, just staring at his opponent in disgust because
he was so weak he had to sit on a stool. I wanted the other team
to look over at our huddle and see how strong and fresh and
confident we were. I wanted them to think about that the whole
minute they were sitting there. I wanted it to bother them, to
distract them, to embarrass them.

In every time-out I'd inspect my team to make sure there
were no shirttails hanging out, no uniform straps twisted and
turned. It was all part of the image. My team looked good,
looked crisp, looked confident. Don't underestimate the psychological values of that.

The other reason I didn't want my guys sitting down was
that they'd be too spread out. One guy would be wiping himself off with a towel, someone else would be looking here,
another guy looking there. I'd get them in a circle around me,
so everyone could hear my voice, and, of course, we could all
hear any players who were asked to speak. We were striving
for communication in an atmosphere of organ music, popcorn
vendors and 15,000 people talking with their neighbors, and
there was no time to repeat everything.

God help anyone I caught not listening. I'd get madder than
hell when someone wandered away from the circle. "Don't you
think you ought to get back here?" I'd say. "If I decide to put

you out there, it might be nice if you knew what the hell was going on!"

We didn't have many problems like that, however. The only two I can think of involved guys who had just come to the Celtics from other teams and didn't know any better.

The first time was in 1955, when Arnie Risen joined us. He was one of the sweetest guys you'd ever want to meet. A real gentleman. But Arnie came from Rochester where Les Harrison was the owner/coach. The Royals used to form a circle and not let Lester in! He wasn't really a basketball coach, but more of an owner than a coach. So the team more or less ran itself during huddles.

Arnie walked into one of our huddles and began to talk. Everybody looked at me as if to say: "How can he talk now? Nobody talks now!" I didn't want to bawl him out. You've got to know the personalities you're dealing with. I spoke very nicely to him. "Arnie, I want to tell you something. You guys did many strange things in Rochester. But over here we have an axiom, a very simple rule that's not hard to understand: You play. I coach. In other words, in common everyday language, keep your goddamned mouth shut!"

He never did it again.

We had a similar situation in 1963 with Willie Naulls. The club was playing lousy this night and I was mad. As soon as we got into our huddle I jumped on Willie. "Goddamn it, Willie, I told you to box out under those boards!" At that point he interrupted me. "I tried to, but I got caught in a switch," he said.

I let him have it. "I don't want to hear any goddamned speeches from you! I told you to do something. If you can't do it, then sit down! I don't want to hear "why?" from you. I don't care why. And I don't want talking in this huddle unless you're asked to talk."

It was a strong put-down, even by my normal way of handling those matters, and I felt kind of bad as soon as I said it. Naulls didn't mean any disrespect by it. But I wanted to make my point very clear.

Later that night I called him aside in the locker room.

"Willie, let me explain what happened out there so there won't be any more problems. When I tell you something in a huddle, or if I'm bawling you out in a huddle, I don't have time to go into any long dissertations. The whole time-out lasts only a minute. I told you that you weren't boxing out and you tried to tell me you got caught in a switch. First of all, you and I both know you never boxed out very well anyway. So in all probability I was right. But even if I wasn't, I don't want any discussions like they have on those other teams. There's no time for them. That's why I gave you hell out there."

He said he understood. I never had another problem with him.

Chapter 23
The Psychology of Coaching

"There have been many great teams ruined by coaches."

Once a year the Boston Red Sox host a fellowship breakfast in their handsomely appointed dining room atop the roof of Fenway Park. Rabbis, priests, ministers and civic leaders gather in ecumenical fashion to extol the virtues of brotherhood. At one such conclave a few years back, Red Sox GM Dick O'Connell listened patiently as speaker after speaker strode to the microphone and sought to capture the essence of people helping people, of people working together, of people subjugating themselves to a common cause.

Finally it was O'Connell's turn to address the group.

"Gentlemen," he began, "I've heard so many speeches about men fighting together on the battlefields of war, unaware of religion and skin color and nationality. That's fine. I'm impressed. But right now you're sitting in a sports building talking about brotherhood. May I suggest the best exam-

234

ple is right down the street from here. There's a team over there in Boston Garden made up of blacks and whites, Catholics and Protestants, coached by a Jew, and they've been world champions for a long time now. Everyone's running around looking for theories and searching into history for explanations. If you want a perfect example of what we've been talking about, just look at the Celtics."

The harmony O'Connell alluded to was at once one of the beauties and the mysteries of the Auerbach empire. Everyone knew why the Celtics won. They were great, great players. But many of those same observers kept waiting for the other shoe to drop. They knew—because the history of professional sports had taught them well—that any team with a superabundance of extraordinary members will eventually fall victim to its own foibles—jealousy, dissension, runaway egos—not unlike Lincoln's "house divided against itself."

"People don't realize how easily that great team could have blown apart at the seams," Macauley says. "You had all these super athletes, each with his own personality and temperament; you had a shifting of race as the league went from predominantly white to predominantly black; you had the very active Boston media fawning over a guy like Cooz and generally understating Russell's contributions; you had great players like Ramsey being asked to sit on the bench. Now you take all of these factors together and you begin to realize what a marvelous job Auerbach did in keeping them all happy.

"That was the greatness of Red Auerbach."

"A lot of guys have the horses," Sid Borgia points out, "but don't know how to ride them."

Auerbach did.

"There was a certain mystique about Red which he liked to cultivate," Sanders explains. "He was very, very tough, and he played on the natural fears of certain athletes. See, Red made it a point to study the character of every Celtic. He knew every one of us quite well. And he knew how to handle each of us. Tommy loved to shoot, so every once in a while Red would remind him the rest of us wouldn't mind holding the ball once in a while. He yelled at Tommy a lot. He yelled at Loscutoff, too. But he'd never yell at certain others. He knew

Cousy considered himself a perfectionist, so he'd get on him for throwing a pass away. All he'd do with Russell was point out how so-and-so was making him look bad, knowing perfectly well what that would do to Russ's pride.

"We'd lose one damned game after a winning streak of maybe ten in a row and he'd go into a rage, telling us we were getting fat, content, lazy. He'd yell something like, 'You're all going out and buying homes!', and he'd look right at Sam, knowing damned well Sam had just moved into a new one. His favorite saying was, 'I'm not married to any of you guys!' That was just another way of reminding us that we could always be traded. He'd go by your locker and whisper, 'You know, I had an offer for you today, but I turned it down.' Then you were supposed to go out and bust your ass because you were so grateful that Red didn't send you away. He was a great con man that way."

Heinsohn and Loscutoff were his whipping boys. "You have to coach those two with a whip," Red once insisted. "They were always so steamed up they couldn't hear him anyway," Ramsey figures.

"He couldn't yell at Russell or Cousy, because they had too much pride," Heinsohn says. "And if you yelled at Sharman, he'd get the red ass. If you yelled at Ramsey, he'd take it to heart. If you yelled at Sam, he'd brood. If you yelled at KC, Satch, Naulls or Havlicek, they'd be hurt and embarrassed because they were basically quiet people.

"So he would give it to Loscy and me almost every goddamned night. But we didn't really care. We understood what he was doing and why."

One of Auerbach's favorite tactics was yelling at the wrong guy intentionally, just to get his message across to a more genteel soul. He took a peek at Wayne Embry one night and then yelled to trainer Joe DeLauri: 'Damn it, Joe, you're letting Embry get fat again!' He even conspired with Russell one day.

"It was at the start of my second season," Bill smiles. "He called me up and asked if I'd meet him at his hotel. 'You know training camp is starting tomorrow,' he began. 'Now if I can't yell at you, I can't yell at anybody. So I'm going to give you hell tomorrow and for the rest of the week, but don't pay any attention to it. It's just for the good of the team. We've got to work together.'

"I said okay. I wanted to be on a winning team. He was the coach. If he thought that would help, then I'd go along with him."

But nothing was quite as effective as his tirades at Tommy and Jungle Jim.

"Whenever Red began by saying, 'Okay, Tommy and you other guys . . . ,' I always knew I was one of the 'other guys,'" Ramsey laughs.

One night Heinsohn—the team's resident comic—stole the Redhead's thunder. The Celtics had run up an insurmountable first half score and now they sat in their locker room, awaiting their leader's arrival. As soon as the door opened, Heinsohn jumped up and said: "Okay, Red. I didn't shoot. I didn't rebound. I didn't block out. What else didn't I do?"

Everyone laughed, including the boss.

One of the biggest problems on any winning team is motivation.

"Red was a master at that," Sharman says. "He knew when to fire us up and when to calm us down. In college coaching the biggest problem is keeping the kids relaxed. They play two games a week and they've got pep rallies and campus excitement all around them. But it's just the opposite in the pros. After a while you get tired of all the traveling, all the airports, all the hotel lobbies. So the coach's job is to make each game seem important, and Red could always find a reason why *this* particular game was one we had to win. He was so good at manipulating players."

Walter Kennedy happened to cross paths with the Celtics one day in Cincinnati.

"I was standing in front of the hotel, waiting for a cab to take me to Cincinnati Gardens. Arnold walked out with Russell, Sam and KC just as a taxi arrived, so he asked if they could go with me. I said yes, of course. We started out, and I'm kind of an effervescent guy, you know, so I began talking and no one answered me. I continued a little bit longer, this time asking Arnold a direct question. He gave me a monosyllabic answer. Now I'm thinking to myself that maybe I'd better shut up. Perhaps they were embarrassed riding to the game with the commissioner, although that didn't make any sense to me.

"When we got to the arena I paid the driver, then looked at Arnold and asked, 'What the hell's going on?'

"He said, 'You crazy bastard. You know as well as I do how psyched up we get for big games like this one—especially those three!—and you're yapping away. Right now they couldn't even tell you their names!'

"I never forgot that ride. To me, it's just one more mark of Auerbach's greatness."

Singer Danny Kaye had a similar encounter one night in Boston Garden. He was sitting with *Boston Record* sports editor Sam Cohen. Red was going to meet them for dinner after the game. Just before the teams were due out for their warmups, Kaye decided he wanted to visit the Boston locker room. Cohen looked at him aghast. Visit Auerbach's locker room now? Kaye was insistent. Cohen sighed, shook his head, and led the way.

"It just happened that the door was partially opened," Sammy recalls. "I spotted Red and got his attention. 'Danny wants to come in,' I whispered. He came right over, grabbed the both of us by the arms and brought us into the room. If the walls had been white, I couldn't have seen some of their faces. I used to hear about how tense they got before games, but I never believed it. Red took Danny from man to man, introducing him, and each player sort of mumbled quietly. Then they got to Russell. Danny said something to him and the big guy started to laugh. Have you ever heard Russell's laugh? Pretty soon the whole room was laughing, and that was the first time I saw blood in their faces.

"Then they went out and won the game so easily it was ridiculous."

A word frequently used to describe Auerbach is "psychologist."

"That's what he was," Havlicek insists. "You could be having a great game and if the team was winning big he'd make you sit down. He did that to Sam quite often and it really made Sam mad. It made him so mad, in fact, that he went out the next night and played harder. Red was always playing these little games with people. Some nights I'd be sitting on the bench waiting to go in and he'd turn around and look at me. Just as I'd start to get up he'd turn his head the other way. It was his way of making sure I was ready. I was supposed to go in after six or seven minutes, but some nights he'd keep me out for a period and a half. That would really piss me off. And when I'd finally go in I'd run my heart out. That was his plan all along, of course."

One night he had Conley on the verge of apoplexy.

"It was in 1959 and we had a game against the Knicks," Gene explains. "Now you've got to understand that in those days the Celtics could practically name the score against New York. My whole family was in the stands, so before the game I was kidding with Loscy and the guys about how I might do a little bit of scoring myself, just to please the relatives. Everyone laughed. I even got taped—something I hardly ever did.

"Well, the game gets under way. The first period goes by and I don't play. Then the second period. By the third period we're killing the Knicks—I mean *killing* them!—and everybody's out there scoring and having a ball. Even Gene Guarilia, a rookie who didn't play too often.

"Now the fourth period is almost over and I still haven't played. I looked around and the people were walking out the aisles. Man, my heart was beating ninety miles an hour. I was boiling.

"All of a sudden Red yelled out: 'Conley! Get out there so Russell can get an ovation!'

"Wow. That was digging a little bit too deep, I thought. I took off like a madman. Somebody fouled me and I had three chances to make two free throws. I just threw them up there—bing! bing! bing!—and missed all three. I didn't care. Boy, was I ever ripping.

"Afterwards Red asked me if I wanted to go out with him for some Chinese food, and I told him where he could store it! Then I stormed out of the locker room and slammed the door."

At this point Conley breaks into a grin.

"The next night Wilt was in town. I played thirty-five minutes and belted him all over the place while Russell was sweeping the boards clean.

"And that's exactly what Auerbach had up his sleeve the night before. He was getting me rested for the big one. Rested and infuriated!"

Those things happened day in and day out in the Redhead's dynasty.

"What Red accomplished was as good as any Viennese psychiatrist could have done with a couch," Kennedy marvels.

Gene Guarilia, the handsome kid who spent the better part of four seasons languishing on the Boston bench, once told *Boston Record* sportswriter Bill McSweeney: "I'd rather play for Auerbach, just sitting on the sidelines, than play for anybody else in the league."

Clyde Lovellette, the mammoth 6'9 center who played nine years with the Lakers, Royals and Hawks before ending his career as a Russell backup, stood off in a corner of the Boston locker room one night shortly after joining the team and pointed at Red. "Now I understand why they're champions," he said to McSweeney.

Did they all love him?

Emphatically not.

"Sometimes I loved him," Loscutoff says, "but most of the time I hated him. Brannum and I both used to say the first thing we planned to do after we retired was punch that sonofabitch in the mouth! Every year I'd go to training camp and worry about my job. Red made me feel that way. He wanted me to feel that way. And I'd go home and take it out on my wife. I'd be mean and bitchy to her. Then I'd realize what I was doing and I'd try to explain to her that I was simply worried about making the team. One year, right at the start of camp, he walked by me and said, 'Minnesota is interested in getting you.' He never mentioned it again. The man could really be mean. I think that's one of the reasons we had such great unity on the team. We played hard together because he gave each and every one of us a feeling of insecurity."

Scolari would buy that. "Red was like Leo Durocher," Freddie says. "He made you dislike him. That way you got along better with your teammates. He was a common bond that way. Instead of picking on each other, you got together and bitched about him."

But the most fascinating relationship in the eyes of the NBA was the combination of Auerbach and Russell.

"Russell was an enigma," one Celtic veteran insists.

"He had a kingly arrogance," another player added.

Russell, quite simply, was the most dominating performer in the history of the game. The record says that. So do the men he played with and against. The dynasty began in 1957, his rookie season. It ended in 1969, the year he retired. No other player—not Cousy, not Heinsohn, not Ramsey, not Havlicek—was there from the beginning to the end. Only Russell. To this day he wears two rings: a 1957 championship ring and a 1969 championship ring, a silent testimony to the enormity of his accomplishments.

He was proud. He was private. And he was fiercely independent.

"If Auerbach had not been able to control Russell," Macauley points out, "there would be no story."

"They knew how to deal with each other," Willie Naulls explains. "Russell knew how far he could push Auerbach, and Auerbach knew how to control the situation without ever embarrassing Bill. Those two were a lot alike."

In Ramsey's words, they shared a "mutual admiration society."

"I wouldn't say Red *handled* me," Russell advises. "I don't like that word."

Then what, exactly, was the relationship between the fiery coach and his elegant warrior?

"Red and I exchanged favors," Russell replied. "He never made any demands of me, and consequently I never made any demands of him. We exchanged favors."

There have been many great teams ruined by coaches.

That could have happened with the Celtics, too, but I made it a point to study my players, to analyze them, to determine which ones would respond to which kinds of motivation. Motivation is a hard word to define. You can be motivated by an outside force. You can also be motivated by an inside force.

And it's possible to be motivated too much. Don't forget, basketball is a game of touch. If a player becomes too hypertensive, it's no good.

I tried to figure the best way to reach each man on my team.

Russell is absolutely right when he says he didn't like to be handled. He had a big hangup about that word and I don't blame him. I respected him for that. I didn't handle Russell or handle Cousy or handle anyone else. They weren't animals. They were men. And without getting too sloppy about it, they were also a family.

My job was to be the head of that family. Sometimes it called for disciplining them. Sometimes it meant they weren't going to like me. I couldn't be their buddy and be their coach, too. I don't care what anybody says, that won't work. But I loved that family, and there wasn't a single day when I wasn't proud of every member of it.

How do you motivate a guy to give you his best? Do you do it through yelling? Through scolding? Through embarrassment? Through reasoning? Through pride? Yes and no. It depends on the situation and it depends on the man. Some you whisper to. Some you berate.

I don't remember ever yelling at KC or Satch, and there were very few times I ever took off after Cousy, Ramsey or Sam. But if I bawled out Loscutoff, I knew he heard me. If I talked softly to him, he wouldn't react. Heinsohn always looked out of shape, so he was easy to yell at.

But I never yelled at rookies. That wasn't my cup of tea.

I learned how to pick my spots. When we lost I very rarely said much until the next day at practice. The worst times I blew my top were those nights when they'd play lousy and just eke out a win. I'd go into the locker room and they'd be laughing and joking and I'd let them have it: "You ought to hang your heads in shame because you were terrible tonight!"

There was one game, I think against Philadelphia, when we went ahead by something like 42 points in the first half. It was one of the greatest exhibitions I ever saw. We ended up winning the ball game by eight points! That was the maddest I ever got in 20 years of coaching. Why did I get mad? Because we'd have no chance at all in our next game unless I brought things to a head right then and there.

When we'd win in spite of what we did, rather than because of what we did, that's when I'd really tear into them. People say, "Why get mad? You should be happy. You won the game." They don't understand. It's the next one that matters.

Sometimes after a loss I'd go in and say, "You blew the game. Goddamn it, you gave it away, and there's no excuse for a great ball club like this, with your experience, to ever give a ball game away."

Other times I'd say, "You played pretty well. I've got no beef. We lost tonight. So we lost. We'll get it back tomorrow." When my guys lost, I knew they felt badly enough. They very seldom heard from me on those occasions.

But when they deserved it, I gave them hell. Immediately.

I can remember nights when Ramsey would come up to me and say, "You were magnificent tonight. That was a fantastic job of coaching." And I'd agree it was, but that can work both ways. I wasn't afraid to admit deficiencies, either. There were some losses which I felt I was partially to blame for. Who's to say every loss had to be their fault? Common sense will tell you that can't be true. Maybe I made a bad move, or called for the wrong play, or made a poor substitution. Or maybe my attitude was bad and the players picked it up.

I'd go into the locker room and they'd be sitting there, expecting me to tear their asses off. "You know, we lost that ball game," I'd say, "because you played horseshit. But I did a horseshit job, too. In fact, I did a lousy goddamned job. Let's all do better next time."

I think the secret to a great deal of my success—forget the playoffs, that's a separate thing—was my ability to get the team up and motivated for 82 games a year. Throughout my career I probably came up with more than 2,000 reasons to win.

I was especially concerned with motivating them against the easier opponents on our schedule. When I talk to college coaches I always stress this point. It's the weaker teams you've got to be motivated against. The big games are self-motivating. The games that catch you off balance break your hump. Check the record and you'll find that schools like UCLA, Kentucky, Indiana, North Carolina, Maryland—all the powers—

go through these stretches where they'll win two or three games in a row by just a couple of points. You preach against overconfidence all the time, yet it's going to happen now and then.

Rather than repeat the word over and over until they got tired of hearing me say it, I wouldn't mention overconfidence. I'd find a different approach. "Look," I'd say, "you guys are already chalking up this win, but you're not going to win it on paper. If you get out there and bust your balls right away, however, you might wrap it up by the third quarter and then you can take it easy. But if you don't, you're going to wind up playing 48 hard minutes. The choice is yours."

One thing that could really get to me was dealing with the media. Personally, I was never big on interviews. I'd stay around the locker room for about five minutes after each game, figuring I owed the writers answers to any legitimate questions. Then I'd get out of there. "Talk to the players," I'd say. "I didn't score the points. They did."

In the early days when I first got to Boston, the writers didn't know a thing about basketball. The more they covered us, the more they started forming their own fan clubs. There'd be pro-Cousy stories, pro-Heinsohn stories, pro-Ramsey stories. Forget the game—they were too busy writing about their heroes. They didn't know what was happening out there. So they'd write, "The Boston Celtics streaked to another victory yesterday, 112–94, thanks to another sterling performance by Bob Cousy, who scored 22 points." Blah-blah-blah! They'd go on and on and never mention the fact that Russell dominated the game. And I resented the fact that so often they gave the wrong people the credit.

This can hurt a team. I'd try to make a joke out of it. "Did you fellows see the paper this morning?" I'd say. "Was that guy really at our game? He sure didn't see what I saw." Then I'd tell them the story about the day Webby Morse, the sports editor at the Christian Science Monitor, called Lynn Patrick, the Bruins coach, and told him he was sending a young writer over who had never seen a hockey game before. Webby asked Lynn if he'd teach the kid a few things. So Lynn spent a couple of hours with him. Within two weeks the kid was criticizing Lynn's line changes!

"So you see," I'd say, "if Joe Blow writes something in the newspaper, it's hardly worth getting upset about. It's just one man's opinion, and we all know how much he knows about the game."

For years the Boston press wrote very authoritatively about a game it didn't understand.

I had only one rule regarding the press, and I was very tough on this. Certain members of the press would cater to certain players, hoping to develop a pipeline into the team. This still goes on. Whenever I'd find out who the player was who kept feeding the writer little scoops, I'd call him into my office. "You want to be buddy-buddy with him? Keep it up and you'll have him paying your salary instead of me, because you won't be here. Let's get one thing clear. You are part of the team. The next time we have a secret meeting and something leaks out, it's going to be your neck. I don't give a damn who you are or how important you think you are to this ball club. You're not going to air your grievances with the press or be a stooge for anybody. No way. This is a team and we stick together. What goes on in our locker room stays in our locker room. Have I made myself clear?"

As far as my relationships with the players goes, there is one thing I'd like to make very clear. As great as Bill Russell was, we never maintained two sets of standards on the Boston Celtics, and anybody who says we did is absolutely wrong. We did not!

I tried to be understanding about little things with Russell. I did the same with Cousy, Sharman, Ramsey and the others. Contrary to what people may think, Russell never tried to push his weight around. Russell was basically a peaceful man who liked his privacy. In all the years we were together—the 10 in which he played for me and then the three in which he coached and played—he never once answered me back when I bawled him out and we never once had a confrontation of any significance. You see, in his heart Russ knew I was fair and that I wouldn't make a big issue out of something unless I was pretty

damned sure I was right. Whenever I went at him, I had a good
reason and he realized it. When a guy puts out the way Bill
did, and gives as much as he gave the Celtics, it doesn't make
sense to jump all over him unless the provocation is legitimate.

Besides, some players need it more than others. That brings
me to my whipping boys. Loscy and Heinie.

I'll tell you what kind of a guy Jim was. One night I was
coming onto the court in St. Louis, and as I passed through the
stands this big kid jumped over a railing above my head and
landed right in front of me in the aisle. He was around 6'3, 220
pounds. He said, "Auerbach, you're no damned good. I ought
to wipe you out." Well it so happened that Loscy had remained in the locker room for something when the team came
out. So now he's right behind me. I said to the kid, in a very
soft voice, "Wait one moment, please." Then I turned to my
friendly bruiser and said, "Jim, will you take care of this mi-
nor problem for me?" Loscy grabbed the jerk and threw him
right back up over the railing.

"Thank you, Jim," I smiled, and we walked away together.

Tommy was a tough kid, too. He was the ideal forward. He
could do it all: great offensive rebounding, great moves, great
shots—including a beautiful soft hook, even great defense
when he felt like playing it. Heinsohn was a winner. Period.
He was always the one who'd stand up in the locker room just
before the team left and say something like, "Okay, let's go
out there and kick the shit out of them!"

One year I put a special play in the playoffs which called for
Tommy to stand in Wilt's way when Chamberlain tried to run
after Russell. Wilt's got to be the strongest man in the world,
and when he realized what was going on, he got madder than
hell and ran right up Tommy's back a couple of times. But
Heinsohn never budged. He just stood there and kept on doing
his job. That's why I loved the guy.

Ramsey was a brilliant player who'd do anything I asked
him to do. I first met him up at Kutsher's when he was a college sophomore at Kentucky. He couldn't understand how
people would eat sour cream. He thought it was ruined cream.
Madison, Kentucky, is not the most progressive town in the
world, you know. He weighed 196 in his first season with us

*and played mostly at guard. I told him I wanted to make him a
swingman in his second season, playing a lot at forward, so he
suggested getting his weight up to 210. I said no, I wanted it
down to 190. He figured he needed the extra weight to fight off
guys like Pettit and Baylor, but I reminded him there were two
ends on the court, and those big guys were going to get plenty
tired trying to keep up with him at our end. His only reaction
was, "Yessir!" And he reported to camp at 190.*

Those are the kind of people we had on the Celtics.

Do you wonder why I loved them?

*But you can talk about motivation, psychology and every-
thing else. To me, the one word which best explains the success
I had with my guys is integrity.*

*And it all began with Walter Brown. He was such a fantastic
man. I believed in the things he stood for and the kind of man
he was, and after he died I tried to carry on that tradition with
the team. My guys knew I'd never lie to them. When they came
in to see me, they knew they were going to get the truth. And
they knew the Boston Celtics organization stood behind them
100 percent.*

*Like Russell says, they were men. We tried to treat them like
men, not like parts of a machine to be discarded when we felt
like it.*

That's what the Boston Celtics were all about.

We were men. We were friends. We were family.

And we were one hell of a basketball team.

PART FOUR

Reflections

Chapter 24
Red: A Closer Look

"I deal in people, not things."

That's where he came from and that's what he did.
Auerbach. The son of a working class immigrant.
Auerbach. All-Brooklyn, Second Team.
Auerbach. Hustling his way through college.
Auerbach. The wunderkind Washington coach.
Auerbach. Unimpressed by a "local yokel."
Auerbach. A dictator. A psychologist. A pain in the ass.
Auerbach. Eleven world championships in 13 years!

What a remarkable journey it was.
To assess the man in a chapter is like trying to summarize World War II in 25 words or less.
Was he lucky? Or was he a genius?
Don't suggest "luck" to his friends. "All someone has to do is mention something derogatory about Red and I'm ready to

go to war," Indiana Hoosiers coach Bobby Knight snapped. "I think the sonofabitch is the all-time great. I just love the guy."

Great. But that doesn't answer the question. Specifically, if that superlative cast—led by Russell, Cousy, and Havlicek—had been the same, if all of the conditions and factors had been the same, but someone else—a Lapchick, a Hannum, a Holzman, a Schaus—had been the coach from 1957 through 1969, would the results have been the same?

"I can't see how," Havlicek says.

"I would have been the same," Russell believes. "I never thought there was a better basketball player than me. But would the results have been the same without Red? I have serious doubts. He was lucky to have me. But I was lucky to have him, too. I think his presence was necessary. I really do."

Freddie Schaus coached against the Redhead four times (1962, 1963, 1965, 1966) in the championship round of the playoffs, and his Lakers were beaten all four times. He is not an Auerbach fan. "You know," he says, "it's amazing how much more successful Red became when Russell became his center!"

"That's a lot of bullshit," Knight fumed. "Fuck him! Nobody knew what Russell was going to do until he got to Boston. That's like nobody wanting Bart Starr until Vince Lombardi came along. All of a sudden Starr is the best damned quarterback in the NFL because he played for Lombardi! Who drafted Sam Jones? Who took people like Sanders and Loscutoff and made them great players? Who took a nonshooting guard like KC Jones and made him a superstar? Áuerbach! That's who. I can guarantee you if any other coach in that league drafted someone as quick and agile as Russell, he'd immediately make him into an offensive player. Anybody who tells me Auerbach didn't know exactly what he was doing can just stick it up his ass."

One evening Knight visited with Havlicek, his old Ohio State teammate, after a Celtics game, and during the course of the evening's conversation Beth Havlicek volunteered: "No wonder you and Red get along. You think exactly alike."

"I thanked her," Knight smiles. "I can't think of a better compliment."

✿ ✿ ✿

If there was a symbol of Auerbach's dynasty, it had to be the victory cigar. At that precise moment when he knew victory was assured, when another victim had fallen into the path of the relentless Celtic attack, Red would reach for a stogie. And it was never a pedestrian act. He wasn't content to simply pull off the wrapper, bite off the end, strike a match and puff away. That would be boorish at best, if not downright gauche.

Indeed, from the moment Red slipped his hand inside his sports coat pocket—quite often at the urging of a vulturous Boston Garden crowd—the entire production was as unpretentious as the closing death scene in *Macbeth*.

"That really started back in Washington," Scolari says. "Talk about rubbing it in! He'd sit there with that big grin and he'd stretch his legs out in front of the bench. Then, very slowly, he'd remove the cigar from his pocket, take off the cellophane and twirl it around, light up with a big flourish, then sit back and laugh. He never changed the act over the years. But later on he did buy more expensive cigars."

"I played for something like eleven coaches in eleven years," Bob Pettit said, "and I don't know of one who wouldn't have loved the chance to ram that cigar down his throat. It irritated the devil out of them."

"It was like the Muhammad Ali Shuffle!" Willie Naulls explains. "A lot of players—especially some of those old Syracuse Nats—hated Red for that. It was his way of telling the world, 'Yeh, baby, we're still the best and you can't beat us!'"

"Arnold didn't just smoke the cigar," Walter Kennedy adds. "He actually glowed!"

What did the Celtics think of the ritual?

"I thought it was funny," Russell says. "It was part of what made us what we were."

Wasn't it just a bit ungracious, a bit unsporting, a bit unkind?

"Ungracious?" Russell laughed. "What's that got to do with it? Red was never gracious. I told you, I knew Red for what he was. That's the basis of friendship. It's like this. Suppose you have a brother who you love. He doesn't always have to be good, does he? You'd love him just as much if you had to get him out of jail. Hell, sure Red was ungracious. Who cared about that? We certainly didn't."

✿ ✿ ✿

By all indications, by the unanimous recollections of those who knew him along the way, Auerbach dominated every situation he came into contact with. Except one.

"Cousy, Red and I were at the dedication of a Catholic school gymnasium," Ed Macauley remembers. "Now I'm a Catholic. Cousy's a Catholic. But Auerbach's Jewish. He doesn't know what the hell to do. We're all standing around, waiting for the arrival of Cardinal Cushing. And believe me when I say Cardinal Cushing was *the* dominant force in Boston in those days. No Celtic, no Red Sox player, no anybody could take that away from him. So Red's asking Cooz and me: 'What do I say to him? Do I kneel down? Do I kiss his ring? What the hell am I supposed to do?'

"He was really concerned, really nervous.

"All of a sudden, up comes the Cardinal in a big black Cadillac with a chauffeur behind the wheel. Right away, Red's impressed. I don't know how he thought the man was going to arrive, but that really floored him.

"Now the Cardinal—who was a striking figure—got out of the Caddy with all his robes flowing and the little old ladies of the parish crowded around him, all shook up.

"He looked at one of his aides and said: 'Okay, I've got twenty minutes. Let's get this show on the road!' Then he spotted us. 'Hi Red! Hi Cooz! Hi Ed!'

"And—zip—he's on his way inside.

"We started to follow him, along with the rest of the crowd, and Auerbach nudges me and says, 'Boy, that's my kind of guy!'"

That was the lone exception. Otherwise, the Redhead dominated.

"That's right," Macauley agrees. "Red always came into conflict with anybody he thought might be a challenge to his authority. He got along super with Walter Brown. But he didn't get along too well with Ben Kerner, did he? And his fights with the referees are a classic example of his kind of personality. Look at the situation he had with Cooz in the beginning. He was determined to show that he was the boss, that Cousy was not going to dominate him—but rather he was going to dominate Bob. It all follows a pattern.

"Do you know where I noticed it most of all? In his driving. Red Auerbach should not be alive today. Neither should any of the players who rode in his car on some of those exhibition trips up into Maine. He had a Chevrolet convertible. In those days, for reasons of economy, you didn't travel by charter plane to somewhere like Maine. You drove. We'd have fourteen guys going in four cars, and they'd all be flipping to see who got stuck going with Red. Sometimes he'd have to single out a few of us and say: 'You're going with me. That's an order!'

"He'd be passing on hills, going seventy to eighty miles an hour on winding two-lane country roads. I guess he was trying to dominate the whole state of Maine. He's got to be the luckiest man alive.

"Those of us with any sense finally said no. I know I did, as soon as I had a family."

He was also known for incredible eating habits, particularly his craving for Chinese food.

One morning a Boston writer walked into Auerbach's hotel room in St. Louis and found the coach munching an early breakfast of Coca-Cola and cream puffs! After which, of course, he had his 8 A.M. cigar.

A killer instinct?

"He'd get us to play one-on-one with him for money, but he'd make us spot him points," Ramsey says. "Man, he'd act like he was dying or something. His face would get beet red and we'd be afraid he was having a heart attack. Next thing you know, he'd pop in two from outside and you'd owe him fifty cents. Sam and I used to play with him a lot. Once in a while he'd play with Heinsohn. Ask Tommy if Red knew how to push!"

Today Jeffrey Cohen is Red's very able front office assistant, but years ago he was just the son of Auerbach's good friend, Sammy Cohen.

"One day Red grabs me and says, 'Let's go outside and play some one-on-one.' I was only about ten years old at the time. So we went out onto the driveway and started. He did everything to me: pulled my pants, grabbed me, tripped me. I was bruised all over. My mother happened to look out the window and she was horrified. She yelled, 'Red, what are you doing to Jeffrey?'

"He said, 'I'm beating him! What do you think I'm doing?'"

A few winters ago Cohen had a much more serious encounter with his boss. It was team picture day at the Garden and Cohen, in keeping with his duties, made all the necessary arrangements. Photographers and writers milled about as he went over to Auerbach with a suggestion. The Redhead screamed at him as scores of heads turned to see what all the commotion was about. It was a prolonged, embarrassing bawling out and Cohen was understandably hurt. His only mistake had been to catch Auerbach in a nasty mood.

But minutes after, he cooled down and realized what he had done. Red went over to his young assistant and apologized. "You were right and I was wrong," he said. "I'm sorry."

"Now the only reason for repeating a story like that is for what it tells you about the man," Jeff says. "Red is everything he appears to be on the surface in terms of his emotional feelings. He lets everything come out, and damn the consequences. But then he is willing to do the necessary thing. Everybody talks about what a great ego he has. And he does. He wouldn't have been one-tenth as successful as he was without that ego. But he is also able to see beyond himself, to see that it's possible for him to be wrong sometimes. Quite often men with egos like that have great difficulty accepting the fact they've made a mistake.

"But he doesn't. Red is a very good man, even though from that story you'd wonder how in the world I could ever work for him."

Clarence Cross is a CBS executive who met Auerbach for the first time in 1975 at the NBA's annual league meetings. He recalls how the Redhead impressed him one day at lunch.

"He got talking about the pressure young kids face, especially young black kids from poor backgrounds. He described a kid living somewhere in northern Florida or Alabama and what it's like for that kid to come from a shack where no one ever paid much attention to him and go right into a big high school where the coach falls all over him, and then go on to college where another coach promises him the world. Then all of a sudden he has the kid completing his eligibility and leaving without a degree, heading back to the shack and a life of welfare or pea picking. He really gets aroused. 'Jesus Christ, they talk about trouble makers, but no one stops to think how the world has been playing Jekyll and Hyde with the kid. They don't realize the stresses that can put on a kid's mind.'

"I was fascinated listening to him. That's a very large understanding. He's talking knowledgeably and forcefully about a culture that, theoretically, he should know nothing about.

"If you only think of the Celtics when you think of Auerbach, you get the impression he worships excellence and winning. And it's true. He does. But he also understands the other side of life."

That was not the same Auerbach that Jim Murray once described in the *Los Angeles Times:* "When he gets mad, which is a good part of the time, he glows in the dark. . . . A top sergeant with corns has a better outlook on life. . . . He's been pelted with eggs in St. Louis, rotten vegetables in Chicago and snowballs in Syracuse. . . . His court-side deportment at times is so bad he would be expelled from a bar brawl . . . the league extracts enough from him in fines to pay its mailing costs each year. . . ."

One of the Redhead's major fines—a $350 stiff—was the direct result of quotes attributed to him by *New York Journal-American* writer Warren Pack in 1962. When the penalty was announced Pack called to say he was sorry—but never got past the first word.

"You sonofabitch! You're out to get me! You stabbed me in the back. I'll never talk to another New York writer as long as I live. . . ."

"He went on like that for another minute or so," Pack said. "Then he paused and asked, 'How's your family?' "

But no writer ever got under his skin more than the mischievous Clif Keane of the *Boston Globe*. If needling had been a professional sport, Keane would have been its Russell. As the leader of the pro-Cousy pack in 1950, Keane automatically headed up the anti-Auerbach forces in town. "He was hostile towards me from the beginning," Red insists. "Auerbach has always been more lucky than good," Clif feels.

One year early in the dynasty, when their feud was still hot, Keane entered a Boston hospital for a gall bladder operation. The very first call he received after surgery came from the enemy.

"How are you doing?" a low voice asked.

"Is this you, Red?" Keane replied, just a bit baffled.

"Who the hell do you think it is? How are you?"

"Okay."

"Good. Hurry up and get better."

That same afternoon Keane's door swung open and Sam Jones walked in, bearing an overflowing basket of fruit and a card which read: "Get well. The Celtics."

"I never got over Auerbach doing that," Clif says.

In his dramatic autobiography, *Go Up For Glory*, Russell wrote:

> Characters.
> So were they all. The old professionals who were playing out the string with us; the superstars who made us champions; the determined, dogged fighters who gave us the juice to keep going; the young rookies who came in and proved they had a place on the squad.
> The biggest character of all was the balding little man with the big bank account.
> Arnold Auerbach.
> The dictator.
> The man who ran this team like a symphony, covering all the discordant notes beneath the sheer momentum of the score.
> Auerbach . . . the real character of our cast.

* * *

It always surprised me to pick up a paper and see myself described as a tough bastard. I never thought that was me at all. People assumed I was flamboyant and outgoing, but in reality I'm a little bit of an introvert, and I also happen to be a very good listener.

I deal in people, not things. I've been blessed with good friends.

I think I'm a good friend, too—but I'm a bad enemy. I may forgive, which is a good point, but I don't forget. By that I mean I'll forgive up to a certain point, but I'll keep watching.

Sometimes I think I was misunderstood. I never allowed myself to get too close to my players. You've got to realize that there's close and too close.

What do I mean? Well, you can get close to a player by trying to understand his problems at home, if he has any; by being aware of his financial situation; by sharing thoughts on the game itself with him. But while he is a player I've always felt you must be careful not to become too emotionally attached to him. That's why I never went to parties with my guys, and I never cared to get real close to their wives and kids. If the time ever came that I decided to trade a player, I didn't want to be thinking about things like how much his wife loved her home or his kids loved their school.

The most distasteful part of coaching to me—by far—was having to tell a guy he was being traded or released or cut from training camp. That aspect of the job bothered me right up until the day I retired. Maybe that's one of the reasons so few Celtics were ever traded. It was always a traumatic experience for me. I felt the same way about rookies in camp. How do you suppose I'd have felt dealing away a guy I was buddy-buddy with? I just could never visualize trading a Frank Ramsey, a KC Jones, a Tom Sanders. Never. I couldn't do it. Even the deal involving Ed Macauley bothered me, despite the fact it meant getting Russell. When Ed says Walter Brown didn't want to allow it, he's absolutely right. Macauley was a Celtic and a great one, but I honestly believed the deal was a good one for Ed as well for us, partly because he loved St. Louis, but mainly because of the situation with his little boy. He left us before we started winning titles, and he even helped beat us out of the 1958 championship, but in my mind he will always be a Boston Celtic, one of my guys.

The players knew how much it killed me to make cuts, so one year they pulled a mean joke. Actually, it was kind of fun-

ny, but I didn't think so at the time. It was at the end of training camp in 1960 and only one more cut had to be made. Either Satch, who was my first draft choice that year, or Jim Smith was going to go. Smith was a big kid from Steubenville, Ohio, who I had drafted a couple of years earlier. He was a free agent trying out again and he really did a wonderful job, but everyone knew Sanders was going to beat him out. I postponed the dirty work until the last possible moment. Finally we came to our closing exhibition game and some of my clowns got a bright idea. They convinced Smith that his only hope was to ignore me when I tried to cut him. They said I'd appreciate that kind of spirit.

So I walked into the locker room after the game and as I passed him I said, "Jim, would you step into the office, please?" I went ahead and waited. No Smith. So I popped my head out the door and yelled, "Jim!" Still no Smith. Now I'm wondering what the hell's going on. It's tough enough I've got to break this bad news to the kid. I didn't need any extra aggravation. I walked out into the locker room and went up to him. "Jim," I said softly, "didn't you hear me?"

He jumped up and screamed, "No, no, you sonofabitch! I won't go."

Jesus Christ, I almost fell over. Then I happened to notice Ramsey, Loscutoff and a few of the others with shit-eatin' grins on their faces.

My fault, I told myself. I should have guessed.

As the years went by my reputation grew. I don't mean the part about being a bastard, but the stuff about being a genius and that kind of crap. Some people said I was lucky. Once upon a time some people thought the earth was flat. What was I supposed to do? Worry about their opinions?

The praise and the tributes and the accolades were something else again. They were very nice, and I appreciated them, but they were also potentially destructive. One of my biggest concerns as a coach was making sure my guys didn't get fat heads with all of their success. There had to be some kind of proper perspective maintained or else we'd have been buried in our own press clippings.

*That went for the coach, too. That's one of the reasons I was
so careful not to hang around the locker room talking with the
writers after each game. Too many coaches get caught up in
this "I, I, I" business: "I did this and I did that . . ." I saw
this happen once with Al Cervi, back in the '50s. He made the
mistake of using the first person too much when he had those
great teams in Syracuse. One year the players got fed up with
it and voted him out of a playoff share. The vote was 10–1. He
started yelling about it on an airplane, so Dolph Schayes stood
up and said, "I just changed my vote. That makes it unanimous."*

*Cervi was a good coach. He was a tough guy from the old
school and he really knew how to motivate, but he never gave
his players enough credit. Finally they rebelled.*

*I learned a good lesson from his experience. "Talk to the
players," I'd tell the writers. "They're the ones who did it."*

I always followed a personal set of rules in my coaching.

*Back in college they convinced me that the best way to go
into a test was not too hungry and not too full—maybe just a
little bit hungry. That way your mind operates better, you
think better, and you do a better job. When I arrived at the
bench before a ball game, I wanted to be like a tiger. I wanted
to be alert, aggressive, maybe a bit hostile. I wanted to be
ready to fight.*

*So I'd eat a sandwich or something very light around two
o'clock in the afternoon, and that was all I'd eat until after the
game. I still do that, even though I'm no longer on the bench.
Many times somebody will come into my office around 5:30
and say, "Hey, let's grab an early dinner." I always refuse.
Maybe it's true what they say about old dogs and new tricks. I
don't know. But I know I'm still hungry every time I watch the
Celtics play.*

*The same thing went for drinking. First of all, I've never
been a drinking man. I don't particularly like the taste of liquor. Once in a while I'd have a social drink, but I'd never,
never have a drop—not even a beer—on the day of a game. I
didn't want a ballplayer to smell liquor on my breath. I never
wanted anyone to think I needed false courage to say what I*

was going to say. And I didn't believe in being sneaky, like having a drink and then using a mouthwash, or maybe drinking vodka because it doesn't smell. I was no hypocrite to my ball club.

Maybe it all sounds like a lot of superstition, but it wasn't. There was a very good foundation in those ideas.

I got hooked on Chinese food a long time ago. It's not fried, so it's easily digestible. It's steamed or quick-cooked or something like that. I could eat a pile of it after a ball game and then go right to bed.

That's really where it started. And then I got to love the stuff.

But knock on wood, I've always been fortunate when it comes to health and eating habits. I can eat anything at any time. Hell, I can go out and eat a corned beef sandwich on top of a salami sandwich at three o'clock in the morning and then sleep like a baby. That's with potato salad, pickles—the whole bit.

I was lucky that way. I never missed a practice or a game because of illness—not once in 20 years on the bench. That doesn't mean I wasn't sick once in a while, of course. I remember one time when I really came down with some goddamned flu or something. It wasn't too bad when I got to the game, but they had the basketball floor set up over the hockey rink. My teeth were chattering all night long. I covered myself with towels, took an aspirin and sat there until the game ended. Then I beat it back to the hotel, drew a hot tub, got all the hot tea I could hold and sweated it right out of my system.

The next day I felt fine again.

One thing that I kept hearing over and over was that I was a poor loser. A lousy loser.

People—especially writers—were always trying to analyze my personality. Overlooking, for a moment, the fact the average sportswriter knows as much about psychology as I know about neurosurgery, let's just say they missed the point.

Did Auerbach have to win at everything? Yes and no.

If you're talking about basketball, emphatically yes. The game was my livelihood, my whole guts. I had to win. I want-

ed to be good in whatever I did. I wanted to be the very best teacher I could possibly be. I wanted to be the very best player I could possibly be. And I wanted to be the very best coach I could possibly be.

Could I be a good coach and lose? To me, that's like asking if a guy can be a good doctor even though his patients keep dying. When it came to basketball—whether it was playing in Brooklyn or coaching in Boston—winning meant everything to me.

Did I have to win at everything? *Of course not. The concept of winning was not basic to my whole personality. I don't care what anybody tells you. I play handball. I play tennis. I play those games to win, sure, but I don't cheat or go into fits of rage if I'm beaten. I'm happy to get a good workout. The same is true of my investments. I could sell some stock and see it go up 10 points the following week and it wouldn't bother me. I'm realistic enough to know that if you hit one out of two, or one out of three, in this life we live, you're doing pretty well.*

Winning has its place. That place in my life happened to be on a basketball court.

After all I've said about controlling my ego and letting my players take the bows, let me explain how the cigar thing got started. It had nothing to do with winning at first, but was intended to irritate the Commissioner's office. It was a symbol of rebellion at Podoloff. Again, let me make it clear: Podoloff did a fine job, and in many ways I liked and respected him.

But I was his whipping boy, and don't let anyone kid you about that. I wasn't a big college coach when I started out. I was some poor, dumb schlemiel who had done a little bit of coaching in high school, and now I had the audacity to think I could compete against Joe Lapchick, Ole Olsen, Eddie Gottlieb, Honey Russell and giants like that. Who the hell was Red Auerbach?

I'd get fined while Joe—if he was really bad—might get a reprimand.

Lapchick used to light up a cigarette and relax whenever the Knicks had a game in the bag. So cool. So confident. It was that New York smugness type of thing.

Podoloff didn't mind it if Joe smoked on the bench, so he couldn't very well object if Auerbach did it, too. But I never smoked cigarettes. Besides, what expresses contentment, relaxation and celebration any clearer than a big, fat cigar?

So I started puffing away and there wasn't a damned thing they could do about it. If Podoloff got upset when I sat back and lit one up, beautiful. That just made the cigar taste sweeter.

Then, of course, the thing caught on with the public and I was trapped. It became a big image. That wasn't the idea in the beginning, but I liked it. Even an introvert can have charisma. When I started winning championships the governor was coming out of the stands to give me a light! Once it caught on the way it did, I couldn't back off.

A lot of people didn't like it. One night we had a game in Cincinnati and I found out the management there had passed out 5,000 free cigars to its customers. It was a big clutch game, back when the Royals had guys like Robertson, Lucas, Twyman and Embry and they were our biggest rivals in the East. The arena was sold out. They thought they were going to run all over us and then have 5,000 nuts blowing cigar smoke in our faces.

I gave my guys a speech that night that got them so hopped up they raced out there and ran them off the floor in the first five minutes. The only guy who lit up a cigar that night was me.

One day, just before the 1965 playoffs started, I picked up a paper and saw a picture of myself. It kind of shocked me. "My God," I thought, "do I look that bad?" I had a dead cigar stump in my mouth, bags under my eyes and a look of complete exhaustion.

Until that moment I hadn't fully realized what I had been doing to myself. That was the year Walter died. I was general manager, coach, scout, everything. I worried about the team's transportation, I ran the front office, I sat in on all of the NBA's Board of Governors meetings, I negotiated our lease with the Garden, I supervised ticket sales, I worked out the deals for radio and TV coverage and I kept as many speaking dates as

*my schedule would allow. Emotionally and physically, I was
drained.*

*A beautiful thing happened early that season. I got a call
from Ramsey. He had retired in 1964 and was now up to his
ears in all of his business activities back home in Kentucky.
"Red," he said, "there's no way you can continue doing this.
You're going to kill yourself. Something's got to give. So, look,
if you ever need me for anything—if I can help you carry that
load for a while—you put in a call to my home and I'll be right
up to do whatever I can."*

*Ramsey was right. I was going to hurt myself. Even if I
didn't, I was going to hurt the ball club. And that was even
worse.*

*You can't always pick your spots. I could have retired right
then, right after that 1965 championship. It would have been
easy and no one would have blamed me.*

*Yet it bothered me. Would people say I was quitting while I
was on top? Would they say I got out while the getting was
good?*

*All throughout my career I operated with the idea that I
didn't give a good goddamn what anybody thought or said
about me. I was me. Take me or leave me. I let my record do
my talking.*

*But after 19 years in the league, I did care. They could call
me a bastard, a poor sport, an egotist—anything they felt like
calling me—but I didn't want to be called a quitter. That was
very important to me.*

*So I made a decision. I would quit. The time had come, but
not while I was on top. They would never say that about me
because I would never give them a chance to.*

*I announced I would retire, but I announced it one year
ahead of time. I said 1966 would be my final year on the Boston bench.*

Freddie Schaus and the Lakers knew it.

Jack McMahon and the Royals knew it.

Richie Guerin and the Hawks knew it.

*The whole world knew. They had one more shot at Auer-
bach.*

There were no guarantees I would go out with a winner.

Heinsohn had just retired. Cousy, Sharman, Ramsey and Loscutoff were gone. We were getting old fast. We had seven straight championships in our pockets, eight out of nine altogether.

No one could possibly predict what would happen in 1966.

That was the longest year of my life, but we won another championship. We were still on top.

When I walked out of the locker room that night there was a lump in my throat. And, yes, I did cry later on. But there were no regrets. I was tired. That part of my life was over and I accepted the fact.

I couldn't have felt that way in 1965, but in 1966 I walked out of Boston Garden beholden to no man.

Except, of course, those beautiful guys who wore the Green.

Chapter 25
The Worthy Opposition

"I'd rather have them adjust to me than me adjust to them."

"I've never known anybody who played under Red Auerbach who didn't like him," Russell once said. "Of course, I've never known anybody who played *against* him who did like him!"

Certainly Harry "the Horse" Gallatin, a Knickerbocker star of the early '50s, would agree to that. "Nobody has to get me up to play the Celtics," Harry explained one day. "All I have to do is look over there at Auerbach."

Unfortunately, history has misplaced the name of one NBA personality who probably best captured the common view of the Redhead. "When I first met Auerbach I disliked him," the *Boston Record* quoted the unknown foe. "But gradually it grew to hate."

Perhaps it's best he remains nameless, for like the Unknown Soldier in Arlington's tomb he represents the multitudes.

The Celtics were a scourge, a menace, indeed a plague visited upon the NBA throughout the years of Auerbach's dynasty, and human nature—not to mention the Almighty Dollar—being what it is, Boston's perennial success did not engender warmth among the brethren.

"If those Celtics weren't that great, we'd have been the best team for a number of years," Ben Kerner wistfully noted. "But there's no room for second best. I can remember so many big playoff games when we'd lose to Boston and nobody would come into our dressing room to talk with our guys afterwards. Everyone wanted to talk with the Celtics. We'd leave Boston the next morning all alone, huddled together on that airplane as if we had lost everything in the world. And, in a sense, as professionals we had lost everything. It was so frustrating."

Jerry West can fully understand Kerner's commiseration.

"It hurt so much to play as hard as you could, year after year, only to find out that it wasn't quite enough. It's such a tremendous letdown to sit in front of your locker, alone with your thoughts, and realize your season is over while down the hall the Celtics are celebrating once again. I don't care who you are, you'd love to know what it must be like to be in that other room."

For 13 years, frustration was the order of the day as Auerbach's Celtics ran amok.

"We used to call them the Green Wave," says Paul Silas, the former Celtics star who played with the Hawks through the last five years of the dynasty. "You just knew that at any moment that wave was going to come swooping down on you. They were awesome because of the pressure they continually applied. That was their whole concept. Pressure basketball. They would pick you up at one end line and beat you all the way down to the other. And if you let up for just a second, they'd run ten or twelve straight points right past you."

Earl Lloyd, a premier forward of the '50s with Syracuse and Detroit, remembers Red's Celtics. "It was so tough going into Boston. You knew your chances of winning were very, very slim. You began the game with the attitude you were probably going to get creamed. They were so tough, so well drilled, so disciplined. The thing that impressed me most was that every single one of them knew his job. KC knew he never had to score a point as long as he played the Big D. Cooz knew exactly what he was doing whenever he got the ball. And Lord knows Russell knew what he was doing! Just when you got rid of Heinsohn, Ramsey came in to kill you. That was the genius of Auerbach. He had everybody playing to his strength. You'd work your butt off, all the while knowing you were about to get killed. Then, with about a minute to go and your tail really dragging, you'd see Red sit back, cross his legs and suck on that cigar. Believe me, it did not make you particularly happy."

It certainly didn't please Freddie Schaus.

"Fred is one of the really nice people in this world," West insists. "But one of the things that bothered him so much was the fact we never beat Boston. He really had trouble accepting that. Quite often he was incensed. If we were behind by ten points with only a minute to go, Red would call a time-out and that would absolutely drive Fred crazy."

Don Nelson played with the Lakers in 1964 and 1965 prior to joining the Celtics. He concurs with West.

"Schaus carried on a private vendetta against Red," Nellie says. "He hated him so much for lighting up that cigar in his face, year after year. Auerbach was never the nicest winner, you know. And that really bothered Freddie. I can remember sitting in the Los Angeles locker room before a game with Boston and listening to him carry on about Red this and Red that. Instead of preparing us for the game, Freddie would rave for five or ten minutes about Auerbach! But no one interrupted. Frankly, we didn't like Red either."

Auerbach, well aware of his adversary's discomfort, took great delight in administering an occasional needle. In the winter of 1961–62, for example, the year the West-Baylor-Schaus Lakers first emerged as a power (54–26), the Redhead raised a ruckus over Baylor's military activities during a Celtics visit to the West Coast. The great star was playing games while on leave. "That's not fair and it should not be allowed," Auerbach told LA writers. "If Baylor plays four times against us, he should play four times against Cincinnati, too! That's only right." It was only horsefeathers, of course, but it certainly caused a furor for days after Boston's departure.

Today, fully a decade after open hostilities ceased, Schaus still finds the subject of Auerbach quite annoying.

"I'll say this," Freddie began. "I admired his ability to

coach. He always kept his team hustling and hungry. But I did not like the man. I didn't like the goddamned way he rubbed salt in our wounds. Red Auerbach will never be known as a gracious winner."

What made the Auerbach dynasty so amazing was the quality of opposition it had to deal with over the years. Those weren't paper tigers on the other benches.

"In pro basketball, every man has been an All-American in college," Russell wrote in *Go Up For Glory.* "There are only eleven—and actually each team plays with its seven best— and when you get the seven best playing out there, you have a game, baby, make no doubt of it."

"There weren't two leagues back then," Loscutoff points out, "and when we first started winning championships there were only eight teams in the whole NBA. With eleven men on a roster, that meant the eighty-eight best players in the world were thrown together. You want to talk about fundamentals? Maybe today's players are bigger and faster and everything else, but modern teams can't compare with those old St. Louis, Syracuse and Philadelphia teams when it comes to being fundamentally sound. And we beat the shit out of all of them!"

"Keep something in mind," Heinsohn suggested. "Not only were most of the teams deep and sound in those early days, but all of them saved their very best efforts for when Boston came to town. There were no soft touches. After a while it seemed like the whole world was against us."

If not the whole world, as Heinsohn saw it, surely whole cities were united in anti-Celtic passion.

"When the fans in Syracuse paid their admission," Johnny Most remembers, "they believed that made them participants in the game. They were never just spectators when the Nats and Celtics went at it."

One night a group of fans actually invaded a Boston huddle and all hell broke loose. "Loscy and Conley were knocking them down as fast as they came," Howie McHugh laughs. "Then a cop lost his hat and Jim belted him by mistake. That certainly got us into some hot water."

Then there was the night Loscutoff's fierce predecessor, Bob Brannum, walked onto the Syracuse court and the fans hurled thousands of paper hatchets at him. "See that, Bob?" Auerbach grinned at his startled 'policeman.' "You don't have to score points to be a celebrity."

Auerbach proved that point in St. Louis, where he was the focus of every Missourian's wrath.

"Oh, boy," Kerner smiles. "Red was really something. Not many coaches or managers sell tickets in sports. Casey Stengel did. So did Durocher and Lombardi. But Auerbach sold more tickets in St. Louis than my whole promotion department! Our fans used to have egg-throwing contests, and you should have heard the cheers when he got hit. Anything was possible when Red came to town, like the time he punched me in the mouth. Red never acted like a visitor. It was incredible. He'd walk into my building and try to take over everything. He'd yell at my scorer, give directions to my announcer, jump all over the referees and incite the crowd to a frenzy. Talk about charisma! Red was the greatest of all time."

On March 1, 1966, Auerbach made his final coaching appearance in the city which had long ago proclaimed him Public Enemy No. 1. Before the game Kerner had Red come out to halfcourt for a good-bye ceremony and the presentation of several gifts. But before a word could be spoken, the 10,000 fans on hand stood up and gave the Redhead a thunderous ovation—waves and waves of tremendous applause which swept across the court and left the guest of honor misty-eyed and shaken.

"My sincere thanks to you," Red responded. "I've taken some potshots at you people and you've deserved them! But this really touches me. I appreciate it. Thank you and good-bye."

Then, just before he left the mike, he blurted out an afterthought: "You're lucky to have Ben Kerner!"

The confidence Red's teams projected was an enormous weapon all by itself.

"We were like Ali going into a ring, knowing he could toy with somebody," Cousy says.

Snatch puts it more vividly. "We were kickin' ass and takin' names!"

More than one opponent—indeed, probably a great majority

of them—would have jumped at an opportunity to wear the Green, for the Celtics had an aura not unlike the romantic phenomenon of Yankee Pinstripes.

"I think if you asked any player back in those days," Earl Lloyd says, "he'd have told you he would like to be a Celtic. No question.

"I almost got traded to Boston once and I remember thinking how much I would have enjoyed playing for Auerbach. Sure, he bothered me with that cigar routine. But I'd watch him stomping around, yelling at the officials and ranting and raving, and I'd secretly admire the way he fought for his players. He had a purpose other than simply infuriating the rest of us. He knew the Celtics would see him doing those things in their behalf, and then they'd say, 'Hey, if he's doing all that for us, let's go out and do something for him!'

"They had a very beautiful tradition. Teams would walk into Boston Garden—a lot of people won't admit this—and they'd try not to look up at all those championship flags. I'm not saying opponents cowered or anything like that. But you tried not to look up. Sometime during the night, however, you'd steal a peek. And there they were: 1957, 1959, 1960, 1961 and on and on and on. Tell me any man would not want to be a part of that!"

The most intriguing match-up of all would have been if Chamberlain and Auerbach had teamed up, rather than Russell and Auerbach.

Their paths had crossed years before Wilt's NBA debut. In the early '50s, when Chamberlain was still a schoolboy sensation in Philadelphia, he spent a summer up at Kutsher's, one of many plush resorts in the Catskills which formed what came to be known as the Borscht Belt. College stars would work as bellhops during the day, then play for resort-sponsored teams by night.

Auerbach was the Kutsher's coach. Eddie Gottlieb, practically swooning over the prospect of having Wilt play for the Warriors, suddenly panicked when he thought of Auerbach and Chamberlain alone. All Red had to do was sell the wondrous giant on the idea of matriculating at Harvard, Boston College or some other New England institution, and there went Gottlieb's dream, for Boston would be able to exercise territorial rights.

"If that kid even thinks about blowing town for Boston," Eddie roared at Milt Kutsher, "I'll turn your joint into a bowling alley!"

Then, in an unprecedented move that has never been repeated, Gottlieb persuaded his fellow NBA governors to guarantee the Warriors territorial claim to Wilt while he was still in high school!

From that day on, Red and Wilt—who might have made a beautiful couple—were embarked on a collision course.

Their paths finally crossed in 1959–60, Chamberlain's rookie season, the beginning of the Chamberlain vs. Russell era.

"I've always had this belief," Gottlieb says today. "If Auerbach had been coaching my Warriors and somebody else was coaching Russell and the Celtics, I think we'd have won with Red and Wilt together. That has always been my contention, because I think Red would have gotten more out of Wilt than any other coach in the world."

Perhaps it wasn't fair, but it surely was inevitable that Chamberlain's stature in the game would be directly influenced by the results of his head-on battles with Russell, despite both men's protestations that the real issue was team vs. team. When West, Baylor, Robertson, Pettit, Schayes and all of the other superluminaries of the game fell before the Boston juggernaut, it was generally understood the Celtics were simply too much to cope with. When the Warriors—and later, the 76ers and Lakers—bowed to Boston, it was always viewed as another example of Russell's mastery over Wilt. In the whole history of team sports, no rivalry was ever as personalized as Chamberlain vs. Russell.

"Russell did a job on him psychologically," Sanders mused, "because Russell is all Wilt ever talked about."

In the eyes of Boston's players, the distinction between the two giants was clear.

"Russell made the talent around him better," Sanders says. "Chamberlain did not."

"There are two types of superstars," Nelson advises. "One type makes himself look better at the expense of the other four men on the floor. The other type makes the other four men look better. That's the kind of superstar Russell was. He made a Don Nelson look great."

In his best-selling book, *Wilt*, Chamberlain says: "Had Wilt been surrounded by the playing cast that Russell was with the Boston Celtics, and had he had a Red Auerbach as coach, his team might have won all those championships."

Then he goes on to a startling rationalization, giving great credence to Sanders's observations about the psychological aftermath of Chamberlain vs. Russell: "It may sound like sour grapes, but I really think Bill is a shallower man for all his basketball triumphs, and rather than my being angry or envious over his victories and his gloating and his raps at me, I feel sorry for him."

He may be the only man in league history who feels sorry for Russell.

Most of the others, it can be safely assumed, would nod in agreement with Havlicek's assessment:

"The whole thing is to win the championship. Talk to players from other teams who have had great careers, but never won a title, and ask them what they would really like to have done in their careers, and the first thing that pops up is: 'I would rather have played on a championship team than to have had all the personal victories I gained.' That's how I felt. That's how we all felt in Boston."

Let's get one thing straight: I never rubbed it up a coach's ass and I never knocked somebody else's ballplayers! Okay?

Check the records and you'll never find me quoted as saying some other coach did a lousy job, or such-and-such a player stinks. I would never, ever make any comments like that about opposing teams. Hundreds of times someone in New York would ask me: "What's the matter with the Knicks?" I'd always answer: "Hey, I've got my own problems. Do you want to know what's wrong with the Knicks? Go ask the Knicks."

I never went out of my way to embarrass anybody. If we got a 20-point lead, sure, I'd want to make it 30. But I wouldn't try to beat someone by 50 or 60 points, as a lot of teams have done. Once I felt we had a safe enough lead I'd just tell my guys to keep playing hard, maintain their lead, keep the game out of reach. There's a big difference between staying in command of a game and trying to humiliate someone. Once my guys had complete command, I was satisfied. The killer instinct was satisfied. I've got him down and I'm going to make sure he stays down, but, goddamn it, I'm not going to kill him 10 times!

"The sun doesn't shine on the same side of the cat's ass all the time." That was another one of my sayings. It's original, isn't it?

The only time I would feel contempt for another team is when I knew they had the material and personnel to do a good job, but didn't. To be specific, a team like the San Francisco Warriors in 1964–65. They had Chamberlain, Thurmond, Attles, Rodgers, Hightower, Meschery—all those good players, although Wilt was traded that winter—and they won only 17 games all year long! Now that was absolutely ridiculous. Yet they had a good coach in Alex Hannum. He put some good teams together over the years, but he just couldn't control that bunch.

Most professional athletes are willing to pay the price, but to what extent? The players on that team, for instance, hustled, were hungry, and worked hard for a while. Then they'd figure: "Gee, it doesn't look like we're going to win, so I might as well get my points." When you talk about a team putting out, that's a very hard term to define. Maybe they don't realize what they've got. There can be a lot of factors, but usually they just aren't willing to play with their heart and blood and guts.

When I saw that happening, yes, I was contemptuous.

I thought Freddie Schaus was a good coach, a bit underrated, and very, very knowledgeable about the game.

But I detected a flaw in him. He was an insecure guy. Maybe that was because of the Los Angeles organization or the California press or just being in a big city. I don't know. I know the LA writers all felt the Lakers should have beaten us more often.

Freddie never exuded strength in his position, and a scared coach is never a good coach. If a man is afraid of his job, it's only a matter of time before he's going to blow it. You've got to go out there and do your best. If you're going to blow it, blow it yourself.

I always felt Freddie could be disturbed or ruffled. Every

*time I made a move that worked, I would make goddamned
sure he was aware of that move and aware of the fact that it
worked. I got to him. Yet I never once knocked him in the papers.*

*We drove Schaus to the point of distraction. He was so wor-
ried about what I was going to do, what new thing I was going
to come up with. Most of the time it was nothing. I just wanted
to play the ball game. We would let them think we were coming up with something unusual and Freddie would get so excited he'd start thinking about me instead of thinking about his
own ball club.*

*That was fine with me, since I always operated on the theory
that I'd rather have them adjust to me than me adjust to them.
And it always worked out that way.*

*Two of Freddie's guys—Elgin and Jerry—were among my
own all-time favorites. Mister Inside and Mister Outside.*

*Jerry was a great, great performer. I had nothing but the ut-
most respect for him. That kid came to play. If he didn't win, it
wasn't because he didn't try. Everyone thinks of him as a great
scoring guard, but in my book he was also one of the greatest
defensive guards who ever played the game. A lot of people
underrated his defense because he was so great offensively,
and quite often that's how they'd get burned. He wasn't one of
the better defensive guards; he was one of the best.*

*He was a great star who never quit. So was Baylor. I knew
Elgin back when he was in high school. He was unbelievably
quick and strong, but the thing I loved about him was that he
simply wanted to win. That made him my kind of guy.*

*What do you do when you're up against a pair like those
two? We tried to play Jerry without the ball, hoping to tire him
out as much as we could so he wouldn't hit his normal percentage of shots. Then we'd try to take him and Elgin out of their
patterns, out of their set routines, and make them play our
game. We'd try to destroy their rhythm.*

*You never completely stop talents like theirs. We expected
Jerry would get 30 and Elgin 30. That's 60. We figure to get
105. So we made sure the rest of those guys didn't get 45.*

That's the way we approached the Lakers.

❊ ❊ ❊

Although his team only had a couple of really big years against us, I want to mention Oscar, too. When people talk about the all-time great guards in NBA history, three names come up immediately: Robertson, West and Cousy.

How would I rank them?

Oscar was different. He wanted to control the game. If you were going to break down the skills of what I called the Big Three, you'd have to say Oscar had more combined skills than Jerry or Cooz. He was a great shooter, but not as good as Jerry. But he was a much better passer than West. He was also a damned good defensive player, but again not as good as Jerry. Yet he was easily the best rebounder of the three. He was also more of a leader than West, but that's mainly because he had the ball most of the time. West was more like a Sharman: he'd get the ball after it was brought down. Oscar liked to set the tempo all the time.

You can talk about Oscar and you can talk about Jerry, but for our type of game. I'd take Cousy every time. Bob could make the plays and see the court better at full speed than any guard who ever lived. If you analyzed all of their skills, Cooz would be a close third, but for running the fast break, he was the all-time great.

And now for a word or two about my friend Wilt.

I had him on my team up at Kutsher's. We were playing this other club and two of its players—Joe Holup from GW and B.H. Born from Kansas—were eating him up. We were behind at halftime when we went into one of the rooms and I started talking.

Chamberlain wasn't even listening. He lay down on a bed and covered his head.

"Hey," I yelled. "You sit up and listen!"

He said, "Gee, I'm sorry. I played so badly I wanted to hide my head in shame."

I said, "Okay, you've hidden your head. Now sit up and listen."

Even in those days, he had his own mind. I tried to explain to him what Holup and Born were doing, and I told him how to guard a pivotman properly. He insisted on doing things his way and I remember thinking that someone was going to have a tough time trying to coach him. He was only a high school kid, but he had his own theories and nobody was going to change them.

I'll give him credit for one thing, though. Chamberlain worked his ass off as a bellhop, carrying that luggage to make a buck. He really did. Then he got big money early when the Globetrotters persuaded him to quit college, and from that point on there was no such thing as anybody telling Wilt what he was going to do.

I've often been asked how I would have coached him.

There's no way to answer that question.

If I could have had him before he quit school, before he got the big dough and the no-cut contracts, that would have been a different story, but Wilt was spoiled very early.

Eddie Gottlieb was one of the greatest men in the history of this game, but Eddie spoiled Wilt badly. I could never have coached him in Philadelphia because I wouldn't have had complete control. It would have been a situation like the Jets had with Weeb Ewbank and Joe Namath. Weeb was the coach, but Sonny Werblin said, "Hey, I take over where Joe's concerned." It was that type of thing with Eddie and Wilt. For years Wilt often didn't travel with the rest of the team. There was no disciplinary control whatsoever. The man did whatever he felt like doing.

Under those conditions, he and I never would have lasted a day together. If I could have had him before he went to the Globetrotters, and if no one interfered with my authority over him, I think I could have disciplined him. But we'll never know.

There was really only one way to play against Wilt and that was to let him get his points, but shut off the rest of his team. Except for some special things we'd try in playoffs, our policy was to forget his offense and concentrate on the people around him. Many clubs would try to double-team him, or even triple-team him, but Chamberlain wasn't dumb. If he got stuck he'd just hit the open man with a pass.

We let Russell handle Wilt alone and he'd have a hard time getting 20 points as long as Bill was concentrating on him.

Many, many times he'd have 15 or 18 points halfway through the third period. We'd be way ahead, so Russ would back off and Wilt would end up with 40. The papers would say we won, but Chamberlain had outplayed Russell. That simply wasn't true.

Chamberlain was a giant among giants. I'll never take that away from him. He really was. I'll tell you something else about him: he was a damned decent guy, too. Every year he'd make it a point to get up to Kutsher's for the Maurice Stokes Benefit Game, and one year he even flew back from Europe just to participate in it. But if you're asking me who was better—Chamberlain or Russell—let me assure you it wasn't even close.

In case you think I'm being too provincial, believe me when I say there wasn't a player in the league who wouldn't have preferred having Russell on his team instead of Chamberlain.

Russell was better because he played with his head and he had the bigger heart. I think he was the better athlete, too.

There were only two times that I saw Russell get upset because of Wilt.

Chamberlain was a lot like Freddie Schaus in that he always seemed to be worried about me. I unnerved him and he didn't like that. One night I was arguing with a referee and out of the clear blue sky Wilt walked over and said, "That's enough out of you."

Immediately, Russell stepped between us. "If you're going after Red, you've got to go through me," he said.

Chamberlain flexed his muscles. "Look at this arm!" he yelled.

Russell just glared at him. "I don't give a damn what you've got," he said. "You've still got to go through me if you want Auerbach."

Bill was madder than hell and Wilt knew better than to push it any further. I've always maintained Chamberlain is the strongest man in the world, but I wouldn't want to bet on who'd walk away if he and Russell ever really mixed it up.

Bill was a great track man. Wilt fancied himself as a track man, too, but he never competed on the same levels as Russell. Bill could have been an Olympic high jumper if he hadn't played on the basketball team instead. He got so tired of reading about Chamberlain running the 440 and doing this and doing that. So one day he said to me, "Why don't you get someone to put up twenty-five thousand dollars and I'll have a one-on-one decathalon with him and beat his goddamned brains out!"

The only other time Russell ever lost his cool over Chamberlain was after the 1969 playoffs when he called Wilt a quitter for sitting down at a critical stage of the seventh game.

Was Russell right? You bet he was.

I was once asked who I would pick for an All-Opponent team.

I said West and Robertson as the guards. No question.

The forwards would be Pettit and Baylor. Again, no question.

The center? Willis Reed. First, he was a leader. Secondly, he was tremendously unconcerned about his own production. He was disciplined, he'd do what you asked him to do, he'd pay the price and—most of all—he was a winner.

All five of them were my kind of guys!

The coach? Freddie Schaus. He was an excellent coach, except against me.

While I'm at it, we'll need two referees. Give me Pat Kennedy for one, and Sid Borgia—if he'll stop making up his goddamned rules.

Chapter 26
Meanwhile, Back Home

"It was a price that had to be paid."

The young man was a bag of nerves as he slowly wheeled his car through the streets of Washington.

"Don't be silly," his date admonished. "He's not going to bite your head off."

He forced a smile. "But what's he *really* like?"

"He's like a father," she replied. "A plain old father."

He felt like saying "plain old fathers" don't coach world championship basketball teams, nor do they strike fear in the hearts of grown men, but he bit his lip and rode in silence.

"There was no way to convince him Daddy wasn't a monster," Nancy Auerbach smiles. "He had read about him and he watched some games on television in which my father got thrown out, so he just didn't know what to expect now that he was going home with me to meet him."

And if he had guessed forever he wouldn't have come close

to the scenario which greeted him upon his arrival in the Redhead's abode.

"Daddy was sitting in the den, watching TV in his under-
wear," Nancy laughs. "I introduced my date to him and he
said, 'Hi, want a salami sandwich?'"

Red and Dot—the striking coed who caught his eye one
long-ago day in the GW Student Club—have been married for
35 years now and their little girls have grown into charming,
sophisticated ladies. Nancy, who was born two months before
Red took over the Washington Caps, still lives in the D.C.
area. Randy, born in the winter of 1952—the year Sharman
teamed up with Cousy and Macauley—has an apartment in
Boston.

There's a new little girl in the Redhead's life. Her name is
Julie. She's seven years old and, as she tells her friends, her
"grandfather is famous."

"Randy and I never used to open our mouths about Daddy's
career," Nancy smiles, "but Julie is his biggest fan. He takes
her bowling, to movies like *Mary Poppins*, to all kinds of
things. It's really beautiful to watch. She's just crazy about
him."

The day Red got the call from Ben Kerner, asking him to
leave Duke University's athletic department and come to Tri-
Cities as his coach, he began paying a heavy price for the
enormous success which would come to him. While Dot and
Nancy went north, back to Washington, Auerbach headed
west to Moline.

Except for that very brief interim between Tri-Cities and
Boston, he never again went home to stay.

The Scriptures tell us man cannot serve two masters at once.
In Red's case the choice came down to his family or his career.
His family *and* his career, he always maintained, was never a
viable alternative.

For 27 years now he's lived alone in Boston, first in a downtown hotel suite, and more recently in a high-rise complex.
Between games and practices and meetings and appearances
he'd rush home and—for a day here, a weekend there, once in
a great while a string of weeks—he'd be the happy family man

again. But there was always a plane ticket lying on the bureau.

In *Go Up For Glory*, Russell described him as " . . . a lonely man, a man who spends the lonely months of the season locked up in his hotel room, eating Chinese food off a hot plate."

"Dot wasn't with him and the girls weren't with him," Macauley said. "He achieved his success in a very lonely manner. He did it all alone."

Was it too great a sacrifice?

"Red really didn't sacrifice anything," Macauley believes. "He was doing what he wanted to do. You've got to bear that in mind. But was it too much of a sacrifice for his family? That's another question."

"I'm twenty-four now," Randy says. "Up until the time I was eighteen I think he was home twice for my birthday. And he couldn't go to my high school graduation. So I didn't go either. I think the happiest memory of my life came on my eighth birthday. I wanted him to be there so much, but it just wasn't going to be possible. I understood. So Mom got a big party together and we were just getting ready to cut the cake when the doorbell rang. I went over and opened it and there was Daddy standing there with his arms open, saying, 'Hi, Randy! Hi, Nancy! Hi, Mommy!' You never forget things like that."

"Did I miss him?" Nancy repeated. "Yeah. Very much at times. If you had a problem, you wanted to talk about it *now*, not in a couple of weeks when he got home. They weren't really big things. Maybe they were even foolish. But they seemed important at the time."

Yet Red shares a relationship with his daughters today that contradicts his absentee record.

"Right in the middle of my wedding reception, the band played a particular song," Nancy remembers. "It just hit me a certain way, and as I walked over to him tears were pouring through my veil. He reached out, put his arms around me and comforted me, and right at that moment someone snapped a picture of us. We had never had a father-and-daughter picture taken, but I've got that one today and it's very, very special to me.

"I've always felt close to my father. No, he wasn't there a lot of the times when I really wanted to see him, but in a way he *was* there. There were phone calls every day, and telegrams and cards and presents. Sometimes he has a hard time showing affection, but he never forgets. Like he'll call me on Mother's Day and say: 'Get your mother some flowers. And get your grandmother some, too. I'll pay you when I get home. Oh! And get some for yourself.' I'd laugh and tell him I wasn't going to buy myself flowers! But that's the way he is.

"The day Julie was born I called him in Boston to tell him he had a granddaughter. Naturally he wasn't in Washington. I said, 'Daddy, I had a little girl.' Right away I could tell he was very touched. He wanted to know if I thought he should come right down and I said no, stay in Boston for his playoff game that night. The next day he walked into my hospital room with Randy and I showed him the baby. He looked at her and didn't say a word for a minute. Then he turned to me and said, 'She'll need a nose job!'

"You know something? My grandmother told me those were the very same words he said when he first saw me."

"People have asked me what it was like not having him around all the time," Randy says. "I tell them I know an awful lot of kids whose fathers worked nine to five and they don't get along with them at all. In our case, it wasn't the quantity of time he spent with us. It was the quality. We always looked forward to him coming home. We'd be all over him and sometimes he'd get mad and say: 'I can handle Bob Cousy, I can handle Bill Russell, I can handle all these ballplayers, but when I get home it's women, women, women and I can't handle them!'

"And he was right. I could twist him around my finger. He wasn't very strict at all. But there were two things he always insisted on, and I can remember him saying this over and over to Nancy and me: *honesty* and *respect*! Those things were very big with him."

When friends from Boston saw him at home in Washington, they were amazed to discover what a homebody the Redhead could be.

"Red could have fun with his kids like very few men I've known," Sammy Cohen says. "It was hard to imagine how a man could be away from home as long as Red was, and then walk in the front door and act as if he'd never been gone."

"I'm sure he's missed a lot in the family scheme of things," Havlicek smiles, "but, believe me, when Auerbach walks into that home he's the Candy Man!"

When you talk with his daughters, you pick up traces of the Redhead's influence.

"When I was about thirteen," Nancy says, "I was playing in a kickball game up at Kutsher's, where we spent our summers. For some reason, a girl on the other team started to heckle me and I really got annoyed. We began exchanging words and then she shoved me. So I hit her. I had never hit anybody in my entire life, but this was a great shot. She had a bloody nose and a black eye. Well, word spread around Kutsher's almost immediately and my father, who had been playing cards, came running over. I was a nervous wreck. But then he grabbed me and said, 'Nancy, that's the greatest thing you ever did. That shows some guts!'

"That was always a big thing with my father: 'Show a little guts, Nancy! Don't let people walk all over you.'

"He always used to tell me: 'Nancy, there's such a thing as being nice and such a thing as being stupid. And sometimes you're stupid!' "

What was the distinction?

"Being stupid is when you're nice and people take advantage of it," she smiled. "That was another one of his big lessons."

The real story of the Auerbach home is Dot.

"She is a remarkable lady," Bob Faris says. "That beautiful family is really a tribute to her because of the way she kept it together all the while Red was traveling around the country."

"That's true," Zang Auerbach agrees. "She's a doll. And those two daughters of theirs are sweet young gals. They've had almost everything they ever wanted from the word go, and yet they've never been in a bit of trouble or caused their parents a day of regret. And I've got news for you. In today's society, that's no small statement. Dot did a wonderful job in that home."

But she paid a stiff price for all those flags in Boston Garden.

"It wasn't easy for her," Nancy says. "The neighbors would throw a party and say, 'You and Red come over!', but Red was never there. And Mom never wanted to be the spare wheel, so she stayed home. It wasn't fun, I'm sure, going to PTA meetings by herself and things like that, but she handled it beautifully. She was great."

"I'm tough and independent," Dot explains. "I was never one who dreamed of someday being the wife of a celebrity and living in the lap of luxury and all that. I never cared about those things. It's like the time Red bought his first Cadillac. I asked him, 'What do we need a Cadillac for? I don't want a fancy car. I want to be able to ride around town in my dungarees.' And he said, 'Dot, when you drive a Cadillac you can wear any damned thing you please!' So I wore my jeans and drove my Cadillac."

She developed a coolness in the face of pressure. No crises alarmed her. No problems overwhelmed her.

One hot summer day as she sat in front of their first home, watching rush hour traffic go by, Nancy came running out to her, screaming that the drapes in Randy's room were on fire.

"I ran upstairs," she remembers, "and there really were flames. The kids were naturally upset, so I told them: 'Don't cry and don't be scared, because we're all fine and that's the important thing.' Then I took them outside and called the Fire Department.

"They went running in with axes and hoses, the whole bit, and there was all kinds of excitement. Suddenly the phone rang. It was Mister Auerbach calling to see how everything was.

"He said, 'Where the hell were you? The phone's been ringing off the hook!' I said, 'I had some trouble getting to it because of the fire.' And he said, 'Fire? What kind of fire?' I said, 'Oh, you know, a regular fire with hoses and engines and hook-and-ladders . . .'"

She laughs at the recollection.

"What was I supposed to do? Panic? It was just one of those things. So I told the girls, 'Let's sit down and enjoy all of the excitement, because there's nothing we can do about it.' And that's what we did."

If there's any question about Dot's acceptance of the unconventional life-style imposed on her by her husband's career, it may be answered in her appraisal of Red's association with the Celtics.

"First of all," she says, "I often thought about the arrangement and wondered if it wouldn't be smarter for us to move up there with him. But then I'd tell myself he's got all these TV appearances, radio shows, banquets, speaking engagements and so on. He wouldn't have time to take the kids to the movies or to go to PTA meetings anyway. It just wouldn't work. He couldn't attain the heights of his career and still be home with us every night.

"So we accepted that.

"And to tell you the truth, I think I'll be very sad when the day comes he leaves the Celtics for good. I mean that. There's been something very special about Red Auerbach and the Boston Celtics. The phone in this home rings all the time with calls from KC Jones, Bill Russell and all of the other great guys who played for him. When Frank Ramsey retired he gave us a silver tray with mint julep glasses, a beautiful thing, inscribed: 'Thanks for ten wonderful years.'

"The Celtics are very special people to the girls and me.

"The night Red coached his last game we talked on the telephone afterwards. Do you want to know what I told him? I said, 'I've been following this game for years. I know what's going on. But I can't even name two-thirds of the coaches in the league today. But whenever you coached—whether they liked you or hated you; whether they came to cheer you or to boo you—they knew who you were! When it came to coaching, you were Mister Basketball.'"

If a guy's going to be a success in coaching, one of two things must be true: (a) he has a super, fantastic, understanding wife; or (b) he's a bachelor.

Did I miss out on a lot in my personal family life? Yes. Yes, I did. Could there have been a better way for me to handle it? No. Absolutely not.

You can't have a normal family life and still do your best at coaching. I don't care what anybody says. That's impossible. You end up bringing your team's troubles into the home and your family's troubles back to the team.

I missed Dot and the girls very much, but I had to have my solitude. It was a price that had to be paid.

You know they always say—and it's true—that an unhappy ballplayer is a bad ballplayer. This might be a weak analogy, but an unhappy wife—even if she's with you all the time—is much worse than a happy wife whom you don't see every single day. Dot and I were realistic. We knew the demands of my job, and we knew the type of individual I am and the emphasis I'd put on achieving success. It wouldn't have been any better if she lived in Boston with me. First, between all of the road games and the local obligations, I wouldn't have been home that much anyway. And second, when I was home I'd be getting pestered like hell by every social organization in town to go here and speak there.

The way we worked it out, I'd sneak home for two, three, four days at a time and nobody would bother us.

Later on in my career it probably would have been different. She could have moved up here then, but by that time our whole pattern was much too ingrained. It was too late in life to rearrange things.

There were many times I'd get up to leave on another trip and really feel like a heel, especially when the girls were young. As a result I think I spoiled my kids a bit. I knew I should have been tougher at times, but I couldn't get myself to do it. I don't know, maybe it was like an atonement on my part. A lot of times I'd think about them while I was traveling around and I'd be troubled by the idea that maybe I was having big success with the team at the expense of having success with my own kids. I'd be thinking along those lines and I'd get a guilt complex.

I've been a very lucky man. They turned out to be beautiful kids. I used to tell them, "If you show proper respect at all times, and if you always tell the truth, I will always love you and do everything in the world that I can do for you. Just don't become a liar. Don't become a sneak. Don't feel you have to hide things from me. Trust me. I'm your father and I'll stand by you."

Julie? She's my sweetheart. I have so much fun with that kid. Sometimes I look at her and I think of Nancy and Randy when they were that age, and it reminds me again of how many good times I missed.

Yet I still can't think of settling down 100 percent, even after all these years. Dot will say, "Why don't you come down to the pool and sit with Julie and me?"

Sit by a pool? I can't do it. If I go to the pool, I jump in and swim. I can't just lie around on some damned chaise longue. I get too jittery.

I've slowed down a lot in recent years, but not that much.

Chapter 27
The Ambassador

"It was a good thing to be doing as Americans."

In Tokyo they call him *"NBA Icheban Honcho-San"* ("the big boss of the NBA"). Drop the name Red Auerbach almost anywhere in the world and someone will be quick to tell you who he is and what he's known for. Every year, for more than two decades now, the Redhead has traveled abroad for the State Department, conducting clinics, demonstrations and seminars in the finer points of the game he's helped make famous. The hand-picked teams he brings with him have included many of his own stars—Cousy, Russell, Heinsohn, Havlicek—and many leading NBA celebrities, such as Robertson, Pettit, Jerry Lucas and Tom Gola. His sojourns have followed no particular pattern: Morocco, Turkey, Iran, Austria, Germany, France, Italy, Yugoslavia, Poland, Czechoslovakia, Egypt, Rumania, French West Africa, New Zealand, Taiwan, Malaysia, Hong Kong, Burma—and the list goes on.

Wherever basketball is played, wherever there is an interest, Auerbach is revered as the sport's international ambassador.

Bill Fitch, the coach and general manager of Cleveland's Cavaliers, joined the troupe for two successive stopovers in Japan.

"I was with Red constantly," he said. "In fact, my clothes still smell like cigar smoke! And I was just fascinated by the way he organized everything. It all starts with the kind of people he selects, just like it is with the Celtics. Red's told me this a hundred times. Ability is fine, but he's wants a guy who'll be tough in the trenches and who'll be nice to the people he'll meet. If you're the kind of guy who's going to be missing boats and trains, you damned well don't want to travel with Auerbach. He'll send you home from Istanbul without a second thought! And I couldn't agree with him more. He's absolutely right. He tells you this before you ever leave this country. He wants no screwing around over there. Sure, there's time for fun and all that, but Red makes it very clear up front just what his players can and cannot do."

Through his travels Red has become one of the most discriminating shoppers in the world, a regular habitué of the marketplaces and specialty shops which line the routes of his itineraries.

"I wish I'd known that the first year I went with him," Fitch smiles. "I got up one morning, put on a new pair of shoes and started out with him. That guy dragged me through every store in Tokyo. When I got back to my room that night my blisters were killing me. But the next morning he was ready to go again."

Bill remembers one particular episode. "Red knows all about ivories and silks and things like that. He can't be fooled. Whether you're talking about price or quality, Auerbach knows his stuff.

"So we went into this one little place and as soon as we stepped inside I saw this beautiful assortment of jade. I started to look at it, but Auerbach poked me in the ribs and whispered, 'That's not real jade.'

"Holy Cow, I'm thinking to myself, this guy's really a genius. He hardly even looked at the stuff, yet he could tell it wasn't real. I said, 'Red, how can you tell that?'

"He said, 'It's too close to the door!'"

❋   ❋   ❋

The trips represent much more than basketball action and shopping excursions to the Redhead, for he still remains very much a patriot at heart and the idea of enhancing the American image abroad excites him to the core.

"I think my brother would be embarrassed to talk about it very much," Zang Auerbach says, "but I know his feelings about our country and, cornball or not, he's goddamned proud of Uncle Sam. It disturbs him very much—hell, it aggravates him—when he hears people shooting down America. Maybe it's because of the home we came from and the background our Dad brought with him when he arrived here as a boy, but Red is very, very determined to show that this is the best damned country in the world."

"He's a bit of a chauvinist," notes Clarence Cross, the CBS executive. "That is to say he's a real patriot. But he carries it off so much better than most people I've heard. Damn it, when Red stands up there and waves the flag, you've got to totally go along with him.

"Let me tell you a very private story about the real Auerbach," Cross volunteered. "I think it's so revealing. On one of his trips he went to Burma. Now that's not exactly the fun spot of the world, but he knew how much the people there would appreciate it. So he went and did his thing. And when he got back home he started sending all kinds of shoes and equipment back to the Burmese people he had met because they had nothing, but he didn't do it through the State Department! He didn't want to wait for all of the red tape to untangle, so he did it at his own expense, except for some merchandise he got a few companies to donate. That cost him money, time and sweat and he did it without a lot of fanfare. I think that says a great deal about the kind of person Red Auerbach is."

So did an incident in Zagreb, Yugoslavia.

It was 1964, an Olympic year, and U.S. prestige was taking a beating in Iron Curtain countries as an AAU-sponsored team, made up of assorted Olympic hopefuls, played less than .500 ball on an ill-planned swing through Europe. Only a year earlier the AAU's entry in the World Games had finished third behind Brazil and Russia.

Red was asked to take an eight-man squad across the waters that spring with appearances scheduled in Poland, Rumania,

Yugoslavia and Egypt. He selected Pettit, Robertson, Lucas, Gola, Russell, Cousy, Heinsohn and KC Jones.

This time it wasn't just a goodwill tour. In the Redhead's mind, it was nothing less than a crusade. Basketball fans in Poland were still glowing over their teams' recent successes against the hapless U.S. amateurs when Auerbach's forces arrived and proceeded to clobber their finest squads by margins as great as 49 and 54 points.

After a complete sweep of their Poland engagements, they moved on to Yugoslavia, which was not exactly a hotbed of pro-American sentiment. After raising a furor over the shabby accommodations provided for his team—the original plans called for sleeping two to a bed—Red arrived in a jam-packed arena and immediately noticed the American flag was not displayed. He summoned embassy officials and local basketball chieftains to his bench and demanded America's colors be raised. When he was told that wasn't allowed in the country, he got madder and more demonstrative, threatening to call off the game.

"I consider myself patriotic, too," Pettit says, recalling the furious showdown, "but to be perfectly honest, I couldn't have cared less about flying the flag at that particular moment because there were 16,000 people against us. I mean they really hated us. They were whistling and hollering and throwing things at our bench, and we were mainly worried about getting out of there alive. The guys just wanted to get the game started and hopefully cool things down, but Red wouldn't budge, not even in the midst of all that hostility. He meant business and he made no secret of it. Yeah, I was scared, but I was proud of him, too."

A compromise was reached. It would take too long to find an American flag that night. If Red would allow the game to go on, the flag would be added by the next night's game.

He agreed.

His stars then went out and beat the Yugoslav champs by 32 points. And the following night, with Old Glory hanging overhead, they won again. This time by 52 points.

Only one other incident marred that year's trip.

President Lyndon B. Johnson had taken time to entertain Auerbach and his players in a White House send-off, and

Secretary of State Dean Rusk had seen fit to bid them a personal bon voyage at the airport. But not a soul from the U.S. Ambassador's office in Egypt—much less the Ambassador himself—bothered to greet them upon their arrival in Cairo.

Seven months later, halfway through another championship season, Auerbach was asked to address the faculty and students of the Fletcher School of Law and Diplomacy at Tufts University. His audience wanted to hear of some of his experiences abroad, but was particularly interested in the flag incident.

So the Redhead gave them what they wanted. He also gave them a special insight they weren't expecting. "Pardon my colloquialism, gentlemen," he said, "but I'd like to report that our Ambassador to Egypt is bush!"

I don't want to use this book as a sounding board against any person, team or anything like that at all, but there are a few things about our image overseas which should be said.

If there's one thing that's always gotten under my skin, that's really upset me time and time again, it's the way this country allows itself to be represented to the other nations of the world. Don't ever make the mistake of believing that a basketball game between American kids and foreign teams is just an evening's recreation. It isn't.

I'll give you a perfect example of what I'm talking about. One year Cooz and I visited a small town in French West Africa. The place was so remote that they didn't even have radios or newspapers. A few months before we arrived, an AAU team went to the Pan-American Games and got wiped out. It was a lousy, lousy team and it had no business being there. I think it came in fifth or something like that. Anyway, Cooz and I were standing on the court in this little-bitty village, getting ready to start our clinic, when a small boy walked up to us.

"You're supposed to be the great American player," he said to Bob. Then he looked at me. "And you're supposed to be the great American coach. How come everybody beat you?"

I was embarrassed, and so was Cousy. There was nothing we could tell that kid. There was no possible answer that he would understand or accept. All he knew was that the Americans had been clobbered by the Russians and everybody else.

That's not an isolated incident. We continually send inferior teams into international competition and our enemies—whose teams are as professional as the Celtics—turn those games into unbelievable propaganda devices. We sit back and allow that to happen.

A private promoter can send a team—ostensibly representing the United States—almost anywhere in the world and get sanctioned by the AAU. There are no grounds to refuse him. I could get a team from Joe's Pool Room and dress it up in uniforms with "USA" printed all over them and then bring it into the Iron Curtain countries and get humiliated. Who's to stop me?

This is wrong, wrong, wrong.

I've always been a great believer in the idea that we should create a cabinet post entitled "Secretary of Sports." Sports has reached a point in this country where it's certainly worthy of that consideration. This goes for pro sports, too, with all of their headaches and controversies over reserve clauses, TV blackouts and so on. But right now I'm primarily interested in our amateur sports. The NCAA has been fighting the Olympic Committee, and everybody's losing. They fight over eligibility, over sanctioning powers, over everything under the sun, because they're all afraid of losing their power and influence.

Bullshit on their power and influence!

What about the power and influence of the American image abroad? By what right can they jeopardize that? But it's done every day.

Very simply, I'd like to see a Secretary of Sports who has the authority to call the shots on Olympic selections, on Pan-American and World Game appearances, on every phase of amateur competition on the international level. He'd see to it that any team representing this country was properly selected, trained and prepared.

When people in other parts of the world see a team with "USA" on its uniform, they think they're seeing the best we've got. As long as countries like Russia are going to use sports to propagandize for their philosophies, then I think the kids who wear "USA" had better be just that—the best we've got!

When we visited the Yugoslavians, they were second to the Russians in a big world tournament that was held a short while before we arrived there. The first thing I was told when we pulled into town was that they didn't want any demonstrations or clinics from us. They had badly beaten an AAU team and now they were offended at the suggestion my guys could possibly know more about this game than they did. I tried explaining that we were professionals, but one of their officials was very smug. He said all he knew was that he saw "USA" on the teams they had beaten before. So I said, "Okay, Buster, you're going to see a hell of a lot more tonight!"

In my pregame talk I said, "Russell I want you to do me a favor. I want you to guard that redheaded scorer tonight, and if he scores one basket I'm going to break your goddamned neck. I don't want you to help out. I don't want you to rebound. Pettit and Heinsohn can take care of that. All I want you to do is make sure that guy doesn't score a point."

The kid I'm talking about later died in a car accident. He was 6'5 and the leading scorer in Europe at the time of this particular game, so he was the big local hero. He was the one I wanted stopped cold.

I can still picture it. The game started. The kid got the ball, faked to his right, bounced once to his left and jumped. He was about 17 feet from the basket and he had the widest grin on his face you've ever seen. Out of nowhere, Russell uncoils his arm and blocks the shot. We get the ball and score. This happened six times in a row. The kid was going bananas. On his seventh try he took two steps backwards and threw the ball at the basket like it was a baseball. I jumped and yelled, "Goddamn it, Russell, you let him hit the backboard!"

Now Russell, in his own inimitable way, decides he has to get rid of this kid, get rid of me, get rid of the whole situation. The next time the poor kid went up for a shot Russell smacked the ball instead of blocking it the way he usually did. It hit the kid in the head and he started to scream. He went into a tantrum like a four-year-old and kicked the ball into the stands. The officials gave him a technical foul and threw him out of the game. We won by 32 points.

Then a couple of representatives of the Yugoslavia Sports Federation came over to me and asked, "How do you think our national team would do against your amateur teams?"

They had never said anything like that before in their lives. But we had convinced them that there are different strata of sports in this country.

They also wanted to know, all of a sudden, if I would put on a clinic. I said, "Hell no!"

You see, I'm from the old school. I am not a trained diplomat. I am me.

They also got mad at me because I didn't observe proper protocol after the game. One of their officials started complaining through an interpreter that I was supposed to line up my guys at the foul circle and bow to the crowd.

I waited until he got done. Then I said, "Now I want you to tell him something. You've got sixteen thousand people here, whistling every time my guys take a free throw and hurling junk at our bench. If you think I'm going to stand out there and acknowledge this kind of bullshit, you're out of your mind."

The next day a lot of kids came around for our autographs and we gave them pictures, sneakers, and all kinds of souvenirs. You see, that's where the goodwill is accomplished. That night we played a second game and they started getting rough. They were still upset over what happened the night before, and I guess they figured the way to even things up was by getting physical.

I called one of their officials over to our bench.

"I'll make this very simple," I said. "You people start playing basketball right now, or two things are going to happen. First, we're going to beat the living shit out of you physically. And second, we're going to beat you so goddamned badly in front of this crowd that you'll want to give up the sport! Now, have I made myself clear?"

Then I turned around and walked away. He went over to the other bench and started talking to the coach, and I guess they understood my message, because they settled down to play the game the way it should be played and we had no more problems. We won that one by 52 points.

That particular episode was an exception. Most of our trips were enjoyable and, I hope, beneficial.

It was never a case of going for the money, believe me. There was no money. The players got a couple of bucks a day and expenses. That's all. So why did they go? The traveling was fun. And I'm sure there was a certain amount of curiosity involved.

I really believe they felt it was a good thing to be doing as Americans. When you're in some other country, doing things to help its people, and you see your own flag and hear your own anthem being played, it's a thrill I can't even begin to describe.

Those were my reasons for going, too, along, of course, with the idea of helping to promote the game of basketball. It's given me everything I've got. Why can't I give back a little?

Chapter 28
Today's Auerbach

"I'm busier now than I've ever been."

Charlie Scott was no awe-stricken kid the day he walked into Auerbach's office in the summer of 1975 for his first meeting with his new boss. After a spectacular career at North Carolina, Scott had gone on to three superstar seasons in the ABA and then three all-star seasons in the NBA with the Phoenix Suns. At the age of 26 he was rich and firmly established. Then a post-playoff trade brought him to Boston in exchange for Paul Westphal, setting up that initial tête-à-tête with the Redhead.

"I always felt the most exciting moment of my life was that first day I stepped onto the campus at North Carolina," Charlie confided a few months later, "but after that meeting with Red, I wasn't so sure. In the short time we talked he made me feel like all of those flags up there in the Garden belonged to me, Charlie Scott, and that I was part of a great tradition, a great aura, and it was up to me to get another flag for the collection. This sounds ridiculous, but I was never so excited about playing basketball before in my entire life! That's where Celtics pride begins. It starts at the top. You see, Red *is* the Celtics. And in order to become a real Celtic, you've got to have that first talk with him."

On November 2, 1974, Auerbach was just sitting down to dinner with some guests in his Washington home when he got a phone call from Tommy Heinsohn, his coach, explaining that he was sick with a flu, and assistant coach John Killilea was on the West Coast scouting, and the team had no bench leader for its game in Atlanta that night.

Auerbach hung up the receiver, excused himself from dinner, packed a suitcase and made it to National Airport just in time to catch a 6 P.M. flight to Atlanta. At 7:35 he hailed a cab which rushed him to the Omni, and just a few minutes before the Celts were due to file out, their locker room door swung open and their boss breezed in.

Except for Havlicek and Nelson, no one else in the room that night had ever been coached by Auerbach.

"So many times in years gone by I had thought to myself, 'Gee, wouldn't it be nice to play for him?'" Paul Silas says. "Now, there he was, but the situation was so rushed and unexpected that I almost felt sorry for him. I couldn't imagine what he was going to say to us.

"This was his speech: 'I really don't believe in a lot of Xs and Os. I believe the game of basketball is basically simple. You've got one basketball, two baskets, five men on one side and five men on the other side. The objective is to put the ball in our basket and stop them from putting it into theirs. Okay? It's that simple. What I do believe in is each man in this room knowing his own job and knowing what his opponent is likely to do. I'm going to use most of you tonight, and when I call you I want you to be ready. I don't care if you haven't played in months. I want you to be ready tonight.'

"That was it. It was so simple I couldn't believe it, yet every word hit home. There's just something about the way Red talks, sort of a command in his voice, and way down deep you respect him because you know he means what he says. It's a feeling you get. I'll tell you, he's something else. For a guy who hadn't been coaching in almost ten years to walk into that room that night and motivate me the way he did, it was kind of overwhelming to me."

The Redhead substituted freely, and during time-outs his players gathered around him and listened intently.

"It was just like old times," Nelson smiles. "In a matter of minutes he had the whole team in the palm of his hands. The young kids were sitting on the edge of the bench, sort of keeping one eye on him. They were simply excited to watch him in action. And to tell the truth, so was I."

But they didn't get their full 48 minutes' worth.

In the second half Red got into a battle with referee Richie Powers and was thrown out of the contest.

Auerbach, perhaps remembering the way he bridled at Ben Kerner's interference in Tri-Cities and later fought off the second-guessers who descended on Walter Brown's office, has remained remarkably detached from the day-to-day operations of his team, giving full authority to Russell, first, and then to Heinsohn.

In Russell's case the hands-off policy was easier to maintain, for the Celtics continued to win in 1967, 1968 and 1969 under Bill's regime as player-coach. But in the fall of 1969, after Russell's unexpected retirement announcement, Heinsohn left a lucrative insurance business to take the helm of a suddenly reeling ship. Without the big man in the middle, and with Sam Jones also newly retired, the aging Celts were at once vulnerable to Willis Reed and the Knicks, to rookie sensation Lew Alcindor and the Bucks, to Chamberlain and the Lakers, to Wes Unseld and the Bullets—to nearly the whole field, in fact. Except for Havlicek, Nelson and Sanders, the squad was staffed with marginal veterans and untried kids and they paid the price, going 34–48 and missing the playoffs, the first time Boston failed to qualify since Doggie Julian's last team in 1950. It had never happened before in the Auerbach era.

"That was not the easiest time to be the Boston coach,"

Heinsohn recalls. "Halfway through that season, when it became obvious we weren't going anywhere with just the older players, we decided it was time to cast our lot with the kids: with Jo Jo White, Don Chaney and Steve Kuberski. The beautiful past was finally over and we had to start planning for our future. It was a situation which was going to need a lot of patience. Red knew that, and as a result he never once put any kind of pressure on me. He knew what our realistic goals were. Sure, I caught all kinds of hell from the fans and writers because they were just looking at the scores. That's all they saw. But all I was looking for was improvement. The next year we got Dave Cowens in the draft and then everyone knew it would be just a matter of time before we were back on top where we belonged. But Rome wasn't built in a day. We were trying to phase out one dynasty and phase in a new one. Publicly, I suffered during those two seasons. But privately, I knew I had all the time I needed, thanks to Red. If you don't know for sure that you're the boss, you begin running scared and second-guessing yourself. I never had to do that. Red stayed clear of my locker room, my practice floor and my players, unless I asked him for help. He put me in charge, then stepped back and let me do my own thing. And he made sure I knew that he stood behind me every step of the way."

In 1972—just three years after Russell's retirement—Heinsohn's Celtics were 56–26. In 1973 they were 68–14, the finest record in the history of the franchise. In 1974 they were world champions. And in 1976 they won the championship again. It was almost as if they had never been gone.

His retirement from the bench never pushed Auerbach away from center stage. Indeed, he became more of a towering figure—a living legend, to use an overworked term—in the city, in the league and in the game.

"I don't remember Red ever getting booed in Boston," Sammy Cohen says. "He was a transplanted guy, but he's all Boston today and people in this city look upon him as a god. To this very day you'll find thousands of fans in Boston who are convinced Auerbach could take over the Red Sox, the Patriots or the Bruins and make them into champions. That's how

much they believe in this guy. And in the last ten years, with
all of the ownership changes and money problems, he's become more like Walter Brown than Walter Brown was. You
can't say one damned word against the city or the Celtics to
him. Not one. And any time there's been talk about some owner moving the club away from here, Auerbach makes it publicly clear they'll have to go without him. It's not because he
loves the mayor or the governor or anything like that. It's because he spilled his guts out for this town. This is where he
did it. Believe me, Red could have gone to any number of other cities and made a lot more dough, but it'll never happen.
This is his town. He's a part of Boston now."

In the league his stature is unmatched.
"I remember the first time I met him," Bill Fitch says. "I
was general manager and coach of the Cavs, just like now, and
we were getting ready for our first season in the league. We
were an expansion club. You know, Red's a very important
cog in this game. So I more or less expected he'd say, 'Who the
hell are you, kid?' But he treated me with so much respect,
and he continued to do that all the while we went 15–67 that
year. That meant so much to me. Of all the people a new guy
meets coming into the NBA, Auerbach is the one he's most
aware of."

The public Auerbach—10 years after he stopped coaching—remains as celebrated as the fiery character who once
rode herd on history's greatest team.
"I can walk across the city of New York with Tom Seaver at
my side and nobody will bat an eyelash," Clarence Cross marvels. "But if I go into the crummiest Chinese joint in the worst
part of town, the waiters—who don't even speak English—
will all be Auerbach fans. You think I'm kidding? Let me tell
you something. The bartenders at the 21 Club have got to be
the most jaded crew you've ever seen in your life. They would
not give Elizabeth Taylor a second look if she walked in.
They're much too sophisticated for that. But when I walk in
with Auerbach, the joint is upside down! The bartenders and
waiters are eyeballing him constantly, giving him tentative

smiles whenever they catch his eye, and sort of clustering around him without being too obvious. They'll try to say something to him—anything at all—just looking for some kind of a response. Believe me, this kind of thing just doesn't go on in there. Auerbach has got to be one of a kind."

"He's certainly been great for the league," Eddie Gottlieb says. "He's primarily interested in the Celtics, of course, and he'll fight like hell for any edge he can get them. But I have never once known him to sacrifice the legitimate good of the league for his own personal gain. He won't do that. Neither would Walter Brown."

"That's absolutely right," Walter Kennedy concurred. "His first consideration is always the Celtics, and it should be. He's bled, fought and died for that team. He'd throw tantrums and yell and scream and everything else, but in my twelve years as Commissioner he never once, when the chips were down, crossed me. I'd say, 'Arnold, this may not be best for the Celtics, but it's best for the NBA and you've got to go along with it.' He would look at me and say, 'Walter, when you put it to me that way, okay.' "

Cross first met Auerbach at the annual NBA meetings in 1974, and during that initial encounter the idea of "Red on Roundball" was conceived. Within a matter of months formal plans were made to launch the immensely popular series which featured Auerbach and selected NBA stars in brief clinics during halftimes on CBS telecasts. Red taught and the stars acted out his tips.

"A group of us had gone to lunch," Cross recalls, "and the conversation naturally centered on basketball. Somehow Red got going on the theme 'The floor is smooth and the ball is round,' and then went into a twelve-minute spiel on the philosophical meaning of the seams on the ball. It just blew my mind. He was telling us how to use the seams, how not to use them, things like that. And everyone's attention was riveted. Here's a guy who knows all there is to know about the game, and yet he can return to base zero and keep you fascinated with a simple discussion of fundamentals. It wasn't so much his knowledge as it was his commanding presence. The hardest thing in the world to do on television is a teaching series. They've never worked out well, especially in sports. They're terrible tune-outs. The only possible way to carry them off is with a strong, engaging personality. And where the hell are you going to get a better one than Red Auerbach?

"So we decided, 'Yeah, that's exactly what we want. Just the way he was that afternoon. With a cigar in one hand and shaking the other hand in our faces, telling us to use the seams!'"

People ask me if I'm restless now that I've retired.
They've got to be kidding me.
I'm busier now than I've ever been: running the office, signing the players, going to meetings, speaking here, appearing there. And I still do the State Department tours.
Do I miss the old days on the bench?
Yes and no.
Yes, because they were a big part of my life, but no, because I knew the day I walked out in 1966 that I'd had enough. And that game in Atlanta a couple of years ago didn't do anything to change my mind. There was a perfect example of what always bugged me: referees not paying attention to the game. That should have been a nice little change of pace for me, an opportunity to get back inside the locker room and meet the guys at game level again. Everything's going fine. I'm having a good time. I'm sure the players were getting a kick out of it. And we were winning the game. Beautiful. Then Richie Powers makes a stupid call. What the hell was I supposed to do? Sit there like little Lord Fauntleroy? So I said, "That was a horseshit call!"
When a coach says something like that, the referee should just look over, point a finger at him and say, "That's enough out of you!" But Powers yells, "Technical foul!"
Why? Because it was me—Auerbach—on the bench. Even after 10 years, they're still watching me instead of the game!
I said, "Richie, what for?"
He said I cussed him.
"Christ," I said, "you haven't been to the movies lately!"
You know, it was absolutely ridiculous. So when he came

back down I yelled, "Well, you've still got the rabbit ears, I guess."

Boom.

"Technical foul! You're out of here!"

I couldn't believe it. So I really let him have it. "You're still an incompetent, pompous little sonofabitch! This is really outrageous."

It didn't change his mind, of course. I knew it wouldn't. I hadn't been away that long.

Down through the years I had a reputation as a lousy public relations man. That started back in the early '50s with Walter. I made the mistake —and I use that word advisedly—of telling people what I thought, and not what I thought they wanted to hear. In the long run that worked to my advantage. Writers came to realize that when they asked me a question, they would get a truthful answer. Is that bad public relations? I never thought so. In the case of the Cousy thing, maybe I could have been more delicate. I don't know.

Now I think I'm a pretty damned good public relations man, in my own way. Every single letter—except form letters—that comes across my desk gets answered by me. This was another little lesson I learned from Walter: the bigger a person becomes, the more accessible he becomes. The self-styled big shot becomes difficult to see. It's beneath his dignity to answer letters and all that crap. But Walter answered every letter he got, and so do I. If any Celtics customer has a problem, he knows he can write to me and I'll get the damned thing solved. I tell my daughters whenever they have troubles with their cars, write to the president of General Motors. If he's any kind of an administrator, you'll get an answer. Write to some flunky junior executive and it'll probably end up in the watebasket. That's why he'll always be a flunky junior executive.

I deal with the public a lot today and I think I do a good job at it. But when you're in the public eye, some people think you're a nothing as far as individual rights and privacies are concerned. They think they own a piece of you, that you're being paid to be at their beck and call.

One day I was having lunch with Jack Waldron, a former owner of our club, in Harry M's at Madison Square Garden. We must have waited 20 minutes for our food to come. At the next table some woman was having a party with half a dozen kids. They were laughing and talking and having a great time. Finally our food comes. I cut into the steak and just about had a piece of it into my mouth when the woman reaches over and grabs my arm. I put my fork down and looked at her. "Yes, ma'm?" She said, "Would you mind getting up and coming over to our table and saying hello to the boys? We're celebrating a bar mitzvah."

I said, "Lady, I've been sitting here for twenty minutes, doing nothing while you ate your meal. Why didn't you ask me then? You wanted to enjoy your meal. Fine. So do I. But you don't give a damn about my meal, do you? The answer is no!"

Five minutes later, while I'm still eating, she shoved a couple of those big two-foot-long menus over my shoulder. They practically fell on top of my food! She said, "Will you sign these?"

Now I was really angry. "Madam," I said, "I will do nothing for you until I finish this meal. Now forget it!"

Was I wrong? This happens all the time.

Sometimes people come running up to me on a sidewalk and try to be witty and funny in 10 seconds. I can't stand that. Maybe if the person said, "Pardon me, I'm sorry to intrude, but I just wanted to say thanks for so many nice memories," it would be different. I'd probably relax and talk for a couple of minutes. But when they start that jabbering, trying to squeeze everything into the first 10 seconds, I just say to myself, "Oh, bullshit."

Or I'll start to sign a few autographs and the next thing I know, people are pulling my sports coat, grabbing my arms, bumping the hell out of me. Half the time they've got nothing for you to write on, so they hand you a piece of Kleenex. Believe me, you just can't win.

I was riding in a New York cab one night and the driver recognized me, so we started talking. He told me he was a big Knicks fan, but he was pleasant, so when the ride was over I gave him a pretty good tip.

He said, "Thanks very much, but the Celtics are still horseshit!"

See what I mean?

❁ ❁ ❁

But overall I'm happy today.

And, no, I've never regretted staying here. Not for one second.

If we had won all those championships in New York, of course, we'd all be multimillionaires today. In most cities the reaction to what we did would have been fantastic, but I don't think it was ever fully appreciated here. Not while it was happening, anyway. Now, looking back, people are realizing the enormity of what took place. If I've one regret at all along those lines, it's that the people of Boston didn't appreciate it more while Walter was alive, so he could have reaped some of the recognition he so richly deserved. Let me say one thing about that. We have never allowed Walter's spirit to die in the Celtics organization. Never. And we never will.

The players missed him because he was their friend and their very best fan, but no one will ever know how much I missed him, nor will anyone ever fully appreciate the difficulties the Celtics faced with future ownerships.

Marjorie, Walter's widow, continued to own the team with Lou Pieri throughout the 1964–65 season, but in the summer of 1965 they decided to sell the club. I didn't blame them. It was too much of a strain on her, and I knew all of Lou's business interests were centered in Rhode Island. There was no way either of them could give the team the day-to-day attention Walter used to.

In the next ten years the Celtics had seven owners!

One was Marvin Kratter, the head of a big conglomerate with offices in New York's Pan Am Building. He was a brilliant man, but like all geniuses he was convinced a little bit of studying and application could make him an expert in someone else's field. One day he had a direct line installed in my office, connecting to his office in New York. I knew he'd be on that phone five or six times a day if I didn't do something about it, so every time it rang I made believe it was out of order! Finally I simply told him, "Marvin, let's get this thing out of here. It's really bugging me." There was no problem. He had it removed, but it was a type of interference I had never had to deal with before.

The worst was to come. The 1968 expansion draft was

around the corner, so Kratter called a board of directors meeting in New York and invited me. We sat around this big table having dinner and I didn't say too much. I knew what was coming. As soon as everything was cleared away, Kratter got up. The purpose of the meeting, he explained, was to decide whether or not to protect Satch Sanders and Don Nelson in the draft. He turned to the first guy and asked him what he thought. "Well, Marvin," he said. "You know what you're doing. If you think we can afford to let them go, I'll agree." Then he turned to his son, who was also on the board. "I'm not totally in agreement on Sanders," the kid said, "but I'll agree we can let Nelson go."

I broke in. "Are you guys through?" I asked.

"Not yet," Marvin said.

So they went on. The lawyer added his two bits. Then Jack Waldron, the president of the team and an employee of Kratter's, got up. Jack had balls. "All I can say, Marvin, is that we're paying Red a lot of money and I think we ought to hear what he has to say."

Kratter turned to me and nodded.

"You mean I can speak?" I asked. Then I let them have it.

"I don't know what the hell's going on here, but this is the goddamnedest thing I've ever seen in my life! Listening to you guys discussing the skills and future abilities of ballplayers is like letting civilians run a war. It's a joke. Would I pick out a piece of real estate and tell you people how much it's worth and what you should do with it? Of course not. But that's what you're doing right now with the Celtics and I want no part of it. If you're going to make these kinds of decisions, then you can take the ball club and shove it. I want nothing to do with it, and I'll call a press conference to say so."

Then I got up and walked away from the table. Kratter came running over to me, put his arm around my shoulder and pointed out the window. "Look at that view, Red," he said. "Isn't it beautiful?"

"Marvin, stick that view up your can! I didn't come here to look at any views. I came here to get something squared away. I meant what I said just now."

Eventually, they came around to my way of thinking. In fact

Kratter and I later became very good friends, after he sold the team, and I made some pretty good money by going into a few investments with him.

But it's like I told Ben Kerner way back in Tri-Cities: a little knowledge is a dangerous thing.

The worst times of all came around 1970, 1971 when a company called Trans-National Communications, based in New York, bought the club. Everything was handled out of New York. They took all of our money and then never bothered to pay our bills. The Celtics had to travel COD all over the league! We owed money to hotels in every city. They wouldn't let us stay unless we paid in advance. One time I had to lay out $9,000 of my own money before our guys could board an airplane!

We were making a proft at the gate, but we never saw a penny of it. Not only that, I didn't have access to any of our financial records. There were people on the Celtics payroll who I never heard of. It was just awful.

Then one day we were notified that our office telephones would be shut off if we didn't pay our bill. On top of that, the phone company insisted on a $2,000 deposit, just to make sure we wouldn't default again. I had to personally visit the business office and ask for an extension to our credit. Embarrassing? You bet your ass it was. It was an indignity the ball club didn't deserve. But what could we do about it?

Finally, Trans-National went bankrupt and ownership of the team reverted back to the Ballantine Brewing Company.

When Ballantine sold us to Bob Schmertz in the summer of 1972, we had our first real security since Walter Brown died eight years earlier. Schmertz made a fortune in developing retirement communities and he bought the team as an investment, but then he fell in love with the players, just like Walter did, and it was nothing at all to see him hop a plane and meet the club somewhere on the road, just to watch the game and give the players moral support. He never missed a home game, even though his office was in New Jersey. When he died in the summer of 1975, we decided to wear black patches on our uniforms the coming season, just as we did after Walter's death.

That's how much we appreciated having good ownership again.

Today, under Irv Levin and Harold Lipton, we're still secure.

Irv comes to most of our games, too, and he's been great to the players. I'm not saying this because he's the owner today. In all honesty, he's conducted himself beautifully. One day last season we were talking about the ball club and he said to me, "Am I the best owner you've ever had?" I said, "No. Walter Brown was. But you've been fantastic to work with and I appreciate it. But remember one thing: we've got a great team, we're doing well at the box office and everyone's happy. If the situation should ever turn around, I want to see your reactions then. I want to see how you'll react if we ever start losing money, losing fans and losing games. That's the test of great ownership."

There were times when it was very tempting to leave Boston, especially in that period around 1970 when the money was tight and we were faced with a rebuilding program. Sure, I had offers to join other organizations, and some of those offers were very, very lucrative. One of them, involving a piece of ownership, would have meant an immediate $400,000 increase.

Twenty years earlier Walter Brown faced a similar decision. He had no dough to work with and the future of the team looked very dark. Everyone advised him to bail out while he could. But he wouldn't do it. He loved this team too much to give up on it. And so do I. When Sammy Cohen says I've become a lot like Walter in my feelings for Boston and the Celtics, he's absolutely right. How could I take someone else's money and run, not caring if the franchise went down the drain?

I'm a loyal person. I've preached loyalty to every Celtic player who's worn our uniform since 1950. We're a family, I tell them. We care for one another. We're proud of one another. We can always count on one another. I didn't say those things because they sounded good. I said them because I meant them. When we didn't have a goddamned nickel to our names, *we were still the Boston Celtics and that meant we were still very special people.*

When Walter hired me in 1950, things couldn't have been worse. But together we built what I've always felt was the greatest team in the history of professional sports. So being broke and being a loser in 1970 didn't scare me. I didn't like it, but I wasn't intimidated by it either.

The thought of leaving never really entered my mind, because there was something special about the name "Celtics" that wouldn't let me go. Money had nothing to do with it. You see, you can't buy what this team's given me over the years.

Of all the things I do today, the most important of all, I think, is making sure we keep that spirit, that tradition, alive.

When a new kid comes to my office, I have a standard speech waiting for him:

"Have you ever seen our team play? You can tell a lot about a team that way, and I'm not talking about talent right now. Our guys are champions, and they have been for a long, long time. But if you're going to be a champion, you've got to feel like one, look like one and act like one. Then you'll play like one. That means paying a price to play here. We're smart enough to know when you're giving us false hustle, and as soon as we spot it, we'll get rid of you because we have no time to go into the whys and wherefores.

"But if you have the desire to give us the best you have, you're going to get all kinds of help here—not just from me and from your coaches, but most of all from your teammates, because they want to win, and they'll do all they can to improve you so that you can help them win. That's the whole concept we have here, and you'll be aware of it right away. Guys like Havlicek will sit with you and talk about your game, your problems, your whole approach to basketball.

"And you're going to notice things. You'll never see a Celtic bawl out another Celtic. Never. You'll never see a Celtic come out of a game and throw down his jacket or express any discontent. Never. We don't stand for that.

"What you will see is unity. You know, more players have started and finished their careers in Boston than in the rest of the league combined. That's a fact you can look up. We're *very proud of it. It tells you two things. One, we're pretty choosy about the people we select. And two, once you've joined us, you've joined a family.*

"We'll help you find summer jobs. We'll help you in business endeavors. Your wife will find that the other wives will be calling her all the time. They stick together. That's another very great tradition in Boston. It's part of the family thing we've got going.

"If we offer all of this to you, how could you even consider dogging it and going through the motions? It's almost impossible.

"If you have problems, we want to hear about them.

"Otherwise, we'll expect your very best. And in return we'll give you all of the things which have made the Celtics famous throughout the world. You'll be a Celtic. You'll be one of us. One of my guys.

"Now you've got to decide if it's worth it."

But here it is, years later, you're thinking. *Players are too sophisticated for that kind of talk.*

Wrong. You couldn't be more wrong.

Let me tell you about Charlie Scott. Do you remember the fifth game of our championship series with Phoenix this year, the one that lasted three overtimes? Charlie was called out of that game on fouls, some of which were really unbelievable. I walked into our locker room before the press arrived and Heinsohn grabbed me. "Will you talk to Charlie?" he said. "He's ready to explode."

Tommy was right. They had given the kid six fouls and a technical and he was so upset he was shaking.

I grabbed him by both arms. "Charlie," I said, very softly, "you've had a great year. You've done everything we've asked you to do. You tell me you want to be a lawyer someday, but now you're ready to blow your stack over a technical foul . . ."

He started to interrupt me. I squeezed his arms tighter.

"Charlie, let me tell you something. I was worse than you are now, on many occasions, but I didn't have someone to grab me and stop me like I'm doing to you. And so I did a lot of *crazy things. But I'm stopping you now. I want you to show me what you're made of. I want you to grit your teeth, take a quick shower and get the hell out of here without saying a word to anybody. Just dress and go. Quickly."*

I dropped his arms. He looked at me and then walked straight into the shower room, came out a minute later, jumped into his clothes and left. He never said a word.

In the next game, Charlie played magnificently. He scored 25 points and led the way. We won the championship that day. As soon as the game was over he came running up to me, threw his arms around me and gave me a kiss. He knew what it was all about. I knew. And the ballplayers knew. No one else did.

In my eyes, and in the eyes of his teammates, he had disciplined himself for the good of the team, and now he had just helped us win the biggest game of the year.

He became a Celtic and that says it all.

Chapter 29
The Legacy

"I wouldn't change a thing."

The Medal for Distinguished Achievement is perhaps the most prestigious civic honor bestowed by the City of Boston. The list of recipients is exclusive and outstanding. It's a tribute set aside for the giants of the community, men like Arthur Fiedler, the beloved octogenarian who presides over the world-famous Boston Pops Orchestra.

It was never associated with sports until the night former Mayor John F. Collins draped the medal, hanging from a blue ribbon, around the neck of Arnold J. Auerbach and presented him with a citation which read, in part: "In the field of competitive sports he stands alone. In the major sport to which he has given most of his life he has made the name Boston synonymous with success."

As the capacity audience in War Memorial Auditorium stood in a rousing, extended ovation, Auerbach was clearly overwhelmed.

"I'm just a coach," he said, almost apologetically. "I can't play an instrument or save a life or create anything . . ."

The medal hangs on the wall of his Boston office today, one of scores of mementos, plaques, photos and souvenirs which form a dazzling still life of the now-grayed Redhead who sits behind the corner desk. There are handsome trophies from the NBA. There's a framed presentation from the Boston branch of the NAACP, the first Man of the Year award it gave out, citing Auerbach ". . . who as coach of the Boston Celtics basketball team has inspired, directed and developed in the world of sports an integrated group of men who reflect his own sense of fair play and deep concern for all people and who thus are champions, not only in basketball but also in the area of dignified human relations." There's even an old, tattered green and gold warm-up jacket with "Washington Capitols" on its back.

It's more than an office; it's a museum.

One very special plaque tells of Auerbach's enshrinement in the Basketball Hall of Fame.

Then, of course, upstairs in the cavernous Boston Garden, there is the breathtaking display of championship banners, all of which are nine feet wide and fifteen feet long. One reads, "Boston Celtics, World Champions, 1957." The next one ends "1959." And then they continue: 1960, 1961, 1962, 1963, 1964, 1965, 1966, 1968, 1969, 1974, 1976.

There's not another collection like it in the world.

Two other banners bear retired numbers: 6, Bill Russell; 14, Bob Cousy; 15, Tommy Heinsohn; 16, Satch Sanders; 21, Bill Sharman; 22, Ed Macauley; 23, Frank Ramsey; 24, Sam Jones; 25, KC Jones.

There's also a number 1. Walter Brown.

But the real Auerbach legacy isn't tacked to a wall or hanging from a dusty girder.

Indeed, it lives in the continuing success of the men who wore the Kelly green.

"It was like having five assistant coaches on the floor," Havlicek says, recalling the days of Auerbach's dynasty. "Red taught us how to take this game apart, how to analyze and understand every facet of it. We found out what it takes to win. So it certainly hasn't been surprising to see how much success our guys have had in their own coaching careers."

Sharman (Lakers), Cousy (Kings), Ramsey (ABA's Colonels), KC Jones (Bullets), Russell (Celtics, Supersonics) and Heinsohn (Celtics) all became head coaches at the pro level.

Siegfried (Rockets), Sam Jones (Jazz) and Nelson (Bucks) became assistant pro coaches.

Loscutoff (Boston State) and Sanders (Harvard) took over college teams.

Conley (Hartford) headed up an Eastern League entry.

All in all, more than 30 Auerbach protégés ended up in coaching positions. Now, when they talk about the days gone by, the days when they lived together, traveled together and won together, they talk about the intangibles they shared.

"It was never a business when I played," Sanders says. "I was very proud to have been a Celtic. I lived it and now I preach it, because I happen to believe this is the way things should be done in sports."

"I feel I've done a lot with my life, just by being a member of those Celtics teams," Ramsey said. "It's something I'll carry with me to the grave."

"Long after I'm retired, years and years from now, I'll still feel we're separated only by geography," Havlicek noted. "We'll always be close, just because of the things we went through together."

"When you're talking about those people," Russell said, "you're talking about people I happen to have great affection for. I guess *love* would be the proper word. Every one of them was a man. I don't mean just a male over twenty-one. And it all started at the top. I remember the first year I was there we lost the last game of the regular season to Syracuse, a team that had eliminated the Celtics from the previous three playoffs. Walter Brown came into the locker room and said, 'You bunch of chokers! I'll never come into this dressing room again.'

"The next game he came in, kicked the floor, and said: 'I'm sorry. I'm just a fan and I was so scared that we were going to lose everything again that I got frustrated. I didn't mean it. I was upset. I apologize.'

"That man owned the team. He didn't have to do that, you

know? But this is the way the Celtics operated, from Walter and Red on down.

"We were a family. We looked out for each other."

That's what Willie Naulls found out in 1963.

"I learned more about professional basketball in one year under Red than in all of my seven previous years put together, and I was a damned good basketball player.

"But that's not what the Celtics mean to me today.

"In life we have our families and our friends. Those are our teams. When you have a victory—whether it's selling a car or putting a deal together—these are the people you like to share it with. We're individuals, but we all like to have our little families to share things with.

"I realized this when I was eleven and my parents separated and I was all alone. My father was never around and I had nobody. So when I started playing basketball I played for myself. I considered myself a team player all through college and seven professional seasons, yet I was determined to be an all-star and never sit on the bench. See, I was still playing for Willie.

"Then Red asked me to come to Boston and it was like finding a family at last. There's a lot said in this world about all for one and one for all, but those aren't empty words with the Celtics. Russell just took over my life. He picked me up and took me every place, including his home. I took his bed. I ate his food.

"Auerbach was like a father figure on that team, a parent image, someone who'd scold you and discipline you, and yet you'd know he was doing it out of love. Russell, KC, Havlicek and the others—they were like brothers.

"All of the concepts you'd normally attribute to a family are actually thriving within the Boston Celtics organization.

"I've often been asked the definition of *soul*. It's what the Celtics are all about. Red Auerbach has it. And so do the guys who play for him."

Just about the time I hit Boston, the most famous politician in the city's history was getting close to the end of his own career. His name was James Michael Curley. A lot of people

*loved him and a lot of people hated him, and I guess the two
sides are still divided. When he finally sat down to write his
own life's story, he entitled the book,* I'd Do It Again!

I thought that was beautiful.

*I wish I could have used it, too, because it's just the way I
feel when I look back on my own life. I wouldn't change a
thing.*

*I'm very proud of the record I compiled, and I'm especially
proud of the records my old guys are putting together today.
Most of them—Russ, Cooz, Ramsey, Sharman, Tommy—were
leaders when they joined us, and it took a strong personality to
lead leaders. I tried to do it in such a way that I didn't destroy
those leadership qualities, and I tried to teach them a concept.
They learned that everybody is an individual and all individuals must be treated differently, yet treated exactly alike in a
team sense. I like to think they got more than just a basic
knowledge of the game here. They learned how to control a
team, and they learned that a team is most effective when each
of its members concentrates on the particular phase of the
game he excels in. They learned that winning is the only statistic that matters. And I think they learned the importance of
honesty and openness in player relations. On top of all that,
they learned what it means to have pride in your organization.*

*Almost every single one of them keeps in regular contact
with me. My phone's always ringing. Sometimes they just
want to say hello, or tell me some news about their families or
careers, and sometimes they want advice.*

*It gives me a good feeling inside to know that they still val-
ue my opinions, and that I've apparently had a good influence
on their lives. Call it respect, if you want to, or call it friendship. In my mind it's just their way of letting me know they're
still my guys, and I hope they always feel that way. That relationship doesn't stop the day they stop playing for me. As Mister Russell says, it goes on until one of us dies.*

*I've always been pleased when people referred to me as hon-
est, as someone with integrity, as someone whose word is
good. I'd rather hear that than all of the accolades about my
coaching record.*

And I'm prouder than hell of what the Boston Celtics have

come to stand for. We've got one of the greatest sports names in the world. In this country people say we're on a par with Joe McCarthy's New York Yankees and Vince Lombardi's Green Bay Packers. But in many countries of the world where they don't play football or baseball, the people still know all about the Boston Celtics. Kids too young to have seen Cousy, Sharman and most of those guys still grow up with a great desire to put on that green uniform. Why? Because the Celtics stand for something very special. The Celtics weren't just Cousy or just Russell or just anybody. They were a team. And they are a team today. And the team, like a family, goes on and on, even though different members must leave from time to time.

One of the proudest moments I ever had came in Milwaukee the day we won the championship in 1974. I was standing in the locker room, just watching the celebration, when Paul Silas walked over and put his arm around me and gave me a hug. He said, "You know, Red, when I first got here I really believed all of that stuff about tradition and so on was a lot of bullshit. But I know better now. It's real, all right, and I'm awfully proud to be a part of it."

Hearing something like that from a 10-year veteran just made my whole day.

It's absolutely true. The Celtics are a way of life.

What about the future? I don't know.

When I was younger I'd get irritated listening to old-timers saying, "Kids today can't do this and don't do that." I don't talk that way. I say kids today are better and better in many aspects of sports. They're bigger, faster, smarter, quicker.

But on the whole, I don't think they're as easy to control. There are a lot of reasons: changing life-styles, exhorbitant contracts, variances in motivation.

You've got to change with the times. You've got to bend a bit. I can be stubborn, like the time I made that stupid statement about never dealing with agents. But I can mellow, too. If I can't change with the times it means I'm stagnating. You just can't live your life in the past. People are always bringing up the past, and from an egotistical point of view that's very nice. But I've got to keep looking forward.

What does bother me—bother me a great deal, in fact—is the

way I see pride and integrity and dedication slipping away in sports. Where are they going? And why? These are values that should last forever. How are we losing them?

I had them throughout my career. And my guys had them. Today's Celtics still have them. But how long we can hold onto them, I just can't say. The personalities coming into the game today are changing. Unfortunately, you don't see many Frank Ramseys and John Havliceks anymore. Kids still come out of college all eager and excited about playing pro ball, but then they get agents—which is right in today's market—and what happens? You're at odds before the kid even plays for you. An antagonism builds up. The kid feels threatened. The team feels threatened by the agent's demands. Before there's even a chance to develop a good rapport, money has hurt the relationship. After that, it hurts the kid's performance. Now they can get their big dough, go through the motions for four or five years, then retire financially secure for life.

Because of all these problems, I've often heard it said that a Joe McCarthy, a Vince Lombardi, a Red Auerbach couldn't coach today the same way they coached years ago.

Bullshit.

I think it would be even easier for me today. It's hard to say this without sounding like an egotist, but I'm sort of living with a legend. As a result, I think players would listen to me even more today.

Will I ever go back to the bench?

No.

Oh, I still get restless once in a while, especially when I see mistakes I know I could correct. But I'm careful to hold myself in check. Our players still come to me with questions about their game, and even though I'd love to give them some answers I don't. Or else I tell them exactly what I know Tommy would tell them. He's their coach. If his way and my way differ on something—and naturally that will happen at times—then his way is right, because he's the coach.

Besides, there are two strong reasons why I'd never go back.

First, everything I might do would be anticlimactic. People would always compare it to the past.

Second? suppose I came back and lost?

Maybe they'd start thinking I was never that good anyway!

Index

323